A CAST OF FALCONS

A CAST OF FALCONS

PHILLIP PAROTTI

CASEMATE
Philadelphia & Oxford

Published in the United States of America and Great Britain in 2021 by
CASEMATE PUBLISHERS
1950 Lawrence Road, Havertown, PA 19083, USA
and
The Old Music Hall, 106–108 Cowley Road, Oxford OX4 1JE, UK

Copyright 2021 © Phillip Parotti

Paperback Edition: ISBN 978-1-63624-088-6
Digital Edition: ISBN 978-1-63624-089-3

A CIP record for this book is available from the British Library

Printed and bound in the United States by Integrated Books International

Typeset in India by Lapiz Digital Services, Chennai.

For a complete list of Casemate titles, please contact:

CASEMATE PUBLISHERS (US)
Telephone (610) 853-9131
Fax (610) 853-9146
Email: casemate@casematepublishers.com
www.casematepublishers.com

CASEMATE PUBLISHERS (UK)
Telephone (01865) 241249
Email: casemate-uk@casematepublishers.co.uk
www.casematepublishers.co.uk

Note:
This book is a work of fiction. Names, character, places, and incidents either are the
product of the author's imagination or, if real, are used fictitiously.

For Judi and John

In the air,
Sometimes,
A cast of falcons
Stooping for prey.

1

Standing beside the rail of the HMT *Tribune*, Lieutenant Devlin Collins Royal Flying Corps (RFC) glanced to starboard, where he saw the Royal Navy destroyer that had escorted them from Malta coming up on their beam. He wondered if the speeding greyhound would eventually move ahead in order to lead them into Alexandria, which remained only a few miles distant over the horizon. All things considered, their transit had been an easy one. Normally, Dev had been told, the Mediterranean could kick up more of a bother during the winter months, but in Dev's limited experience, the opening winter days of 1916 had produced nothing but unruffled waters, even if the air had remained cooler than he had expected. Egypt, when he stopped to think about it, had been the last place on earth he had expected to wind up, and what it might bring struck him as wholly unknown. How, he could not stop from asking himself, had things come to such a pass?

First, he supposed, there had been Derry, Londonderry, his birthplace in Northern Ireland. The Collinses, his grandfather had told him, had settled on land east of there in the 17th century as a part of the Anglo-Irish Ascendancy, and as far as Devlin knew, remained in comfortable possession of Oak Hill, the family estate, ever since. Sir Colm Collins, the hereditary baronet who happened to be his grandfather, continued to enjoy a good return from the land—property which, owing to the laws of primogeniture, would eventually devolve onto his Uncle Ryan. His other uncles, Connor and Sean, and his father, Doyle, would continue to seek their own ways in the world, something all three had done together in a shirt factory that had enjoyed steady profits through the 1890s but entered a slow decline when foreign competition had started to develop around the turn of the century. There, at the age of ten, Devlin had been entered at Foyle's College, an old and respected school which, after his year as a new boy, he had come to love, playing rugby owing to his size and occasionally keeping the wicket for his house on the cricket pitch. But in 1904, all of that changed—and changed abruptly.

"What has been wonderful for three," his father said one evening at table when Devlin happened to be home during an end of term break, "is now only adequate for two, so I've sold up to Conner and Sean. At the beginning of June, we will move to the United States, to a place named New Brunswick, New Jersey, southwest of the city of New York where Liam Kelly and I have bought a motor business. We are going to sell Maxwells. They are made in Tarrytown, New York, and in Detroit, Michigan, and from all reports, they will provide us an excellent opportunity and set us up in the same style that we've enjoyed here."

The move had given Dev something of a shock—the surprise announcement, the rapid packing, the hurried leave-takings, the swift voyage across what should have been a placid Atlantic, but which turned out to be a storm-tossed saga of sea sickness and ending finally with a quiet passage beneath the Statue of Liberty. After processing through Ellis Island and spending two nights beneath the towering skyscrapers of New York, the family finally disembarked from the train in New Brunswick. There they found themselves warmly welcomed by the Kellys—the Kellys who had moved months before and made prior arrangements for receiving them. And then, to Devlin's additional surprise, he found himself fairly welcomed into the public schools he attended, replacing rugby with football and cricket with baseball, while adjusting to a wholly new style of teaching in classrooms which, to his additional shock, turned out to be co-educational and none so demanding as the curriculum in which he'd been immersed at Foyle's. Occasionally, the friends he made commented on his accent, but considering the array of immigrants with whom he went to school—Irish, German, French, Italian, Polish, and even Russian—he was not singled out for his country of origin. He assimilated fairly swiftly to the atmosphere in which he found himself, excelled in both his studies and the sports to which he dedicated his time, and accommodated himself to his new surroundings with the ease that only the young can indulge.

In keeping with his father and Mr. Kelly's business, Devlin learned to drive early—even before his 14th birthday—qualified for his license, and began spending his weekend and vacation time in his father's automotive garage. It was there that two former blacksmiths, Todd and Pringle, taught him everything they knew about engines, so that, by the time he was ready for college, even his father considered him to be a skilled mechanic. As a result, when Devlin entered Rutgers in 1910, he opted for a course in Mechanical Engineering, continued to work for his father on weekends and during summer vacations when not otherwise engaged, and helped to support himself during his college tenure. It was not that he needed to—his father and Mr. Kelly's business had thrived almost from the moment that they'd established it—but whether it had developed from an ingrained sense of responsibility or his sudden immersion in a culture where hard work and manual labor were taken for granted, Devlin had developed early on a serious turn of mind. That mind continued to equip him with what he believed necessary if, like his father, he was to be expected to make his own way in the world.

Socially, Devlin remained a fairly serious young man. Without ever indulging in what would have been considered "walking out together" in Derry, he escorted Colleen Kelly to the occasional New Brunswick tea dance, school events, promenades, and, after his entrance into Rutgers, to college functions. Colleen, an intelligent, pretty redhead, followed her own course of studies at Barnard in New York City. Their relationship, based largely on their fathers' partnership, never passed beyond a comfortable friendship formed in their youth, and both seemed perfectly content that it should remain so. What might have been considered serious courting simply didn't occur to either of them, so committed were they to their individual pursuits.

And then, on a summer afternoon in 1912, hearing a sudden sound overhead, Devlin looked up and spotted something that changed his life. Soaring like a bird, free on the air and directly over New Brunswick, Devlin saw his first airplane—what he believed to be a Wright Brothers Model B-Trainer, something he had only seen in one or two photographs that had appeared in the illustrated papers. The sight, when he first apprehended it, sent something like an electric shock down the back of his spine, and in the same instant he knew absolutely that he wanted to learn to fly, to pilot one of those machines which, he imagined, might take him anywhere he wished to go with the freedom of an eagle.

Without mentioning to his family what he was doing, Devlin made inquiries. He learned that the Wright Brothers maintained an aviation school in Dayton, Ohio, something which he determined to be out of his reach for both expense and distance; however, he also learned that they were running a summer course in Mineola, on Hempstead Plain on Long Island. So, equipped with monies accumulated through his work in his father's garage, and still without telling anyone in the family what he was doing, Dev enrolled, making weekend trips to Hempstead Plain by train. He camped out overnight on the grounds on Saturdays and Sundays, completed the ground school with stellar marks, and, after three hours of dual-seat instruction, made his first solo flight at the age of 20 in August 1912, on a Wright Model B Trainer of the type that he had first seen in the air over New Brunswick.

"I think ya might be a bit of a natural," Tedford Scott, his instructor, told him after he'd seen him solo twice more, "but I want to warn ya, Dev, being a natural can kill ya as sure as if you was an incompetent. Check your engine, check your rigging, and then, when ya gets behind them controls never, ever, let your concentration wander. These birds are dandy when they behave, but it don't take 'em two seconds to go wrong, and if ya let your mind wander, two seconds is long enough for them to kill ya. Mind what I'm telling ya?"

"Yes, Sir," Dev said.

Across the remainder of that year, Devlin Collins accumulated more than 12 hours of flying time in his log book, and then, in 1913, he accumulated 45 hours more, with even more hours following in 1914. Sometimes, he flew planes at the Wright Flying School or rented a plane from the Long Island Flying Club. By this time, he'd acquainted his family with his aspirations regarding flight. While he'd given his mother a fright with the news, his father, always one to seize an opportunity, had been supportive and given him encouragement, suggesting that while no one knew anything about the so-called future of flight, it might lead to business ventures in the future that had been as unforeseen as what the automobile had originally provided.

And finally, on a warm morning in early June, with both the Collins and the Kellys attending, Devlin walked across the stage at Rutgers, received his diploma, and graduated from his university as a fully qualified engineer. Two days later, the families reassembled to watch Colleen receive her diploma at Barnard. To everyone's surprise, by means of connections she'd made through a classmate with whom she'd gone through her final two years, Colleen went almost immediately into a sub-editor's position with a respectable publishing house in lower Manhattan. Dev, determined to consider his options before committing himself to a place, continued to work for his father and Mr. Kelly, spending six days a week in the garage and flying on Sundays. But that work only continued for four weeks, until his father sat him down one evening after supper, flashed him a smile, and said, "Your uncles wish to install an entirely new steam plant with which to run the factory. They'd like you to go to Derry, on salary, and oversee the installation. I doubt that the work will require more than three or four months to complete, and after your efforts at Rutgers and your work here, it might give you a vacation as a part of the bargain. Feel like visiting the family back in Ireland?"

Faced with such an unexpected opportunity, Dev felt delighted to be able to go. Dev arrived in Derry during the second week in July and went straight to work overseeing the new installations at the factory. In order to reacquaint himself with his uncles, his aunts, and his many cousins, he lived for the first month with his Uncle Conner, his second month with his Uncle Sean, and then moved to Oak Hill to live with his Uncle Ryan's family not long after the Germans invaded Belgium, launching The Great War. Almost immediately, his uncles bid for and received government contracts that called for the production of an array of uniform shirts. The work went ahead even more swiftly than originally planned, while Uncle Sean oversaw the factory's extension into an adjacent building so that production capacity could be increased. Dev designed and oversaw the power plant, while his uncles saw to the extension's layout and the hire of additional staff.

On the streets, in the pubs, in the music halls and theaters, Dev detected what almost amounted to a euphoria about the war. Everything seemed to be festooned with the Union Jack or red, white, and blue bunting. Rallies and recruitment drives seemed to be going on daily, and there appeared to be a general feeling that the war would be quickly won and conclude within months, if not weeks. Marches and parades clogged one street or another at more than frequent intervals, and twice, after listening to recruiting sergeants deliver their spiels from elevated platforms and turning to walk away, sharp-eyed young women with looks of contempt on their faces had hurried up to him and deposited white feathers into the breast pocket of his jacket. America, as the newspapers were quick to point out, would not be entering the war, President Wilson committing the country to remain neutral. A part of Dev tended to treat the white feathers as amusing dispensations from ignorant girls who didn't know the first thing about him, where he came from, of what he was doing there. But after a few weeks of this sort of thing, Devlin Collins began to feel a rub, a rub which soon began to chafe and then feel downright raw.

As Paris was threatened and the BEF dispatched to hold the line on the Marne, Dev began to feel more than a little conflicted about the war. New Brunswick was his home; his family was there, he'd largely grown up there, gone to school there, and planned his life there. But from the start, the family had maintained dual citizenship, meaning that no matter how he looked at it, he remained in some part a subject of the crown. Dev couldn't deny that Derry, regardless of the distance that had for so long separated him from her, also remained his home—the place where he'd been born, the city in which he'd spent his tender years. Being back, almost accidentally at this particular moment, reminded him that he loved his first home as much as his second. And with that realization, he felt some kind of responsibility to defend her.

Meanwhile, work at the factory went on without a break, Dev sometimes laboring as many as 14 hours on a Saturday and even into Sundays as yet more government contracts accumulated, Uncle Conner landing a contract to expand production to manufacture webbing for such things as belts, knapsacks, duffle bags, and brailing loops for tents. Commensurate with the need for doing the job right and doing it safely, Dev rushed his own work as productively as he could, with the final result that the factory, now expanded into three buildings, had started working three shifts by the middle of November, Dev's uncles declaring themselves more than satisfied with what he'd accomplished and awarding him a generous bonus to underwrite their thanks.

With the job concluded, Dev might have returned to New Jersey—but he didn't. Instead, sitting down before the writing table in the room at Oak Hill in which Uncle Ryan had installed him, he wrote a long letter to his parents and concluded by saying, *Being back in Ulster has reminded me that I'm as Irish as I am American and that I have a responsibility to defend our United Kingdom. I think I can contribute. I intend to join up.* And then he went to have a talk with his Uncle Ryan.

By virtue of his position in society, having inherited the baronetcy from Sir Colm, Sir Ryan was particularly well connected and well placed to help Devlin when Dev finally approached him about entering the unformed service of his country. In the beginning, feeling a responsibility to his brother and motivated by a genuine liking for Devlin, Sir Ryan tried to talk him out of making the commitment.

"With your engineering expertise, Dev," Sir Ryan said, "I think you could be of more help to the cause by staying right here in Northern Ireland or establishing yourself somewhere in the Midlands where you could help us increase our production of war materials."

"That, if I'm rejected, I will most certainly do," Dev said, "but if I don't attempt to join and offer to take the risk, I fear that I will never be able to stand straight again and face myself in the mirror when this thing ends."

They talked on, the two of them, for more than an hour, but when Sir Ryan knew finally that Devlin remained firm in his intention, he acceded to his nephew's request for help, made the requisite telephone calls, and sent him to Victoria Barracks in Belfast for an interview with a major in the Royal Irish Rifles.

Major Mumford, when Devlin met him, at first treated Devlin's request to become an officer candidate—what Mumford called a "temporary gentleman"—with skepticism, but after an hour's interview and in consideration of Devlin's background, education, and practical training, his view changed.

"Normally," he told Devlin, we draw our officers from Sandhurst, Woolwich, or an OTC connected with public schools like Eton, Harrow, or Rugby. However, at Aldershot, an experimental company has formed, a Cadet Training Company, which the Army intends to expand into a battalion should more officers be needed later in the war. If you are agreeable, I think we might be able to fit you into it.

Devlin declared that he was indeed agreeable, and during the week following Christmas 1914, he took ship, crossed the Irish Sea, and made his way to Aldershot. There, he quickly passed his physical examination, held up his hand, swore his oath, and took the King's shilling as an officer cadet in the training company. To his surprise, he found himself included in a mix of recent public school graduates, bank clerks, former sergeants and former warrant officers, all of them blended together for three months of square-bashing, classroom instruction, and rigid military discipline. Devlin found the course in no way difficult and passed out near the top of his class with his King's commission as a second lieutenant. He returned to Victoria Barracks in Belfast just in time to be dispatched—again on an experimental basis, to see what a "temporary gentleman" could do—in a draft of replacements to fill officer gaps in his regiment that had resulted from the battle for Neuve Chapelle which had been fought in March.

Based on his three-month stint in the trenches, Devlin later found that he could not look back on them with pleasure. Aside from the drenching spring rains, the mud, and the rats, there had been the vermin, the smell, the noise, and what had sometimes seemed a never-ending stream of Bavarian bullets piercing the air immediately overhead. Then, finally, in the high heat of July, with nearly everyone soaked and bedeviled by their own sweat, his battalion had gone over the top in the battle of Fromelles, his own platoon losing three dead and seven wounded, including himself when a machine gun bullet shattered against a steel picket and threw a sliver into his thigh. The sliver had not been large and, in the field hospital to which he had limped, it had been quickly removed by a medical attendant who next poured in enough tincture of iodine to make him feel like his leg was on fire. Thereafter, bandaged but limping, he returned to his trench, resumed his duties, and three days later put himself forward when his battalion commander announced that the Royal Flying Corps had sent down a bulletin seeking recruits.

"Sorry, old chap," said the lieutenant colonel, somewhat contemptuously, who had stopped at Division Headquarters to interview potential candidates for the RFC, "but we are not presently taking *temporary gentlemen* into the RFC."

"Not even temporary gentlemen who are certified aviators with more than 80 flying hours in their log books?" Devlin asked, immediately producing his.

"Ah," said the lieutenant colonel, pinching his lips even as his eyes narrowed, "spot of difference, there, if you see what I mean."

"Quite," Dev agreed.

Three days later, still limping slightly, Devlin Collins boarded ship at Calais, disembarked at Dover, took the train to London, and enjoyed a week's convalescent leave before boarding yet another train which put him down at Montrose, Scotland, where he went through preliminary flight school and passed out first in his class. Four of the group of 20 with whom he had started the course failed to complete it, each of them killed in flying accidents before the course had half ended. At the time, Dev found the deaths distressing, but there were so many in the flying schools that he also knew he had to accept them as routine. From there, Devlin was dispatched to the Central Flying School at Upavon on the Salisbury Plain. There, graduating to more sophisticated planes and training, he not only learned to fly more demanding aircraft but also had to master a variety of associated skills, including bomb dropping, photography, artillery observation, distance flying, formation flying, fighting practice, and finally, machine gunnery. The course on machine gunnery lasted a full week in which the pilots sat on hard benches, memorized the parts of the Lewis gun, learned how to take them down and put them back together, how to load their ammunition canisters, and how to clear jams. Finally, months after he'd returned from France, Devlin received his passing-out certificate, granting him permission to sew on his RFC wings. This time, three more of his classmates had died in training—one when the wings on his plane folded back in a dive, one who flew into a tree, and one when his engine quit on takeoff and he made the unforgiving mistake of trying to turn back. Then, as fully prepared as the course could make him, Devlin once more prepared to return to France, where the Huns, as they were then known, seemed to be shooting Allied pilots from the sky as swiftly as the RFC could train them and send them into combat. What, Devlin had wondered at the time, would he be flying—a Sopwith, a Neuport, a Vickers? His flying school marks attested to his high performance and his competence as a pilot, and in the meantime he'd been promoted to Lieutenant. Although he could not foresee developments, he fully expected to be assigned to fly a scout and looked forward to getting into the air with a front-line squadron. But his passing-out interview did not turn out as expected.

"France?" said Major Horton, the balding, overweight assignments officer who interviewed Devlin, the man's eyes and lips screwing up with a smile as he said so. "Oh, I think not, Lieutenant. Dispatched three drafts of new pilots to France yesterday, don't you see. For the moment, France is full up, with pilots to spare, so you're not needed in France. So, I'm sending you to where you are *most* needed. Most needed indeed. You're going to Egypt, Lieutenant, to defend the Suez Canal. Vital, the canal, don't you see? Passage to India, and all that. Absolutely vital, the canal! And just at the moment, the Bosche are making a fuss about it. Trying to take it, if you see what I mean. You're needed there, and with your flying skills, I should imagine that they will make you a flight leader straight away."

"But Sir—" Devlin started to say.

"No buts, Lieutenant," interrupted Major Horton, handing Devlin a manila envelope containing a train ticket to Southampton, a steamship ticket to Alexandria, and a set of orders. "New horizons await, so off you go, and let me wish you good hunting to speed you on your way." And so, two days later, Dev boarded HMT *Tribune* and steamed for Egypt.

2

Dev saw very little of Alexandria when the *Tribune* tied up alongside the quay and put over her brow. In the moment he stepped ashore, his duffle slung over his shoulder, he found himself met by Captain Trevor Rotham—a short, slightly built, impeccably dressed officer who might, in civilian life, have easily passed for a jockey but for the ribbon of an M.C. that adorned his blouse.

"Lieutenant Collins, are you?" Rotham said as Dev put down his duffle and saluted.

"Yes, Sir," Dev said, standing to attention as Rotham returned his salute.

"Rotham, here," the man replied, "commanding B Flight, 14 Squadron. Pick up that duffle and come with me."

Devlin grabbed his duffle and hastened to catch up with Captain Rotham who had turned and immediately started walking toward a Crossley tender at a rapid pace.

"Toss your duffle in the back and get in," Rotham said, instantly hoisting himself into the driver's seat and starting the engine.

Dev did as he was told, and as soon as he sat down, Rotham popped the clutch on the tender, bolted down the quay and onto the street, and sent what he called the gyppos flying in all directions as they leaped out of his way.

"Won't do to waste time," Rotham said as the tender accelerated. "There's a do on in the desert, and we've been called for."

The intensity with which Captain Rotham spoke signaled to Dev that things were going to develop much more rapidly than he'd ever imagined they could. Rotham seemed to be talking about action—something immediate, something demanding—and Dev hadn't been disembarked for as much as five minutes.

"Now listen up," Rotham said, "because I'm going to give you the drill. Off to the east in Sinai, Colonel Friedrich, Freiherr Kress von Kressenstein, the Bavarian artilleryman, is threatening a fuss with the probable expectation of seizing the canal. At the moment, he seems to be the principal adviser to the Turks, who will be doing most of the fighting. What that means for practical purposes is that he's commanding them, and he appears to be a man who knows his business. That's bound to be a big do when it unfolds, but it hasn't quite developed yet, and in the meantime, we've got trouble to the west, which is where, as you've probably noticed, we're heading."

Where they were heading at that moment, more precisely, appeared to be straight toward two donkey carts, their white-robed Egyptian drivers screaming curses at the tops of their lungs while beating their donkeys to move them out of the tender's way. With a deft touch on the wheel, while Dev thought his stomach might turn over, Rotham swept around them with mere inches to spare.

"Our problem," Rotham continued, unmoved by the disaster he'd barely avoided, "are the Senussi. German and Turkish agents have gotten out into the desert west of here and agitated the Berber and Arab tribes. The Senussi are a religious sect, and with those buggers, the agitation seems to have taken hold, so much so that they have been raiding British outposts and killing British personnel. In December, a force of some twelve or thirteen hundred of them, armed with both machine guns and artillery, attacked our Western Frontier Force near Wadi Shaifa and made a considerable disturbance. They were vigorously repulsed, of course, but in the wake of their attack, their forces swelled to possibly as many as 5,000 rifles. We've kept tabs on them from the air, and working in company with the WFF, we've substantially reduced their numbers and given them one bloody nose after another, but right now, south of Alexandria about 50 miles, they seem to have collected a concentration around Wadi Moghara. That's an oasis of sorts where water is plentiful."

With a sudden leap, the Crossley bounced over a pothole, scattered a flock of chickens, and sent a herd of goats leaping for cover, the herder, screaming with fear, pressing himself against a wall to avoid being run down.

"Yesterday," Rotham went on, "Yates, flying from El Hammam which is about 20 miles distant and where we're headed, reconnoitered Moghara, but apparently his plane broke up in the air on the way back. We found it last evening before sunset, and both Yates and his observer were dead. This time, we're taking two planes out, you and I, with bombs instead of observers."

Devlin Collins felt his stomach tighten. Fifteen minutes ashore and not yet outside of Alexandria, and Rotham was talking about a mission—a combat mission—as though it were some kind of Sunday flight over the Hempstead Plain.

"If I might ask, Sir," Dev said carefully, "will we be flying Bristols, Neuports, or Vickers?"

Hunched behind the wheel, his small stature necessitating that he peer through it in order to drive, Rotham's jaw dropped slightly open. Then, much to Dev's surprise, he broke into such rollicking laughter that he nearly ran them into a ditch.

"The lads, when you finally meet them, will be much amused, Mr. Collins. No Sir, I'm afraid not. As far as I know, Bristols, Neuports, and Vickers have never been seen on this front. Anything resembling a new scout or a new aircraft of any kind goes to Western Front, which means that our masters, benighted though we believe them to be, send us nothing but the lame and the halt—the castoffs that can no longer compete in the air over France. 14 Squadron's aircraft consist of BE2cs, a single DH1, and Martinsydes. The Huns, what little we've seen of them, fly much better machines."

To Dev, what Rotham told him sounded not unlike the kiss of death. BE2cs, which Dev had flown in training, were notorious on the Western Front as "flying coffins." It wasn't that they were unstable and unreliable—for limited kinds of duty, they were both stable and reliable—but they were also slow, extremely difficult to defend, and easily shot down for the simple reason that they didn't muster a forward-facing machine gun. In a BE2c, the only Lewis gun that could be mounted had to be mounted for the use of the observer, the plane's struts and rigging preventing that observer from firing forward. The Martinsyde, which could offer a forward-firing Lewis gun, seemed so underpowered with its 80hp Gnome engine that it was essentially a sitting duck for a new German Albatros or Eindecker monoplane, which fired forward by means of a cleverly contrived interrupter gear. The DH1—a pusher airplane with the prop and engine mounted behind the pilot and observer—at least offered the front-seat observer a clear range of vision and defense with its forward-firing machine gun; but aside from the fact that it was both old and not particularly fast, 14 Squadron apparently had only one of the machines. So, Dev imagined, he wouldn't be flying one of those.

"So," Dev said, trying to hide his disappointment from Rotham, "we'll be flying BE2cs when we go out?"

"Yes," Rotham said at once.

"Bomb racks controlled from the cockpit?" Dev asked.

"Racks to hold 20-pound Cooper bombs attached to either side of the cockpit," Rotham said. "Easy as pie. When a pilot is ready to bomb, he pulls out one of the Coopers, holds it over the side, and drops it when he's over the target, all by what we like to call 'airman's eye.'"

Holy Mother of God, Dev thought, and then, on the instant, found it surprising that they weren't armed with spears.

"And when, might I ask, Sir, do we fly?" Dev said, his voice remaining restrained.

"Just as soon as we reach El Hammam," Rotham said cheerfully, "and you can get into your flying togs."

Within the space of a heartbeat, Devlin Collins' blood ran cold.

El Hammam, when Rotham raced the Crossley into it, struck Dev as not much more than an Egyptian farming town, most of the houses that he saw consisting of single-storied, whitewashed structures thrown up haphazardly in order to provide shelter for the farmers who went out to their fields in the morning and returned at nightfall. Dev imagined that life within the mud brick walls offered few home comforts. The field from which the BE2cs would fly seemed even less impressive—a hot, dusty flat flanked by a single canvas hangar, something that looked to Dev like it might blow away in the slightest wind.

Leaving the road, Rotham fairly sped the tender across the field toward the hangar, screeching and sliding to a stop beside it before leaping out and reaching for his own flying togs, when one of his fitters brought them out to him from the hangar.

"Quick as you can," Rotham called to Dev. "It may be winter here, but the desert's going to heat up fast, and the more it does, the less efficient our engines are going to be, not to mention the evaporation of our petrol."

While the men changed, the fitters pushed out their planes, two BE2cs, neither of them new, both of them showing patches on their fabric where they'd been holed and repaired. One of the wings on the craft that Dev was to fly looked to him like it had developed a slight warp along its trailing edge, something he was quick to ask Rotham about.

17

"The dry heat and the sun," Rotham said quickly, tugging on his flying coat. "Depending on exposure, the air mechanics have to strip the fabric, sand down whatever varnish hasn't blistered, and refit the frames. Never ending, it is, but your bird's more than fit to fly, so let's hop it while we can." And without another word, he raced for the cockpit of his own plane, climbed in, and while Dev made haste to scramble into his own bird, signaled his fitter to spin his prop.

Dev had flown BE2cs before in training, but that did not change the fact that this, without preliminaries of any sort, was the first time he'd flown on anything like a combat mission. He had no idea where he was going, or how, if things developed badly, he would get back. Tense to the point of shaking, he glanced out, found the fitter in front of his plane standing ready, signaled the man to swing his propeller after he'd adjusted choke and throttle, and felt his engine burst into life. Seconds later, trailing a cloud of dust kicked up across the hard-baked field behind him, he lifted into the air and raced to catch up with Rotham, stationing himself slightly off to the side and behind the captain's port wing.

The air over the desert that morning in the midst of the Egyptian winter seemed nearly as warm as a dry summer's day in England. Below, beneath the morning sun and once beyond the green fields surrounding El Hammam, the desert seemed to glisten, the sun reflecting from its infinite grains of sand. In the Egyptian summer, Dev was quick to understand, the midday heat might become so intense as to make flying difficult, if not impossible, but on that morning, his first in the air over the Sahara, conditions seemed both conducive to flight and downright pleasant.

Steady on a southwest heading, Rotham took them up to an altitude of 3,000 feet, leveled off, and never deviated from their course. The terrain, when Dev deigned to look at it—momentarily breaking his concentration on the two-plane formation in which he was flying—differed slightly from the wave-like sand dunes that he had expected. Much of it, from what he could see, seemed to resemble what he'd gleaned from photos of the American Southwest, mixing a dry wadi here and a dry wadi there with some scrub, outcroppings of rock, immense treeless flats, and the occasional patch of grass fed, he imagined, by some undetected and unexplained seep of water. Of landmarks, he saw none that he thought that he could identify or remember, but he committed to memory the compass bearing down which they were flying, in the event that he would have to reverse it in order to fly out when the time came to return to El Hammam.

On the drive from Alexandria to what passed for their base at El Hammam, Rotham had been careful to brief him about his intentions for their mission, going over more than once the sequence of operations he expected to conduct, hand signals that they would use in the prosecution of their maneuvers, and the distance that they ought to maintain between their machines once they found the Senussi camp and began flying over it.

"One hundred yards, at least," Rotham had said as he bounced them over yet another bump in the Crossley. "Don't want to cluster in case they start shooting at us. Don't want them shooting at me and hitting you by mistake because we're too close, if you take my drift. Photographs first, for the Western Frontier Force, and a count of both tents and camels as far as you're able. And then, once we've done the job we've been sent to do—a thorough reconnaissance—the Coopers. Easily armed, and I assume you've done it in practice?"

"I have," Dev said.

"Right, then," Rotham said. "Best, I think, to come at them from two directions. You bomb on a north–south axis. I'll come at them on an east–west line, and we'll turn our attack lines 45 degrees clockwise for each pass. Take my meaning, do you?"

"Yes, Sir," Dev said.

Forty minutes into the flight, with the BE2c's engine roaring in his ears and with the wind rushing past his windscreen, Dev caught

Rotham's hand signal to begin their descent, and then, very swiftly Rotham took them down to 2,000 feet, leveled off, and gave Dev yet another hand signal indicating that he was to load his camera with the glass plate that would record the desired image of the Senussi camp. Ahead of him, Dev could see nothing, but knowing that his was not to question *why* but merely to *do*, he put the stick between his knees as he removed one of the glass photographic plates from the pouch that the fitters had given him. Then, he eased away from Rotham to avoid any possible collision while he performed the evolution, reached over the side of the cockpit to where the camera was attached, and did as he'd been taught to do in training, by inserting the plate into the camera. And then, once more, he looked ahead with his hand on the stick and saw, far out in front of him, tiny black specks rising from the desert floor and imagined them to be the date palms that he could not yet actually identify.

Less than a minute later, he knew absolutely that he was looking at date palms and, seconds after that, not only date palms but the outline of tents scattered beneath them, and then, finally, tethered in the adjacent wadi, camels—an entire massive herd of them with here and there a few horses. One quick glance in Rotham's direction showed him the precise moment in which Rotham closed his fist, and in that second—with the Senussi camp directly beneath them as they ripped through the sky with only moderate power on their throttles—Dev snapped the photograph that he'd been assigned to take. Still flying south, still flying safely distant behind Rotham's port wing, within another ten seconds they had flown beyond the camp, where Rotham led them in a wide turn to bring them in for a second time on an east–west axis for a second photographic pass.

In changing the glass plates in his camera while their turn took them down to the much lower altitude of 500 feet for their next pass over the camp, Dev experienced some minor difficulties but managed to accomplish the feat just in time to snap the button and expose the second plate. And in the instant that he did so, and much to his sharp surprise, he suddenly saw a single hole appear in the center of his starboard wing, not 3 feet from where he sat in the cockpit—someone on the ground had struck his plane with a rifle round.

For Dev, the moment was unsettling, and on the instant, he found himself glancing at the bottom of his cockpit and wondering, for the first time, what kind of protection it afforded him. To say that his heart pounded seemed inadequate, as his heart rate had increased the moment he entered the plane, but the stress and tension he suddenly felt was of a new kind. Someone down below had tried to kill him. Possibly, several someones had tried to kill him, and in the split-second that Devlin Collins stopped to think about it, he found that he didn't like it. But this was no time for self-reflection. Very swiftly, in order to hold his place beside Rotham, Dev knew that he had to put both the sudden revelation and the sensation that it produced behind him and concentrate on the job that he'd been set to do.

Without immediately flying back directly over the camp, Rotham led him on a wide turn around the perimeter of the encampment— not once, but three times in succession—for the purpose of counting both tents and camels. Then, finally, with yet another hand signal to indicate the commencement of their predetermined tactics, the two fliers separated, Rotham turning immediately west and descending for his first bomb run, Dev continuing on around the circle until he reached the southern foot of the oasis, removed and armed one of the 20-pound Cooper bombs from the rack fixed to the outside of the BE2c forward of the cockpit, gripped it by the narrow neck at its tail, and turned north to make his first dive over the camp.

Dev came out of his turn and leveled out just in time to see Rotham reach the foot of his dive, cross the camp, and begin to climb near the western side. From the distance, he could not actually see Rotham drop his bomb, but in the seconds after Rotham leveled out, the plume of fire and dust behind him indicated an explosion directly in the center of the camp. Cooper bombs did nowhere near the damage that the 100-pounders could do, but they did do damage and had the effect of creating absolute consternation where they fell. So, by the time that Dev descended to 300 feet and dropped his own bomb not 40 yards from where Rotham's had fallen and exploded, he could see tents on fire, a few bodies on the ground, and robed and frightened Senussi running everywhere and not a few of them firing up at him with raised rifles as he roared over the camp. Then, just as he pulled back on the stick and started to climb out from his attack, he saw something else that swiftly caught his attention before he was over, out, and gone, concentrating on making his escape and reorienting his position with the 45-degree clockwise change that Rotham had called for them to make on their second run.

On Rotham's second attack, an attack he made by flying low up what turned out to be the conveniently arranged path of the wadi, he dropped his bomb directly in the midst of the Senussi's camel herd, killing not a few while stampeding those which the Senussi had not taken the time to tether. The few horses that had been mixed with the herd and tied to their own line simply broke from the camels and disappeared like streaks, three or four of them climbing the wadi and stampeding through the camp. As Dev made his second pass, he saw the horses knock down two or three tents and one or two men in their terror-stricken departure. Then, concentrating on releasing his second bomb at least a hundred yards from where he'd dropped his first, Dev allowed himself to descend almost to 200 feet, let go of his bomb over what appeared to be a huge black tent, and quickly took at least three more rounds through his lower port wing, one of them causing a 3-inch strip of fabric to peel back, exposing part of the rib to which it had been attached.

On their third pass over the camp—Rotham this time coming up from the south while Dev continued to move around so as to make his run from the west—he saw clearly, in an interval between two of the date palms, two men mount what looked like a machine gun on the top of a post and begin firing at Rotham. Whether or not Rotham had seen them, Dev didn't know, but once he'd seen the machine gun burst into action, he dived directly toward it, saw the men turning the gun in his direction, and saw more bullet holes strip fabric from his starboard wing. He dropped his third and final bomb as nearly over the offending weapon as he thought he could before pulling back on the stick and lifting his plane into the sky. Dev never knew whether he had done for that machine gun or not, but as he flew out, glancing only once over his shoulder to see where his bomb had fallen, he thought he had. Whatever the case, what he had seen going in confirmed what he had seen on the ground during his first run—and that would be something he would have to tell Rotham and which would have to go in their reconnaissance report to the commanding general of the WWF.

Almost from the moment Dev rejoined Rotham, he could see that Rotham's machine, while still flying, seemed to be sputtering. Judging from the holes that Dev could see in Rotham's port wing, Dev knew that the ground fire from Rotham's last pass over the camp had struck him, most likely from the machine gun that Dev had tried to bomb, and imagined that at least one round had struck the BE2c's engine, damaging it in some way for which he couldn't account.

For 30 minutes as they flew back northeast toward El Hammam, Dev continued to see Rotham's plane jerk occasionally. Then, quite suddenly, Dev sensed that Rotham had started to slow and dip and saw that his air screw had stopped turning. And there, in the middle of the Egyptian desert, as Dev circled, Rotham began a gliding descent, searching for one of those flat patches on the desert floor which they had flown over on their way to Wadi Moghara and the Senussi camp.

Moments after he'd started down, Rotham found what he was looking for—a less than rocky flat, its barren, obviously sterile, hard-packed pan devoid of grass, bush, or stone—and put his BE2c down not more than 50 yards into what looked to Dev like half a mile of utterly open space. Dev, after circling twice and seeing Rotham climb from his cockpit and wave, took his own plane down, made a bumpy landing not far from Rotham's machine, and taxied into a nearby position before cutting his engine.

"You shouldn't have done that, cutting your engine like that," Rotham said, when he walked over to where Dev had climbed from his cockpit. "Might not be able to get it started again, and then the two of us would have a very long walk ahead of us."

"Sorry, Sir," Dev said, taking the man's point. "Thought I might be able to be of help, on the engine I mean. I know a bit about them."

"Do you now?" Rotham said, his manner easing slightly. "Well, then, let's take a look. Caught a packet, I think. Never saw one, but I think they had a machine gun down there somewhere."

"They did," Dev said. "I saw it about the time they hit you and tried to bomb it in my last pass, and while I can't be sure, I'd say that they were either Germans or Turks manning the machine gun. They were wearing uniforms rather than robes, and I saw another one running from one of the tents when I went over during my first pass; judging from the cap he was wearing, I think that one must have been an officer."

"That is information worth the trouble we've been put to," Rotham said quickly. "How many tents did you count?"

"I can't be exact," Dev said, "but I'd estimate between 60 and 70."

"Right," Rotham said. "If we count five men to the tent, that would make it a camp of at least 300, unless they have their women with them, and I didn't see any women."

"Nor did I," Dev said.

"Three hundred men, possibly 350, and at least one machine gun."

"And at least three Germans or Turks," Dev added.

"Yes, and at least those, if you didn't reduce their number when you dropped your last bomb," Rotham said. "Well, here's the plane. Take a look and tell me what you think. If you can't do anything with it, you can take me back, and I'll fly a fitter down here to mend it."

Dev climbed up on the wing, eased himself up onto the cowling, and inched his way up toward the engine.

"Fuel line's crimped, for one thing," he said. "It's a wonder that it wasn't severed and that you didn't catch fire."

"Perish the thought on that," Rotham said quickly, "and let us drop a curse on old Brother Trenchard for not letting us have parachutes."

"Amen," Dev said. To Dev and to most of the pilots with whom he'd flown in training, General Trenchard's refusal to equip pilots with parachutes, to save them from burning to death when their flimsy planes were set on fire, was tantamount to murder. Either they stayed with their planes and burned to death or they leapt into space to escape the flames with an immediate death upon impact. Balloon observers had parachutes, so it seemed to Dev that giving them to pilots made perfect sense. Refusing them seemed insane.

"One of the magneto wires has been shot away," Dev said. "If we can take a bit of wire from somewhere, I think I can fix this, and if you have a pair of pliers or an adjustable spanner anywhere handy, I might be able to open your fuel line without breaking it. One of the fitters can replace it once we get this bird back."

"Bright lad," Rotham said. "I've a vice grip in the pocket inside the cockpit. Sit steady, and I'll hand it to you. I think I can find a span of wire in there as well."

Dev didn't need more than a few minutes to make both repairs, and then, after he'd slid back down to the cockpit and climbed from the plane, he swung the propeller for Rotham in order to get his engine going, after which Rotham, leaving the BE2c to percolate, rushed over and performed the same function for Dev.

Five minutes later, with Rotham leaping first into the air and with Dev taking off after, both of them were once more headed back to El Hammam.

—o—

In El Hamman, while the fitters and air mechanics fell at once to repairing whatever damage Rotham and Dev reported to them, the two pilots, still wearing their flying outfits, leaped into the Crossley and drove at what Dev considered an unsafe and impossibly dangerous speed 3 miles farther west to the encampment of a yeomanry regiment, where an RFC photographic intelligence detachment also happened to be billeted. There, acting swiftly but with care, an RFC lieutenant and two corporals quickly developed, printed, and read the photographs that Rotham and Dev had taken, the resulting numbers for Senussi rifles, tents, and camels confirming the rough estimates that the two fliers had made. Those results were instantly turned over to the yeomanry regiment's intelligence officer who'd been standing by. After a quarter of an hour's wait, Rotham and Dev were summoned to confer with the regiment's colonel and his squadron commanders. Questions were asked, answers were given, short and precise, and estimates were confirmed. Then, acting with both purpose and dispatch, an operation was laid on, and orders sent down for the regiment to be prepared to march at 1600 hours that afternoon in what would amount to a night operation with an expected engagement to take place the following morning. Captain Rotham and Dev were assigned to fly out at dawn, one hour apart, each making his way to Wadi Moghara independently to maintain a reconnaissance umbrella over the heads of the yeomanry throughout the supposed period of action. In order to aid the attack, each would carry four Cooper bombs but had instructions not to drop them within 300 yards of any of the men in the mounted squadrons.

Content to let Dev drive back to the hangar at El Hammam, Rotham leaned against the passenger seat so well as he might, put his feet up against what passed for the tender's dashboard, pulled out his pipe, crammed it with tobacco, and lighted it.

"Not quite what you expected for your first day in Egypt?" he said, grinning broadly around the stem of his pipe.

"Not quite," Dev said, responding with a grin of his own.

"And still, one more day to go before I can send you east where the living is good but the action is slow," Rotham said.

"But where it is expected to pick up?" Dev asked.

"Absolutely," Rotham said, "but exactly *when* is a question for the Ascot odds-makers. Meanwhile, we must do what we must do. I'll be sending you out later tomorrow. The yeomanry, I suspect, may be a trifle late. They've at least 50 miles to march, which means that the horses will have to be stopped, rested, fed, and watered along the way. So, while the colonel hopes to attack at dawn, I'm betting that he won't come within sight of Wadi Moghara or be in a position to attack tomorrow morning much before 0800 or 0900 at the earliest, regardless of what his incredible optimism has led him to believe."

"How under the sun does he expect to feed and water his mounts?" Dev asked. "In going down there this morning, I don't remember seeing a pool of water anywhere or grass enough to feed more than a few goats."

"Ha," Rotham smiled. "Camels, old boy, about 900 of them carrying everything from rations and ammunition for the men to fodder and water for their mounts. Regiment of about 550 men with almost double the number of camels in support to carry supplies. Regular circus on the move. Just wait until you see them. Sort of takes the breath away, if you see what I mean."

"I shouldn't wonder," Dev said. "But won't the Senussi see us coming, with all the dust those hooves will raise?"

"They probably will," Rotham said, "if they're paying attention at all, but if the colonel circles round to take them from the east where the sun will be in their eyes, which seems his present intention, and if he gets his squadrons down there early enough, he may go a long way toward hiding his movements from them. It may give him exactly the edge he needs."

"I thought an attack like this was always supposed to be made with a three to one advantage" Dev ventured.

"Oh, it is, old boy, it *is*. But out here, we have to make war with what we've got, not what we'd like to have, so if the colonel doesn't straggle half of his men going down there, he'll be going in with almost … almost a two to one advantage, and that's not bad. And besides, a lot of the Senussi rifles are old, while our lads have good equipment and enough training to know how to use it. They did very well at Mersa Matruh. Sent the Senussi packing, they did. Ran 'em like rabbits."

"So," Dev said, "how, exactly, are we to go about our business down there?"

"Pad, pencil, and paper," Rotham said quickly, "and at least half a dozen drop bags. You want to communicate a piece of information to the colonel or one of his squadron commanders, you write a brief note, put it in the bag, and drop it over the side as you fly over him. The yeomanry know the drill; they will race it to the right man quick march."

"And what about getting word back to me about what they want me to do for them?" Dev asked.

"They won't," Rotham said. "As you know, our birds aren't presently equipped with wireless, so communication is all one way. So, if you do communicate anything to the ground, be sure that your message is precise and clear. Won't do to have the colonel misunderstand you and send in an attack which will get the yeomanry slaughtered, if you see what I mean."

Dev saw. He didn't like what he saw, but accepted nevertheless what he had no choice but to accept.

"One other thing," Rotham said. "You will probably arrive over Moghara before I leave to return here, but whatever the case, the last thing I'll do before I start back is stampede whatever camels and horses the Senussi have been able to reassemble overnight. It would be nice to think that I might be able to time that attack so that I catch them flatfooted around the time the colonel launches his own attack. Not only might I add to their confusion, I might also be able to prevent any number of them from getting away into the desert."

"Understood," Dev said.

"When you see me go in," Rotham continued, "and if the colonel is attacking by that time, drop at least three of your bombs on the oasis. That's bound to multiply the confusion factor, but save at least one for any unforeseen need you meet."

"Yes, Sir," Dev said.

They dined that night, sitting alongside the fitters, on hard biscuit, boiled bully beef, and scalding mugs of tea brewed up without the benefit of either tinned milk or sugar. After folding tarps into mattresses of a kind, they bedded down inside the hangar, under a double layer of blankets, still wearing their clothes, and slept fitfully.

By 0400 on the following morning, no matter which way he turned, no matter what he did to try to warm himself, Devlin Collins found that he could no longer take the cold and crawled out, feeling half frozen, wondering if the desert winter might not exchange for an arctic summer replete somewhere nearby with surrounding sheets of ice. What he found instead when he stepped outside of the hangar was fog—dense fog, and dew—the fog having rolled in from the Mediterranean, the dew having come, he supposed, from the moisture collected in the farm fields surrounding El Hammam.

Outside the hangar and at a safe distance away from it, two of Rotham's fitters had already poured petrol into the sand-packed cans, lighted them for cooking fires, and started brewing up tea for the morning while an air mechanic named Hastings had started boiling the oatmeal that would pass for everyone's breakfast.

"Care for a cuppa?" one of the fitters asked Dev, holding out a steaming cup toward him.

"Yes, yes I would," Dev said, taking the cup. "Always this cold in the mornings, is it?"

"Aye, Sir," the man replied, giving his head a shake with a mild laugh. "But a good day for a war, I've 'eard 'em say."

"Oh, aye," the second fitter said with a smirk, "them as knows what they's talkin' 'bout."

The tea might have looked scalding when the fitter handed it to Dev, but by the time Dev finally raised it to his lips, it was merely hot and strong, warming him all the way down to his stomach. When Rotham stepped from the flaps of the hangar only a few minutes later, Dev was able to greet him with a degree of equanimity that would have been beyond him only moments before.

"Damn near froze to death last night," Rotham said as he took the mug of tea his fitter handed up to him. "Winter nights in the desert can be perfect hell, and blankets are no substitute for sleeping bags. The squadron has them, of course, at Kantara and Ismailia. Probably give you one when you get where you're going. Word to the wise on that. Hang it up during the day, well off the ground and your cot, otherwise you're liable to find a scorpion has crawled into it during the day or, worse yet, a snake. And mind your boots in that regard as well."

"Just like in the boy scouts?" Dev laughed.

"Just like in the boy scouts," Rotham said. "Good old Baden-Powell, bless the man, one and all, for what the movement taught us in our youth. Well now," he said, looking around, "first a cuppa then a mug of oatmeal, and then we'd better be ready to fly."

With the sun threatening a pink dawn to the east, Rotham took off at 0700 that morning, leaving Dev to cool his heels—heels that had only barely begun to warm from the night preceding. At 0800, on signal, the fitter standing in front of Dev's patched-up BE2c spun his propeller, backed away as Dev's engine sprang to life, and waved once as Dev opened the throttle and lifted into the sky.

Dev's flight down to Wadi Moghara that morning was nothing like the flight he'd made on the preceding day. Rotham had warned him beforehand, and Dev had paid attention to that warning, so he'd flown prepared, wearing a sweater, his flying coat, thick socks, two pairs of them, and his flying boots. Still, no amount of warning had prepared him for the cold that he encountered flying at that hour and at an altitude of only 4,000 feet. The desert would warm, he knew, but it would obviously warm at an hour later than he'd expected. Next time, he thought, he would procure a pair of wool gloves to wear inside his flying gauntlets, which seemed so stiff with the cold that they almost froze his fingers.

Slowly, as the sun climbed, he did warm, the rays from the east, little by little, conveying their first heat to the exposed side of his face and his flying coat. Down below, as he glanced to either side, things looked much as they had the previous morning—a treeless waste punctuated here by an outcrop of stone and there by a patch of grass or scrub, but always wide, empty, and lonely. Without ever having seen them, Dev found himself wondering if places in Arizona, California, New Mexico, and Texas looked the same. Then, quite abruptly, he gave up such thoughts, when he once more sighted the specks on the horizon that indicated the date palms and moments later, descending, circled Wadi Moghara and found it empty, the entire Senussi contingent having packed up, tent, rifles, and camels, and decamped to parts unknown. This sudden development, coming as a total surprise, troubled Dev, but what troubled him more was the fact that the yeomanry and Rotham were also nowhere in sight. However, knowing that he had seen neither hide nor hair of them on his way down from El Hammam, he reasoned that they had to be somewhere in the vicinity and began a search, circling the oasis and stretching his circle 2 miles to either side with each circuit that he flew. Sure enough, within 15 minutes, he sighted the column by its dust, well off to the west down the wadi, and turned to catch up with them.

Minutes later, now at 3,000 feet, Dev flew over the rear of the column, the string of camels stretched out behind it, the yeomanry squadrons already deploying to either side, forming with horses and camels a huge T below, with the deployed rifles of the yeomanry spread north and south less than a mile from yet another tiny oasis. There, too, after a careful search, he finally saw Rotham, the BE2c looking like no more than a dot in the distance but reflecting just enough of the morning sunlight from its wings for Dev to keep it in view.

Immediately, Dev put his machine into a steep descent, went down to an altitude of 2,500 feet, and joined what Rotham had previously described to him as yet another attack circle—one designed to repeat the previous day's tactics, with Rotham making his first bomb run from east to west, while Dev made his run from south to north before rotating their attack axis 45 degrees.

By that time, the yeomanry were obviously on the move and had closed on the oasis to within half a mile. Dev marveled as he watched the yeomanry break first into a gallop and then into a run, their horses stretching out, the entire regiment bursting into a cavalry charge of the kind that Dev had only read about in history books. Transfixed by the sight, he nearly missed seeing Rotham dip toward the newly erected Senussi camp, but the flash from Rotham's first bomb brought Dev back to himself. He put his stick over and began the dive that would take him down over the camp for his own bomb's drop. In the flash of a second, Dev realized that he hadn't even removed and armed one of the Coopers from the rack outside his cockpit—an idiot's mistake, he thought—which almost made him miss his own drop. As he sailed in over the camp, men running everywhere, he got off his bomb less than 40 yards from the northern edge of the camp before pulling up sharply to gain altitude on his way out to rejoin Rotham's circle.

Furious with himself for having broken his concentration, for having allowed himself to be so foolishly distracted by the spectacle beneath him, he had double cause to curse his failure when he happened to glance at his starboard wing. He counted five holes stitched across the fabric, the obvious residue of a machine-gun burst that he hadn't even noticed as he flew down over the camp. Failure to have spotted the machine gun—and to know where it was located—was a failure in spades, one for which he could not forgive himself, because it might easily kill him or kill Rotham when the two of them dived down to make their next pass and bomb run over the oasis.

But to Devlin's intense relief, Rotham turned sharply away from the camp and instead fixed his attention on the camel herd. The yeomanry, having burst into the Senussi camp, had become so mixed with the Senussi that neither pilot could bomb the tribesmen without bombing the yeomanry.

Rotham, using two of his Cooper bombs, made two swift runs over the camel herd, stampeding them once more in all directions while killing any number of the pitiful beasts. Then, while Dev hovered overhead, flying back and forth on a north–south axis, Rotham left off his attack, climbed to Dev's altitude, and with a hand signal and a salute, turned northeast toward El Hammam, heading back there before he ran out of fuel.

For one more hour, Dev remained above the battlefield, circling and observing. Down below, while he had witnessed here and there some hard fighting as the yeomanry had reduced this or that pocket of resistance, the fight had been quickly concluded, the whole of it lasting not much more than 15 minutes before the yeomanry began to set fire to the tents and reorganize along the northern flank of the former encampment. Around 0950 that morning, because he'd decided to make a slightly wider circuit around the position than he'd formerly made, Dev had cause to make—aside from the bomb that he'd dropped—the one contribution to the engagement that might have carried any significance.

Out to the west about a mile and a half along the wadi from where the Senussi had been encamped, Dev spotted a second, much smaller collection of camels sheltering beneath an escarpment with as many as 25 or 30 dispersed men attending them. Rather than try to bomb the dispersed group, Dev swiftly produced pencil and pad and wrote *25–30 Senussi, 1.5 miles down wadi southwest of you.* Hastily he signed the document, ripped it from the pad, thrust it into one of the weighted cotton bags he'd been told by Rotham to carry, and returned to the oasis, where he spotted what he imagined to be the yeomanry's staff. He sailed directly over them and dropped the bag over the side, turning his plane on his way out in time to see one of the staff dismount and run to pick up the bag where it had fallen. Fifteen minutes later, moments before he turned north to return to El Hammam, Dev had the satisfaction of seeing two squadrons of the yeomanry mount and ride in pursuit of the Senussi he'd described.

By noon, Dev was back on the ground at El Hamman, eating more hard biscuit and more bully beef alongside Rotham and the fitters. And then, changing quickly from his flying togs into his uniform proper, Dev once more seated himself in the Crossley and bolted forward with Rotham behind the wheel, driving hell bent for Alexandria.

"Pinched you off, don't you see?" Rotham said. "Orders were to send you straight from Alexandria to Port Said and 14 Squadron headquarters at Kantara, but with Yates dead, I needed you here, not tomorrow or next week—but yesterday. Squadron CO's a good chap. He'll understand. Tell him Trev sends regards. Sorry about having to press gang you that way, but no other choice. Too big of a job for one; just right for two, if you see what I mean. But if you're assigned to B Flight, I'll be more than pleased to have you aboard. What?"

Stunned, his mouth hanging open, Devlin Collins faced up to the fact that he'd been shanghaied and then, unable to help himself, broke into laughter.

"You have an interesting way of doing things out here," Dev said, as the Crossley rocketed over a bump in the road that left the two of them bouncing up and down in their springless seats.

"Oh, aye, that's a fact," Rotham said, skidding around a slight turn in the road and accelerating away from it. "And while we're on the subject," he continued, drawing an envelope from his pocket, "here's your train ticket, good for any day, and your travel orders. When you reach Port Said, see the station's transport officer, and he'll lay on something that will get you down to Kantara."

"Thank you, Sir," Dev said. "I'll hope it isn't a donkey."

"Right," Rotham said. "Good man. Glad to have had you with me."

3

Devlin's train trip from Alexandria to Port Said involved a jolting seven-hour ride through much of the Nile Delta while sitting in a compartment with a pinched and elderly Anglican minister who seldom said a word and a sweating Syrian businessman who had no words at all. Sporadically, the Anglican minister slept; the Syrian merely fanned himself throughout the entire journey and seemed to make his exit from the compartment with relief once they arrived in Port Said. With his own duffle in tow, Dev was the last to leave the compartment, and after a quick exchange with the guard, he made straight for the workplace of the transport officer.

"You were supposed to have reported here two days ago," the transport officer, a captain, said, looking Dev up and down with a waspish glance. "Why didn't you?"

"Spot of trouble with the Senussi," Dev said. "I was dragooned to fly, and did."

"Where? In the flesh pots of Alexandria?"

"No, Sir," Dev said, trying to maintain an even tone. "In the skies over Wadi Moghara."

"Right," snapped the transport officer, "and if your commanding officer swallows that one, he's as likely to swallow a camel. I shall be sorry to miss your court martial. Now, Mr. Smarty, march yourself out to that Crossley tender you can see through the window there, and make it quick if you expect to reach Kantara before dark. This time, be quite sure that you don't stop anywhere along the way!"

"Right, Sir," Dev said, making the martinet a salute and turning on his heel.

The rating behind the tender's wheel, a gnarled corporal named Fox, seemed to have attended the same driving school as Captain Rotham, with the result that as he raced the machine south through Port Said and out onto the dusty road flanking the canal, Dev found that he had to clutch the sides of his seat with both hands to avoid being thrown from the vehicle. Twice the Crossley clipped the edge of standing fruit baskets, spinning their contents all over the street behind them; once Fox narrowly missed taking a donkey down, and the numbers of men, women, and children he sent fleeing for safety as he raced down the narrow streets nearly defied counting.

"Make this trip often?" Dev asked the corporal, once they emerged from the chaos of Port Said and fairly flew down the road toward Kantara.

"Aye, Sir," Fox said, "most ever' day, carryin' parts for 'em an such. Back and forth like a stoat, I goes, but 14's air mechs got 'em a good mess, and they feeds me right well an' bunks me for the night, but thems eat early so as to work late. Spected ya yesterday, I did, an' the day before. What happen?"

Fox's question, in no way insolent, struck Dev as amusing.

"Trouble with the Senussi, west of Alexandria," Dev said by way of explanation.

"Oh, aye," Fox said at once, "thems a right nasty lot of buggers, ain't they?"

"So it would seem," Dev said. "But there are fewer now than there were two days ago."

Corporal Fox dropped Dev in front of a tent he called C Flight's Headquarters shortly before 1700 that afternoon whereupon Dev, still shouldering his duffle, raised the flap and went in to find a rotund, semi-bald captain named Tuck looking up at him from behind a makeshift desk, a pen poised in his hand.

"Sir," Dev said, dropping his duffle, coming to attention, and saluting, "Lieutenant Devlin Collins RFC reporting for duty, Sir."

"Well, Christ Almighty," Tuck barked, setting down his pen, standing, and returning Dev's salute. "Where the devil have you been?"

"With Captain Rotham, Sir," Dev said quickly, "I'm afraid that he roped me into his do against the Senussi. Said you'd understand."

"Oh, I might understand," Tuck said quickly, "but whether Major St. Clair will is another question entirely. Lucky you, however, because he's on station today, so you'll be able to tell him all about it in the mess. Pick up that duffle and set it on the chair. Scorpions about, if you see what I mean. And then you can follow me."

Dev did as he was told and followed Tuck back outside the tent, where the man seemed to be stepping a lively pace toward a much larger tent erected on the ground some 30 yards away.

Dev quickly found himself inside the mess tent, which had been arranged for supper—trestle table thrown up by the mess waiters, with tin plates and tin mugs arranged alongside battered cutlery. He might have noticed more, had he taken the time to look, but before he could give the space a second glance, he found himself standing in front of a tall, narrow-faced major whose coal black hair was roughly parted in the middle above a pair of dark gray eyes which seemed to bore straight into Dev like a pair of drills.

"Major St. Clair," Tuck said swiftly, "Lieutenant Collins, freshly arrived after whatever odyssey has prevented him."

"Where, Mr. Collins," Major St. Clair asked pointedly, "have you been keeping yourself?"

"With Captain Rotham, Sir," Dev said forthrightly, "over the Senussi. I gather that Lieutenant Yates was killed three days ago, so Captain Rotham took me straight to El Hammam the minute I debarked from my ship, and we flew two missions over the Senussi. He said to give you his regards and imagined that you would understand."

"*Ah*," Major St. Clair said after a moment's hesitation, "perhaps I might, after I hear the particulars in detail, something we will put off until after we dine. In the meantime, let me introduce you to 14 Squadron's adjutant, Captain Sims."

Sims, graying, portly, and stepping with a limp, looked old enough to Dev to have been a participant in the Boer War—a notion that proved true when Dev noticed the ribbons on his uniform. While it seemed clear that Sims deferred to St. Clair in most regards, it also seemed clear to Dev that Sims probably filled a role as old counselor to the squadron, his age more than twice that of any man in evidence. St. Clair next introduced him to the other officers in the flight: Lieutenant Crisp, a blond-headed flier from Kent; Lieutenant Bivin, a young man who nevertheless seemed already to have developed a heavy set of jowls; and Second Lieutenant MacNab, a red-headed Scot youth whose eyes tended to dance. Lieutenant Peters, the officer in charge of maintenance and armaments, rounded out the assortment, and then, very quickly, Dev found himself with a bottle of beer in his hand—a beer only slightly chilled—and involved in conversation with the other officers of his standing, who quizzed him lightly about his background and flight training and what life had been like in America.

Their meal that evening was not one that Dev intended to write home about. The main course consisted of mutton with steamed carrots and a boiled potato on the side—not exactly gourmet, but still a huge step up from the bully beef, hard biscuits, and oatmeal upon which he'd survived since he left the boat. Washed down with a second bottle of lukewarm Egyptian beer, he found it thoroughly satisfying.

No one sat long at the table that night, each officer largely focused on his food following the before-table preliminaries. Then, their plates emptied, each officer requested permission and paid the proper respects to St. Clair, before exiting the mess, anxious to make whatever preparations were required for operations on the following day.

"All right, Mr. Collins," Major St. Clair said, pushing back slightly from the head of the table and lighting his pipe while both Sims and Tuck did pretty much the same, "the time has come to hear about your travails with the Senussi. Proceed."

Selecting his words carefully, neither gilding what he had to say nor clipping the salient facts from his report, Dev offered his justification for his absence while describing the actions that he and Captain Rotham had taken.

"I suspect that seeing the yeomanry make their charge must have been a stirring sight," St. Clair said when Dev finished.

"Yes, Sir," Dev said.

"Distract you a mite from what you were supposed to be doing?" St. Clair asked, studying Dev's face as he waited for an answer.

"Yes, Sir," Dev said, "at first."

"I'm not surprised," St. Clair said.

"And kudos to you for having spotted that second band farther down the wadi," Sims added.

Dev acknowledged the remark with a slight nod but said nothing.

"Good enough," St. Clair said. "Captain Rotham did the right thing about you, and you seem to have done the right thing by him. Well done, Mr. Collins. Now, to business, so as to put you in the picture."

"Yes, Sir," Dev said, feeling a sudden sense of relief.

"As I'm sure you are well aware," St. Clair said, "we have both Germans and Turks to the east in Sinai. Our job, 14 Squadron's job, is to help protect the Suez Canal, so C Flight is based here at Kantara, while A Flight is based 30 miles to the south at Ismailia—that's where Captain Sims and I are presently headquartered. Eventually, when this Senussi disturbance is fully quelled, B Flight will return and be quartered somewhere alongside of us. Following me, are you?"

"Yes, Sir," Dev said.

"A road of sorts—the most probable line of advance for the Germans and the Turks—runs all the way from Kantara to El Arish, which is about 100 miles east of us and about 30 miles south of Gaza. El Arish is at the junction of three roads: the one that leads here, one that leads south into Sinai and to Bir Hasana, and another which leads southwest to both the Maghara Hills and Rodh Salem. Those roads, if they may be called that, are the main routes to the canal. Most of the Sinai, you must understand, is a virtual wilderness inhabited by isolated Berber tribes, and those rascals, those who aren't absolute devils, are by no means civilized according to our standards. 17 Squadron, who we've relieved, had at least two fliers go down out there, and when they were found finally, they'd been stripped naked and had their throats cut. We've had a couple of pilots go down as well; they were also stripped naked and then sold back to us for 50 pieces of gold. Two others that we know of and according to air intelligence were turned over to the Turks, who only paid five pieces of gold and who seem to have as little use for the Berbers as we do. I tell you this because it is best that you know what you may find in the Sinai before you ever attempt to fly over it."

"But fly over it we must, I take it, Sir," Dev said.

"Absolutely," Major St. Clair said. "That is our entire purpose here. Our job at the moment is reconnaissance; we're here to alert the Army in the event that the Hun makes a move toward the canal. At the same time, we are doing an extensive photographic survey in order to map everything between here and El Arish, and when and where we are able, we intend to bomb Turkish water stations and wells in order to reduce the kinds of supplies they will need if they are ever to come forward in any substantial way."

41

To Dev, the tasks assigned seemed mundane, pedestrian, and possibly boring, and upon hearing them, he thought, not without seeing the irony in his perceptions, about how greatly they differed from what he'd imagined he would be doing when he first reported to the Central Flying School.

"I would suppose," St. Clair said, anticipating him, "that our work differs considerably from what you imagined you would be doing when you first put on your wings."

"Yes, Sir," Dev said, showing the man a hint of a grin.

"Yes, well," St. Clair continued, "the same, I think, has been true for all of us. But do not think we are on a picnic, Mr. Collins, because we are most assuredly not. We may not yet have encountered more than a few Hun fliers, but the Hun and the Turkish infantry are present in numbers at El Arish, Bir El Mazar, Magdhaba, the Maghara Hills and in any number of other places. Those who aren't armed with machine guns and rifles are armed with some very deadly Archies that can shoot you out of the sky with sometimes fearful accuracy."

"Archies?" said Dev.

"That's our word for the Turk's anti-aircraft guns," Sims said, registering a mild smile.

"Nasty, they are," said Tuck, "and the Huns seem to have given the Turks an unlimited number of them. Sudden puff of smoke, heat and compression of the blast wave, and shrapnel flying everywhere."

"Do we bomb them?" Dev asked.

"Right you are," said St. Clair. "Even with an observer to fire the Lewis gun, the BE2c is severely limited in its ability to fight back, and when you're out alone, your only recourse is to bomb the Archies if you can find them and outmaneuver any Hun or Turk you may meet in the air. At the moment, all of our observers are sergeants, but most of them are fair shots, so you do have some protection behind, and they can also get off bursts to the ground.

But if you're out alone, you will be carrying at least four Coopers with the understanding that you will make them count."

"Understood," said Dev.

"One other thing," St. Clair continued. "Should you encounter and fly through cloud over Sinai, pay particular attention to your altimeter. Some of those rugged and barren mountains out there rise to considerable heights, so remaining above 2,000 feet in those conditions is always wise."

Dev, instantly sitting up straighter and registering made a mental note of the fact.

"Well, then," said Major St. Clair, "for the moment, I think that covers what I have to tell you, save for one thing. Be up and ready to fly in the morning. You and I will do an early breakfast, and then the two of us are going up together. C Flight received a Bristol Scout today, our first, and I want to try it out. You'll be going along because I mean to see what you can do. Written reports on you that we've received are good, but the proof is in the flying. Okay?"

"Yes, Sir," Dev said.

"Right," said Major St. Clair. "Captain Tuck will show you where you're to bunk. I'll see you in the morning, Mr. Collins. And welcome to 14 Squadron. May your tenure with us be long and safe."

Leaving the mess tent with Captain Tuck, the two men walked directly to the supply tent where Tuck drew a sleeping bag for Dev, handed it to him, and then walked him a few steps down the tent line before raising a tent flap, flashing him a smile, and saying, "You're in with Crisp. I rather think the two of you will hit it off. Glad to have you aboard, Collins. Make yourself at home."

Crisp was not in the tent when Dev entered it, but his arrangements were clear enough, Crisp's cot, footlocker, chair, and wash basin all arranged on the left side, with a hurricane lamp sitting on a small camp table between the empty cot, footlocker, and chair that were obviously to be Dev's. Throwing down his bedroll, Dev flipped open the footlocker, removed and stowed the contents of his duffle, and had just started unrolling his sleeping bag when the flap once more opened, and Lieutenant Crisp came in.

"Ah, welcome to Oxford East," Crisp said with a laugh as Dev turned to greet him. "All of the discomfort of an OTC tent on the Christ Church meadow with none of the amenities."

"The amenities being?" Dev said with a grin.

"Pubs and shop girls, near to hand," Crisp said. "After a week in Kantara, one begins to feel deprived. After a month, the deprivation seems like an eternity. Like life without char, if you see what I mean."

"Sorry," Dev said with a slight smile, "but I'm afraid I don't."

"You mean you don't know about pubs and shop girls?" Crisp said. "How odd!"

"I mean I don't know about char," Dev replied. "What the hell is it, if you don't mind me asking?"

"Oh, I see," Crisp said, his eyes lighting up with amusement. "*Tea*. Indian word, I suppose, corrupted from *chai*. In common use amongst our fitters, or so I'm told. Not used in Ulster, then?"

"This is the first time I've heard of it," Dev said.

"Interesting, that," Crisp said. "Evolution of language, and all that."

"Your course of study?" Dev asked.

"In a manner of speaking," Crisp said. "Modern languages— French, German, Italian, that sort of thing. And you?"

"Mechanical engineering," Dev said, "at Rutgers, in New Jersey."

"Might surprise you," Crisp said, "but I've heard of it. Once called Queen's College, wasn't it? Before the Americans so unwisely severed their connections with us?"

"Ha," Dev said, "but I think you're right." And then, very swiftly, Dev changed the subject. "Question," he said, "if you don't mind?"

"I will agree to answer, of course," Crisp said, seating himself in his chair, "as long as you agree to come clean about your experiences over the Senussi."

"Fair enough," Dev said. "So, what's it like to fly with Major St. Clair?"

"Demanding," Crisp laughed. "Not to worry. Sooner or later, every new boy gets the same treatment. St. Clair takes them up and puts them through their paces. Wants to see what people are made of, I suppose. Not a problem as long as you don't draw BE2c Number 24 for your flight. That one has an engine that acts up. If I were you, I'd march myself right down to hangar number 2, see Sergeant Banes, and tell him to set you up with something better for tomorrow. Don't want you coming down east of the Quattuya Oasis and getting picked up by the Berbers. Nasty lot, those, the Berbers. Downright uncongenial."

"What seems to be the problem with Number 24?" Dev asked.

"No idea," Crisp said quickly. "Our air mechs are pretty good, but whatever it is that bedevils that bird has remained a mystery." Then, his eyes lit up as he changed the subject. "So, what about the Senussi?"

Dev once again recounted his experiences with Captain Rotham.

"And there were actually Germans out there, in uniform?" Crisp said, registering a sense of wonder.

"Germans or Turks," Dev said. "At the altitude, I found it difficult to distinguish. What happened to them, I really can't say, but I would guess that the yeomanry either killed them or captured them."

"What one wonders," Crisp said, "is how they reached the Senussi in the first place."

"Good question," Dev said. "And I have no answer, but I would guess that they landed from a boat or submarine, well to the west of El Hammam."

"Stands to reason, doesn't it, because I don't see how they could have crossed Sinai, gotten over the canal, and hiked around south of Alexandria or Cairo without being detected," Crisp said. "So, a submarine sounds about right."

"Yes," Dev said.

Crisp, also slated to fly in the morning but not with Major St. Clair, then declared his intention of turning in early. When he did, Dev strolled down to hangar number 2, found the man Crisp had identified as Sergeant Banes—a former blacksmith in his forties whose handshake felt as hard as a hammer—and made his intentions about not flying BE2c Number 24 on the following morning abundantly clear to the man. Then, Dev took the liberty of quizzing Banes about what in particular seemed to be occurring with the faulty engine.

"Pilots seez that it sometimes tends to cut out on 'em after an hour in the air," Banes said, his brow furrowing with the wonder of the unknown. "We've stripped her down, me and 'im that's 'er air mech an all, an' we ain't found ought' ta account for it. New engine when we put 'er in."

"From what you've told me, Sergeant, I don't think the problem is in the engine," Dev said. "I'd say it's in the ignition system. Something around the magneto may be overheating with a connection separating when it heats up. Might be worth your time to check it."

"Aye, Sir. Ah will," Banes said. "Knows sometin' 'bout 'em, does ya?"

"A little," Dev said.

By the time Dev returned to his and Crisp's tent, the temperature had dropped at least 20 degrees, the desert's winter night coming on fast without restraint. In the minute he crawled into his sleeping bag and dossed down, Dev knew at once that the sleeping bag was going to make all of the difference and slept like a rock, regardless of Crisp's snoring, which, at first, Dev rather thought might be enough to resurrect an Egyptian mummy.

46

By 0700 on the following morning, with Major St. Clair in B Flight's newly arrived but previously flown Bristol Scout and Dev flying BE2c Number 16, the pair were 10 miles east of Kantara flying at an altitude of 4,000 feet. It was there, very rapidly, but as St. Clair had warned Dev in their pre-flight briefing, that the major began to put Dev through what he had called "a few exercises." Because the Scout could fly at a speed approaching 90mph, it had at least a 20mph speed advantage over Dev's BE2c, which, going all out, could barely make it to 70mph; nevertheless, St. Clair set out to "work" his new pilot, doing a very sudden, very unannounced, double Immelmann turn which took him directly up and over Dev's head and brought him almost instantly back down on Dev's tail. Dev, in response, immediately cut his throttle, dropped down, and caused St. Clair, who still had speed on, to pass directly over him while Dev pulled into a tight turn at the slower speed—a turn which would, had he been carrying an observer, have unmasked the observer's machine gun and given the man a clear shot at St. Clair as the Scout whipped away from him.

Together, for the following hour, the two pilots sparred as combatants might, and then, finally, St. Clair turned northeast with, as he had previously announced, the intention of reconnoitering the eastern limits of the Quattuya Oasis. As far as Dev could tell—as they approached what appeared to be a scattering of date palms interspersed with a few brown fields and three or four that appeared to be green—human beings, Egyptians or otherwise, seemed to be virtually nonexistent below them. But when they moved to within half a mile of the edge of the oasis, wholly without warning, a black puff of smoke exploded in front of them and off somewhat to their left, and St. Clair instantly began to fly a dipping and weaving course as Dev came face to face with the fact that he was encountering his first Archie. Then, very swiftly a second shell burst to the right of them. Up ahead, Dev could see Major St. Clair remove a Cooper bomb from the rack that had been attached to his cockpit and swiftly did the same.

Dev, concentrating on following St. Clair, had seen neither men nor a muzzle flash on the ground to indicate where the challenging anti-aircraft gun might be located, and it seemed its presence at Quattuya had come as a surprise; from what Major St. Clair had told him before they flew out that morning, the nearest to the canal the Turks were thought to be was somewhere in the vicinity of Bir Salama, another 15 miles east in the direction of El Arish. The "practice reconnaissance" that St. Clair had planned had uncovered not only the unexpected but an increased threat. As Dev felt his bowels cramp and a bead of sweat roll down the side of his face, a third burst of smoke erupted to his side, something the size of a fist instantly punching a hole through the leading edge of his upper wing. Quick as darts, St. Clair and Dev shot in over the oasis at an altitude of no more than 200 feet, Dev dropping his Cooper bomb in the same instant that he saw St. Clair lose his. In the next second, swooping up and away, the two planes put yet another exploding black puff of shrapnel behind them as they turned to see the results they'd achieved with their bombs.

Seeing St. Clair motion him to dive and circle the oasis—something he had briefed Dev about as a possibility before takeoff that morning—Dev quickly put his stick forward and, with the wind whistling past his ears, dove the BE2c back down to 300 feet. He began making a wide circle around the oasis, climbing and dipping so as to change his altitude every few seconds while weaving in and out along his circular course, so as never to present a constant range or altitude that the Turk gunners might be able to judge. In the meantime, on the opposite side of the circle that Dev continued to fly, St. Clair had climbed for altitude, always maintaining something like 180 degrees, not to mention several hundred feet of elevation between their relative positions. Dev sensed the extent of the difficulty that St. Clair was attempting to force onto the Turks. If the Turks had no more than one gun on the ground, St. Clair had worked them into an impossible position. If they fired at Dev, thinking that he was preparing to attack them, they would have to depress the elevation of their gun while leaving St. Clair unattended and high above them. If they turned their attentions to St. Clair, they would have to break themselves physically as the pointer and trainer manipulated the hand wheels to elevate and train their weapon on St. Clair; and if they did, they would leave Dev unattended to make his bomb run. If the Turks had two guns on the ground, that, as Dev knew, would change everything by ramping up the danger for both Dev and St. Clair when they made another attack.

In less than a minute, the Archie fired at Dev twice—and this time, Dev located the gun's position by detecting its flash. The gun seemed to be firing just to the left of a cluster of palms, with mules and a number of camels apparently tethered not far distant. Dev could see the camels, but he could not see any of the men manning the gun, as he had only caught its flash before, high above him, he saw St. Clair point the Bristol's nose down and begin his dive in order to bomb the Archie. When he did, Dev knew that the major had timed his attack perfectly—that unless another gun opened up on him as he descended, St. Clair had a better than even chance of making his attack unopposed while the Turks fired at Dev. And in that instant, as Dev forced his attention back to what he was doing, the Turks did, exploding yet another round out to his starboard side, a piece of shrapnel instantly tearing away the top of his cowling and, he thought, damaging his air screw in such a way that he could feel a vibration beginning to develop in it. As soon as Dev perceived the fact, he turned away and headed toward Kantara. And that, too, he did by prearrangement.

"In the event of damage to your craft," St. Clair had told him, "damage to your engine, your controls, or your prop while leaving out holes in your fabric, you are to return to Kantara at once. We've too few planes to risk losing one that a good pilot can fly back here and land safely where the air mechs can patch it up. No false heroics, if you see what I mean. No sticking around to watch the results of anything we might get into. You are directed to fly low, count your own safety first, and get your ship back in any way you can, and that's an order."

Moments after Dev had started back, St. Clair slid the Bristol in beside him, holding up one finger to indicate, Dev imagined, the number of guns that he'd attacked and then showing Dev a thumbs up sign. Dev, for his part, pointed straight to his prop and then showed Major St. Clair a thumbs down, indicating, he hoped, the kind of trouble that had started him back.

Thirty minutes later, with Dev landing first, the BE2c and the Flight's new Bristol Scout taxied across the dirt field and cut their engines in front of hangar number 1, and when his propeller stopped spinning, even from where he remained sitting in his cockpit, Dev could see that a sizable chuck of laminated wood had been torn from one of its blades. As with the damage that had been done to Number 16's cowling, both would be easy for the air mechs to find and repair. But before climbing down from the machine, Dev instructed Sergeant Banes to make a meticulous examination of the engine to be certain that nothing about it had been damaged by the blow that the plane had taken. And then, Major St. Clair came walking toward him as Dev finally lowered himself to the ground.

"Damage?" St. Clair asked.

"She'll need a new air screw," Dev said quickly, "and either the fitters will have to mend the cowl or replace it, but I believe her engine remains sound, Sir."

St. Clair acknowledged Dev's report with a mere nod of his head. "Not exactly what I'd planned for you this morning, Mr. Collins," he smiled, "but no matter. You acquitted yourself well, and I shall tell Captain Tuck to integrate you into his flight schedule without further training. It seems doubtful that you will be doing something like what we've just done on a daily basis, but from time to time … well, who knows what the morrow may bring."

"If you don't mind me asking," Dev said, "did you get him, Sir, the Archie?"

"Nothing certain, and I didn't stick around to find out," St. Clair said, "but I think we might have eliminated that one. If we didn't, we at least blew the pants off a few Turks, and that might be just the thing to keep them out of Quattuya for another week or two."

"A couple of those rounds seemed almost too close for comfort," Dev said.

"For all we know, those might have been Huns who shot at us," St. Clair said. "The Turks are not bad shots, but the Germans are slightly better, and if those were Germans, intelligence will want to send in a friendly Berber or two to confirm their presence. Put a line in your report about the apparent accuracy of the rounds, and I'll do the same. That will arouse the interest of the staff without committing us to a positive identification."

"Yes, Sir," Dev said.

"Well, then," said Major St. Clair. "This is the last I'll see of you for a time; Captain Sims and I are off to Ismailia as soon as I change. So, welcome to 14 Squadron, and let me wish you good hunting, Mr. Collins. I pass you as ready and fit for duty."

When Dev stepped back into his tent that morning, he found Crisp, his legs propped up on the table, sitting in his chair reading Trollope.

"So," Crisp said, greeting Dev with a grin. "How'd it go? St. Clair tie you in a knot and hang you out over some Berber's herd of goats?"

"Not entirely," Dev said, removing his flying coat and throwing it onto his cot along with his gauntlets before sinking onto his chair. "We flew up to the Quattuya Oasis and took out an Archie."

"Did you now?" Crisp said, suddenly leaning forward with interest. "Do tell?"

"Not much to tell," Dev said. "Air bursts around us as we dove down to reconnoiter, and then, I circled to the south and sort of drew fire while St. Clair, who had climbed to the north, dived back down and unloaded a Cooper on them."

"You didn't drop anything yourself?"

"One, on our first pass over the oasis," Dev said, "but I merely dropped by following St. Clair's lead. I didn't know where the gun was located; I hadn't seen it. Spotted it finally when I started around in that low circle to distract them."

"Turks or Huns?"

"No idea," Dev said, "and St. Clair said that he hadn't stuck around to find out, but whoever they were, he thought he'd done for them. Let's hope."

"From what you've just related," Crisp said, "I think you must realize that you've seen more action in your first three flights out here than most of us are likely to see in three months. Nothing doing on my hop this morning. I'd call it downright boring."

"How so?" Dev asked.

"Went out with Bivin," Crisp said. "We flew out 30 miles to the east, scanned for Turks, and then began taking photographs. Exposed 12 plates, each of us, flying level at 3,000 feet. Came back and landed. Dull as dust, if you see what I mean. Sent the plates off to intelligence as soon as we landed. They're developing them and using them to make maps, or so we've been told."

"How many trips like that have you made?" Dev asked.

"One every day and sometimes two for the past three weeks," Crisp said. "Reconnoitered Bir El Abd once. Didn't see a thing.

The word *dull* seems to have been invented to describe what we've been doing. I suspect our lads in France would be driven into the madhouse if they had to face the same thing."

"Or get down on their knees to thank the Lord for their deliverance," Dev said. "From all reports, they appear to be dying like flies up there. Six from the class before ours at Central Flying were dispatched to France the week before my bunch finished, and from a report we had, four of them were dead before the following Thursday, and a fifth had gone to hospital."

"Yes," Crisp said, taking on a more meditative tone, "I suppose that we should be grateful for small favors."

"Well," Dev said, "this is certainly not what any of us expected, but with all things considered, it does seem to have its advantages."

Two days later, Dev had good cause to remember what he'd said when another new pilot, a fresh-faced 19-year-old named Billingsly, came to them straight from the Central Flying School after leaving a public school in Manchester. Billingsly, ebullient and uncharacteristically loud for a man from the Midlands—"anxious to get at the Hun," as he told everyone he came across—took off for his inaugural flight with Tuck and instantly made the most colossal blunder of his life. Over the end of the field, when his engine suddenly cut out and died, rather than fly straight ahead and glide down for a safe landing, he foolishly tried to turn back, lost his lift, and plowed straight into the desert floor at a more than mortal speed.

4

Following Billingsly's unsettling demise, Second Lieutenant Symes reported for duty with B Flight. Symes had been at Cambridge for a year prior to his enlistment, obtained his flying certificate from a civilian flying school during that same year, and been sent direct from his officer training course to Central Flying School. There, Tuck said, he had shown himself to be a careful, competent flier with what one of his instructors had called a "calculating attitude." Circumspect in speech, with a dry wit he didn't often show, the man found himself welcomed in the mess, for the simple reason that there wasn't a thing about the man that could offend anyone.

Dev, during his first week with B Flight, had found himself in no way taxed by his duties—duties which, as Crisp had warned him, revolve around the mundane and largely unexciting. Given his Flight's assignments, he'd flown eight times in six days, going out at least once with MacNab, twice with Biven, and flying three times with Crisp, as the pilots with whom he associated himself acquainted him with Sinai. All of their flights had combined standard reconnaissance with photographic missions. Their primary job was to take clear photographs to assist with mapping Sinai, but their secondary role was to keep a sharp eye open for Turkish penetrations in the direction of the canal. In pursuit of that aim, and without regard to the fact that each pilot carried an observer to assist in the photographic work, they also carried at least two Cooper bombs, with standing orders to bomb any Turkish patrols or units that they happened to uncover.

Dev's observer, Corporal Trent, came from London, where, prior to the war, he'd been employed as a solicitor's clerk. Short in stature, with cropped hair but a full mustache, Trent, according to Dev's estimation, was around thirty, and much to Dev's satisfaction, he did not speak with anything resembling a Cockney accent. Dev was also gratified to learn, when he went down to the butts one morning to observe some of the men take target practice with the Lewis gun, that Trent also seemed to have a good eye for striking whatever targets he happened to be shooting at when he pulled the trigger. Furthermore, as Dev quickly learned, Trent had a quick hand on the camera they were using and didn't make mistakes while inserting and extracting the fragile glass plates they were forced to use.

Corporal Trent, for his part, showed Dev just the right degree of deference without ever behaving in any way that Dev would call subservient. He went about his work professionally, enjoyed a mild joke whenever Dev attempted to deliver one, worked meticulously with both the plates and the maps that the two carried, and showed, after his three months' experience on the station, a high degree of knowledge about the terrain—something that Dev found exceptionally helpful as he worked to become familiar with it. As a result, while no one would have accused the men of developing a particularly strong friendship for one another, the two developed a bond of the sort that aided considerably in the work they were assigned to do and lent an added efficiency to the reports they submitted, which Tuck was quick to notice. It wasn't that Trent always flew with Dev; on Dev's off days, Trent often went out with the other pilots who were flying. But when Dev did fly, he could be fairly sure that Tuck would send Trent to fly with him, and Dev learned more and more to rely on their relationship as the days went by.

Twice during that period, Dev and Crisp flew once more to reconnoiter the Quattuya Oasis, but in neither case did they meet anti-aircraft fire. When they first passed over the site, Dev quickly spotted the place where the Archie had fired from—the ground around it blackened enough to indicate the spot—but the gun itself had apparently been removed, and Dev saw no Turks or Huns to suggest a continued presence. Over Ghratina, however—a collection of mud huts a few miles east of Quattuya, an area over which Bivin was assigned to fly later in the day—Trent noticed a cloud of dust rising from somewhere along what he imagined to be the road. He reported it to Dev as soon as he could scribble a note to hand to him, voice communication over the roar of the engine being utterly beyond possibility.

As a result, Dev turned and flew once over Ghratina, but by the time he did so, the dust had dispersed, and later that afternoon, Bivin also failed to sight anything that might indicate a Turkish presence on the ground.

Later that evening, as the two sat in the mess talking about it, Bivin raised the possibility of a Turkish or Hun vehicle having raised the dust—something that could be parked in the shade of a palm grove or beneath an overhang so as to avoid notice from the air.

"We must talk to Tuck," Dev said, "and see if he won't assign us to make another pass. Might be something down there. Might not. If we don't go to look, we'll never know."

"Righto," Bivin said. "And let's be sure to take a Cooper or two with us. Potting a staff car might be just the thing for lifting the spirits of the moment."

"Want to lift the spirits of the moment?" Crisp said, entering on the tail of their exchange and instantly sitting down across from them. "I'm just back from Ismailia with a tale to tell."

"Don't let us stop you," Bivin said quickly. "Pour forth. Traveling show with debs? Loose women on the march? Or better yet, real beef steak coming through supply?"

"Those are mere youthful dreams," Crisp said. "The news I have is genuine. C Flight's made a raid on Bir Hasana."

"I've heard of Bir Hasana, but only once," Dev said, "so you're going to have to explain."

"It's well out to the east," Crisp said, "about one hundred miles east of Ismailia on the most southern of the possible routes to the canal, and it has a very good water supply. If the Huns or Turks ever want to approach the canal from that direction, the water at Bir Hasana is an absolute necessity for them. We know that, so we've attacked them."

"That's all very good on grand strategy," Bivin prodded, "but very short on detail."

"And if that place is one hundred miles out," Dev said, "that means a 200-hundred-mile flight to go there and return, and that's a mite beyond our range."

"Not if you don't take an observer and put an extra gas tank in the front cockpit," Crisp said, rounding on them with a grin.

"Yes, yes, continue," Bivin said, coming forward to the edge of his seat. "You have our attention, I'm sure. No need to draw things out."

"Well," Crisp said. "As we all know, Captain Blackburn is in command of the Flight down there, and Dev, for your information, because Biv already knows, Blackburn is an innovator. He's the man who tried attaching metal deflectors to a propeller so that we could mount a forward machine gun on the BE2c without shooting ourselves to pieces."

"I'm guessing that idea failed its ground test," Dev laughed.

"Yes, well," said Crisp, "so the next thing he got to working on was a bomb sight. He fixed that to Lieutenant Hill's machine and sent the man out to practice with cloth and sand practice bags. According to Major St. Clair, that looked like a bust as well, but apparently Hill kept at it and got better and better to the point where St. Clair gave approval for a mission. So, on the morning of

February 27, Blackburn sent Hill off to Bir Hasana loaded with a single 100-pound bomb slung under the belly and two 20-pound Coopers. And if you can believe it—and you'd better because I've seen the photograph—Hill popped the 100-pounder dead center in the concrete reservoir, fracturing one of its walls."

"You jest," Bivin said skeptically. "You're telling us a porky, Crisp. You ought to be ashamed of yourself."

"Heart's honor," Crisp said, raising his right hand, "it's the absolute truth! And as if that weren't the whole of it, he got one of those Coopers right onto the roof of one of the buildings at the station as well. Must have given the Turks perfect fits, if you see what I mean."

"And what were the Turks doing while all of this was going on?" Dev wanted to know.

"Blasting away at him with every machine gun and Archie in the place, apparently," Crisp said. "How he got out of there alive and all the way back to Ismailia is as much of a wonder as getting the bomb in the right place."

"Sort of gives us something to shoot for," Dev said.

"But not with a second tank of petrol sitting in the front seat, I hope," Bivin said.

"There's that against it, sure," Crisp said. "Nasty stuff, petrol. One tracer through it, and you're a fireball rather than a plane.

"I think I'll park the whole idea somewhere else and try to forget about it," Bivin said quickly.

"Too soon the hero, too quick the death?" said Dev.

"Something like that," Crisp said.

"Suddenly makes our photo recon work look inviting," Bivin said.

"Point taken," said Crisp.

"Quite a feat, though, wasn't it?" Dev said.

"Yes," both men replied, "quite."

By the time that Devlin had reported for duty with 14 Squadron, General Sir Archibald Murray had been appointed Commander in Chief of all British troops in the Egyptian Expeditionary Force, and by the time Dev actually started flying with his Flight, General Murray seemed well on his way to making himself more than a little disliked by the men under his command. Field Marshal Kitchener, it seemed, had gone so far, during his visit to Egypt, to suggest that the troops were supposed to defend the canal rather than the canal being in existence to defend the troops—a prompt, many imagined, designed to get Murray moving with a view to securing Sinai, to ensure the safety of the canal. And indeed, the man had begun to make plans in that direction—plans that apparently involved endless delay and endless detail, most of which Murray was reported to go over himself, meticulously, before sorting it all out for further attention to a staff whose ever-growing numbers seemed to rival, according to one wag, the number of angels Michael had mustered when he drove Satan into the deep. Not a few other wags, Tuck and Rotham among them, compared the staff to Satan's own minions, an aspersion they backed up with only mildly suppressed fury whenever they heard that Murray was about to go anywhere outside of Cairo by automobile or train.

"What do you suppose is at the root of that particular flit?" Dev asked at the beginning of his second week of flight as he and Crisp left Tuck's tent after submitting the written reports they'd prepared following that morning's photo reconnaissance mission. Tuck, when they'd left him, had been virtually dancing up and down behind his desk, cursing the air and cursing the unnamed "General" for all he was worth.

"I don't suppose," Crisp said flatly. "I *know*. Murray is about to make an inspection of some facilities up around Port Said, or at least directly across the canal from Port Said. That means a train trip, and for 14 Squadron that means a flap. Murray is a virtual old maid, like the most pinched and waspish spinster aunt that any man could imagine. Apparently, he had a breakdown once—nervous, that is. Brought on during the retreat from Mons in 1914. He's recovered now. After a fashion, if you ask me, and they sent him here, the Imperial General Staff, but the man's thought to be touchy, temperamental, obsessed with artillery, and most certainly obsessed with detail. He is also known to be a brilliant staff officer, so since his arrival here, he seems to have remained in Cairo and devoted his time almost wholly to staff work, or so the rumor goes, while giving virtually no attention to the troops."

"And that's what Tuck is upset about?" Dev asked.

"No," Crisp said as the two of them proceeded toward the mess tent for a sit down and a cup of tea. "What Tuck's about to have a fit over is Murray's train trip to Port Said. The issue, you see, is that the Huns slipped a couple of flying machines over Port Said the week before you came. If I had to guess, I'd guess that they loaded up with extra fuel the way Hill did for his do at Bir Hasana, and then flew down to Said from El Arish and dropped two or three bombs. So, 'The Spinster,' as I like to think of him, is riding an armored train to Port Said and has put out a standing order that anytime he goes anywhere in that train or away from Cairo in an automobile, he is to have three of our birds flying directly above him as added protection."

"You're kidding," Dev said, his jaw dropping slightly.

"I'm not," said Crisp. "And with Rotham's lads flying against the remains of the Senussi, he can only put up two birds, which means that Tuck himself has to fly to Cairo and then waste his time and at least two days 'escorting' The Spinster to Port Said and back."

"We have an expression in New Jersey," Dev laughed. "'There ought to be a law.' Against such misuse of time and resources, if you see what I mean."

"Oh, I see it and see it only too well," Crisp said, as they walked into the mess tent, "but who's going to tell that to Murray, or make him see the point of it? Somewhere there, I detect a degree of timidity, insecurity, or downright cowardice that seems just a trifle reprehensible."

"What, I wonder, has prompted him to go all the way up to Port Said for an inspection?" Dev said.

"Water, I think it must be," Crisp went on, picking up a tin cup for himself and handing Dev another. "If we ever plan to move on El Arish, we are going to have to move along the coast. For men, horses, camels, and vehicles that will require huge amounts of water, so as we speak, Egyptian labor gangs are already building a pipeline, 12-inch, that will carry the water forward from freshwater reservoirs on the Nile, carry it right under the canal, and move it along beside the troops. I talked to an engineer involved in the project, and it's a big one: pumping stations, filtration plants, miles and miles of pipe … the works. And paralleling the pipeline, other Egyptian labor gangs are starting to build the rail line east of Kantara that will bring up the troops' supplies. I flew up in that direction on a recon about a week ago, and at the moment, I believe they are somewhere in the desert about halfway between Port Said and Romani. Enormous undertaking, don't you see. When or if the troops will start to move is another question altogether, but you do see why the Huns and the Turks are showing an interest in the Quattuya Oasis. It's right on the road down from El Arish, directly south of Romani, and probably the best positions from which to attack it, and from which to stop the pipeline and the rail line."

"Yes," Dev said, as a mess attendant filled their cups with murky tea. "I don't think I'd want to give odds, but somewhere around there, probably in the not too far distant future, I think the Hun will make a move."

"Right you are," Crisp said as the two of them sat down, "and that's the particular bee in Tuck's bonnet. Tuck knows that every resource we have ought to be watching the Huns and the Turks; instead, the general has him off playing nanny to an armored train, during the day, at an hour when the Hun wouldn't dare try to fly to Port Said."

"Useless muddle, isn't it?" Dev said.

"Absolutely beyond reason," Crisp replied.

On the following morning, prior to his departure for Cairo, Tuck dispatched Bivin to do a photo recon mission around Ghratina and MacNab, and Symes to cover Romani. Dev and Crisp, Tuck called in last.

"Major St. Clair has four machines down for maintenance," Tuck said swiftly, "and two flying west for some assignment that the staff wants performed, so he's well short of what he needs, and you two are going to fill in. You're to reconnoiter southeast in the direction of Rodh Salem, with a special emphasis on Rodh Salem, and there are mountains down there, so mind how you go. Downdrafts and such, and there could also be fog because you're flying so early. Trent will be flying with you, Collins, and Crouchbank will be in your ship, Crisp. Off you go, and watch your fuel."

They took off that morning just as a faint pink dawn had begun to break, and for 30 miles they had clear flying. But as they approached the mountains to the north of Rodh Salem—the tiny oasis sandwiched to the south of that first high range—they met fog, climbed to get above it, and flew on for 15 more minutes before they began to find it breaking up. They dropped down through whatever wisps of it remained to find themselves approaching the black specks they took to be Rodh Salem from a flying altitude of 1,000 feet.

Flying twice over the oasis while Trent and Crouchbank exposed as many as four plates, Dev sighted nothing of note, beyond a few Berbers and an assortment of no more than six camels. But having twice crossed the oasis from north to south, as Dev once more turned east to come around and point his machine back to the northwest toward Kantara, he spotted something that caught his attention. Out to the east, two or three miles distant, Dev saw the morning sunlight reflecting from particles of dust in the air, particles of dust that did not look to him like they'd been raised by a swiftly whirling dust devil. Off to his side, Crisp's hand signals showed that he had apparently spotted the same thing. So, both pilots eased back to the south in order to sweep well around the dust they had seen, circle it at no more than 100 feet, and come up behind it with the sun at their backs. The turn into which their maneuver took them required nearly five full minutes to complete, given the wide radius of the circle they'd decided to fly. Such flying required concentration, more concentration at the low altitude, in the event that one or the other of their machines acted up.

By the time Dev and Crisp had worked fully around to the south of the dust they had spotted, Dev knew—or thought he knew—absolutely that what he was seeing had to be a column of Turkish horsemen stretched out along whatever path, trail, or road they were following for more than a quarter of a mile or, perhaps, an even greater distance. What he believed he was seeing amounted to a Turkish cavalry troop or a mounted company, probably numbering between 50 and a hundred men, depending on whether they were marching by twos or threes.

A swift glance over his shoulder showed Dev that Trent was already on his feet, preparing the Lewis gun for action, and another swift glance in Crisp's direction showed him that Crouchback was doing the same.

Tensing, once more feeling his stomach cramping almost to the point where Dev found it difficult to sit still, he continued on the course he was flying, moving east, hopefully beyond the sight of the Turkish column. Then, finally, about a mile and a half behind them, Dev eased once more into a turn that brought him slowly around onto a reverse course that would take him straight back in the direction from which he'd just flown but bring him up directly behind the enemy.

Quickly raising an upturned palm to Crisp, off to his left, Dev made as if to inquire whether or not Crisp wished to lead them into the attack, but Crisp promptly waved the offer off. Dev took the lead, dipping the BE2c to an altitude of 75 feet and angling out to the right side of the dust cloud that was now coming up fast, so as to give Trent a clear and uninterrupted line of fire on the left side of the machine.

Possibly owing to the noise made by their column of march, the Turks failed to detect the impending attack until the two planes had closed to within 500 yards. Even then, surprised and stunned, thinking possibly that they were about to be overflown by their own aircraft coming up behind them from Bir Hasana, they appeared to freeze. It was in that moment, as Dev sailed down beside them for a straight run up the right side of the column, that Trent cut loose with the Lewis gun and began to take them down, Crisp and Crouchback following less than 100 yards behind and repeating the stunt.

Dev's run up the column didn't last, he thought, more than 15 full seconds before the head of the Turkish column disappeared behind him. However long it had been, it had been long enough for Trent to expend the 47 rounds in the ammunition pan on the Lewis gun, and glancing once more over his shoulder, Dev could see the man methodically laboring to remove the empty pan in order to replace it with a fresh canister. In that second, as Dev pulled out, gained altitude, and brought his machine around, he also reached for the first of the two Coopers that he'd carried out with him that morning.

By the time Dev got around and started his bomb run, the Turks, although initially caught flat footed, had started to disperse. Crisp quickly caught up with Dev so that the two of them could go forward side by side with 25 yards between them and drop their bombs together, to catch as many of the breaking enemy as possible as they turned from the road and fled to both sides.

The two Cooper bombs that the men dropped as they dove in on the column from no more than 200 feet created pandemonium on the ground, the entire forward stretch of the formation disintegrating as men on horseback, men on foot, and riderless horses ran in all directions. But after Dev dropped his bomb and climbed above the rear of the column, the Turks who had avoided the bombs had the presence of mind to fight back. A rifle round thrown up from the ground snapped a guy wire on his port wing, while another, splintering the deck beneath his feet, destroyed his altimeter.

Balancing the need to attack against the danger from the ground, Dev led Crisp into their next bomb run at 300 feet. By the time that they had maneuvered to make it, and while both Trent and Crouchback fired off their Lewis guns in brief but hopefully effective bursts, the Turks were so dispersed that Dev didn't imagine that either of the bombs they had dropped could have been very effective.

Once more, as here and there an isolated Turk fired back at them, Dev and Crisp circled the remains of the column, attempting to estimate the amount of damage they might have done. Then, without hesitating and in observance of the fuel they had remaining, they turned to the northwest and headed for Kantara, landing there with what both later estimated to be as little as a 15-minute reserve of fuel left to spare.

Commending Trent for what Dev called a stellar performance, Dev sent him to turn in the photographic plates he'd exposed. Then, after informing Banes of the damage that he taken—at least what he knew about—Dev walked over to where Crisp was dispatching Crouchback with his photographic plates and delivering the same damage report to his own fitters.

"Well?" Dev said, when he first approached Crisp.

"Apparently," Crisp said, showing Dev an ironic smile, "if a man flies with you, he can expect to be shot at. At least now, I suppose, I can say that I've actually made some kind of contribution to the Allied effort in this war. By Crouchback's count we did for at least ten or 15 of those beggars, and that doesn't include their poor horses."

"Yes," Dev said, "and one or two of them nearly did for us, or at least me. I had a round punch straight up through the deck and do for my altimeter."

"Then your luck is holding," Crisp said. "One round apparently punctured my tire, so I was damn fortunate that I didn't fold up on landing. Did you see the Hun?"

"No," Dev said.

"Riding at the head of the column, right beside what I took to be the Turk in command. If Crouchback can be believed, we sent him sprawling when we dropped the first bombs."

"Let's hope that we sent the Turkish officer sprawling with him," Dev said. "Reckon we ought to inform St. Clair about this?"

"I think we must," Crisp said. "This is precisely the kind of thing that he and Tuck sent us down there to look for, and with Tuck gone, I believe a telephone call should come now, well in advance of any written reports that we send in later. Want me to make the call?"

"You're the man with most time on station," Dev said. "Seems fitting. In the meantime, I'll get onto Barnes and the fitters because I have a feeling that we'll be going straight back down there in the morning, on St. Clair's direct orders."

They did go back to Rodh Salem on the following morning, flew over the oasis several times at no more than 100 feet, and didn't sight a thing. Even the Berbers had removed from the vicinity, leaving nothing to see. Carefully, extending their search, Dev and Crisp flew a widening circle out to 4 miles from the oasis and found nothing save for a few dead horses and a number of sand mounds where graves had been dug alongside the road where they'd made their attack. The Turks had pulled out, probably to Magdhaba, 25 to 30 miles farther to the east, but acting on St. Clair's orders, Dev and Crisp did not try to fly there to check. Instead, finding Rodh Salem utterly empty, they returned to Kantara and reported their findings to St. Clair by telephone. The following day, when Tuck returned to the Flight and learned what they'd done, he commended them wholeheartedly for their actions.

Slowly, March gave way to April. On the desert floor, slightly to the north, Dev, when he flew in that direction, noticed both the rail line and Murray's pipeline going forward, large gangs of Egyptian laborers, looking like beetles from the heights Dev flew, laboring in swarms. In the meantime, at least one yeomanry regiment of which Dev had heard went forward to occupy the Quattuya Oasis and guard Romani's southern flank while also providing an advance guard for the labor gangs that were advancing Murray's projects. In the days that followed, aside from their normal photographic responsibilities, Dev and Crisp found themselves, along with the other pilots in the Flight, being dispatched farther and farther to the east in order to reconnoiter places like Ghratina, Bir Al Abd, and Bir Salama, all three south of Bardawill Lake on the coast but within 30 or 40 miles of Quattuya. And what they found out in the desert east of Quattuya was in no way reassuring.

The first indication that things were changing came on a morning when Symes and Bivin flew up to do a photo reconnaissance over Bir Al Abd, and Symes returned with a wounded observer, 14 holes in the fuselage directly behind the observer's seat, and the tip of his lower starboard wing shot off.

"Archies and machine guns, both," Symes said. "I'd say that there's a battery of the damn things parked at Bir Al Abd, and if there aren't 300 Turks moved in there, I put their numbers at four."

The following morning, Bivin and MacNab ran into virtually the same number of wasps while over Ghratina. This time, everyone came back whole, but they also reported a battery of Archies located down among the palms, guarded by machine guns. MacNab had tried to bomb them, dropping three bombs which his fitters had suspended from racks beneath his kite, but while he said that he'd raised considerable dust, he could offer no direct evidence that he'd actually done any damage on the ground nor put even so much as a single machine gun out of action.

"I dropped my bombs at 600 feet," he explained, "with the Archies popping everywhere around me, so I didn't linger to make any handshakes."

Two days later, Dev and Crisp took off in order to reconnoiter Bir Salama, faced a stiff headwind going up, and made one good pass over the settlement before not only machine guns but at least three anti-aircraft weapons opened up on them. Their single pass over Bir Salama had been enough to convince them that at least one and perhaps two Turkish cavalry battalions were present in the vicinity. Having carried at least two Coopers on the mission with them, Dev and Crisp dropped them over a tented camp which the Turks had been foolish enough to erect in the open, taking mild satisfaction in watching a number of tents catch fire. But it was on their way out that they entered a whole new dimension to the war.

As both pilots climbed for altitude following their last bomb run, but with Crisp still far out in front of him, Dev became aware of a sudden change—when the Archies inexplicably stopped shooting. In the next moment, as Trent swiftly clapped him on the shoulder, Dev heard the Lewis gun begin to pop, saw bullet holes appear in his wing, and glanced over his shoulder to find a German Eindecker—its single forward-facing machine gun spitting gun flashes—descending on him from astern. Instantly, Dev knew that he and Trent were in trouble. The Eindecker, Fokker's quintessential and much feared monoplane, carried a machine gun synchronized to fire through the propeller, and for all practical purposes, Dev knew that it also had nearly a 20mph speed advantage on the BE2c.

Dev quickly threw the BE2c into as tight a turn as he could manage—something the Eindecker would have to match if it intended to continue the combat and a turn that would give Trent the best possible advantage for defending the two of them. The Eindecker, good in a dive according to the intelligence that Dev had been given, was none so good in a climb, so if Dev got the chance, he intended to climb. But after flying twice around in a tightening circle with Trent cracking away at the Hun in every way that he could think of, the Hun inexplicably broke off, dove once more for the ground, and disappeared, leaving Dev free to rejoin Crisp, who had already turned back to assist in helping Dev to drive off his attacker.

They'd had a narrow escape, Dev and Trent, and as they flew back to Kantara side by side with Crisp and Crouchback, Dev could feel his hands shake with the tension he'd been under. Twice reaching over the cowling, Trent had given him claps on the shoulder in apparent confirmation of the action that he'd taken. While they went far to confirm Trent's loyalty to Dev, they did not relieve him of from the stress he felt in having been caught out by the Hun, who had swept down on him so swiftly without detection. In that instant, Dev determined to find a shaving mirror that he could fix somewhere above him to give himself a possible way of seeing behind him when he sat in the cockpit.

On the ground in Kantara, once down from the wing, Dev felt wobbly from the fright the Eindecker had given him. Why had the

Eindecker turned away? Why hadn't it continued with its attack? Had Trent with the Lewis gun beaten the Hun off? Had the tight turn Dev had put the BE2c into somehow dissuaded the Hun from attempting to follow him into a climb? Or had the Hun merely had enough and decided to break off while the breaking was good? Dev had no idea but knew that too much thinking about it would lead him nowhere and felt relieved when Crisp finally caught up with him after landing his aircraft.

"Everyone whole? Nobody wounded?" Crisp asked hurriedly as he approached.

"We're whole," Dev said, clapping Trent on the shoulder by way of thanks for the defense Trent had given them, "but I can't say I'm very happy for not seeing that bastard coming down on us in the first place."

"That's my job, Sir," Trent said. "He must have been right above us somewhere and dropped straight down, straight down from directly above without first showing himself anywhere behind and distant. Neither of us could have seen him without looking straight up, and that, we weren't like to do, and he knew it. Dead spot, up there, if you see what I mean."

"It's a dead spot that we're going to have to bring alive in the future," Dev said.

"Aye, Sir," Trent replied. "Stands to reason."

"Well," Crisp said, "whatever the tactic and at long last, we now have definite proof that the German Flying Service is about."

They found more proof when they approached the mess tent, saw MacNab standing outside the flap, and immediately heard from him that he had seen an enemy scout in the distance that morning while flying over Bir El Abd.

Inside, seated across from Tuck who was having a late breakfast, and with mugs of tea before them on the trestle table, Dev and Crisp delivered their preliminary reports orally before the mess attendant delivered them breakfasts of their own.

"For the past few days," Tuck said, sticking his fork into a banger, "I've emphasized the fact that I think the Turk is preparing to make a move on Quattuya."

"And?" Crisp said.

"And," Tuck continued, "I'd say that GHQ has ignored me, or at least that is St. Clair's opinion, and St. Clair has not only written them, he's been on the telephone with them. Staff wallahs he talked to laughed, told him he was seeing things, told him the Turks wouldn't dream of moving beyond El Arish."

"Obviously, the comfortable rooms of Shepheard's Hotel and probably the bar are very convenient places from which they are able to make their observations," Symes said in a voice dripping with sarcasm.

"Staff duty corrupts," Crisp said, "and red tabs corrupt absolutely."

"I shall advise them to think twice," Tuck said, placing a bit of the sausage into his mouth and beginning to chew. "This sudden appearance of enemy kites ought to alert them that things are on the move."

Across the three days which followed, Dev, Crisp, and the remainder of the Flight saw more that indicated Turkish movement: a broken-down staff car midway between Bir El Abd and Bir Salmana, distant enemy aircraft that did not seek to engage, and what looked like a poorly camouflaged dump of supplies beneath a few sparse palms north of Ghratina.

According to Tuck, each of the reconnaissance reports he sent in were written in more and more pointed language, language that St. Clair allowed to go forward, all of it virtually shouting on paper about the operation that the Turks seemed to be mounting. From the word that St. Clair sent back, however, the staff wallahs had become downright waspish in their denials that the Turks had anything afoot, declaring that their own intelligence—gleaned in whole or in part from "reliable" Berber spies that they'd sent into the field—ran counter to anything that could be seen by the naked Royal Flying Corps' eye.

"Miserable bastards!" Tuck said mere moments after speaking to St. Clair one morning over the telephone. "Whatever has possessed the staff at GHQ to trust Berber spies will be one of the great mysteries of this war. A Berber spy will take money from any party that's willing to pay, and the same Berber is as willing to take gold from a Turk as he is from one of our lot. Getting money out of a Turk is usually like trying to pull the incisors out of a tiger, but in this case, I'd bet money that the Turks are paying one or more of those untrustworthy rascals to tell Cairo exactly what Cairo wants to hear so as to cover their own tracks."

Dev and Crisp, not to mention the remainder of the Flight—men who had seen the evidence with their own eyes—thought the same thing.

But on the morning of April 23, 1916, beneath a dense fog that had blown down from the sea, the Turks finally moved, and moved fast, pushing the yeomanry straight out of Quattuya with the apparent strength of a Turkish regiment. Suddenly, with the barn door ripped from its hinges and the stock fleeing, cocktails at the Shepheard bar were overturned, egg was left dripping from any number of faces, and consternation became the order of the day. Suddenly, the staff wallahs—those most in fear of losing their cushy jobs in Cairo—seemed to fairly burn up the telephone lines to 14 Squadron's headquarters in Ismailia. At that moment, 14 Squadron ceased to be the goat and began to look to any number of people at GHQ like a form of deliverance that they'd somehow misplaced and only recently rediscovered.

"I gather that the yeomanry regiment, the same one that must have been sitting on their duffs in Quattuya, is in disarray," Tuck said, as he called the Flight together that evening. "Two other cavalry regiments are on the move, as well as at least three battalions of regular infantry, but it is going to take them a few days to move into position. I need not tell you that, through no fault of ours, GHQ has been caught with their pants down, and now, as you might suspect, they are begging for us to save them from being caned. See to your machines, have your observers see to the ammunition in their Lewis gun pans, and load up with Coopers, at least ten per kite. Major St. Clair and Captain Blackburn will be bringing up at least four planes in the morning for a joint operation, and as far as I understand it, we are going to take off from here at a few moments after dawn and bomb the hell out of the Turks to try to drive them back out of Quattuya. Any questions?"

On the following morning, with Tuck leading his Flight and St. Clair up from Ismailia, lately landed and refueled, leading 14 Squadron, a total of eight BE2cs left Kantara for the 40-minute flight up to Quattuya. Given the early hour, the moisture-laden atmosphere that prevailed so close to the dawn, and the number of kites in the air, the planes flew in a gaggle rather than anything resembling a tight formation so as to give each pilot room to maneuver. Dev and Crisp, flying on the right flank of the formation, had been detailed by Tuck with special instructions. Each of them were to limit their bombing runs over Quattuya to five drops at approximately 500 feet, but with five Coopers left in their racks, they were then to draw off, stand aside to the north, and wait. If, following the action by the remainder of the Flight, St. Clair deemed the damage done satisfactory, they were to fly on east toward Bir Al Abd in an attempt to bedevil anything else they found moving west toward Quattuya.

"Apparently," Crisp said to Dev as they strode toward their planes that morning, "your action over the Senussi and our attack down at Rodh Salem have suddenly turned us into independent experts at this sort of thing."

"Or so our masters think," Dev laughed.

The flight up to Quattuya with the BE2cs bobbing up and down on the thermals went swiftly enough. Over the oasis, most of the morning fog had dissipated by the time St. Clair led them to within 2 or 3 miles of the place. But even at 2,000 feet, the air remained both cool and humid, so that regardless of the temperature, in anticipation of the action in which Dev knew that he was about to involve himself, he could feel sweat forming around the edges of his goggles and taste salt from a drop that rolled down alongside his nose and into the corner of his mouth.

Then, very swiftly, St. Clair took them down, spreading out the Flight so that the planes covered as much as 1,000 yards. As the oasis came whipping toward them, its date palms reflecting the light of the morning sun, Dev could see tents, horse lines, at least one machine gun on the top of a post, and men, brown-uniformed men, running in all directions, many of them stopping to raise rifles. He dropped the first of the two bombs he unloaded in the midst of his pass, and then, before he flew out and over the northern limit of the oasis, his second, all the time audibly aware that behind him, manning the Lewis gun, Trent was busy firing off every round in the first of the several ammunition pans that he had loaded for the trip.

Only after he had flown out and gone into a slight climb to rejoin the remainder of the squadron did Dev, glancing quickly right and left, notice that he'd been twice hit by ground fire—rifle rounds, each of which had produced tiny holes through the fabric of his wings. To his gratified surprise, he had seen nothing that suggested Archies on the ground, but if he'd managed to pickle the machine gun on the post that he'd seen going in, he knew he would be grateful.

Owing to the wide turn that St. Clair put the squadron into, when they finally prepared to attack again, this time from the north, Dev found himself flying in over the western edge of the oasis at less than

500 feet, the two bombs that he dropped falling amid a collection of horse lines and supply wagons. Something—possibly petrol or ammunition—exploded behind him with such an instantaneous blast that Trent later claimed to have felt the heat.

Coming out from this particular run, St. Clair showed the squadron a hand signal that allowed them to break formation in order to attack targets of opportunity. As a result, on his third and final pass over the oasis, Dev dropped all the way down to 200 feet in order to bomb yet another machine-gun post, the Turks manning the weapon wholly unaware of his approach as they fired south toward one of the planes crossing the central portion of the oasis. As Dev flew out and climbed north to join Crisp and stand off from the remainder of the attack, he didn't know whether he had done for the machine gun or not, but he felt fairly sure that, to use the Flight's expression, he had "blown the pants off the gunners" if he hadn't actually done for them.

Circling overhead, Dev and Crisp did not have to wait long for Tuck to find them. When he did, considering the thoroughness with which the remainder of the squadron seemed to be working over the Turks on the ground, he swiftly sent the two of them flying east toward Bir Al Abd and dropped back down to reenter the fray.

This time, while flying east, had anyone outside their ships been able to see them, Dev and Crisp gave the appearance of whirling dervishes, their heads going everywhere as they scanned the skies for Hun opposition. Things had changed; the silk scarves with which they had wrapped their necks were no longer put on for warmth or Royal Flying Corps fashion. Now, with actual Huns in the air over Sinai, the scarves were essential if they weren't to chafe their throats raw from constantly turning their heads to look for trouble coming from all directions.

Upon their approach to Bir Al Abd, with the wind rushing fast past his face, Dev instantly imagined that the Turks had gotten above themselves—that with Quattuya in their possession, they'd imagined themselves safe at Bir Al Abd and relaxed their guard. Even from the distance, as Dev and Crisp approached, Dev could see Turks everywhere, hundreds of them, with horses, wagons, and various kinds of equipment disposed about the settlement with no apparent effort to conceal their locations.

Pushing their throttles to give them full-out speed, Dev and Crisp, with perhaps 30 yards separating their planes, dove straight in to make their attack from an altitude of 200 feet, each dropping two bombs as they sped down the length of the settlement. That they attracted rifle fire there could be no doubt, but with regard to counterfire by machine guns, the pass seemed blissfully free. The Turks, merely resting on the march, seemed to have erected no anti-aircraft defenses nor did they seem to be making their move with the benefit of machine-gun wagons for protection while underway.

Dev and Crisp did not linger, turning swiftly at the end of their pass and reversing course for a second, and as they went in, Dev did see at least one Turkish crew attempting to lift a machine gun from a wagon in order to set it up in one of Bir Al Abd's dusty streets. But if they managed it, Dev never knew; he was down and over them at 400 feet, losing his last bomb before the three Turks could even extract the machine gun's tripod from the wagon that carried it. Given the strength of the explosion that resulted from the bomb that Dev dropped, he could not be altogether sure that he had not done for both the gun and its crew.

West of the settlement, Dev and Crisp once more turned to make their third and final pass. As they did so, both at once spotted yet another Hun machine dropping down from above to attack them and so put themselves into a tight turn designed to give Trent and Crouchback as clear a shot at the approaching enemy as the men could deliver. Both pilots were stunned to disbelief when, after firing only a few shots at them, the Rumpler—for that was what the enemy machine proved to be—turned instantly away while still as far as 500 yards distant and fairly burned up the air flying away from them in the direction of El Arish. For some reason—one that Dev couldn't even begin to fathom—the Hun fliers, if met with any resistance, real or anticipated, seemed reluctant to engage. Dev hardly imagined that they were cowards and therefore wondered if they'd been ordered to conserve their planes unless they could be absolutely certain of a kill.

Turning once more on El Al Abd so as to make a diagonal pass over the location, Dev did spot one machine gun that the Turks had managed to get into action. But given the direction from which the two planes made their approach, the Turks only had seconds for a clear shot before one of the mud houses interposed itself between the Turks' line of fire and the two aircraft. It was at that point where, still taking rifle fire from the ground—rifle fire that punched more holes through the fabric—Dev and Crisp unloaded their last Cooper bombs, pulled out to the southeast, and headed southwest toward Kantara, landing there slightly less than an hour later with their tanks nearly dry.

News they brought about the Turks at Bir Al Abd caused Major St. Clair to lay on a second strike for later in the afternoon—a strike delayed until 1600 owing to the time that the fitters and air mechs needed to patch up all of the planes in the two flights, arm them, and bring them fully back into flying condition.

In the mess, in the meantime, over lunch, the pilots of the two Flights exchanged what they knew about the raid, this one reporting that he'd set a staff car on fire, another claiming a hit on two machine guns set up nearly side by side, his bomb falling between them, while a third, Bivin in this case, mentioned potting a water tanker that had been mounted on some kind of six-wheeled wagon of elongated size. Two of the pilots from Ismailia claimed to have seen identifiable Huns on the ground, several of them standing around a staff car or a staff truck located near the eastern edge of the oasis. Whether or not their bombs had done for the collection, they couldn't say, but when quizzed by Major St. Clair and Tuck, they stood by their report and wouldn't be shaken from it. The men they'd seen were German; they were absolutely sure.

Once more in the air over Quattuya by 1700 that April afternoon, with a much warmer sun beating down from above before descending into its late afternoon slant, the eight planes of 14 Squadron found that the Turks had cleared out, the entire oasis showing no sign of its recent occupation by them, other than here and there a burned patch to show where the Coopers had fallen. Thirty minutes later, the squadron was over Bir Al Abd, and there, too, they found no sign of what both Dev and Crisp had estimated to be the 1,000 Turks they had attacked earlier that morning. The Turks, faced with an obstacle for which they had not been prepared had decamped, leaving the Sinai clear all the way to El Al Abd and, as subsequent reconnaissance would show, to Bir Salmana as well.

Over supper in the mess that evening, St. Clair ventured a word.

"I believe that we can now hope," he said straightforwardly, "that GHQ will take our work more seriously. One could almost begin to imagine that after what we seem to have achieved today, a few of the more astute among them might begin to see the potential of air power and recognize that we aren't out here flying for recreation."

"Hear, hear," the men were quick to respond.

5

For 14 Squadron—after months of having the Sinai virtually all to themselves—the war changed and plunged into a new dimension. Where before the air had been clear, all of the squadron's pilots were now aware that German and, perhaps, Turkish aircraft might be met anywhere at any time. And, as if to underscore their presence, the Huns did not remain idle. Three times in succession, they bombed Ain Sudr, which was about 35 miles east of Suez; then, very swiftly, they mounted yet another raid on Port Said—an attack that seemed to give GHQ fits, resulting in a flurry of hastily placed telephone calls between GHQ and Ismailia.

In response, on St. Clair's orders, Dev's Flight began flying morning and evening, machine gunning here and dropping Cooper bombs there around every Turkish detachment or installation that they could find up and down the road to El Arish. Then, on May 17, St. Clair once more flew up from Ismailia and laid on a raid of particular import.

"We're going up to El Arish," he said, briefing Tuck and the others that evening after he'd arrived. "Captain Tuck, Crisp, Bivin, Symes, and MacNab will carry extra petrol in the observer's cockpit to offset the weight of the bomb load they'll be carrying. Lieutenant Collins and his observer will fly top cover at 6,000 feet and stand by to fend off any Hun who attempts to interfere. Our objective is to find the Hun airdrome, locate whatever hangars and planes are parked there, and bomb them. Rather than fly up the road, which would alert the Turks to our coming, we'll leave here, strike the coast, and fly east directly up over the sea and about 1 mile out before we finally turn south and go in over El Arish. In the event that one or another of you gets into trouble, you will be delighted to know that the Royal Navy has graciously agreed to station three trawlers along the route. So, if one of you actually has to set down, you can find one of them, set down nearby in the sea, and expect to be recovered. I'll be going with you, of course, and leading the raid, so check your ships and be sure that everything is in perfect flying condition before we take off in the morning."

"Christ," Crisp said as he and Dev walked back to their tent following the briefing, "the thought of carrying an extra tank of petrol in the rear seat, rather than Crouchback with a well-oiled Lewis gun, twists my knickers. Do bail me out, you and Trent, should you see me in trouble."

"I shall consider it an honor," Dev said.

"I should feel a sight more comfortable if I knew they had you flying something a good bit faster," Crisp continued, "like a Nieuport 11, let us say. A plane like that would give the Huns fits."

"Flying a plane like that would give me fits," Dev said, "fits of joy and no little confidence. If I have to dive the BE2c on a Rumpler, it is as like to run straight away from me as not, without ever letting us get close enough to give it a burst."

"Just as long as it runs away," Crisp said, "without taking a shot at me."

"Yes, well, there's that, most assuredly," Dev said.

The raid, when they made it, turned out to be a total bust with regard to finding and bombing the Hun airdrome because no one could locate it. In other respects, the raid came off fairly well. The route they'd flown had proved secure, no Hun had taken to the air in order to come up after them, and considerable damage had been done in El Arish, St. Clair and Bivin dropping their bombs on a Turkish tent camp on the northern extremity of the settlement, MacNab striking and breaching a water reservoir nearby, and Symes potting what he imagined to be—after considering the numbers of men gathered around it—either a battalion or a regimental headquarters. On the way back, not 4 miles west of El Arish, Crisp, previously unable to find a target, finally unloaded on a column of at least 500 Turkish cavalry troops making their way west toward Bir El Mazr. The 100-pound bomb that he released above them so scattered the formation that when he flew once more around to unload his Cooper bombs, he could find only individual horsemen bolting from the sight full tilt in all directions.

By the time the squadron returned to Kantara and sat down in the mess tent for debriefing, the men were utterly exhausted. Theirs had been the longest flight that any of them had ever made under combat conditions. The wonder, to Dev as he sat beside Crisp for the debriefing, was that not a single man had been wounded or killed, because the anti-aircraft fire that the Hun had put up that day had seemed fierce. Even from the altitude at which Dev and Trent had remained, they had seen Archie mushrooms exploding everywhere. According to what Crisp told him when they came back, he'd flown with his heart in his mouth, fearful every moment that this or that tracer coming up from the machine guns on the ground would penetrate the petrol tank behind him and turn him into an instant flamer. But if flesh and blood had come through unscathed, the BE2cs that the squadron had flown had not.

Material damage done to the Flight over El Arish, Tuck said after hearing their reports, would probably keep almost the entire Flight on the ground for at least one, if not two, long days. Bivin, for example, had seen two wing ribs broken and one rudder cable cut and had flown all the way back from El Arish holding the stick with one hand while clutching the rudder cable with his other. A part of MacNab's port elevator had been shot away, while a hole the size of a dustbin lid had been punched through the fabric on his upper wing. St. Clair had collected at least 14 holes from the ground as well as a damaged strut, Tuck had seen three of his guy wires shot away and worried all the way back that his port wing might fold up, and Symes's engine had been struck in such a way that it had choked and coughed throughout his return, threatening at every minute to quit outright and set him down like a man called Peters who the Berbers had taken captive. Crisp had seen his fabric holed four times not more than 2 feet from where he sat, but aside from that slight damage, his ship remained whole. At the altitude at which Dev had flown, he and Trent had wholly escaped attention, leaving his ship the only one in the Flight that didn't require significant repair. Banes, the fitters and the air mechs, he knew, would be working overtime to get the Flight back into a condition to fly.

When, finally, reports had been taken, and St. Clair had chewed over the effects the raid achieved, Dev put up his hand and ventured a word.

"I don't believe this could be seen from the altitude the squadron took when it flew in to make the raid," Dev said, speaking slowly and with care, "but off 3 or 4 miles to the east, from the altitude where we were flying, Trent and I spotted a wide, very flat-looking wadi with a grove of palms along the western side. We could not see beyond the palms, but given the angle of sight, those might very well have provided cover for hangars, and we both wondered whether or not the wadi might provide a hard surface and ample space for the airdrome that we didn't find."

For a moment, the mess tent went silent, and then St. Clair came to a swift decision and turned to Tuck. "I'd fly tomorrow myself," he said, "but I have to be back in Ismailia tonight, so as soon as Banes patches my kite, he's to patch Crisp's." He turned his attention to Dev and Crisp. "You lads are going to answer this question about the wadi tomorrow morning," he said swiftly. "Take off at dawn, fly up well south of the road to El Arish where you can't be seen on your way, and do a reconnaissance over the wadi that you spotted. We'll want photographs, but you are to carry at least four Coopers each, and once your plates are exposed, you may bomb with care without going below 1,000 feet so that you will have a reasonable chance of getting back here with the plates. If you do turn up something, I'm sure we will have no difficulty in convincing GHQ that we need to lay on another raid."

"I believe," Symes said as the three walked back to their tents following the debriefing, "that Dev's good eyes have rather dropped the two of you into the soup."

"Yes," Crisp said. "Keeping company with Mr. Collins seems to have a bad habit of doing just that on an regular basis."

"I don't know what the two of you are talking about," Dev said. "Quiet flight up in the morning, gentle breezes over Sinai, morning outing with Aurora shining pink on the horizon. Why, it could almost be a picnic that we're headed for."

"And you can be damn sure that's what the staff wallahs in Shepheard's bar will think as well," Symes laughed.

"One might almost wish for Moses' rain of toads to descend upon them," Crisp said.

"Almost?" Symes said. "*Almost*? If it were within my power, I would wish their bed clothes invaded by a plague of locusts. Serve the uppity bastards right for sitting around in posh chairs, sipping cocktails, and letting the rest of us carry the load for them."

"Now, now," Dev laughed, "I'm sure their mummies raised them to be very good boys and polite to their seniors."

"Why is it, I wonder," Crisp said, "that when I came through Cairo, all of the staff officers I saw looked like they'd just gotten up off their knees after kissing the shine on their senior's boots?"

"Careful," Dev said, "because exaggeration will get us nowhere. Fancy a drink, either of you? I've been hiding a bottle in the bottom of my footlocker."

"Why, you naughty boy," Symes quipped. "You'll never get staff duty by following that course in life."

Dev and Trent, Crisp and Crouchback took to the air at dawn on the following morning, timing their takeoff for the moment when they had no more than a faint gray horizon to the east, with just enough light for them to make out the field and assure themselves that they could take off without hindrance. Knowing that they would both be flying into the morning sunrise, when Aurora finally did show them the pink of her complexion, both carried sun shades for their eyes but refrained from using them until the moment when they knew that they would really be needed.

Given their line of approach, given the nearly 100-mile distance that they had to fly, they'd calculated their time over target, if they found the target, to last for less than 15 minutes if they were to return without running out of gas. In the event that they risked running out, both Trench and Crouchback had packed in two gallon tins, which, if an extremity were experienced, might give them enough to make their return. Trent was the one who'd come up with the idea for carrying the additional fuel and used it on their previous flight over El Arish, but given the speed with which St. Clair had conducted the raid, Dev and Trent had never had to use the additional petrol and returned it intact to supply upon landing.

The flight east went well. Aurora blushed, her cheeks faded quickly to pale pink, and were soon overcome by gold in the seconds before the sun came up to burn on the horizon, and the two BE2cs operated beautifully as they had been designed to do. Flying by compass at least 5 miles south of the road, neither Dev nor Trent saw a single thing they would have thought out of the ordinary; to Dev's eye, the desert floor in northern Sinai looked almost exactly like what he had seen flying south from El Hammam with Captain Rotham. After an hour and a half in the air, off to the north, Dev spotted El Arish, angled his flight, with Crisp following, toward the unnamed wadi that he and Trent had detected the day before, and flew directly over the palm grove that he had mentioned to St. Clair and the squadron pilots during the debriefing. In that moment, as Trent clicked the camera, changed plates, and clicked it again on their second pass over the grove, everything became abundantly clear to both Dev and Crisp, who immediately pulled a quick turn, went down to 1,000 feet, and dove steeply for a bomb run after seeing a Rumpler on the ground in front of two partially concealed canvas hangars, the Hun kite apparently warming up and preparing for takeoff.

Disregarding St. Clair's instructions to them, both Dev and Crisp went down to 500 feet to drop their bombs, Dev pickling his Coopers directly over the Rumpler, causing it to lift from the ground and come down on its back before bursting into flame. Crisp, meanwhile, unloaded his bombs onto the first of the hangars, causing an initial explosion of some considerable size with secondary explosions following shortly thereafter. Neither pilot had had time to see the results and only sensed that damage had been done when their observers signaled them that success had been achieved. Each, as they later said to one another, would have liked to have known more at the time. But with the amount of machine-gun fire that was coming up at them from the ground, by the time they'd flown down over their targets and with the fact that Dev, at least, and possibly Crisp, had both sighted a Pfalz E. II monoplane dropping down toward them from somewhere out of the western sky, their attention was so suddenly riveted to the approaching danger that neither had time to think of anything else.

Once more, as they had done over Bir Salama, Dev and Crisp turned into an upward spiraling circle so as to unmask their observer's Lewis guns. Then, with the Pfalz closed in to within 500 yards and already shooting at them from its forward-firing machine gun, both Trent and Crouchback opened fire of their Lewis guns, the vibrations shaking their planes in mid-flight.

Nothing that the Pfalz threw at them struck home. Dev knew little about the rate of fire the Pfalz might have been able to achieve, but given the brief burst that the Hun had tried to throw at them, he counted them lucky for not having had to endure a fully committed attack by the German, who swiftly turned away from both of them before he had closed to within 300 yards. And, given the last glance that Dev had thrown in the Pfalz's direction, he was also aware that the Hun had made a mistake. Rather than drop straight down and away from the two BE2cs, the pilot had turned, exposing the entire length of his ship to Dev and Crisp's two observers. Dev felt fairly certain from what he had seen that at least one or the other, Trent or Crouchback, or perhaps both, had gotten a few rounds into the German, because Dev had seen a strip of fabric tear back from the Hun's rudder and flap like a pennons in the wind.

With the Hun inexplicably gone and one more example of the Germans' present reluctance to engage—even when Dev imagined they had a considerable advantage in terms of height and firepower—Dev and Crisp descended toward the desert floor and struck a course for Kantara, flying at 500 feet with the desert whipping beneath them. For the first hour of their flight all went well; then, with what Dev imagined to be slightly more than 30 minutes to go before the home field could be spotted, Dev's engine choked once and quit, causing him to begin a fairly rapid descent while Crisp continued to pull ahead.

Seized at first by fear of crashing, Dev reacted swiftly to this new emergency, spotted a flat stretch out in front of him perhaps a mile away, and tried to glide there with the remains of whatever lift was left to him. Trent, alerted to the problem the moment the engine quit, had swiftly seated himself and buckled his safety belt.

Without Dev knowing what he was doing, the man had also tipped the Lewis gun toward him, removed the canister that he'd half spent firing at the Pfalz, and replaced it with a fully loaded 47 round pan, by the time that Dev finally set them down. They'd flown low over a wadi, which they'd left only a little less than half a mile beneath their undercarriage as they went in, settled onto the sand, and ran straight ahead for some two or three hundred more yards before the BE2c finally came to a halt.

As far as Dev was concerned, it was not time for resting and taking stock. Crisp, having seen Dev's swift descent, had turned and started to circle above, but as Dev had glided over the wadi toward the desert pan upon which he landed, a single glance had shown him at least two tents pitched on the wadi's floor near one of its banks, with a scattering of blue-robed Berbers raising their antiquated rifles in his direction as he flew over them. Trent had also seen them, with the result that even before the plane came to stop, both men had released the catches on their safety belts. In the same instant that Dev snatched up a spanner, a screwdriver, a rag, and a piece of wire, heaving himself from his seat onto the cowling and toward the engine, Trent had also stood, turned the Lewis gun in the direction from which he expected the Berbers to make their most likely approach, and prepared himself for action.

"Downright insulting," Trent ventured as Dev crawled forward up the cowling. "First we have a perfect flight, then we put in a perfect raid and explode a Rumpler, explode a hangar, get away without damage, and then the kite packs up and leaves us to take on a pack of camel jockeys. Why, our mothers wouldn't believe that it could happen to a couple of good sons like the two of us."

"Right you are," Dev shouted back. "You see if you can't blow some sand in the Berbers' faces if they try to come after us, and I'll see if I can't blow some sand out of the fuel line."

Dev had no way of knowing exactly what had gone wrong with the engine, but when he saw that everything else seemed to be intact, clearing a blocked fuel line was the first thing that occurred to him. So, working rapidly with the spanner, he removed the connections at both ends of the maintenance section of the line that fitted alongside the engine block, tried to blow air through it, and to his surprise as well as his delight, found that something in the thin tube refused to let air pass. And if air couldn't pass through that section of the line, petrol most assuredly could not.

Even as Dev thrust the length of wire that he'd carried onto the cowling down the offending section of the fuel line, well overhead where Crisp was flying Dev could hear the sound of Crouchback's Lewis gun rattling out short bursts. Then, perhaps a second or two later, Trent cut loose with three short bursts of his own, and as Dev glanced back over his shoulder he could see that Berbers, six or seven of them, were up out of the wadi, racing toward the plane on foot. Crouchback's burst of machine-gun fire had sent them to the ground, and for a moment, Trent's kept them there. Swiftly, Dev ran the wire down the length of the tube he was holding in his gloved hand, felt resistance, and pushed the wire through, dislodging a glob of what looked to him like grease combined with sand. Three times more he ran the wire through, wiping the mess on the rag he'd snatched up in order to clean the wire and remove the residue. Then, putting the pipe to his lips and blowing air down it once more, he knew that the line was clear and made haste to reattach it. While he did so, Trent fired yet another short burst at the Berbers, who appeared to have shortened the distance between themselves and the plane while Dev continued to work.

By the time Dev managed to reattach the fuel pipe and slide back down the cowling into the cockpit, the Berbers had managed to close to within 200 yards of the plane and were shooting at them with regularity, here and there a round zinging through the air close enough to be dangerous.

Crouchback, firing from well overhead, seemed to be struggling with a jam that had interrupted his shooting, and to make matters worse, the Berbers had spaced themselves out by the time they'd approached to within such a short distance.

"Mr. Collins," Trent said, his voice hardening, "these bastards mean to take us or kill us—or both."

"Yes," Dev said, "it seems pretty obvious that they do. If one or another of them shows himself and tries to come forward, take him down. Then, quick as you can, hop out and give the prop a spin, and we'll be off because I feel fairly certain that I've got our engine problem solved."

Not two minutes passed before two of the Berbers rose to their feet and ran forward in the direction of the plane, firing off their rifles as they came and screaming enough gibberish that Dev could hear them. Trent fired, throwing first one of the Berbers straight backwards into the air and onto his back before he shifted target and took the second out at the legs; then, moving faster than Dev might have believed that Trent could, the man was out in front of the plane and spinning the prop on Dev's signal. The engine did not catch on the first spin, but it caught and coughed to life after a deal of choking on the second. As more rounds from the remaining Berbers kicked up dust around the base of the machine, Dev didn't even wait for Trent to fully seat himself before he opened the throttle and began to taxi while the man was still climbing over the lip of his cockpit. Within less than a minute and with Trent once more behind the Lewis gun and firing at the remaining Berbers behind them, the BE2c lifted off and once more took to the air.

By the time Dev and Crisp returned to Kantara and landed, their machines were running on fumes; indeed, Crisp's ship sputtered to a stop in the middle of the field, forcing the fitters and air mechs to run out to it and push it the remainder of way to the hangars. Dev and Trent, having poured an additional gallon of petrol into their tank while their plane was on the ground, managed to taxi all the way to the hangar, but when Banes checked the tank with a dip stick, he found barely a quarter inch of fuel remaining.

Trent and Crouchback, after being commended for the defense they had given their pilots, made their way first to the intelligence officer to drop off the plates they'd exposed, then headed to the sergeant's mess for a cuppa. Dev and Crisp, wrung out and exhausted from their flight, dragged themselves to Tuck's tent and went in to make their reports.

"So," Tuck said, looking the two men up and down, "you, Collins, think you destroyed a Rumpler?"

"According to Trent," Dev said, "it upended and exploded. I'd say the Huns have one less machine, Sir."

"And you think you set the hangar on fire, Crisp?"

"Oh, no doubt about that," Crisp said cheerfully. "I had a glance back on my way out, and the canvas was burning nicely with a few additional explosions to help it along."

"And now we know where their airdrome is," Tuck said, a smile spreading across his face. "Good job, the both of you. Write up your reports, give them to my clerk to type, and you can take the rest of the day off. I'll telephone St. Clair and give him the good news."

"Think he'll lay on another raid?" Crisp asked.

"Bound to," Tuck said, "but not tomorrow, I think. The air mechs and fitters are still working on our kites. Oh, but before you go, show me on the map the approximate position of those Berbers you ran into. Lucky you were, Collins, you and Trent both, to get shunt of that lot."

On the map that Tuck unrolled—one prepared on the basis of the plates that the squadron had exposed while flying reconnaissance missions across the preceding weeks—the wadi where Dev thought the Berbers to be camped showed up clearly as a single black line.

"About there," Dev said, putting his finger on the spot.

Tuck made a pencil notation. "Good to know," he said, "and best to avoid going near there, although if I know my Berbers, the lot you dealt with will be up and 10 miles away before the sun sets tonight."

"Fearing that we'll return and drop a pair of bombs on them?" Crisp ventured.

"And rightfully so," Tuck said, "because if I thought they'd still be there, I'd have the two of you right back out there with eight or ten Coopers to make sure that bunch don't surface again."

Rather than head for the mess tent and luncheon that day, whipped physically by the flight from which they'd returned, Dev and Crisp went straight to their tent, changed from their flying togs into shorts, shared a quick whiskey from the bottle that Dev had kept by, and piled onto their cots. Both were swiftly sinking into sleep when Bivin, Symes, and MacNab suddenly barged into their tent, rousing them and demanding to hear the full details of what they'd found at El Arish and whatever kinds of action they'd encountered.

Dev, reclined against his pillow, deferred to Crisp, who made a more than colorful narrative out of their mission, not the least of which he devoted to Dev and Trent's engagement with the Berbers.

"Ten? There were *ten* of them?" MacNab exclaimed.

"Well," Crisp said laconically, "there are two less now."

"And Tuck has marked their position on his map where all of us may have a look at it?" MacNab continued.

"Yes," Dev said, "but they are probably already on the move as we speak, changing their location and hiding as well as they might, in the event that we return to bomb them. They seem an ever-present danger out there, but where or when one is most likely to meet with them is anyone's guess, so don't put too much store on where Tuck set down the mark. By suppertime they will be miles away from there."

Eventually, interest waned, and when the three who had not flown that day saw that the two who had could barely keep their eyes opened, they departed for the mess, leaving both Dev and Crisp to plunge gratefully into sleep, and sleep they did, rising only minutes before the evening meal was to be served.

———o———

The Flight's supper that night, a combination of bully beef cooked up with hard biscuit that had been mashed into crumbs, was not one that appealed much to anyone in the mess, but hunger drove them to eat it, and once they did, two bottles of beer seemed to be the most dessert they were likely to find. Not that it mattered much, because while Tuck had returned to his tent immediately following his meal, he was back again before his fliers finished their beer, with the details of a morning mission that St. Clair had laid on for them over the telephone.

The fitters, working throughout the day, had managed to get Bivin's BE2c back into flying condition, and the air mechs, swarming onto MacNab's machine, had also readied it for flight. The planes that both Dev and Crisp flew had seen their fabric quickly patched and also returned to the flight line. The ships that both Tuck and Symes flew needed more work, so the earliest that Banes would promise them would be in the late afternoon on the following day. Tuck and Symes would therefore not be flying on the mission.

"El Arish is not on for tomorrow," Tuck said. "That will give the Hun at least one more day to recover a sense of comfort and lull himself into inattention. Tomorrow, however, those of us who can fly are on for reconnaissance. Bivin, you and MacNab are to reconnoiter Bir El Mazr while Collins and Crisp do a flight over Mustabio which is a few miles west of there. St. Clair wants at least four good plates exposed over each target, and once your observers have exposed their plates, each of you may bomb, going no lower than 800 feet, with the four Coopers each of you will carry. St. Clair recommends that you once more fly up over the sea, but bear in mind that there will be no trawlers waiting out there to pick you up should you opt for that route. I will leave the choice up to each of you individually, but you are to inform me about your route before you depart in the morning. Bivin and MacNab take off at 0700; Crisp and Collins start to taxi at 0715."

On the following morning, with the sun only beginning to rise, Dev and Crisp climbed into their BE2cs and waited expectantly for Bivin and MacNab to take to the air. Fifteen minutes after they'd gone off, Dev pressed the throttle forward, taxied out onto the field with Crisp moving to his side, and then, with each showing the other a thumbs up sign, they moved their throttles forward, picked up speed, and took flight.

The flight to Mustabio that morning took them slightly over one hour, the both of them flying north of the road from Kantara to El Arish but well inland from the sea and slightly south of Lake Bardawill. Flying four times over Mustabio, Trent and Crouchback swiftly exposed the photographic plates that St. Clair had required. Then, dropping down once more to a lower altitude, Dev and Crisp searched for targets of opportunity, saw absolutely nothing to indicate a Turkish presence on the ground, defied orders by searching once more at 500 feet, saw nothing yet again, and turned to begin their flight back to Kantara. This time, rather than try to hide their presence, they flew above the road, sighted a Turkish column east of Bir Salama, and unloaded two bombs each amid a troop of horsemen who were already scattering as they dove to bomb, the sound of their engines having alerted the enemy to their coming. In recovering from the low dive through which their bomb run had taken them, Dev imagined that they'd been fired on by the Turks, but a glance to either side of him showed him no holes in his lower wings, and a farther glance toward Crisp showed him that Crisp, by hand signal, saw no reason to repeat the bomb run. So, the two of them set a course for Kantara and landed there safely by the end of the following hour.

Bivin and MacNab, when they returned, seemed fairly alight with excitement. Their flight over Bir El Mazr had drawn air bursts from the Archies on the ground, and when they'd dropped down to 800 feet to make their bomb run, they'd also drawn machine-gun fire, some of which had penetrated and holed MacNab's port wing, while at least three rounds had struck Bivin's stabilizer. But the cause for their excitement could be found elsewhere, owing to the fact that once they'd dropped down and started their bomb run, they'd spotted two German planes on the ground, a Pfalz and yet another Rumpler, both of them parked partially under makeshift hangars 50 yards apart that seemed to be fashioned from palm fronds. Bivin seemed confident that he had done for the Pfalz after having unloaded his entire stick over it. MacNab, pushed sideways by the concussion of an exploding anti-aircraft round, believed that his bombs had exploded out in front of the parked Rumpler and could not say with any degree of certainty that he had managed to do the plane any damage. Whatever the case, both men came away from the raid with a sense of accomplishment and with the revelation that the Turks and Huns were seeking to push their aircraft forward and closer to Kantara.

Three days later, with Tuck and his entire flight standing beside their planes—which had been fueled and bombed up for the raid—St. Clair and four of the ships from Ismailia landed. All were quickly refueled, and following a few words between the flight leaders and a quickly delivered plan of attack which St. Clair spoke to all of the pilots assembled, the entire swarm of collected 14 Squadron pilots took to the air, flew immediately to the east in a gaggle, and set their course for El Arish and the Hun airdrome.

14 Squadron made their attack approximately an hour and a half later. In the beginning, the raid went well; St. Clair and his pilots, having split away from C Flight while still 5 miles west of the target, elected to come up from the south over the airdrome. Once over the hangars that remained partially concealed beneath the palms and with the sun shining bright to the east, they unloaded their sticks, dropping multiple Coopers with admirable accuracy, catching the Huns on the ground completely by surprise before they swept out, leaving exploding pillars of fire and smoke behind them.

For C Flight—for Tuck, Bivin, Symes, MacNab, Crisp, and Dev—things were altogether different and far more dangerous. Attacking from the east with the sun at their backs, they were making their bomb run only a minute or two after St. Clair and his fliers had pulled out. But the Archies and the machine guns had already awoken to the threat, and without regard to the fact that C Flight's BE2cs were coming at them out of the sun, the rattled Turks were filling the air with every round of anti-aircraft fire that they could muster. Dev flying on the northern flank of the formation spotted what he imagined to be a fuel dump and dropped his entire cluster of eggs over it, the instant mushroom of exploding fire and smoke which rose behind him nearly pushing his plane straight over onto its nose before he could regain control of it. When he did, glancing swiftly to his left, he met a sight he would never forget: MacNab being blown completely out of the air by a direct hit, his plane disintegrating at once in a hail of flaming wood and fabric. In that second, Dev felt a new kind a fear grip him—the fear, not just of death, but of being lost without a trace..

They didn't linger, the pilots of 14 Squadron. Instead, with St. Clair's flight already circling to the west, Tuck led his survivors immediately to join them. There, 5 miles southwest of El Arish, the remains of the squadron joined together in a more formal formation and flew west, heading for Kantara.

What Dev did not know at the time was that one pilot from St. Clair's Flight, landing at Kantara to refuel 15 minutes after the raid, had departed for El Arish and had arrived over the Hun airdrome well after the raid had done its damage in order to photograph the results from several thousand feet. Dev only discovered this three or four hours after the squadron returned to Kantara, the reconnaissance flight following them in approximately an hour later and disgorging the photographic plates its observer had taken before rushing them to air intelligence. By suppertime that night, the squadron found themselves treated to an array of developed photographs that showed them the damage they had done; in one, Dev and Crisp also saw the remains of what they imagined to be MacNab's plane on the ground, the Turks not yet having cleared the debris.

"I wonder if they'll find his body," Dev said quietly as he studied the photo.

"Seems doubtful," Crisp said adopting the same tone. "Direct hit, from what I could see of it. Better than being a flamer. Instantaneous, if you see what I mean. Probably never felt a thing, but that's not much consolation."

"No," Dev said, "it isn't."

Two days later, with St. Clair still on station, and with Tuck and Bivin having returned from a photo reconnaissance flight over the Hun airdrome, the photos developed from the plates they brought back showed clearly that the Hun had cleared out and abandoned the airdrome at El Arish. Added to the photographs that Dev and Crisp had brought back the day before after a reconnaissance flight over Bir El Mazr, the squadron's air intelligence officer and St. Clair reached the same conclusion.

"Gentlemen," St. Clair said, scanning every face in the mess tent as he spoke to them after they had examined the photographs, "for the time being, I think, we've driven the Hun fliers from northern Sinai. My guess, and I only speculate, is that we've forced whatever Turkish or Hun squadron the Germans had moved down here to withdraw, probably to Rafa in lower Palestine. I congratulate you all on a job well done. I do not say that the Hun will not return, but for the time being, I believe the pipeline and the railroad can move forward with less of a threat."

Later that afternoon, with an Army chaplain to lead the assembly, a memorial service was held for MacNab and his observer, all of the men on the station attending.

6

For three days following MacNab's service, owing to a dust storm that blew up out of southern Sinai, 14 Squadron did not fly. At Ismailia, tents were torn from their pegs. Things were not quite so bad at Kantara, but in the mess tent, Dev, Crisp, and the others made jokes about their attempts to separate what they were trying to eat from the grit that seemed to settle over it. With the men largely confined to their tents, the living was less than pleasant, sand and more grit seeming to filter into every stitch of clothing that they owned until the lot of them felt like they were wearing sandpaper. When the storm finally blew out after days of trial which tested their patience, they nearly ran the station's water tank dry in their futile attempt to wash the grime from their bodies.

In the wake of the storm, two spanking new second lieutenants showed up to join the Flight. Lieutenant Lofton, a pear-shaped man from Chester who appeared to have the personality of a badger, had flighted up from being a sergeant observer and had seen action over France, which had permitted him to gain entrance into flight school. From what Tuck revealed, Lofton had already shot down two Huns over the Somme and acquitted himself well in flying school. Lieutenant Wells seemed to be a character of a different stripe. Beneath a mop of thick, wavy, blond hair, Wells had eyes that shifted everywhere over a protruding nose that gave him some resemblance to storks Dev had seen in photographs. When the man spoke, his every sentence seemed clipped in a way that reminded Dev of Mr. Jingle in *The Pickwick Papers*. "Good show," the man said, upon shaking hands with Dev when he first arrived. "Nasty trip. Dust. Fine grit. Can't abide. Better this. Much." Dev's first reaction moved him to laugh, but thinking better of it, he restrained himself and welcomed the man to the mess.

With the raid on El Arish behind them, 14 Squadron returned to what passed for mundane duties, at least two planes taking to the air in the early mornings to photograph the ground east of Romani and Quattuya, with another two flying off to perform the same task over other stretches of the same desert in the late afternoon. All the while, air intelligence and the appropriate staff officers at GHQ continued to blend the photos they brought back into a mosaic from which maps would be made of the uncertain country extending all the way up to southern Palestine.

Although the airdrome at El Arish had been virtually destroyed by the raid, and whatever planes had been trying to use Bir El Mazr as their base had been cleared out and driven back, the Hun did not entirely avoid penetrations into what 14 Squadron had come to think of as British territory. Bivin and Symes—while on a flight over Bir Salmana—were attacked by an Eindecker that tried to drop down on them while they were taking photographs of the site. Before their observers could get their Lewis guns into action in order to drive the attacker off, both of their planes suffered enough damage that Bivin had difficulty making a safe return, one of his struts so weakened by a Hun round that he feared it might give way in the air, and did, in fact, crack and break upon landing in such a way that his upper wing collapsed when he finally touched down. A day or two later, over Bir El Abd, Dev and Crisp ran into a Pfalz that tried to do much the same thing, the Hun diving on them from out of a late afternoon sun. Given the way that Bivin and Symes had been caught out by the Eindecker a few days before, Crisp and Dev had anticipated trouble. So, as they made their runs over the areas they were to photograph, using prearranged hand signals, either Trent or Crouchback kept watch on the skies above while whoever wasn't manning his Lewis gun devoted himself to exposing the photographic plates—a set-up that left the pilots free to maintain the level flight that was required if the photos were to be of value.

As a result of the tactic, when the Pfalz did attempt to drop in on them, Trent, manning his Lewis, caught sight of the offender and opened fire on him at 400 yards, the tracer rounds that Trent had packed into his ammunition drum alerting the Pfalz to the fact that he had sprung no surprise and warning him off even before the German tried to open fire.

In the days that followed, and as the year pushed on into June and early July, Hun planes—apparently flying out of southern Palestine—dropped a few more bombs on Port Said, made one hasty raid over Kantara in a night attack that woke everyone but achieved no more than a few small craters in the surface of the airdrome, and struck variously at British dispositions in places like Quattuya, Romani, and along the railroad. In one instance, the Huns attempted something that Dev thought ingenious but also rather hopeless, when two of their machines set down west of where the Egyptian labor crews were pressing forward. There, they tried to blow up a section of the already completed rail line by loosing a pair of German sappers who had gone on the mission in place of their observers. In this instance, the problem that the Huns faced—and one they hadn't taken into account—turned out to be the mounted patrols that the yeomanry regiments sent out along the rail line to prevent Berbers from trying to do the same thing that the Huns attempted. The Huns managed to land and disgorge the two sappers and their explosives without difficulty. Before the two men reached the rail line only a few hundred yards away, however, one of the patrols appeared, the patrol's presence causing the sappers to drop the explosives they were carrying and race for the planes that had delivered them. Both aircraft barely got back into the air before the yeomanry drove them off with a volley of well-aimed rifle fire.

At about this time as well, another event occurred at Kantara that changed 14 Squadron's situation and offered the opportunity to make life a deal easier for everyone. One morning, Dev's Flight at Kantara had the airdrome to themselves, but on the next they awoke to find that a Flight of BE2cs belonging to Australia's 1 Squadron had joined them at the field, their BE2cs dropping down from the skies to double the numbers of pilots and planes available for the work. Without hesitation, the Australians immediately took to calling the RFC personnel, including Dev and Crisp, "pommies," while Dev and the others countered by referring to the Aussies as "diggers." Nevertheless, and regardless of the Australian accent that tended to grate on 14 Squadron's ear, the pilots in the two Flights met, bonded after their fashion, and got along extremely well, both carrying forward their missions with what the Aussies' commanding officer as well as St. Clair and Tuck called "spirit and drive."

Although Dev, Crisp, and the others continued to go out armed with Cooper bombs during this period, they seldom found cause to drop them and usually returned to Kantara fully loaded. West of El Arish, save for whatever the Turks and Germans might have been doing at night, the settlements up the road seemed to be clear of enemy activity. The threat of Huns in the air remained ever present, and here or there, evidence of that threat showed up regularly. Yet another Rumpler two-seater put rounds through Wells' wing the third time he went out on a photographic mission with Bivin, Bivin's observer driving the attacker off with three well-aimed bursts from his Lewis gun before the German could bring Wells down.

"Ugly. Great beast. Fangs like a snake. Not to be liked," Wells said over bully beef in the mess that night.

"Quickens the blood, doesn't it?" Crisp said in return.

"Froze mine," Wells said hurriedly. "Constipation results."

"Yes," Dev said, "it does have that effect."

Two days later, flying north of Mustabio, Symes was winged by a round when a Pfalz caught him coming out of a turn while his observer was changing plates in his camera, and Lofton's observer—not yet fully broken in to the drill—had not known quite what to watch for while supposedly protecting the two-plane Flight. Symes's wound was not severe and limited, fortunately, to a single slice across the flesh of his forearm. While he managed to bring back his kite and land it safely, the Flight's medical assistant, after slapping a field dressing on the wound, sent him to the field hospital in Kantara, and there the attending doctor virtually grounded him for the week after keeping him in hospital overnight.

In the meantime, two of the diggers flying even farther east toward El Arish had detected something that they rushed back to report, with the result that when the word spread, special flying was laid on.

"According to the Australians, and we have no cause to doubt their report," Tuck said when he drew his pilots together after getting the word, "the Turks are on the move with something like seven or eight thousand of them marching west from El Arish. According to what Major St. Clair tells me, we have some of our own units out to the east. The New Zealand Mounted Rifles and the Australian Light Horse are somewhere near the eastern edge of Lake Bardawil and will probably try to block the enemy's advance for a time, but on first sight, it looks to St. Clair like General von Kressenstein intends a major drive on the canal. As it stands, with the railroad being routed through Romani, that looks to us like the place where General Murray will attempt to give them battle. So, we'd best prepare ourselves because it seems a distinct probability that we are going to be dropped into the thick of things."

14 Squadron didn't exactly "drop" into the thick of things, but across the two weeks following the discovery of the Turkish and German movement, they most certainly "flew" into it, sometimes going up as many as three times a day in an attempt to keep tabs on the enemy's movements. What they found—or so intelligence types at GHQ informed them, after piecing things together bit by bit from whatever they gleaned from their Berber spies and the air reconnaissance that 14 Squadron and 1 Squadron returned to them—was that von Kressenstein's Fourth Army seemed to be moving as many as 11,000 men forward over a variety of routes across northern Sinai. And the Turks, acting the role of perfect allies, seemed to be advancing even more men—16,000 by some counts—in parallel with the Germans. Whatever the final number, the force with which the enemy was attempting to approach the canal appeared to be more than formidable. What particularly caught Dev and the rest of the fliers' attention was that if large numbers of men were on the move, they were dragging or driving with them exceptionally large numbers of Archies and chattering machine guns. No matter what site or settlement Dev and the others thrust their noses into, they were met with multitudes of bursting anti-aircraft rounds—so many that Dev couldn't help wondering how the Germans had managed to manufacture so many guns and get them all the way down to Palestine from which point he imagined that they had been brought into Sinai.

Aside from the Archies, aside from the machine guns that stuttered continuously anytime the Flight attempted to go low, Hun flying machines also appeared over the advance in numbers that 14 Squadron had never before imagined that the Germans were capable of putting into the air. Tuck, in an attempt to offer his pilots additional protection each time they went out, began flying the Flight's one DH1—the only plane in the Flight that had a forward-firing machine gun. In that nearly antiquated contraption, he drove off Pfalz scouts and Rumpler two-seaters from over some of his pilots several times in the closing days of July.

Returning from one flight, his third of the day, and only after submitting his report in writing, Dev sank down to a late supper in the mess, still wearing his flying togs. He felt like he might keel straight over into the plate of rice and curry that the mess attendant placed before him.

"What day is this?" Crisp said, coming in only seconds later and throwing himself into a chair beside Dev.

"I wrote '26 July' on my report," Dev managed to say, "but whether this is Wednesday or Thursday, I couldn't tell you. I've lost track."

"Wednesday. Just," Wells said, sliding into his seat and begging for a mug of tea. "Not to worry. Thursday follows. Then Friday. Weekend, what? No time off. Utter exhaustion. Better Blighty. Summer drinks. Chilled sandwiches. Cool breezes. Silk frocks. Slim ankles. Alluring popsies. That sort of thing."

"Devilish thoughtful," Crisp said. "Often thought?"

"Just so," Wells said. "Every minute. Waking, and some not."

"I'm afraid I've been too tired to dream," Dev said, realizing that his hand was shaking from stress and exhaustion as he tried to raise his fork to put the first helping of curry into his mouth. "*Good God*, is this curried bully beef?" Dev exclaimed, his outrage showing as he sank his teeth into his first bite.

"Just so," Wells laughed. "Inventive, what? The mess cook?"

"If this continues," Crisp ventured, "perhaps we can give him to the Turks, as a gift. I hear that they will eat anything, because anything is just about what they are fed."

"And this is an improvement?" Dev said.

"That's what I mean," Crisp said. "They'll never know the difference."

"Thank God for Tuck," Symes said, coming in and sliding down into his chair across from them.

"Save thy bacon, did he?" Dev asked, forcing down yet another bite of the curry.

"Yes," Symes said. "Chased a two-seater off of me over Ghratina at 6,000 feet. As if the Archies weren't bad enough up there this afternoon, we had a Rumpler drop on us out of the clouds. Never saw him coming. But Tuck was up there somewhere beneath the overcast and dropped on the Hun with eagle eye. Didn't do for the kite, but I think he may have wounded the observer, for that man's gun went silent on Tuck's first pass."

"And the Rumpler?" Crisp asked.

"Oh, the Rumpler. Well, with that big Mercedes engine up in front, it just ran away from the DH1. If Tuck had been on the ground, he would have been left in the dust."

"Thoughtful of London to condemn us to flying these old heaps," Crisp said.

"Yes," Dev answered acidly, "the wonder is that they didn't send us a crate of feathers and ask us to fashion a set of wings that we might try by flapping our arms."

"War effort. France. Ninety-eight percent," Wells said.

"War effort. Sinai. Two percent," Symes said.

"Mental penetration. Symes. One hundred percent!" Wells replied.

"Exhaustion. Dev. One hundred percent," Dev said, rising from his chair and leaving at least half of the curried bully beef untouched on his plate.

"Mummy won't like it if sonny doesn't eat his beefy weefy," Crisp mused.

"Mummy was a good soul," Dev laughed. "The worst she ever served was Irish stew, without the potatoes." And with that Dev took himself off to his cot where he fell asleep without having taken time to so much as remove his flying coat or his boots.

Once von Kressenstein had decided to bring his army, he didn't hesitate or plod or linger. Instead, swiftly bumping the small and isolated scouting detachments of the ANZACs located near the eastern edge of Lake Bardawil, he quickly caused them to withdraw and continued his march toward Romani. Murray—once alerted to the threat by the persistent air reconnaissance conducted by 14 Squadron and the diggers' sorties conducted for the same unremitting purpose—moved methodically, establishing a defense line slightly east of Romani by placing the brigades of the 52nd Division, the Lowland Division, facing east, with the Plain of Tina to their backs, while stretching their line south from Mahmedia on the coast, through Romani, and off into the desert toward Quattuya. On the 52nd's southern flank, the 1st and 2nd Australian Light Horse Brigades and the New Zealand Mounted Rifles nearly doubled the length of the line. Back at Kantara, around which they were based, the 42nd Division entrained and started forward to reinforce the strength of the position.

During the entire period, while the Germans and Turks advanced and the British moved into position to oppose them, Dev flew as many as three times a day. Sometimes he merely marked von Kressenstein's progress, scribbling notes, and returning to drop them over this or that divisional or brigade headquarters; sometimes he dropped a Cooper here or there when a fat and inviting target presented itself. Thrice he flew a pattern that nearly resembled a pretzel as he did his best to fend off attacks by individual Eindeckers and a Pfalz, while attempting to place Trent in a position where the man could have a clear shot at his attackers with the Lewis gun.

The thing that infuriated Dev the most about those encounters was that the Huns had machine guns synchronized to fire through their propellers, while he did not. In every instance Dev had to turn away from his attackers in order to unmask Trent's Lewis gun; invariably, he felt that he was being forced to cut and run, when what he really wanted to do was turn on the Huns to give them a burst from a machine gun that would fire forward. Why the RFC lagged in developing synchronization for firing forward mystified Dev, tortured him mentally, and made him want to stamp his feet and roar with fury every time he returned to the base with bullet holes through his kite. But if the new ships flying over the Western Front in France and Belgium had the system installed, the old boats flying over Sinai did not, and there seemed precious little that Dev could do about it.

As the collision between the two armies approached, St. Clair brought up part of the Ismailia Flight, adding its strength to Tuck's, and when he did so, St. Clair took over the DH1 with its forward-firing machine gun while assigning Tuck, Bivin, and Lofton to spot for the artillery and for the Royal Navy monitor that had been stationed offshore north of Mahemdia.

"Crisp, Collins, Symes, Wells, and my boys will carry Cooper bombs with which to attack Turkish and German infantry and cavalry formations," St. Clair ordered when he briefed the two Flights. "I will do my best to give you top cover and keep the Huns off of you, but watch yourselves, because the Archies and the machine guns that von Kressenstein has brought with him appear to be plentiful, and the lower you fly, the larger the target you present to the enemy below."

On the morning of August 3, 1916, while flying up from Quattuya, where he was trying to mark the progress of the Turkish left flank—the flank that seemed to be within only a few miles of making contact with the New Zealand Mounted Rifles—Dev and Trent suddenly found themselves attacked by an Aviatik, the first Hun plane of its kind that Dev and Trent had seen in the air. Dev knew at once that the Huns were putting up everything they could find and send down into Sinai. This time, Dev banked so steeply as he threw himself and Trent into an escaping turn that he nearly lost control of his ship, lost altitude swiftly, and only recovered in time to avoid the flattening pancake of a crash landing that would have put him down amid a company of Turks. The Turks flattened themselves on the ground before the next enemy company up the line began to pepper his BE2c with every rifle that the Turks could raise, rounds coming up through the bottom of the plane like hornets as he flew over them. All of them, miraculously, missed both Dev and Trent but several of them did so much damage that Dev knew instantly that he had to abort his mission and try to get back to Kantara before he was forced to bring the plane down in the desert. Stable to a fault, the BE2c, coughing and spitting from whatever rounds had struck the engine, managed to remain aloft until Dev had flown them back to within half a mile of the base. Then, with only a second's warning, the engine quit, forcing Dev—with only a gliding second or two in which to think—to put down hard onto a stretch of broken clay that carried them straight over enough rocks and bushes to crack the horizontal axle that joined the plane's wheels while ripping all the fabric behind Trent's cockpit straight from the plane's belly before they stopped.

Once down, neither man remained in the plane for long, each worried that it might be in danger of catching fire. Carrying the Lewis gun between them in order to share the weight, they counted themselves fortunate that they didn't have miles to walk and set out for the base. Halfway to the hangar, Banes and some of the air mechs who had seen them come down met them in a Crossley tender as they prepared to go out and tow the BE2c back to the hangar.

"Sorry," Dev said, "but it's going to take a deal of work. Aviatik attacked us out there north of Quattuya. I barely recovered her before we would have plowed into the ground. And while that was going on, the Turks shot us full of holes. She's a mess. I hope you can reclaim her, because I think this thing to the north is about to kick off."

"Aye," Banes said. "We'll fix her, Sir. Don't you worry 'bout that. Have her good as new 'fore a dab of butter can melt."

Trent, true to form, didn't say a word. Dev remained doubtful. He hadn't taken the time to inspect the airframe and wondered if it might not have been cracked by the landing. He wondered if he and Trent might need an entirely new plane, and where it might come from. Finally, putting both thoughts behind him, he took solace in the fact that they had gotten down safely without catching fire. He didn't realize how badly his hands were shaking until he returned to his tent and tried to write up his report for the mission.

At some time during the night, and Dev never knew when, the Ottoman 3rd Infantry Division and a large portion of Pasha I collided with the New Zealand Mounted Rifles and a part of the ANZAC Division. Fierce fighting erupted immediately and continued through the night, with the result that NZMR and the ANZACS, with the Turks overlapping their flank, were eventually forced to give ground, thinning and extending their line while bending back from the south until they formed almost a 90-degree angle with the 52nd Division to their north, their entire front having gone from facing east to facing fully southeast toward Quattuya. Eventually, when the 42nd Division finally came up in strength, elements of that division would strike the Turks on their own western flank and drive them backwards as their attack collapsed. But at the time, no one, save perhaps for Murray and his staff, had any inkling that such a move might take place. When he got up in the morning and found that Banes and the air mechs had restored his kite, Dev didn't know it either, intelligence and St. Clair reporting to them that while the 52nd Division had held firm, the boys from down under were experiencing a spot of trouble.

"We must do what we must do, to help them get out of that trouble," St. Clair said when he gathered the Flights together that morning for their early briefing. "I'd send you with 100-pounders strapped to your bellies if I thought you'd be safe, but with so many Huns flying down from Rafa and probably from El Arish once more, I think it best to send you out with your observers and their Lewis guns. Therefore, those of you making the bomb runs are to carry ten Coopers each, and I advise you to make them count, because our troops on the ground are hard pressed. Observers, save one pan for Huns in the air, *always*, but carry additional pans for strafing the ground, and don't waste ammunition. Any questions? Right, then let's be about it!"

They flew in pairs that morning, Dev and Crisp going up together, flying moderately high at 4,000 feet to allow themselves a good look at the ground before they dropped down to try to harass the enemy. Symes and Wells, flying lower, also flew farther, aiming for the junction of the line where the ANZACs joined with the brigades of the 52nd Division. Dev and Crisp—believing that the greatest danger to the line fell where the Turks threatened to get around the NZMR's flank—flew to find that point in the line, while the fliers from Ismailia angled more to the east to make their drops over the lines center and in front of the ANZAC's main strength.

Dev and Crisp's first run that morning—a run they only made after thoroughly reconnoitering what they could see of the position on the ground—they made with the sun behind their right shoulders, dropping from the sky after shutting off their engines, gliding down until they were only three or four hundred feet from the ground, before turning them back on, and then pulling on the cables attached to the racks beneath their wings so as to release four Cooper bombs each as they flew low over the heads of a unit of Turkish cavalry that appeared to be riding west in order to get around the NZMR's flank. The sound of their engines once more cutting in startled the riders on the ground and created a moment of confusion. And while it didn't stop the column's movement, it caused sufficient chaos that the Turks, possibly expecting their own planes to be over them, worked to recover control over their mounts which had been spooked by the sudden sound. Then, with the column in sporadic disarray, the Coopers fell among them, causing wholesale consternation and a myriad of casualties, wounding or killing Turks and horses by the dozen as others bolted away from the line of march in all directions. The last thing that Dev and Trent, Crisp and Crouchback saw as they pulled out of their bombing run and climbed for altitude was a company of New Zealanders issuing from their trench and racing over the sand on foot in order to engage the remnants of the Turkish formation at close range.

With six bombs remaining, Crisp led their second run, an attack they drove in from 500 feet over a Turkish battery that they located approximately 2,000 yards behind the line—a battery of four guns that Crisp had apparently noticed when he had seen gun flashes in the distance while he and Dev had climbed out after making their first attack on the enemy. The problem they faced—as both of them knew before they attempted to attack the site—was that the artillery in use would not be unprotected. Indeed it wasn't, because as the two of them circled away from the cavalry that they had bombed and once more gained some altitude, the Archies began to bark at them, throwing up bursting black mushrooms even as they flew in a wide circle with the intention of repeating their performance and making their attack with the sun at their backs.

Pushing their throttles nearly to their stops, Crisp and Dev once more put the sun over their shoulders and flew straight toward the battery, diving and then climbing before diving again, in an attempt to confuse the anti-aircraft gunners as they made their run. Once started in, their approach didn't require more than 30 seconds before they were down over the battery, the Turkish guns fully visible beneath them, and releasing the remains of their bomb load.

Dev, his face swimming with sweat, his hands almost awash with it inside his gauntlets, felt every muscle in his back tighten like twisted rope as he pulled back on his stick and tried to climb out from the run. Even as he did so, he could hear the chatter of the Lewis gun at his back and knew that Trent had found a target and was attempting to strafe it, the recoil of the Lewis gun fairly shaking the frame of the plane to his back.

Not content to make their departure without taking some notice of any damage they might have caused, Crisp and Dev doubled back at low altitude, at an altitude that they hoped would befuddle the enemy gunners. From there, approximately 1,000 yards out from where the battery was located, Dev could see that they had indeed unseated one of the guns and spun it onto its side, exploded at least one caisson farther up the gun line—a caisson that appeared to be burning while setting off secondary explosions from the rounds that were exploding in the fire—and so thoroughly disrupted the battery that it had ceased to fire as Huns or Turks or both raced for cover to avoid the exploding ammunition.

In the wake of their attack on the battery, they might have returned to Kantara fully satisfied that they had done what they'd flown out to do and done it well. But, while Dev knew that he didn't want to make yet another run and that Crisp was no more anxious than he was to do a strafe with the remaining pans of Lewis gun ammunition that remained unspent in Trent and Crouchback's ready pouches, he also knew that the NZMR and ANZACs needed every ounce of assistance that 14 Squadron could provide. So, he took the lead, led Crisp a mile farther east, turned north toward the Turkish line, and came around smartly no more than 200 yards behind the line where the Turks were attempting to press their attack forward. Almost immediately, both Trent and Crouchback began to fire on the enemy line. Glancing out to the north, even at the distance, Dev could see men and animals falling, dust rising where individual bursts of machine-gun fire had missed their targets, and at least two small explosions resulting from tracer rounds that had struck small stores of ammunition or hand grenades or, perhaps, a store of signal rockets that had been left in the open. Whatever had caused the explosions didn't matter to Dev; the fact that the hail that Trent was sending out added disruption to the enemy's attack was all that mattered. When Trent finally clapped Dev on the shoulder to indicate that he'd expended as much ammunition as he was wont to do, Dev was only too pleased to turn away at once, fly low to the south to put distance between himself and the Huns, and know that he'd escaped from their threat.

Flapping fabric on the frame forward of the cockpit and on the starboard wing showed Dev that he had not escaped damage as completely as he'd hoped. The Turks, firing from whatever machine guns or rifles they'd pointed in his direction, had done damage, but as far as Dev could tell, the kite was in no danger. The BE2c still flew with as much stability as she had always delivered, and neither he nor Trent had been hit. It was with relief and a considerable decline in stress that he landed at Kantara after a 45-minute flight and saw Crisp and Crouchback put down safely behind him.

While Banes' fitters began slapping patches onto Dev's kite, and while the air mechs worked to once more bomb up the racks that the BE2c now carried, Dev and Crisp dispatched both Trent and Crouchback to the sergeant's mess for a late breakfast, while the two of them, already feeling the drag of fatigue, trudged toward the officer's mess tent for their own ration of oatmeal and fried bread.

"Sticky wicket?" Wells asked from where he sat as the two of them entered the tent.

"Not particularly," Crisp replied. "Dispersed some cavalry and turned over a Turkish battery before doing a strafe on our way out. You?"

"Blew up a Hun truck," Symes said cheerfully.

"Big smash!" Wells said at once. "Ammunition, probably."

"Sent the bastards diving everywhere," Symes laughed. "And generated a camel stampede not 200 yards distant."

"Small stampede," Wells said. "Thirty beasts, at most. Lickety-split."

"And after oatmeal, 'Now all the youth of England are on fire?'" Dev said.

"*Oh, very good!*" Wells said, his stork's beak lifting slightly over a widening grin. "Shakespeare, yes? Eton, what? Harrow? Winchester?"

"New Brunswick High," Dev laughed. "An American institution of superior academic achievement."

"Oh, I dare say," said Crisp, glancing at Dev with narrowing eyes.

Before they could even finish their oatmeal and down the coffee that all four of them took that morning, one of Banes' minions was at the entrance of the tent to inform them that their kites were patched, bombed up, refueled, and once more ready to fly.

Theirs were the swiftest turnarounds that Dev could ever remember. Sucking air to regulate their breathing, each man made a special effort to finish his oatmeal slowly, as though he intended to linger over his breakfast that morning for an hour or more. Then, drinking down the last of their coffee to the dregs, they rose slowly, strode to the flap of the tent, and once more feeling their muscles tighten, began to run for their planes.

Dev and Crisp, Symes and Wells and their observers flew twice more that day, doing as much damage to the enemy attack as they could—bombing trench lines, horse lines, vehicles, supply dumps where they could find them, and shooting up two more batteries of artillery that had the misfortune to reveal themselves while the planes of 14 Squadron were overhead. When Dev and Crisp finally put down and landed at last light, the two of them were so fully exhausted that they could barely drag themselves to the mess tent for their supper and barely eat it when it was finally served to them. The fact that they dined on mutton and potatoes that night, rather than some combination of bully beef and overcooked vegetables, went a long way in helping them to recover from their fatigue, giving them enough energy to lead them to their tents and their cots. Once inside, beyond managing to remove their boots, both men took to their bunks in their flying togs and didn't stir again until their batman greeted them the following morning with mugs of dark tea.

On the morning of August 5, even before Dev and Crisp took to the air, the summer heat on the field had become searing. At 5,000 feet, the altitude toward which the squadron flew up to the lines, things were better and continued better until 14 Squadron's gaggle of planes broke up as each pilot went to pursue targets of opportunity. Then, very swiftly, Dev saw something that made his blood run cold and left him shaking behind the stick.

Out ahead of Dev by what he estimated to be at least 800 yards, one of the pilots up from Ismailia, while flying straight and level, was apparently hit, the plane beginning to smoke as its nose dipped. Then, it began to burn, the flames creeping back to engulf the cockpit in mere seconds. Horrified and shaking as he watched in terror, Dev saw the pilot rise and leap from the cockpit, throwing himself into empty space while plunging to his death, his observer raising his hands and arms to shield himself before the flames engulfed him and the plane exploded in mid-air.

For several seconds, Dev could not get control of himself, the BE2c under his hands wobbling everywhere in the sky. When he finally did bring it back under control, he realized that he'd been screaming, although not anyone, least of all Trent, could have heard the sounds flying between his teeth. Gritting those same teeth, suddenly looking upon the Hun and the Turk with a whole new attitude—one of utter hatred, hatred that burned as hot and bright as the flames that had exploded the plane from Ismailia—Dev put his stick forward and dove for the Turkish positions. He dove with all the speed that he thought his kite could take without her wings folding back, pulled out not 40 feet off the ground, and drove straight ahead with the throttle pushed all the way to the extreme until, directly over a trio of Archies, he loosed his bomb load. He came away with the satisfaction of seeing the entire trio disappear beneath a cloud of fire, smoke, and flying debris behind him, Trent pounding his shoulder multiple times in an outburst of excitement. Then, after a quick strafing run down a thousand yards of the Turkish line, Dev pulled away and returned to Kantara, leaving the battle to proceed in his temporary absence from it.

And the battle on the ground did proceed, von Kressenstein throwing in everything he had—some 28,000 troops by the estimates that GHQ intelligence conveyed to the squadron. But if von Kressenstein had decided to go all out, so had Murray, who, with the late arrival of the 42nd Division, seemed just on the verge of mustering 50,000 men with which to oppose the Ottomans and the Huns. Fighting on the ground over the blistering heat reflecting from the dunes was reported to be intense, neither side making much headway, casualties rising in high numbers, degrees of heat prostration bedeviling every man who carried a rifle. By mid-day, after grueling hours of unremitting ground combat, forward elements of the 42nd Division were finally coming forward on the Turkish left flank, and slowly, very slowly, the Turks were being forced to give way.

Dev and Crisp took off for their second mission shortly before 1100 hours that morning, flew up to the line at 3,000 feet, which was just enough to dry some of the sweat from their faces, and stumbled onto what they believed to be the headquarters of an enemy brigade. By means of two quick bomb runs, they left it in a shambles, unloading the whole of both of their sticks directly over the tents that they supposed harbored the brigade's communications and control centers. Immediately thereafter, catching the movement of an infantry company making its way toward the enemy trenches, they gave Trent and Crouchback a free hand to cut loose on the marching men, with the result that their observers reported halving the unit's strength on the first pass and pretty much taking it right out of action by the time they'd completed their third run over the target.

Back in Kantara, as the fitters and air mechs refueled them, patched the bullet holes in their fabric, and once more loaded their racks with bombs, Dev and Crisp sat in the mess tent, drinking strong coffee, and stared at the walls of the tent with hollow eyes. At first they said little, giving way to the fatigue that had swept over the two of them like a thick wet blanket. But finally, leaning forward on his elbows and without looking at his fellow, Dev spoke.

"Did you see the flamer this morning?"

"Yes," Crisp said, the words barely sounded from between his tightened lips.

"Doesn't bear thinking about," Dev whispered.

"No," Crisp said, "but from now on, we won't be able to put it from our minds."

"No," Dev said, "we won't."

They didn't go up again that afternoon until 1530, with the intention of flying into their attacks by passing over their own lines to put the afternoon sun at their backs. When at last they reached the vicinity of Romani, unable to exchange any information about it, both nevertheless saw that things on the ground had changed. In fact, owing to a number of indications, Dev saw at once that von Kressenstein was beginning to pull back and give way. On the line itself, the enemy's rear guard seemed to be fighting with determination. But to their rear, battalion, regimental, and brigade headquarters—for headquarters is what Dev took them to be—seemed to be packing up, removing equipment and tents to wagons and vehicles, and preparing to pull back. One of these, a regimental establishment Dev thought, was a target upon which he unloaded four of his Cooper bombs, turning over at least one truck and setting it on fire, while another of his bombs did for one of the wagons associated with the unit. And then, finding a single piece of artillery still firing at the ANZACs, Dev plastered the area around it, leaving several of the enemy stretched out on the ground and once more causing a caisson to explode. After one more strafing run to bring Trent fully into the action, Dev departed for Kantara, where, upon landing, he found Crisp, Symes, and Wells already returned and only then dismounting from their planes and briefing Banes and the fitters before heading for the mess tent.

In the mess, with a double whiskey in his hand, Dev once more realized that his hands were shaking. The tremor was none so great that anyone noticed it. Considering the stress that he'd been under while flying that day and after witnessing the flamer that he'd seen that morning, Dev took it to be the natural reaction of the body—something which no one, no matter their character, could wholly control. Regardless of a college course in psychology that he'd been forced to endure at Rutgers, Dev had never once imagined that he knew very much about the subject, and therefore, he did not consider himself to be given to moments of deep self-analysis in what might have been called clinical terms. But whatever the case, he knew that he was smart enough to detect a physical reaction to the tension he'd been flying under. Knowing that there seemed to be little that he could do about it, he resolved to accept it, adjust to it as necessary, and try to ease the condition with a drink or two—drink that he did think he had character enough to imbibe with moderation.

Symes, on the other hand, took to the bottle with a more definite intent and said so. "I find it helps me sleep," he said flatly. "Mummy wouldn't like it, but mummy doesn't fly, doesn't do what we have to do, and doesn't know what we're doing, and what mummy doesn't know can't hurt her. What's important is that Symes sleeps so that Symes can fly again the following day. That's the long and the short of it for me, and I'm making no apologies."

"Just so," Dev said. "Whatever serves, and no apologies required."

During the morning apparently, while the fliers had been out, two of the sergeants in supply had gone out with bird nets—acquired from sources that Dev couldn't even begin to imagine—and netted enough early migrating quail to feed the entire Flight that night. As far as Dev and Crisp were concerned, the quail made a wholly acceptable substitution for bully beef. So, at table that evening, the two of them dined for what they considered the first time since they'd arrived in Sinai, and the dining proved good—good enough so that following the meal, the pilots, rather than racing for their bunks as they'd been wont to do, actually stuck around for an hour and a few bottles of beer, which, for their Flight, substituted for port.

"Pity we don't have a box of cigars to pass around," Tuck said when he and Bivin finally returned from their artillery-spotting mission.

"We must make a list," Crisp said. "First man who gets to Cairo should return with several boxes."

"Al Cairo," Wells laughed. "Fat chance."

"Not altogether true," St. Clair said quietly from the head of the table. "Once this do completes and we have von Kressenstein shoved back into Palestine, I mean to begin giving leave, two men at a time, three days in Cairo, with half a day to get there and half a day to get back. Good rail connections from Kantara. Swift trip, the ferry across the canal included."

Immediately, cheers went up along both sides of the table along with orders for another round.

"Special passes required, to get into Shepheard's?" Dev laughed.

"If anyone asks me for one," Bivin said, "after what we've been doing, I believe that I shall pass my boot right between his legs and upward."

"Hear, hear!" said Wells.

"Not to worry," St. Clair said. "There will be plenty of leave henceforth, on a regular schedule. I proposed, the medicos advised, and the staff types at GHQ relented, reluctantly, for the good of everyone's health."

"Leave for the good of the service?" Tuck asked.

"Something like that," St. Clair said, "as well as for the relief of the mind. Medicos warned the staff that you lot might go around the bend if you were kept to it without relief. Very adroit, that. Downright inventive, I thought."

"Yes," Dev said, once more feeling his handshake. "Nothing further from the truth."

By August 7, von Kressenstein's forces were in full retreat, brigades of the Light Horse and the NZMR following hard on their heels, bumping them and pushing them back toward El Arish. Dev and Crisp went out early that morning, dropping four of their bombs over a column of Turkish cavalry near Bir El Abd and another four on a convoy of supply wagons west of Bir Salmana.

Later in the afternoon, once more dropping down over Bir El Abd, Trent and Crouchback turned their Lewis guns loose on a formation of Hun infantry, dropping more than a few while dispersing the entire battalion that they attacked into the shallow wadis and behind the rocks that flanked their road back. Twenty minutes later, finding three Archies in tow farther up the road toward Bir Salmana, both Dev and Crisp unloaded their eggs over the targets, overturning all of them while setting some of their transport on fire. But in the process, as Dev dropped down to let Trent have another strafe, he suddenly felt a needle-sharp stab in the right cheek of his buttocks—a stab that seemed to sear with fire, a stab that threw him hard against his safety belt and momentarily left him feeling faint with the shock. In that moment, he knew that he'd been hit. With no Archie bursts anywhere in the vicinity, Dev also imagined that he'd been struck by a rifle round or a machine-gun round, from what point below him he had no idea and didn't care. Instead, already feeling blood seeping from his wound, he turned away quickly and headed back to Kantara.

7

"Here now, bite on this," said the doctor, a major in the Royal Army Medical Corps who prepared to attend to Dev's wound at the field hospital in Kantara and who handed him a rolled-up battle dressing to place between his teeth.

"No painkiller?" Dev protested.

"Oh, *no, no, no, no*," the doctor replied, his cheerful tone grating on Dev's ear. "Small wound this, hardly worth mentioning. Just relax and stay still on your stomach, and I'll have the bullet out straightaway."

The Hun bullet, as far as Dev was concerned, did not come out *straightaway*. Instead, it forced the cheerful doctor, chattering away while he worked, to probe with what felt to Dev like a red-hot steel hemostat that sent burning waves of pain shooting through him with every movement that the doctor made.

"There now," the doctor said triumphantly, thrusting the hemostat and the round in front of Dev as Dev's eyes seeped tears of pain. "Beauty, this! Mauser C96 round, if I'm not mistaken. One of those machine pistols, if you've seen them. Ubiquitous among the Huns, or so I'm told. Want to have it, for a keepsake? Something to show the grandchildren when they come of age?"

"No," Dev said, fighting back the pain and looking up at the doctor with something like murder in his eyes. "On the whole, I think I would rather have had a painkiller first."

"Oh no. No, no," the doctor said, showing Dev a broad grin. "We save those for the seriously wounded. Why, this is merely a minor penetration. I don't think that round was in there more than 2 inches, if that far. You'll be up and around in no time."

"In Cairo?" Dev asked. "On leave?"

"Possibly," the doctor said, "but only after two or three weeks here at Kantara, on your stomach, under a fly net, after eating bland wholesome foods and enjoying the attentions of our beautiful nurses. Why, I almost envy you, Lieutenant. You simply have no idea the number of good things we have in store for you."

The good things that the field hospital had in store for Dev turned out to include daily doses of castor oil, occasional enemas, injections, interrupted periods of sleep as the male attendants came in to dispense medicines or change dressings, stifling heat, bully beef as a standard dietary foundation, and Nurse Cribbon. Nurse Cribbon, a representative of Queen Alexandra's Imperial Military Nursing Service (QAIMNS), struck Dev as having all the warmth and personality that he might find in what he imagined as a 30-year career sergeant major in one of the Guards regiments. Dev didn't know if the QAIMNS had ranks or not, but if they did, he knew from the start that Nurse Cribbon, weighing in at a good 180 pounds of rock-hard muscle, would have had a troop of nurses doing the high step on a barracks square in a matter of seconds.

"You, there," she barked at him the first time he came in contact with her. "Put out that pipe *at once*! No smoking in hospital, no drinking in hospital, no chocolate, fruit, or meats not prepared by the hospital's mess, and no visitors outside visiting hours. Take note, young man, or you will have me to contend with, and that is something you may dislike intensely."

Dev felt certain that she was right, which was why, when Crisp and Symes came to visit, he secreted the chocolate they brought him as well as the pint bottle of whiskey inside the folds of his pack.

"Who is the Medusa standing watch at the door?" Symes wanted to know as he and Crisp stood beside Dev, trying to mask with their bodies the gifts that they had brought him.

"That," Dev said, "is Nurse Cribbon, England's gift to the halt and the maimed."

"Not exactly a substitute for Helen of Troy or Mary Pickford, is she?" Crisp said.

"I've come to think of her as Attila the Hun's direct representative to the forces," Dev said "If she finds the stuff you've brought—and many thanks for bringing it—she'll probably try to skin me alive."

"I thought the QAIMNS were supposed to be beauties?" Symes said.

"The beauties, if there are any," Dev said, wishing that he could get off his stomach, "seem to be assigned to other wards."

"Probably the ones taking care of staff officers," Symes rejoined.

"Undoubtedly," Dev said.

Nurse Cribbon, when she came to Dev's bed moments after Crisp and Symes left to return to the airdrome, needed less than 30 seconds to ferret out where Dev had tried to hide the chocolate and the whiskey, both of which she instantly confiscated before reading him the riot act and threatening to have him up on charges if he ever deviated from the path of purity again. This went a long way, Dev imagined, to explain why, when he left the hospital three weeks later to go on a week's convalescent leave in Cairo, he didn't bother to say goodbye.

Dev's train trip down to Cairo—brief though it might have been at slightly more than two hours—was nevertheless a journey that he

124

did not find comfortable. In the first place, the desert temperatures proved more than warm, and in the second, a part of that trip was bumpy. Dev's wound, mostly healed, remained tender, and as a result, sitting for two long hours on the wooden seats in his compartment did not seem a good idea. As a result, Dev stood in the passageway outside his compartment and smoked his pipe for as long as he tried to sit inside and viewed with indifference the dunes, fields, and gyppos that he saw along the way.

Reaching Cairo's central station in the middle of the afternoon, Dev did not linger on the street. Instead, swiftly finding a taxi, he had the driver speed him to Shepheard's, went in, and after negotiating with a Royal Navy lieutenant who seemed to be in the same financial shape as himself, the two of them managed to convince the desk clerk to give them a room with a bath while agreeing with each other to split the expense. Red tabs—who appeared to look down their noses at the two—seemed everywhere in evidence.

The Royal Navy lieutenant, a man named Dobb, seemed to be one of the few naval officers evident at Shepheard's, and after dropping their kit in their room, the two decided to do what nearly everyone in Cairo did, sooner or later: to go down to the terrace facing the street and the Ezbekiyya Gardens, find two wicker chairs, have a drink, and watch the world go by.

"Stationed in Port Said?" Dev asked, as a waiter brought each of them a whiskey.

"Passing through," Dobb said, sipping his whiskey after voicing an obligatory *cheers.* "Taking ship at Suez next week. Heading for Mombasa. Stink on in East Africa, don't you know. Von Lettow-Vorbeck seems to be giving Smuts fits on his drive into German East. Joining a destroyer down there. *Invictus* by name. Blockade, to keep Hun supplies from landing. That sort of thing. You?"

"Flying the BE2c over Sinai," Dev said. "Been chasing von Kressenstein away from Romani, or at least I was until I caught a packet in the ass and wound up in hospital."

125

"I'm afraid I can't quite place the accent, old man," Dobb said cheerfully. "There's a part that sounds Irish, but the other part sounds almost American?"

"Right you are," Dev laughed. "Born an Ulsterman but grew up in the States. In New Jersey to be precise."

"Ah," Dobb said. "Met an American this morning, coming down on the train from Port Said. Nice chap. Older. Gray-headed, if you see what I mean. Business fellow, apparently; merchant banker, I think. Over here to represent his establishment and oversee their office staff. And he was from New Jersey. Told me so himself. Place called Perth Amboy, if I'm not mistaken."

"That's only a few miles from my home," Dev said, his face lighting up.

"Really?" Dobb said. "You should drop by. Pay respects. That sort of thing. He asked me if I'd met any Yanks in the forces, and I said that I hadn't. And now, you show up unannounced, almost on cue. Name of Winslow … first name Mortimer, I think. He's the one who said I ought to come here, to Shepheard's. Said he thought I would like it. His bank's only two blocks up the street. You ought to drop in. Could be a free meal in it for you, or a letter of introduction to one of the clubs. Americans, and all that."

"Thanks for the tip," Dev said. "I may give it a try."

Content to sit, talk, and observe the prospect, no few fashionable lovelies included, Dev and Dobb remained where they sat for more than two hours, sipping whiskey, trading notes about the service they'd seen, the course the war seemed to be taking, and the political situation in London. Then, when the sun finally began to set, they went into the dining room and treated themselves to the first fine dining that Dev thought he'd enjoyed since he'd left Derry to join his regiment.

"Good but not great," Dobb said, delivering his review. "Rather liked the chicken, however. Tandoori, would you say?"

"Whatever the method," Dev said, "it is a colossal improvement over curried bully beef and hard biscuit. I doubt that it rivals the Ritz, but it is the best that I've had since I came out here."

"Up for a brothel?" Dobb asked. "Fellows in Port Said put me onto a fine one."

"No one could accuse me of being a Puritan," Dev said carefully, "but I'm just out of hospital. It's been a long day, and frankly, I'm bushed, so I'm going to pass. But don't let me stand in your way. I will merely send you off with best wishes for good hunting."

"Right then," Dobb said, as he put down enough currency to cover his part of the tariff. "Have a good sleep, and I will do my best not to wake you when I come in." And with that, leaving Dev to his coffee, Dobb went off to look for a taxi that might speed him to his place of indulgence.

The following morning, once more acting on advice that Tuck had provided before signing his leave papers, Dev found the ornately tiled entrance to Groppi's Cafe and went in to take his breakfast. Sitting at a small, marble-topped table beneath the high ceilings and ornate chandeliers, Dev indulged himself with a steaming cup of chocolate accompanied by a variety of pastries which were, he thought, as good as anything that Vienna, Zurich, or Paris might be capable of offering. Groppi, the man who had apparently opened the establishment originally, appeared to have been Swiss, and that, in Dev's view, explained both the tone of the cafe and the high quality of the preparations that it served. For the rest of it, the place was packed with men from the forces, red tabs, ANZACs, British, a few French, and even one or two naval officers and a handful of naval ratings down from Alexandria or Port Said on their way, possibly, to the same place that Dobb was going.

When Dev finally rose from his table, sated for the time being on the plethora of good things he'd had to eat and with the sun not yet having raised the temperature of Cairo's streets to the boiling point, he treated himself to a stroll. The stroll he took—one that ran its course through central Cairo—showed him a city that reminded him of photos he had seen of Paris. Here and there, glancing up long streets beyond the buildings which immediately surrounded him, he could detect the minarets of mosques and, once, what might have been the bell tower of a cathedral, Coptic or otherwise—a reminder that the Coptic church at least had survived in Cairo alongside the Moslem faith for centuries. Twice he took a stroll through this or that bazaar that seemed to be wedged between one or another of the higher buildings, but mostly he contented himself with walking beneath the shade on the still shadowed sides of the street. Then, as he gradually worked his way back down to the vicinity of the Ezbekiyya Gardens across from which he knew Shepheard's to be located, he suddenly found himself standing in front of a structure that carried the words "First American Bank of New Jersey" on its exterior window. Mildly winded from his walk, almost on an impulse, Dev turned, opened the door, and went in, asking the teller behind the cage if, perhaps, Mr. Winslow might be in. Within less than a minute, after knocking once on a frosted glass door and hearing "enter" from the other side, Dev opened the door, walked inside the banker's office, and found a meticulously dressed, distinguished-looking man with gray hair and pleasant eyes rising to greet him.

"Mr. Winslow," Dev said, standing straight and extending his hand, "I'm Devlin Collins, from New Brunswick. Lieutenant Dobb, who I think you met yesterday, and I are sharing a room at Shepheard's. I don't mean to impose, Sir, but when Dobb heard that I am also from New Jersey, he suggested that I stop and pay my respects."

"Mortimer Winslow," the man said at once, breaking into a smile and giving Dev's hand a hearty shake. "Might you possibly be related to a Mr. Doyle Collins of Collins and Kelly Motors in New Brunswick?"

"My father," Dev said, surprised by the sudden question.

"Well," Mr. Winslow said with a welcoming degree of enthusiasm, "I know your father. We met before the war started, when I arranged a loan for your father and Mr. Kelly. It is a smaller world than one imagines, is it not?"

"Smaller indeed," Dev said, "When I stopped, I never imagined ..."

"Nor could you have," Mortimer Winslow said quickly, "nor could I have imagined when I came to work today. You're in the forces, I see, with the RFC by the look of things. Been anywhere near Sinai?"

"Just in from Sinai," Dev said.

"You must have lunch with me and tell me about it," Winslow said. "That Hun general, von Kressenstein, gave everyone around here a bit of a scare a few weeks back. Any number of people thought he might seize the canal. Some were even packing to leave. The newspapers are now reporting that he's been driven all the way back to Rafa, so we are all in hopes that we have seen the last of him."

"Yes, Sir," Dev said, "that's what my squadron is hoping as well."

"Oh, you've been flying out there, have you?" Winslow said. "Over Sinai?"

"I have, Sir," Dev said. "Picked up a Mauser round somewhere near Bir El Abd. Nothing very serious, as you can see, so I'm here on a spot of convalescent leave."

"Your parents will be most relieved to hear that," Winslow said at once.

"I'm afraid," Dev said, with a somewhat sheepish grin, "that I have neglected to mention the wound and plan to avoid doing so if at all possible."

"Understood," Winslow said, showing Dev an approving nod. "Mum's the word. But do join me for lunch, won't you? My wife will be arriving at El Baqara, where the kabobs are delicious."

"Only if you will allow me to pay for my own lunch," Dev said. "I really didn't mean to impose when I stopped."

"We can talk about that later," Mortimer Winslow said, glancing quickly at his watch, "but if you don't mind, I think we will go ahead now and grab a table before the ladies arrive."

The mention of "ladies"—rather than the one lady that Winslow had referred to when he first spoke about lunch—gave Dev a start. What, he asked himself mentally, had he gotten himself into? One possibility centered on a second doyenne, a friend of Mrs. Winslow's age and demeanor, a woman of years to whom he would have to be particularly polite. Another possibility centered on a possible relative or daughter. Once, during his years in high school, Dev had let himself in for a blind date and been thoroughly disappointed by it, with the result that he had very carefully avoided ever letting himself in for a second, not in high school or later at Rutgers. So, if a daughter were to be imagined, would she be the kind who sewed her own clothes with loving hands and who other girls described as having a lovely personality while she weighed in at double his own weight, or would she be a sharp-tongued shrew, a Bible-thumping Puritan of impeccable virtue, or a repressed mouse so timid as to barely utter a word unless forced to speak? All of those possibilities crossed Dev's mind as he entered a taxi outside the bank and alongside Mortimer Winslow. But like the flamer of his recent experience, Dev buried the notions and bravely went forward to deal with what fate had in store for him.

What fate had in store for Dev when the *maître d'* at El Baqara finally showed "the ladies" to the table where Mr. Winslow and

Dev rose to greet them interrupted Dev's every expectation. Mrs. Emilia Winslow, fashionably dressed in the Parisian style, greeted Dev warmly, particularly when she found that he hailed from New Brunswick. Miss Lily Winslow, dressed smartly in the American style that had prevailed when Dev had left home in 1914, showed Dev a smile that seemed both poised and indicative of a sharp intelligence that restrained itself behind a flawless complexion, inviting blue eyes, and a coiffure of dark brown hair meticulously arranged beneath one of the immense hats of the day.

"You've been in Cairo long?" Dev asked, as the quartet sat down to table.

"Mother and I came over just before the war began," Lily Winslow said very matter-of-factly. "Dad was already here. Originally, we hadn't intended to stay for more than a few months, but with the war on, Dad doesn't like to think of us crossing the Atlantic in the face of the German submarine threat."

"I shouldn't like that either if I were in his shoes," Dev said.

"Yes," Lily said, "so here we are, doing our best to make the most of Cairo."

"And are you," Dev asked, "making the most of it?"

"Oh, I think we are," Lily said. "We've seen the pyramids, of course; we've boated down the Nile to Luxor a time or two, and we've made enough friends here—English, as well as the few Americans in residence—so that we don't altogether wither socially."

"I find it difficult to imagine you withering," Dev laughed.

"As you might imagine," Emilia said, "Lily very much misses her college friends. Cairo isn't New York, but it has been a wholly new experience for us, so we have adjusted."

"Lily had hoped to be started on her career by now," Mortimer Winslow added. "But for the time being, until the Royal Navy once more clears the seas of Hun U-boats, it appears that she and Emilia will be cooling their heels here and putting up with me."

"And what career did you have in mind?" Dev asked, turning back to Lily.

"I had the promise of a place in Congressman Jenkins's office," she said, "but when Jenkins spoke out in support of the United States joining the war in 1914, he lost his place in Congress, so there was no place for me to go back to, if we'd been able to go back."

"So how, if I may ask, aside from family and social obligations, might you be occupying your time over here?" Dev asked.

"If it won't sound frivolous to you," Lily said rather pertly, "I've been writing."

"And she has been published as well," Emilia added.

"And paid quite handsomely, too," Mortimer said. "We're rather proud of her, as you can imagine."

"And what do you write?" Dev said, once more addressing Lily.

"Fiction, mostly," Lily said, "but I have also done two articles on the war's effect on Egypt, both published in the States, and like most women and men who try to call themselves writers, I have a novel underway. But enough of that, Mr. Collins. I think I've divulged almost as much as I'm prepared to for the moment, so what about you? Suppose you tell us a little about what you've been doing, how you came to join the Royal Flying Corps, and something about this latest entanglement in Sinai. With things as quiet as they are in Cairo—if we leave out perpetual beehive activity on Shepheard's Terrace—we could all stand a little excitement."

As the waiter set plates containing El Baqara's stunningly good kabobs before them, Dev spoke of flying and of the desert, describing the sunrise, the sunset, the dunes, the Berbers, and telling a little about the war, while avoiding the kinds of details that might send the table into shock. He did not describe the bombs that he and Crisp had dropped, aerial encounters with Hun ships, strafes, or mention anything about the battle for Romani that went beyond the most general and innocuous description. About the railroad and the pipeline, he found that Mortimer Winslow knew more than he'd imagined, the bank that he headed having extended a loan to the British to finance a part of its construction.

"I suspect, Mr. Collins," Lily Winslow said when Dev had finished, "regardless of the wonderful local color with which you have entertained us, that you are holding a great deal back, including the details of *why*, precisely, the RFC has sent you on convalescent leave here."

"*Lily!*" Mrs. Winslow said, appearing to be mildly mortified by the comment.

"I'm afraid," Dev laughed, "that in order not to horrify you, I rather avoided a description of Nurse Cribbon, she who the Royal Medical Corps has installed to combine draconian methods of recovery with a sergeant major's brand of warmth. I simply cannot begin to tell you how swiftly we've all tried to heal in order to escape from her tender ministrations."

The smile that barely showed at the corners of Miss Lily Winslow's lips, lips that Dev suddenly found exceptionally attractive, also indicated a fine appreciation of irony.

"One always imagines the nurses attending the forces to be swans," Lily said adroitly.

"At our field hospital," Dev said, "any swans attending must have been gliding gracefully across other lakes. Our particular bird, a mean goose of the first order, honked like a bugle and pecked with the sharpest beak imaginable."

"Perhaps I should travel to Kantara, visit the hospital, and prepare an article regarding the care the forces are receiving."

"If I may, without offending," Dev said, glancing quickly at Lily's parents, "I believe, Miss Winslow, that if you were to appear in any of the wards at Kantara, you might immediately create a minor riot. Those are good lads, our boys, but most of them have not seen a woman of your ... refinement in going on for more than a year, so the sight of an attractive young woman, even backed up by such a formidable force as Nurse Cribbon might provide, would probably produce instant chaos."

"I'm sure," Lily Winslow said, barely able to stifle a blush, "that you overspeak, Mr. Collins. By combining a measure of tranquility with force of character, I rather think I might give Nurse Cribbon a run for her money and transform your lads, as you call them, into lambs."

For the length of a split second, Dev tried to imagine Miss Lily Winslow quelling a disturbance in one of the wards at Kantara, and then, rather abruptly, considering the expression on her face and the penetration of her eyes, he came to the conclusion that she could do it.

"Miss Winslow," Dev said with a smile, "I concede your point. I believe you just might bring it off, and I can only wish that I could be present to see you put Nurse Cribbon in her place."

"Speaking of place," Mortimer Winslow said, "I very much need to be in mine, for I have an appointment at two o'clock this afternoon. So, if you three will excuse me, I must be going. Dev, so nice to meet you. We must meet again, soon."

And with that, Mr. Winslow was gone, paying for the entire lunch on his way out as Dev was later mortified to learn. In the meantime, Dev, Mrs. Winslow, and Lily lingered for a few more minutes over their coffee, and then, rising, Dev accompanied the ladies to the door and found them a taxi.

As she prepared to step into the taxi, Mrs. Winslow turned and handed Dev her card. "Come to supper this evening, Mr. Collins. We're having a few friends in, all of them much older than you and Lily, and Lily will enjoy having someone her own age with whom to converse."

"Thank you," Dev said. "Formal occasion, is it? I'm afraid that I have only uniforms with me at Shepheard's."

"Your uniform is more than formal enough for any occasion in Cairo these days," Mrs. Winslow said. "Eight o'clock, shall we say?"

"I will be present," Dev said, "and thank you."

Mrs. Winslow's suggestion that Lily needed someone her own age with whom to converse struck Dev as a ruse. Lily Winslow could clearly hold her own with anyone twice her age with twice her experience, so Dev was not misled. In Mrs. Winslow's mind, whether true or not, a spark had been struck, and Mrs. Winslow, at least as far as Dev was concerned, meant to give the spark an opportunity to catch fire. Whether Miss Lily Winslow was of the same mind was an altogether different matter, but as the taxi pulled away from the curb, Dev rather hoped that she might be.

When Dev arrived back at Shepheard's, he quickly spotted Dobb sitting on the terrace, sipping a drink of some kind, not far from the steps, and joined him.

"I tried to slip out without waking you this morning," Dev said, sitting down and calling upon the waiter for a beer. "I hope that I succeeded."

"Never heard a pin drop," Dobb said. "Late night, last night. Very. Interesting place, *Le Chat Blanc*. The proprietress turned out to be Argentine rather than French, but most of the girls seemed to be from Montenegro and Spanish Morocco. Studied a spot of Spanish once, so I spent most of the evening talking to the Argentinian. Very cultured, very chic. The Argentine accent was rather different from what I understand of the language, but we had no difficulty, and what that woman didn't know about Paris wouldn't constitute a paragraph. Eventually went up, came down, returned here, and slept like a brick. You? Been out seeing the sights?"

"I took breakfast at Groppi's," Dev said, "went for a stroll, and wound up meeting Mr. Winslow. Very congenial. Turned out that he knows my father. And then we went to lunch where I met his wife and daughter."

"Oh, I say," Dobb said at once. "Full turnout? Smart set, one hopes? Nothing in the elephant or rhinoceros category?"

"Decidedly not," Dev said. "The mother was entirely gracious, and she's invited me to supper."

"And the daughter? Small infant with her hair still in braids?"

"No," Dev said.

"Do tell." Dobb said, moving toward the edge of his chair.

"Twenty-something. Appears to have completed college about the same time I did. Writes and publishes. Quick mind, lovely eyes, beautiful lips. That sort of thing," Dev said. "I'm guessing that she'll have none of me, but who knows? He who hesitates is lost, and I do not mean to hesitate."

"Good lad," Dobb said. "Let me suggest flowers. Take a bundle and watch their eyes light up. I'd suggest wine, but in Cairo, one can never be sure of quality, and with Americans, one risks a confrontation with teetotalers. I don't wish to criticize your country, mind, but one hears rumors of a drive toward prohibition. Perfect madness, that. Takes all the fun out of life, and it will be bound to lead to dyspepsia."

"What it will be most bound to lead to is criminal behavior," Dev said. "I don't like to criticize the States, because I rather like being as much of an American as I am a Brit, but there is a Puritan steak in the American character that too often wants to force its religious proclivities down the throats of everyone else, and I find that revolting and always will."

"Too right you are," Dobb said, once more reclining in his chair. "For your sake, I will hope that the delectable Miss Winslow, as you describe her, is not among their persuasion."

"Amen to that," Dev said. "Once William Tyndale translated the Bible into English, one rather wishes that the Puritans had crawled back into their holes and given it a rest."

"And amen to that, too," Dobb said.

The Winslows' flat, located on the third floor of a spacious and rather attractive Parisian-style apartment block and with a balcony overlooking the Nile, was not far from the British residency. When Dev showed up there shortly before eight o'clock that evening, he was admitted by an Egyptian butler of sober mien who deposited his cap on a table in the foyer and then took the roses he carried, a full dozen, before turning them over to a houseboy, who quickly placed them into a vase and followed behind the butler as the man led Dev to the sliding doors of a drawing room and announced him.

Inside, Mrs. Winslow, as Dev knew she would, welcomed him graciously, thanked him for the flowers that the houseboy carried, and then introduced him around—first to the Hortons, Mr. and Mrs., from Philadelphia, Mr. Horton representing a shipping firm which specialized in supplying the British in Egypt with everything from agricultural beef products to munitions. A Mr. Tolliver and his wife apparently hailed from Virginia—Norfolk to be exact—Mr. Tolliver's firm helping to supply the tobacco which the troops most like to smoke. Unlike Dev, who had come in his uniform, the guests were more formally dressed, the men wearing dinner jackets, the women wearing gowns, and as he was introduced to them and presented with a whiskey, Dev could not help noticing that Miss Lily Winslow appeared to be nowhere in sight.

When Lily did arrive, finally, after Dev had had time to exchange a few words with each of the couples to whom he'd been introduced, Dev felt his pulse quicken. Lily Winslow, he saw at once, really was a rather beautiful girl, the emerald-green gown in which she appeared setting off perfectly the tint of her hair, all of it piled above her, washerwoman style, so as to show off her delicately featured face.

"I see you've had no trouble finding us," she said to Dev as she came forward and shook his hand.

"No," Dev said. "Perfect location for access to the residency, I imagine."

"Perfect," Lily said. "Easy walk for Dad, and he seems to confer with the particular minsters engaged in finance at frequent intervals. Much better there than at the bank, if you see what I mean."

Dev saw and said so.

When it came time for dinner, Dev took Lily in, the two of them seated across from one another at the foot of a table that was not so wide that it discouraged conversation. Neither of them desisted from speaking with the others at the table and joining in the round of general subjects that were discussed. But as the dinner proceeded—one that featured a curry that Dev found utterly delightful and for which, he found, Mrs. Winslow's cook had become justly famous—he and Lily nevertheless drifted into more and more semi-private conversation, Lily initiating the talk by asking him if he had gone to college in the States and where.

"Rutgers," Dev replied. "Mechanical Engineering."

"I thought you might be an engineer," Lily smiled. "It's written all over you."

"Oh?" Dev said, not having a clue as to what she might be talking about.

"Oh yes," Lily said, with a slight lilting laugh. "Steady, seeing the world open-eyed, optimistic in outlook with just enough of the imp and risk taker about you to be a flier. I think you are probably a rather inventive individual with the kind of determination that will lead you to solve problems in a creative way and something more than due diligence."

"May I write all of that down and appended it to my resumé?" Dev asked with a chuckle. "Apparently, you see no mystery about me at all."

"Not so," Lily said at once. "I should think that you are most mysterious when you want to be, particularly about your intentions. Right now, for example, I am finding your intentions with regard to me to be one of the most mysterious things about you."

Somewhat to Dev's shock, he found that the spark which Mrs. Winslow had apparently apprehended had exploded in his face.

"My intentions," Dev said, "as though you hadn't seen them for yourself, were to ask if I might see you again tomorrow, added to every day remaining until I have to go back to Kantara."

"That will be splendid," Lily said smoothly, coolly, "but early Thursday afternoon is out because I have a dress fitting. Mother seems to think my outfits drab and means to take me for an update."

Dev couldn't stop himself from laughing. "If your mother finds the outfit you are presently wearing drab," Dev said, "I can only beg to differ. I find it rather stunning."

"All the better to keep you interested," Lily Winslow said, batting her eyelashes in Dev's direction.

"Keep that up," Dev said. "It will get you everywhere."

When the ladies left the table, a bottle of brandy rather than port was set beside Mortimer Winslow, and then, very quickly, the talk turned to the war. The question on everyone's mind was if and when the United States might commit to the conflict.

"I would have thought," Horton said, lighting a cigar, "that the sinking of the *Lusitania* would have changed the majority of the minds in the States."

"It changed many," Tolliver said. "Of that, I feel certain, and the telegrams I've received from the president of our firm seem to back up my understanding."

"My guess," Mortimer Winslow said, speaking slowly and with the appearance of long thought, "is that Wilson will maintain a neutral stance until after the election. At the moment, he's got Pershing's expedition into Mexico on his plate, and that can't be convenient. From what the home office tells me, that penetration seems to have caught fully the attention of the country, and while I'm no strategist, I would also suspect that it is a bit of a dress rehearsal and a testing ground for anything that might come next. He might elect to stay out of the European war altogether, but if the Kaiser lifts another finger against us in some way, I think Wilson will find means to bring the majority around and throw U.S. weight into the fight."

"And do you think the banks and Wall Street will back him?" Horton asked.

"Speaking only for myself," Winslow said, "I think they will. One can never be sure, of course, but my guess, all things considered, is that the British and the French are already in such deep debt to our financial institutions that they will be years paying us off when this thing ends. We will want them to pay us off, you can be certain, and therefore, it behooves us not to let them go under, which is what would happen were the Central Powers to prevail."

"Mr. Collins," said Horton, "do you speculate upon the subject?"

"From time to time," Dev said, "I do, Sir. I have dual citizenship, you see, so I'm here defending one of my homes and rather wish that the other would join us in the fight. If the United States does declare war, I'm doubtful that we will ever see our army on this particular front, but a large American army thrown into the conflict on the Western Front in France might make such a huge difference that the Hun would capitulate."

"There's talk of a revolution brewing in Russia," Tolliver said. "That could make things tricky. Germany's Eastern armies being shifted to the west and so forth."

"Yes," Mortimer Winslow said. "That could increase the difficulty enormously."

For the length of a second brandy, the men talked on, but without lingering overlong, they rejoined the ladies and found them sitting in the drawing room engaged in what Dev imagined to be polite conversation seeded with just enough gossip to keep things interesting for them—the object of the gossip being some outfit or other which the wife of the Second Secretary of the British legation had recently worn to a soirée.

"You don't play cards, do you?" Lily asked Dev almost as soon as he rejoined her.

"No," Dev said. "Never learned. Never wanted to."

"Good," Lily said, "that means that the two of us may adjourn to the balcony while our elders can indulge themselves as they wish."

On the balcony, Dev found the evening air refreshing, the feluccas making their way north and south along the river intriguing, and Lily Winslow nothing short of enchanting.

"I've heard one or two of the Australian pilots talk about trying to overturn the feluccas," Dev said. "Apparently, they fly down as low over them as possible, fill the feluccas' sails with as much wind as they can drag behind them, and attempt to upset them in the river."

"The Aussies have a rather strong reputation for high jinks and rough humor," Lily said. "The Egyptian police declare themselves fit to be tied because the Aussies have a bad habit of tossing carriage drivers from their vehicles and conducting chariot races with them on city streets. The wonder to me is that they can make the horses run. Most of them are so old and worn out to begin with that they seem barely alive."

"Trust an Australian to know what to do with a horse," Dev said.

"Yes, well, when they take to shooting up things on the street, which they have, it all becomes rather too much," Lily said.

"I shouldn't wonder," Dev said. "But to change the subject, where might I take you tomorrow and at what time?"

"All things considered," Lily said, "if you have a hankering to see the pyramids, considering the heat, I believe that I will leave you to make that trip by yourself. But the Museum of Egyptian Antiquities might be a nice substitute, and given the height of the ceilings and the spacious interiors, it promises to be comfortably cool. Shall we say around 10:00 am?"

Later that night, upon returning to Shepheard's, Dev found Dobb hastily packing.

"Sudden change of orders," Dobb said by way of explanation. "First lieutenant on the *Venture*, a destroyer out of Port Said, is down with appendicitis. Replacement needed immediately, so I'm off. Sorry to leave you so abruptly. Rather enjoyed our visits. Expect you'll get along without me. Steady as you go."

"Well said," Dev offered. "Best of luck, and good hunting to you."

Dev's week of leave in Cairo breezed by so swiftly and so intensely that he found that he could barely keep track of the time. On his second day in the city, he and Lily Winslow spent five hours touring the Museum of Antiquities before he dropped her at her flat and picked her up later for a dinner at the Savoy. On his third day, the two of them went to visit the Coptic cathedral, dining later together in the garden restaurant at the Belvedere. On a fourth evening, as Mortimer Winslow's guests, they dined at the Turf Club, and a fifth evening took them, again as guests, to the dining room at the Gezira Club across the river. And finally, on the Saturday night before Dev was to catch the train back to Kantara, he escorted Lily to the weekly dance at Shepheard's, where the two remained late.

From time to time during the week, Lily had taken Dev's arm for their entrance into this or that restaurant, one or the other of the clubs, but only at Shepheard's when they first went out to dance did Dev find that he was finally holding Lily Winslow in his arms. The fact that she did not remain at arm's length when they danced rather surprised him, for while Dev had in no way found her to be a prude since he had come to know her, he had also found her to be a young woman who did not invite advances and might deflect or resist any that he attempted to make. But on the dance floor at Shepheard's, Lily Winslow pressed herself into his embrace in a way that rather stunned him, the warmth of her melting against him all the way down. Rather than separate from him when they turned, she instead clung to him in a way that he had never experienced before when dancing with any of the girls he had known.

Later, in the taxi as their driver careened through the still busy streets on their way back to the Winslow flat, Lily scooted over close beside him, lifted his arm, and placed it around her shoulder, and said, "You do know how to write, I hope, because I shall expect letters from you, Devlin Collins, if not daily, at least on a schedule of once every other day."

Dev broke out laughing. "Letters on a schedule such as that might be taken for the establishment of a serious relationship," Dev protested. "Don't you think your parents might notice and disapprove?"

"Oh, for heaven's sake!" Lily Winslow said, reaching up and kissing him passionately. "My parents, Mr. Smarty, Mr. all-reserve-and-too-much-the-gentleman, have nothing whatsoever to say about my relationships, and if you'd paid a little more attention, you'd have noticed that our relationship became serious over the first lunch we shared together! Now, suppose you kiss me again so that we may seal an understanding."

"You're on," Dev said, leaving Lily Winslow slightly breathless when he finally let her go, helped her from the taxi, and escorted her to her door.

The following morning, Lily Winslow made no bones about kissing Dev at the station, and then, with her eyes moist, she simply said, "How soon?"

"I haven't seen a leave schedule yet," Dev said straightforwardly, "but given the number of pilots in our two squadrons, I would think that I might be able to wrangle three days within a month or six weeks."

"Look after yourself, Love," Lily said swiftly, "and don't trifle with any of the Berber girls that you meet in the desert."

"The Berber girls are all armed with sharp knives," Dev laughed, "and murderous intent. So you may rest easy on that point."

"I will rest easy," Lily said, "when I have you back here all to myself. I love you, Devlin Collins."

"I love you too," Dev said, kissing her one more time before he boarded the train and found himself a seat to Kantara.

8

By noon on Sunday, September 11, 1916, Dev was back in Kantara, back on the airdrome, and standing just inside the flap of Tuck's tent, reporting himself present and ready for duty.

"Oh, good show!" Tuck said, rising and shaking Dev's hand by way of welcome after his return. "And you couldn't have come at a better time. Wells is down and over at the hospital with a touch of fever, and Crisp is in there with him. Caught a slight splinter in the arm while over Bir El Mazr, so we're short-handed by two, but with your return, only by one."

"Want to fill me in on what you've been doing while I've been gone?" Dev said.

"Can do," Tuck said, sitting back down once more in his chair. "Good leave?"

"Couldn't have gone better," Dev said. "I found I rather liked Cairo."

"Hope you stayed out of the brothels," Tuck said. "Can't have you coming down with a dose of the clap short-handed as we are."

"No worries there," Dev said.

"Good lad," Tuck said, showing Dev a smile before turning thoroughly serious. "Now, about our situation. The Hun has moved back into El Arish and made a bomb run or two on Port Said. We've retaliated, of course, but our lads have had a spot of trouble finding the Hun hangars, and on their way back, we've had a Martinsyde go down out there. Picked up the pilot without difficulty, but we had to burn the machine. And the Germans are back at Magdhaba as well. I'll be sending you up this evening, with Symes, the two of you to drop a few eggs over Salmana, but you're going to have to watch yourself. The enemy's putting up more machines, and it suddenly appears that they're a trifle more aggressive. Rumors abound—New Hun commander, that sort of thing—but thus far, intelligence hasn't turned up a thing. And there are also supposed to be Austrians embedded with the Huns, but we're not sure about that yet either. Word to the wise: be alert. Things are changing in the air, and you don't want to be caught out."

"No," Dev said, "I don't."

"Right then," Tuck said. "Let's have a spot of lunch. I hear we're having bully beef on toast."

"Oh, lucky us," Dev said.

In the mess tent, Dev was roundly welcomed back, and as soon as he sat down beside Symes, Symes proceeded with a story that left Dev both laughing and pleased.

"The famous Nurse Cribbon has suffered a bit of a setback," Symes laughed. "Want to hear?"

"Absolutely," Dev said.

"Well," Symes said, "as with you, the minute Wells went down with his fever, Bivin and I proceeded to take him a bit of chocolate and a half-pint of whiskey with the ultimate same result that you encountered. In the first place, Wells complained that the infamous Cribbon had treated him like sack of potatoes when she had the beds changed in his ward, doing everything to him short of pitching him straight onto the floor. And then, the old cow discovered what we'd taken him the moment we departed and fairly raised holy hell over our generously conceived gifts. Wells, more than miffed by her ministrations, managed to con one of the orderlies into supplying him with an emetic, and low and behold, that emetic mysteriously found its way into Nurse Cribbon's cocoa. Apparently, every man in the ward enjoyed the results."

"If I'm not mistaken," Dev laughed, "I think that Jonathan Swift and Alexander Pope did that to a literary critic who'd once been saucy enough to attack them in print. Wells must have had the benefit of more education than we'd give him credit for."

"Either that," Symes said, "or a ready wit all of his own."

When Dev and Symes flew that afternoon, late in the day, they flew with something more than the few eggs that Tuck had indicated. In order to scout Turkish forces that GHQ intelligence types had discovered to be moving forward into the area, the red tabs had also laid on a reconnaissance in force, which meant that units of the Light Horse were moving up toward Salmana with the intention of scouting the enemy and, probably, driving them out. Dev and Symes were specifically tasked with keeping any Hun kites in the air from spotting the Light Horse as they made their approach. As a result, Tuck sent his two pilots up armed not only with their observers' Lewis guns but with flare guns, very pistols, with which to warn the Light Horse if the Huns managed to elude their protective screen.

Dev did not like carrying the flare gun or the additional cartridges that went with it. Weeks before, a Hun tracer had struck a similar packet of cartridges when one of the Ismailia pilots had been in the air, and the cartridges had exploded instantly, setting his ship on fire and plunging the man to his death. Furthermore, any use of a flare gun, as far as Dev was concerned, would only alert whatever Huns were about to the fact that a larger formation of some kind was being warned by an exploding flare—and that, in Dev's estimation, defeated the entire point of the exercise.

"Yes," Tuck said before he sent them off, "stands to reason, of course. But the very pistols have been ordered by red tabs at the highest level, and ours is not to reason why. Take them along, and avoid using them if at all possible, and let's just hope that the Light Horse get up there without incident."

The Light Horse, two full squadrons of them, did get up to Salmana that afternoon, late, with the western sun at their backs, and attacked at once, forcing a Turkish cavalry squadron to take to their heels and move into a rapid retreat along the road to Bir El Mazar. Dev and Symes, however, did not manage to carry out their mission without incident. In fact, Symes did not participate in the mission at all. When his engine faltered and threatened to fail over Bir El Gandadi—a few miles short of Salmana and almost immediately over the Light Horse where they were moving on the settlement from the southern flank—Symes had no choice but to turn back and attempt to make Kantara once more before his engine quit and dropped him onto the desert floor amid the Berbers.

Dev, resolved to carry out his assignment, proceeded on toward Salmana and dropped two of his eggs over a Turkish machine-gun position that he spotted. Then, glancing swiftly to his left when Trent began to fire the Lewis gun, he began a series of swift maneuvers, all of them designed to avoid fire from an Eindecker that had dropped upon them suddenly and appeared to be loosing its machine gun in their direction.

As Dev pulled into what he intended to be a tight turn so as to give Trent the best angle of fire upon the Eindecker, he nearly froze on the stick. From the opposite direction he spotted a Pfalz flying straight toward him at no more than 500 yards distant, the Hun pilot's finger already on the trigger of his forward-firing machine gun which had started to spit tracers. With his heart pumping almost to the point of bursting, and wholly without thinking, Dev seized the very pistol, pointed it in the Pfalz's direction, and fired the round in an attempt to drive the Hun off. But the Hun flew straight into the bursting round, particles of the burning explosive setting the Pfalz's wing on fire. At once the Hun pilot took his plane down in a frantic attempt to put out the fire by the rush of wind around it. And in that attempt he failed, putting the plane into such a steep and rapid dive that the port wing folded back in mid-flight, the smoking ruin dropping straight down onto the desert floor not 2 miles from Salmana.

In the meantime, the Eindecker, seeing what had happened to his fellow and more than troubled by a round or two which Trent appeared to have poured into his radiator, also tried to drop to the deck amid a hasty withdrawal. But the last thing that either Dev or Trent saw of the Hun was a sudden second plume of smoke that rose from the desert in the spot where they imagined the Eindecker had gone down.

Dev, during the hour that followed—while he and Trent remained on station over Salmana as the Light Horse came up—could not stop his hands from shaking. The BE2c he was flying seemed to jerk all over the sky as he tried to bring himself back under control, regulate his breathing, and take a firm grip on himself. He had not fired the very pistol with the firm intention of killing the Hun by setting him on fire, and try as he might, Dev could not quite stifle the sense of horror that followed quickly in the wake of what he had done. In the beginning, he felt nauseated by the recollection of the German flying straight into the explosion of the flare. The upset to his stomach, he managed to fight down, but the upset to his mind—the sight of the burning Pfalz—seemed to be another thing in a class by itself. He doubted that if he lived to 100 that he would ever be able to eradicate it from his thoughts.

War, Dev knew and knew very well, was war, and the Hun, whoever he was, had been doing his best to kill both Dev and Trent, but that certain knowledge did nothing to alter or reduce the gross result of what he had seen. So, it was in that moment—one that could never be changed—that Devlin Collins finally came to know fully what it meant to have to live with and bear the complete responsibility for his actions.

In the mess that evening, when it became clear that Dev preferred not to talk about the Hun that he'd downed that afternoon, the pilots in the Flight turned their attentions to the Hun that Trent had apparently brought down, or so everyone thought. Dev's act of destruction—although Tuck carried a pistol that he sometimes fired at Huns who came within range—appeared to be the first instance in which a pilot in the Flight had actually destroyed an enemy ship in the air. The others for which the Flight had accounted were chalked up to the efforts of the observers with their Lewis guns. Planes on the ground like the one Dev had destroyed during the raid over El Arish did not count. They were recorded and appreciated by everyone from Tuck and St. Clair to the red tabs at GHQ, but none of them figured into what various of the pilots had begun calling "the score." As far as Dev was concerned, a clean hit with a forward-facing machine gun was one thing and seemed acceptable, but setting an enemy kite on fire with a very pistol stuck in his craw in a way that he found it difficult and distasteful to swallow.

"Walk with me," Tuck said to Dev as Dev emerged from the mess tent following the meal.

"Sir?" Dev said, looking up.

"Walk with me, now," Tuck said. "We need a bit of a talk."

Dev straightened up and fell in beside Tuck, who struck a path out toward the middle of the airdrome.

"Having thoughts about the engagement today?" Tuck asked after they had taken no more than a few steps.

"Yes," Dev said.

"Don't," Tuck said forcefully. "Talked to a chap in the Lowland Division, the 42nd. A major, he was. Lost two men going into their attack, not to the Turks, not to the Huns, but to adders. As you've noticed, we have more than a few of them out here. Those men knew it going in, but by accident they stumbled across them and were bitten. No one's fault, no one to blame. Accidents, both of them, but the men died, and there was nothing for it. So don't get in a fret about the Hun who collided with your flare burst today. Accident that. You did the right thing, thinking he would break off and run, but he didn't, and for not running, in this instance, he paid the price. The man made a choice, Collins, and he made the wrong one, and it killed him. Simple as that."

"That's the second time I've seen a man burn," Dev said.

"And it won't be the last," Tuck said. "And I'm sorry to have to tell you this, but whether you kill men with bullets or set them on fire doesn't amount to a pinch of salt. We've been sent here to put the Hun and the Turk down, and it doesn't matter a lick how we do it, as long as we do it. If that Hun had come for me the way he came for you, I would have fired that very pistol straight into him if I'd remembered that I had it, and if one comes at me tomorrow and I have a flare gun with me, I will. Catch my drift, do you?"

"Yes, Sir," Dev said. "Basically, what you're telling me is that we're here to kill," Dev said.

"I'm afraid so," Tuck said, "and the flying, the bombing, the photo reconnaissance, and the strafes are all in aid of it. No one likes killing, Collins, but the faster we kill and the more we kill, the quicker this thing will be over, and then we can all go home and live spotless lives following peaceful pursuits. Unfortunately for the two of us, we've been born into an age which has brought us to this course, and in for a penny, in for a pound."

"One would like to have lived differently," Dev said.

"Yes," Tuck said, "one would, but we're doing this, I submit, so that our sons, or our daughters, or both, may have that choice. Now, go back to your tent, pour yourself a whiskey, and get some sleep because I think St. Clair may be up here early in the morning to lay on a raid to the east."

The raid St. Clair laid on forced Dev from his cot at 0400 on the following morning, not two full minutes after his batman threw back the tent flap and presented him with a tin of strong coffee that remained scalding hot.

"Them's 'nounced a brief in the mess, Sir, at 0500," the batman said as he shook Dev awake.

The coffee, something nearly as strong as the Turkish coffee Dev had enjoyed in Cairo, hit him like a hard slap in the face, jolted him awake, and seemed to burn all the way down.

"*Whoa!*" Dev exclaimed. "Where'd you get this stuff?"

"'im that cooks," the batman said, his face breaking into a grin that looked almost ghoulish beneath the hurricane lamp that he'd lighted. "'e drop a whole bag 'stead of 'alf in 'is pot."

"I'll say he did!" Dev said, pulling on his trousers. "Sort of gives the word *shock* a whole new meaning."

"Aye, Sir," said the batman. "'ad a cuppa myself. Strong, that. Curled me toes."

In the mess tent, Dev almost laughed when he glanced at some of the others. Their eyes, he imagined, looked like they were open wider than he'd ever seen them at that hour.

"If Crumpler's coffee doesn't have you lot wanting to stand on your heads this morning," St. Clair began, "try to take a strain and listen to what I have to say. We're going east to raid Magdhaba; that's west of Wadi El Arish and southwest of El Arish itself by a good 25 miles. No observers flying this morning because you'll be carrying one 100-pound bomb slung beneath the belly and eight Coopers, four per wing rack. I'll fly top cover in the DH1 and do my best to keep brother Hun from bedeviling you, but your job—Captain Tuck, Bivin, Symes, Collins, and Lofton—is to strike whatever hangars and planes you can find on the ground. Yesterday, some Huns unloaded over a troop of the Light Horse at Salmana, and given their line of departure, the red tabs think they came from Magdhaba. If so, they're probably relatively new there and just moved down from El Arish, so let's not let them get comfortable. We'll take off before sunrise, fly once more to the south of Magdhaba, and come up around the place so as to attack with the morning sun at our backs. Once you unload your 100-pounders, you are to bomb targets of opportunity with your Coopers."

The fitters lighted them a bit of a flare path for their takeoff that morning, and once in the air, flying with very little light to the east, the gaggle St. Clair assembled spread the flight out with at least 50 yards between each plane, no one wishing to risk collision with his fellow in the darkness. An hour later, beyond the dunes, as the Flight approached Magdhaba and with the sun coming up directly ahead of them, the pilots edged more together, dropping down to 2,000 feet before flying a wide circle around the supposed location of the target and dropping down to an altitude of around 400 feet as Tuck led them forward for their bomb run at full throttle.

Unlike the German drome at El Arish, Dev saw no trees shielding the big canvas hangar at Magdhaba. Instead, as the Flight rushed in from the direction of the rising sun, he saw a single hangar, smaller tents that he imagined to be living quarters, as well as three or four square, mud-brick buildings which he imagined to have been adopted by the Huns for use as their headquarters and communications center. Not far away, behind one of those buildings, he also spotted what appeared to be a small water reservoir, the source of the station's water supply. In front of the hangars, to Dev's surprise—and, he thought, to the surprise of every other member of the squadrons—he also spotted two Aviatiks on the ground, both of them a pale yellow in color so that they nearly blended with the ground upon which they were parked. When he saw the red and white half-moons adorning their wings, he knew for the first time, and knew without mistake, that the fliers in possession at Magdhaba were not Germans or Austrians but Turks.

One of those Aviatiks, its pilot apparently alerted by the sound of Tuck's approaching flight, began to taxi, the plane's throttle seemingly opened full even before the Flight could approach to within 500 yards of the airdrome and before Dev or any of the others had time to notice and identify the insignia on its wings. The attempt was futile, because as Tuck and the others swept in over the base, Dev, flying on the far-left flank of the attack, waited until what he believed to be exactly the right moment. Then, saving his 100-pounder for a more important target, he unloaded four of his Coopers just beyond but directly in the path of the Aviatik. Glancing swiftly behind him as he pulled up in order to escape from the concussion of his bombs, Dev saw with satisfaction that amid the clouds of dirt and dust raised by his bombs, the Aviatik had run straight into one of the shallow craters produced by a Cooper and flipped over onto its back.

Elsewhere, Dev's glance also showed him that Tuck's 100-pounder had scored a direct hit on one of the mud buildings, while another pilot's bomb happened to be exploding along the edge of the hangar. Without taking time to glance farther, Dev climbed another one or two hundred feet, turned to his left, flew immediately around in a circle, and once more dove his plane toward the airdrome. This time he approached it from the south with the sun off his starboard wing, speeding in for his second attack quickly, but apparently not quickly enough, because by the time he began his bomb run, the Turks had manned their Archies, with the result that black explosions began to blossom on both sides of him. Stamping the rudder pedals as though his life depended upon it, Dev flew a twisting course, threw his ship down as low as 200 feet, and pickled his 100-pounder as close to the water reservoir as he could drop it, hoping to release his bomb directly on top of it so as to explode one of its sides. Whether he achieved his aim or not, he didn't know, because a Turk machine gun cut loose upon him almost in the same second that he released his bomb, and with rounds coming straight up through his wings, Dev felt hard pressed to escape the danger in which he suddenly found himself. Instinctively, perhaps, Dev banked and turned to the right, and that turn, back toward the sun, seemed to mask him from the machine gun that was erected between two of the mud buildings and didn't have a clear field of fire given the angle of Dev's escape. Either that, Dev thought, or the Turkish gunners had shifted target toward one of the other pilots who had timed his run to follow after Dev's and from a different angle.

Someone, who would later be identified in the mess as Bivin, bombed the assembled tins of the Turks' fuel supply at that moment, the fireball exploding from those tins shooting straight up into the air in such a way as to catch Lofton's wing on fire as he flew through the upward spiraling mass. So, Lofton did the only thing that a man in his position could do: without hesitation, he dropped straight down, landed at once before the flames engulfed his wing, leapt from his ship, and struck a beeline for the nearest bomb crater in the runway, raising his hands above his head and waiting for his unavoidable capture.

There was nothing, absolutely nothing that the others could do for him, and they didn't try. Dev felt fairly certain that if he or any of the others tried to unload on the Turks who raced out with rifles to take Lofton prisoner, the Turks, probable privates with rifles, would simply shoot Lofton. Instead, as Dev made his last run and unloaded his remaining Cooper bombs over what remained of the Turks' hangar, he was later able to report that he had seen two of the Turks on the ground marching Lofton, at rifle point, toward one or another of the mud buildings that remained unscathed.

Glancing at his watch, Dev calculated that the raid had lasted five minutes, perhaps six, but no longer. With the Flight once more gathering to the west and St. Clair descending from above in the DH1 that had never been called into action, the remainder of the flight, with Tuck leading, collected into a loose formation and set their course for Kantara. Another quick glance to either side of him showed Dev that the Turk gunners on the ground had got in more than a few licks on the Flight. Bivin's ship seemed to be tattooed with holes right down its side, while Symes had pieces of fabric fluttering from the wings that Dev could see on the left side of his ship. With regard to Dev's own kite, he counted at least eight holes to port and three holes as well as a large flapping rip to starboard, the obvious result of a shell fragment from one of the Archie bursts. What his fuselage might look like, he had no idea, but about his feet, he felt a wind that was extraordinary and imagined that he'd been hit somewhere to the front beneath his engine. No one fell out or experienced a forced landing on the way back, all of them landing by 1030 hours that morning with no loss other than Lofton, the man whom none of them could have picked up or saved from becoming a prisoner. During the immediate debriefing that St. Clair conducted, he commended them for the results they'd achieved and set Dev and Bivin to fly a reconnaissance on the following morning to photograph the results. Then, giving the Flight the remainder of the day off, St. Clair gave them a hearty well done, got back in the air, and returned to Ismailia.

Owing to an unexpected and furious rainstorm that struck Kantara the following morning, Dev and Bivin did not fly their reconnaissance mission to Magdhara. The rain that descended in sheets so soaked the field that none of the Flight's ships could have gotten off the ground before sinking up to their hubs in the mud that the storm left behind it, and elsewhere, as reported by telephone, the wadis were suddenly running hip high with swirling torrents.

"Like as not, we've had two year's rainfall in a matter of six hours," Tuck said, sitting in the mess tent, positioning his chair between two dripping leaks. "Who could have imagined it?"

Dev and Bivin did not take to the air until around noon two full days following the raid, but once the field became dry enough for a good landing, they went, flew up to Magdhara in record time, took their photographs, and returned with well-exposed plates.

"They're gone," Dev said, as soon as he and Bivin reported back. "The Turks have pulled out of Magdhara. We didn't see a kite or a warm body anywhere. The hangar is burned, and there are skeletons of at least three planes burned inside it as well as the two we upended on the field."

The photographs they brought back, once air intelligence had developed them, backed up the oral reports they had made and the quick telephone call that Tuck had put through to Ismailia to inform St. Clair about their apparent success. And as Dev examined the photographs, he also spotted one additional fact that he had not reported orally. The east wall of the water reservoir over which he'd dropped his 100-pounder showed clear signs of damage. He had not wholly cut off the Turks' water supply at the airdrome, but in studying what he could see in the photographs, he believed that he had cut that supply by a third or a half.

"I could be wrong," Tuck said over supper that evening, "but I think we may have driven the Turks out of Magdhara, and I'm prone to think that we've done it for good."

Crisp returned the following morning, having caught the train out of Cairo at midnight following a four-day convalescent leave.

"Toured the flesh pots, did you?" Dev asked, as Crisp came in and sank quickly onto his bunk.

"Oh yes," Crisp said, "oh yes, indeed. Lovely place called *Le Chat Blanc* provides all the amenities. Bit of the bubbly, scintillating conversation, that sort of thing."

"I've heard of it," Dev said.

"*Really* now?" Crisp said, "Go there yourself, did you?"

"No," Dev said, "but met a Royal Navy lieutenant who did. He recommended it highly."

"And what, then, did you do in Cairo?" Crisp wanted to know. "Beside sit on the terrace at Shepheard's and ogle the lovelies."

"Met one of them," Dev said.

"I say," Crisp said, perking up. "Do tell?"

"Not on your life," Dev said. "Keeping her to myself."

"Here now!" Crisp said. "Is that any way to treat a friend? I apprehend sedate teas at the Savoy. Luncheons at the Grand Continental, perhaps a tea dance at Shepheard's, all suitably chaperoned and dull as ditch water."

"Not so," Dev laughed. "American girl from my neighborhood, or thereabouts. Struck a spark, if I don't mistake. Attractive, refined, accomplished—she writes and actually publishes—and she's intelligent."

"Stop," Crisp protested. "You are making me ill, but do introduce me to her sister, or if she is an isolated child, her best friend."

"In your dreams," Dev laughed.

"And you accomplished all of this, in *Cairo*?" Crisp said, voicing his disbelief.

"It is a city of many parts," Dev said, "some of them more inviting than others."

"You've exhausted me," Crisp said. "But do wake me for supper, and if Tuck comes looking for me, make some excuse."

"Before you pop off," Dev said, "how's the arm?"

"Good, but a trifle sore," Crisp said, sinking into his pillow. "It needs sleep."

"I shall try not to wake you," Dev said.

"Good fellow," said Crisp, closing his eyes.

Bivin, Wells, and Symes flew the reconnaissance that evening, going out to have a look at things east of Salmana. Not long after they'd departed, as Dev sat in the mess tent reading a newspaper, Lieutenant Stevens put in his first appearance.

"I'm Stevens," the man said simply, throwing back the tent flap and walking in. "Is this where the meals are served?"

Dev looked up. The man who had called himself Stevens could not, Dev thought, have stood more than 5 feet 2 inches in height, standing on his tip toes. Freckle-faced with a head of red hair over a pug nose and childish blue eyes, the man struck Dev as a refugee from the fifth form of the school that he'd formerly attended in Derry.

"Collins here," Dev said, standing and shaking the man's hand. "Joining us, are you?"

"I am," said Stevens. "Only just arrived. Captain Tuck told me where to stash my kit and then suggested that I come here, to meet the fellows and so forth."

"Not many of them in at the moment," Dev said. "Just me. Crisp is sleeping while Biven, Wells, and Symes are out on patrol. I take it that you are Lofton's replacement."

"And what happened to Lofton?" Stevens asked.

"Down over Magdhaba," Dev said. "Captured by the Turks. Unfortunate, that."

"Very," said Stevens.

"So, from where have you come to us?" Dev asked.

"Central Flying School," Stevens said, "and before that, the Royal East Kent Yeomanry."

"Kent your home?" Dev asked.

"No," Stevens said, "but I have an uncle who knew someone who got me in. Nice fellows, if you know what I mean, but I found that I wasn't much on horse soldiering and put in for the RFC."

"Egypt what you expected?" Dev said.

"No," Stevens said. "Rather expected a posting to the Western Front. Never anticipated Egypt. Not for a second."

"You'll find, I think," Dev said, "that neither did the rest of us. Still, we're here, flying antiquated ships, and the action is plentiful, with the single restriction that we don't have forward-firing machine guns and have to rely on our observers for defense. The Huns are putting up a few more kites these days than when I first reported in, so whatever flying skills you've developed will be more in demand than ever."

"*Ah*," Stevens said, taking Dev's point without thrilling to it. "Carry pistols, do we?"

"Always," Dev said, "which brings up the subject of the Berbers."

Dev told him about the Berbers, and Stevens's eyes opened wide. The Berbers were something that he'd never taken into consideration, something he'd never heard about or even imagined.

"I can see," he said finally, "that I shall have to nurse every ounce of power out of whatever ship I fly to always get her back here in one piece."

"Yes," Dev said. "That would be best. Had a tussle with those rascals once. Fortunately, my observer held them off until I could clean out my fuel feed."

"What is a fuel feed?" Stevens asked.

"Come along," Dev said. "We'll go down to the sheds, and I'll show you a couple of things that might just be useful enough to keep you in the air."

The following day, Dev and Boy Stevens—"Boy" being the nickname with which Crisp and the others had dubbed the lad—flew out to the east to do a photo recon flight over El Arish, breaking the trip at Romani. There St. Clair had established a satellite field for the men to top off with fuel before long flights to places like El Arish and Magdhaba. To Dev's relief and also to his satisfaction, he found that Boy Stevens flew well and seemed to fly with confidence, sticking to Dev's port wing in a way that showed he was more than familiar with formation flying.

Down below as the two of them flew low over the road to Salmana, Dev could see that the rail line and what he took to be the pipeline were moving forward at a clip, the both of them nearing Salmana, which was now firmly in British possession and entrenched with a tent city a mile or two back and supply sheds going up along both sides of the rail line.

East of Bir El Mazar, Dev sighted Turkish columns of cavalry on the desert floor—probable patrols out to scout for a British presence. But with Murray moving so directly forward, Dev doubted that anything other than ANZAC patrols of the same kind would be anywhere in evidence and resolved to drop a Cooper or two on the Turks as he and Boy Stevens returned from their mission.

Over El Arish, flying at 4,000 feet, the two BE2cs were pounced on by two Pfalz scouts, both of them dropping straight down from the heights and with the sun behind them. But while both Huns got a few machine-gun rounds into each of them, the tight turn that Dev put them into—a turn to which Boy Sevens continued to fly on Dev's wingtip—so unmasked their two observers' Lewis guns that the Huns apparently believed they had done as much damage as they dared to risk and continued their dive straight down until they disappeared beneath a low cloud that had formed north of El Arish. The last that Dev saw of them, he believed them heading farther in that direction toward what he imagined to be their field at Rafa.

On their way back, following the exposure of at least six of Trent's photographic plates, Dev did spot one of the Turkish patrols—a column of cavalry riding west, two by two—and went down to only 400 feet to unload his Coopers over their heads. Boy Stevens, dropping back and following some distance away, loosed his own bombs not two seconds after Dev had made his drop. Without making a second circuit to survey any damage that they might have done and with Trent's Lewis gun percolating as they climbed out, Dev knew that they had not only scattered the Turkish patrol but probably had done for some of them.

Back on the ground at Romani, Boy Stevens, in the few words he exchanged with Dev while the air mechs refueled them for the flight to Kantara, showed what Dev considered a proper restraint. The lad might have been young, but as far as Dev was concerned, he was steady, the rounds that the two Pfalz had put into them catching his notice but in no way unnerving him.

"So," Tuck asked Dev when the two of them returned, and waiting to hear Dev's report after he had dismissed Boy Stevens to the mess tent, "how did the lad do, in your estimation?"

"He flew well," Dev said, "and the Huns didn't seem to upset him, regardless of the fact that they punched a few holes through the fabric on both of us."

"Excellent," Tuck said. "Not a wilting lily, then?"

"No," Dev said, "and a good formation flier into the bargain. Stuck right to me. United front, if you see what I mean. I'd say that's why the Huns didn't try it on for a second attack."

"Good," Tuck said. "He sounds like he will hold his own with us."

Crisp, who flew with Boy Stevens the following day, came back to report the same thing. Together, the two had once more flown over Magdhaba, found the place deserted, or relatively so, and bombed yet another Turkish patrol south of Bir El Mazar in the area of the dunes on their way back.

"Good lad," Crisp said as he and Dev sat in their tent, sharing a whiskey, before taking their supper that evening. "Stayed right with me the whole of the way. Steady. Nothing too exuberant upon landing. Just the right attitude, I think. Job well done. Reasonable satisfaction but without euphoric comment afterward. Where did you say he came from?"

"Aside from the Kent Yeomanry, he didn't say," Dev said.

"Let one comment drop," Crisp said. "Told me that his father owns four mortuaries, but I can't remember how the subject came up."

"Good Lord!" Dev said. "Perhaps that explains his steadiness in the face of things."

"So I imagine," Crisp said.

In October, with the pipeline and the railroad now extending east of Salmana and with more and more of Murray's troops moving up beside it, air reconnaissance showed that the Turks had once more moved into Magdhaba. Turkish infantry units, with some artillery, were entrenched in the area so as to establish a block on El Arish's southern flank. Hun air units did not make the move with them, but given the advanced activity in the area, St. Clair established another satellite airdrome at Salmana in order to rearm and refuel 14 Squadron's flights going to and from the areas that most required their attentions. It was from there, on the morning of October 15, that Dev, Crisp, Wells, and Boy Stevens set off to bomb and overfly Rafa for the first time, Tuck himself flying the DH1 to give them all the protection that his forward-firing machine gun could provide.

Rather than fly up over land for the whole of the way, Tuck took them over the Mediterranean to cut the distance they would have to go and afford them, he hoped, a degree of surprise over the target. To prevent a Turkish or Hun attack down the coast, Royal Navy monitors were stationed at intervals off the beach, none of them so close that German artillery could bring them under fire but close enough that the pilots might be able to fly over them with a reasonable hope of being picked up if they were forced to ditch owing to damage or some engine malfunction that they couldn't resolve in the air.

As flights went, the run up to Rafa proved long, but the course Tuck set in taking them up proved successful, their flight in from the sea catching the Turks flatfooted. So, when they did indeed locate the Hun airdrome, no enemy kites rose to meet them. The Flight was able to unload a total of 32 Cooper bombs over the field and the hangars from 1,000 feet, the observers exposing a full array of photographic plates to record the damage on the Flight's second run over the target. But if the Huns remained on the ground, the Archies and the Turk machine guns surrounding the field kicked up a perfect kind of hell for the Flight. Black mushrooms exploded everywhere around the well-separated planes, bullets and scraps of steel fairly lacerating their planes from nearly every angle. One such tiny fragment lodged itself in the heel of Dev's flying boot, while two more ripped slashes in the sleeve of his leather flying coat, another tearing a rip across Trent's trousers while cutting his leg. As far as Dev could tell, his engine remained whole, but much of the plane seemed to look like a sieve once he emerged from his last pass. From what little he could see of the others as they gathered around Tuck for their return to Salmana, the ripped fabric showing everywhere about them made it appear that their planes had been shot through by a brace of shotguns.

Physically, coming away from the attack, more than Dev's hands shook. In fact, as he wrestled with the controls, he could feel his entire body shaking as though struck by a sudden ague. So pronounced was his body's reaction that he only barely brought himself back under control after 20 minutes of flying, and even then, his heart continued to pound in a way that reminded him of repeated hammer strokes. And then, as he finally managed to bring the pounding back under some kind of control, the fatigue set in—a fatigue that felt more extreme than anything he'd ever felt before, a fatigue that left him barely able to hold his eyes open and keep his hand on the stick, not to mention his feet on the rudder pedals.

Once back on the ground at Salmana, Dev recovered somewhat, enough so that he was able to fly on to Kantara. Back at Kantara, he wanted nothing more than to throw himself onto his cot and sleep the sleep of the dead.

"I was on leave in Cairo two weeks ago," Tuck said after he'd heard everyone's reports. "Wells and Symes were there last weekend. Boy Stevens won't be due to go for another month, but in looking at you, Collins, and you, Crisp, I would say that you could both do with a three-day bender in the metropolis. Any objections?"

"None," they said at once.

"But starting tomorrow," Dev said, "not now. We both need some sleep. "

"Yes," Tuck said. "Well, tie up your tent flaps, because if you happened to look south on your way back, you must have seen that we're in for a dust storm."

With a thick cloud of dust rolling in over Kantara, the last thing that Dev did before retreating to his tent was to send Lily a telegram: "*Arriving Cairo 1100, 16 October. Lunch, Shepheard's?*" And then, with Crisp already piled onto his own cot, Dev collapsed onto his without bothering to remove so much as his flying coat, mindless of the dust that seemed to be filtering in everywhere and settling over his body.

9

If Dev had expected to meet Lily at Shepheard's when he and Crisp checked in, he never had the chance; Lily, with another young woman beside her, happened to be waiting for him on the platform when the train from Kantara arrived.

With no hesitation that Dev could apprehend, Lily reached up and kissed Dev immediately, not long but warmly, before turning to the others and saying flatly, "We share an understanding." Then, looking Crisp swiftly up and down, she turned back to Dev and said, "All right, Mr. Divulge-Little. Don't you think you ought to introduce us to your friend?"

"This is Lieutenant Crisp," Dev said, "and this, Crisp, is Miss Lily Winslow, the obvious girl of my dreams who has so suddenly manifested herself in the flesh. And this lady, I take it," he said, turning in the other woman's direction and smiling, "must be her chaperone for the morning."

"I'm Ruth Steel," the other woman said, showing both Dev and Crisp an inviting smile from a pair of rosebud lips that seemed to go well with her faintly green eyes and red hair. "What did you say your name was again, Lieutenant, if I may ask?"

"Crisp," Crisp said.

"I got that," Ruth Steel said pleasantly, "but I don't believe I caught your first name."

"And you never will," Crisp laughed, "if I can avoid revealing it."

"Nonsense," Lily said at once. "We're Americans, Crisp; we go by first names. Do tell."

Crisp tried to hedge, but pressed by both women, he failed. "Bentley," he said finally, "Bentley Wayson Crisp."

"You've got to be kidding," Dev said.

"Alas, I have an uncle," Crisp said, "the kind who gives male infants names against their wishes."

"Oh, I don't know," Ruth Steel said. "I think I rather like it."

"Just as long as you don't call me 'Bent,'" Crisp said.

"So wise of you to have brought Ruth along," Dev said.

"Young ladies of good breeding and perspicacious education do not meet trains in Cairo unaccompanied," Lily said pertly. "And besides, I rather imagined that you wouldn't be coming alone and tried to anticipate."

"Intuition?" Dev asked.

"You will find, my dear," Lily said at once, "that women are particularly gifted in that way. Now, come along, the both of you, and we'll drop off your kit at Shepheard's before we go on to Ciro's."

"What's Ciro's?" Dev asked.

"A French eating establishment with which we are very familiar," Ruth said, "but modestly priced. A place where gold diggers are not likely to take their beaus."

"And is that what you meant by 'perspicacious education'?" Dev asked.

"Why, you clever boy," Lily said, taking Dev's arm.

At Ciro's, beneath ceiling fans that circulated the air, air now cool enough amid the Egyptian October to keep things pleasant, Dev and Crisp lunched on a well-turned omelet and a chop, while Lily and Ruth refreshed themselves on a combination of peeled fruit, sliced carrots, and thin strips of roasted chicken.

"And how, may I ask, do you occupy your time in Cairo, Miss Steel?" Crisp asked politely, as the four of them waited for what Lily had referred to as "Arab" rather than "Turkish" coffee—a mixture that tasted to all of them, when they received it, more like sweet tea than coffee.

"My father is at the American consulate," Ruth said, "so from time to time I fill in there, and occasionally, I act as a guide for some of our country's important but first-time visitors to Cairo, the city's flesh pots not included."

"Ruth," Lily said, "always sees to it that 'Sloth effuses her opiate fumes in vain.'"

"Don't I detect an aberration in that line?" Dev grinned.

"Never you mind," Lily said smartly. "Dear Dr. Johnson would have perfectly understood me."

"I suppose that we can only hope," Crisp said, capping Ruth's point, "that Beauty does not blunt her fatal darts on fops."

"The fops whom my father sends me to guide," Ruth laughed, "usually range from a salt and pepper 60 to a thoroughly gray 80. The only fops we ever see are Egyptian touts, overdressed, wearing the tarbush, and floating in scent. Creatures to be avoided, you may be sure."

Following lunch, with the men to escort them, Lily and Ruth suggested a spin through the Khan El Khalili bazaar.

"There will be a plethora of tourists," Ruth said, "but no matter; it is a sight that shouldn't be missed."

"It is reputed to be one of the most immense souks in the Middle East," Lily said. "I believe that it was established during the Mamluk era, and as far as we know, it has never been closed. Caravans met here, don't you see, bringing goods from every direction."

Khan El Khalili was indeed filled with a plethora of tourists, many of them in uniform, their escorted ladies bobbing here and there beneath their massive umbrella-style hats. But if the tourist clientele seemed large, the native clientele counted as larger, and very quickly Dev saw every kind of person wearing every kind of clothing that he could imagine. Berbers from the desert alongside suited Syrians alongside native Egyptians alongside Moslem women clad from head to toe in burkas alongside their more modern sisters decked out in the latest Parisian styles. And in the shops that flanked both sides of the arcade-like street through which the souk wound, Dev noticed everything for sale from massive Persian carpets to Moroccan leather, Italian shoes, and Turkish tobacco, not to mention Chinese silk, Indonesian spices, and faux Egyptian artifacts.

"It's rather like going to a carnival in the States, isn't it?" Dev said.

"It is," said Lily, "only by means of a sharp eye, Mother and I have been able to pick up some very nice things here, and the variety is an absolute delight."

"I concur," Dev said. "I don't think I've ever been anywhere that has exhibited such a wide assortment of goods for sale, and while I rather imagine that a seasoned shopper could bargain down anything, the prices look rather good to an untrained eye."

Moments later, Lily and Ruth went to work on one of the shopkeepers, bargaining for pieces of silk yardage that had caught their eye, and gave Dev and Crisp a lesson in what a pair of seasoned shoppers could really do when they put their minds to a bargain.

"I had been told," Dev said as the four of them threaded through the crowd and away from the shop, Lily and Ruth carrying parcels they had wrangled for half the asking price, "that Arabs were not only gifted traders but capable of extracting a camel's teeth without its notice in a business transaction. You fairly skinned that poor man. His family are liable to wind up destitute."

"Ha," Lily laughed. "That the shopkeeper made a profit on our sale, you may be absolutely sure, or we would never have been allowed to leave with the goods."

"We paid a little more than we might have liked," Ruth said, "but if young ladies wish to look fetching so as not to embarrass their escorts, modest expenditures are never out of order."

"How much more fetching could you possibly look?" Crisp asked, feigning a sense of wonder.

"Oh, what a bright boy," Ruth said quickly. "Just wait and see what Madam Pico manages to whip up for us. There's a dance at Shepheard's on Saturday. You'll be taking me, won't you?"

"Jinns and leprechauns couldn't keep me away," Crisp said, as Ruth took his arm.

"You two will be attending yourselves, won't you?" Ruth said over her shoulder to Lily and Dev.

"If Lily intends to trick herself out in something more 'fetching,' than what she is currently wearing," Dev said, "I think it safe to say that I will be fetched."

Following a late afternoon period for rest, bathing, and, in Dev and Crisp's case, an early evening drink on Shepheard's terrace, the two couples dined elegantly at the Intercontinental and, afterwards, shared a brandy in the hotel's lounge where female guests were permitted—the hotel's long bar, like the long bar at Shepheard's, being wholly given over to male guests only. Here and there, red-tabbed officers with their ladies graced this table or that while a few standard tourists—Europeans mostly, seeking to escape from the atmosphere of conflict in their own lands—took up other tables along with a smattering of what Dev imagined to be civil servants.

"Interesting clientele," Dev said in the spirit of throwing the remark away. "I wonder how many actual spies come this way?"

"Oh goodness," Ruth laughed. "If you listen to my father, Cairo seems to be filled with them: German, Hungarian, Bulgarian, Ottoman, Arab, Greek, Syrian … the list is endless."

"Along with the ubiquitous warning that idle talk tends to sink ships, not to mention giving away the family goose," Lily said. "These chaps with the red tabs on their lapels are thought to classify their laundry lists *Most Secret*, but if you sit and listen to the talk—and I've done that a time or two when out with my parents—their tongues seem to wag with the regularity of warblers."

"To the point," Ruth added, "where one can almost imagine a host of drab little men wearing dark suits sitting at every other table snatching words straight out of the air and writing them down with pencils in little notebooks."

"That does sound like what we might expect from the men wearing the red tabs," Crisp said.

"Yes," Dev said, "it does."

"There was a case of which we have heard," Lily began, "in which a rather smart woman, always beautifully decked out—a woman that the two of us caught sight of several times—hoodwinked a French staff colonel in that way. She put herself forward as a rich Swede, arrived at Shepheard's with an array of steamer trunks, put the women to shame by the quality of her gowns and daywear, danced a whirl with a regular bevy of those red tabs you are talking about, finally settled on a French colonel in General Murray's entourage, and was eventually discovered to be someone other than who she had claimed to be."

"Yes," Ruth said. "In the beginning, I believe that she announced herself as a Baroness Lindstrom, or something close, from Stockholm, with an old title going all the way back to Charles X. But by the time that British intelligence got around to running a check on her, they found that she was a countess—an Austrian countess named von Strumm, closely related to the chief of one of the Austrian intelligence services—and had been putting it around, in Egyptian and Arab circles, among their Illuminati, so to speak, that the Kaiser had secretly converted to Islam. Tricky woman, that one. Armed to the teeth with beauty, grace, and poise and trying all the time to foment an Islamic jihad so as to throw the Allies out of Egypt and seize the canal by subterfuge."

"And?" Dev prompted.

"Arrested," Lily said.

"Tried by court martial," Ruth said.

"And shot?" Crisp offered.

"Without hesitation," Ruth replied. "And there have been a few others as well."

"If you ask me," Lily said, "the newspapers have been rather full of them. I remember Emin Adnam, a man British intelligence caught just after Mother and I came over. He appears to have been working as a waiter, right inside Shepheard's. Turkish, of course. And then Berishav Kuzaim, a Bulgarian, showed up not long after his country entered the war. Seems to have been a bit of a lout and not very intelligent, that one. Tried to knife a British officer in an alley and got knocked down with a thick swagger stick for his efforts. The Red Caps found him carrying papers that completely gave him away. And then, there was Mattias Huber; he was Austrian, like the countess, but a man of small parts apparently, the smallest of the parts being his brains, or lack thereof. Signed on as a janitor and was caught rifling through the contents of the waste bins in one of the British staff offices."

"Which seems to show us one thing," Ruth continued. "While the countess appears to have been fairly intelligent and resourceful, the other three appear to have been dunderheads. And if that is the best that the Central Powers can throw at the Allies, the Allies seem to have the advantage."

"Which makes one wonder," Crisp said, sipping his brandy, "how our own people stack up beside the opposition."

"One can only hope for a better showing," Dev said. "How is it, exactly, that the two of you have followed this subject so closely?"

"We are confidants," Lily said brightly.

"And Lily, whether she will admit it or not, is attempting to write a thriller, about an unnamed British intelligence officer who is trying to catch a spy in Cairo," Ruth said. "So, when I find something in the newspapers that is pertinent, I telephone her at once, and when she finds something worthy of my notice, she does the same, although I am not attempting to write anything beyond grocery lists for my parents."

"What a very bright pair you are," Dev grinned.

"So perceptive, so astute, this boy of mine," Lily said, reaching over and squeezing Dev's hand.

Outside on the street near the hotel entrance, Dev and Crisp had planned to hire a carriage in order to take their ladies for a ride. But as they looked on from the terrace, two packs of well-oiled Australians leaped into the only two carriages waiting, tossed the drivers into the back seats, cracked the carriage whips into the air over the horses' heads, and took off side by side in a tear around the Ezbekiyya Gardens that forced taxis onto the curb to avoid them and sent pedestrians running.

"So much for a carriage ride in the moonlight," Crisp said, watching them go.

"And so much for the race," Dev said, as he and the others watched one of the carriages turn too tightly and roll over at the end of the street.

"Somewhere," Ruth said, registering mild distaste, "the ANZAC Command should erect a playground for them where they can roughhouse to their heart's content."

"I think," Dev said, "that roughhousing describes what they've been doing, in the desert. It isn't fair to the Egyptians to have to put up with that sort of behavior, and it doesn't do much for making lasting friends of them, but it is a sight better than having the Hun in control of the canal."

"You're right, I know," Ruth said, "but still …"

"You're right, the both of you," Crisp said. "I suppose we are left with no other choice but to chalk it up to the war."

"Which we all wish to end soon," Lily said.

Setting a meeting at Groppi's for the following morning and because the flats to which Ruth and Lily were returning stood in opposite directions, the couples took separate taxis to their destinations.

"Come up and have coffee," Lily said when the driver stopped in front of her parents' apartment block. "Mother and Dad will be in bed, but we won't bother them, and they will have no objection to your coming up."

"All right," Dev said, "and thank you."

In the flat, after Lily turned on the lights, she left Dev in the drawing room, went down the hall "to tidy herself," she said, and inform her parents that she was home, and returned moments later, looking bright and more refreshed than Dev had imagined that she would. And then, she walked straight over to where Dev had stood beside the mantel to examine some family photographs, threw her arms around his neck, and kissed him long and passionately, longer and more passionately than Dev had ever imagined possible.

"There," she said, "a little something to welcome you back to Cairo."

"Do I dare ask," Dev said, some of his breath taken away, "what brought that on?"

"All the better to show you what is waiting for you each time you tumble in here," Lily said, showing him a sly but inviting smile. "I find I rather like it, if you don't mind, so let's do it again, and then I shall make you the coffee I promised."

Dev didn't care if Lily never made coffee and knew that he would be content to go right on kissing her until the sun rose in the morning but didn't say so before he folded her into his arms a second time and left her nearly panting when they finally separated and went into the kitchen.

With the coffee made and set on the table, the two of them did not adjourn to the drawing room; instead, they took up seats on either side of the Winslows' breakfast table, picked up their mugs, and simply gazed at one another.

"I find that I'm rather in love with you," Lily said finally, "so it's time for some serious talk, Devlin Collins."

"Go right ahead," Dev said, "talk seriously."

"Is that all I'm going to get out of you?" Lily said, her eyes sparking fire, "after a declaration like the one I just made."

"No, it isn't," Dev said, just as forcefully, "but you started this, so let's hear what you have to say."

"All right," Lily said, not giving an inch, "I want to know something about your plans for the future, about what kind of life you intend to live."

"To see if it fits with your own?"

"Absolutely," Lily said. "I want to know if there's likely to be room in it for me."

"If there isn't," Dev said, "I will make room. And if the room I make at first isn't big enough to fit you, I will make it larger, much larger."

"And is that a proposal?" she said at once.

"If you think you can give me time to get around to it," Dev said. "I'll tell you, Lily, you are an uncommon girl, and I love you for it, but whether you think so or not, I already had a proposal in mind for Saturday night at Shepheard's and worried that you'd think I was rushing you by 12 times too much. What's made you want to move so fast?"

"Like I told you before you left the last time," Lily Winslow said, "I've loved you, Devlin Collins, since the first time I sat down across from you at El Baqara. My mother spotted it at once, and I think my father only guessed it later. Ruth, of course, knows everything. We have no secrets, she and I. And I intend to be right up front with anyone else who takes an interest. So, Dev, what are your plans? I want to share them."

Dev looked at Lily with a more serious expression on his face than he thought he had ever showed her before, reached across the table, and took her by the hand.

"My plan, Lily, is to try to stay alive," he said forthrightly. "And for the time being, that puts almost everything else on hold."

"Not for me," Lily said. "Not by a long shot, Dev. I know you're going to stay alive. I *know* it, Dev. And because I know it, I don't want to wait, and I am not one of those girls who is going to sit here with her hands pressed gently together over her breast wistfully pining for her distant flier who is wandering about somewhere in the vaporous ether. If you feel as strongly about things as I do, let's get married, if not tomorrow at least on your next leave."

The look on Lily's face showed Dev that she was entirely serious.

"What about your parents?" Dev asked. "I would imagine that they'll be sure to object."

"No, they won't," Lily said. "I've already discussed the matter with them. So they know that I intended to marry you the second you popped the question."

"My next leave?" Dev said. "Before a judge, a minister, whatever you like, the minute I get off the train? Will that be fast enough to suit you?"

"Not quite," she said, getting up, coming around the table, sitting in his lap, and kissing him again, "but I'll take what I can get. You've made me the happiest girl in the world."

"Then I've at least done one thing right," Dev laughed before he kissed her again.

The following night, while Ruth and Crisp went to a concert, Dev and Lily once more dined at the Intercontinental, on pheasant accompanied by a bottle of the establishment's bubbly. In the background, an Egyptian string quartet contended with Vivaldi's *Four Seasons*, but not, Dev thought, terribly successfully. The music, however, didn't matter. With Lily wearing a lavender frock that seemed to cling to her in all the right places, Dev found that she wholly absorbed his attention in a way that threatened to leave him breathless.

"To resume our conversation from last night," she said, suddenly shifting from whatever subject they'd been talking about, "where, do you imagine, we might settle once this thing ends and we go home, wherever that home is to be? Are we going back to Northern Ireland, or will we be returning to the States? I object to no choice that you are considering. It's just that a girl likes to know so that she can plan ahead."

"Mapping things out with a T-square and a pair of dividers are you?" Dev grinned.

"Now stop that," Lily said, reaching across the table and slapping his hand. "I want to have Madam Pico whip me up a winter coat and a frock or two before we go where we're going, and I would like to have a rough idea about the climate we might be moving into."

"I think I'm betting on the States," Dev said. "I have no doubts whatsoever that Britain and France are going to prevail in this thing, but once they come out of it, I believe that both countries will be in debt up to their ears, and that, to me, spells diminished opportunities. Your father has a much better understanding of the economic issues than I could ever hope to have, but I believe that he will tell you the same thing."

"He already has," Lily said. "He thinks that even if the United States enter the war, we will come out of this a world power with a decided economic advantage over everyone else. Germany will be broke and be years getting back on her feet, and in a manner

177

of speaking, both the U.K. and France will owe their souls to the Wall Street banks."

"Limited as my knowledge of such things may be," Dev said, "that's the conclusion I've reached. And there's something else to consider. Germany will wind up stripped of whatever empire she's tried to assemble, and the next question seems to be to ask how long Britain and France will be able to hold onto theirs? This thing with white Europeans fighting white Europeans will have shown colonial people that their overlords have feet of clay—something they may not have been aware of previously—and when they find that out, I suspect that places like India, Kenya, and the French possessions in Africa are going to begin pressing for independence with a desire to handle their own affairs. I don't know how long the dispossession will take, but I think it's coming, and when it comes, I think the U.S. will be picking up the pieces and enlarging its sphere of influence."

"It's clear to me," Lily said, "that you and my father are singing a similar tune, one far more harmonious than the attempt at Vivaldi behind us."

"Be kind," Dev prompted. "Every violinist is someone's son."

"I promise to mind my manners," Lily said. "So, my Love, where, in the States, do you intend to build my palace and set me up in the style to which you expect me to become accustomed?"

"I've had a letter from the Curtiss Aeroplane Company," Dev said. "For the moment, they are based in Hammondsport, New York, but the letter suggests that they are moving to Buffalo, where better transportation is available as well as better facilities and capital. The parent company is interested in hiring engineers, and someone—probably my father or Rutgers—gave them my name. The salary mentioned is good, and they say that they will be ready to hire me, if I'm interested, when the war ends, with a suitable time off during my return home."

Across the table where she sat, Lily's face shone.

"And you will never do military flying again?" she said.

"Not if I can help it," Dev said. "After my months at Kantara, I find that the urge has left me."

"This is the second time in 24 hours that you've made me the happiest girl in the world," Lily said. "But I want you to know, Devlin Collins, that if you elected to stay with the Royal Flying Corps that I would have followed you anywhere. I hope I know, Love, that a man's choice of occupation has to be his own; if it isn't or if he's forced into something that he doesn't want to do, he's bound to be miserable, and that makes for a very bad marriage. I shouldn't like that for us. Not at all."

"No," Dev said. "Well, on that point at least, you can rest easy. After you've lived with me for a while, I hope you won't want to revise your standards and send me off to prospect for gold so as to keep me away for months on end."

"You won't have time," Lily said, raising an eyebrow. "You'll be too busy diapering our children."

"Here now," Dev said. "None of that right off the bat. I'd like for us to have a few years to ourselves before we get going in that direction. And if it's all right with you, I'd like to be making enough money when we do consider it so that we don't have to raise them on smashed bananas and whatever we can scoop out of tin cans retrieved from the dust bins."

"Agreed," Lily said. "But bear in mind, ye who hath so little knowledge about women's bodies, that future mothers have to contend with the thing called the body clock—and it ticks. If it is kept waiting too long, unsatisfactory results might develop, and that we must not have."

"Two years?" Dev said. "Once we're home?"

"Done," Lily said.

When Dev and Crisp removed Lily's and Ruth's coats in front of the cloakroom at Shepheard's on Saturday night, they swiftly agreed that the unseen Madam Pico was a genius and that Lily and Ruth looked ravishing in the new gowns that the genius had fashioned for them. Lily, wearing something long in a pale and icy shade of light green, looked so stunning to Dev that she left him slack-jawed, and when Ruth stepped forward in a gown of pale lemon, two red tabs coming up the stairs missed their step entirely and stumbled, owing to the sudden excitement the girls had generated.

"Those two idiots rather look like they might enjoy tearing us limb from limb," Crisp laughed, whispering a response as he spoke to Dev.

"Yes," Dev said. "Best to let them eat their hearts out after making such obvious fools of themselves. What say we take these beauties of ours into dinner?"

Dinner at Shepheard's, always good but never quite on the level of the Ritz, more than satisfied them that night, particularly the soufflé, which Ruth and Lily thought a triumph.

"I would say," Lily observed, "that a new pastry chef has been hired. This is perfectly scrumptious."

"Rather a change from when we came with your parents, don't you think?" Ruth said. "The one we had that day could have passed for a soggy pudding."

"So true," Lily said.

"You've mastered the preparations for one of these?" Dev asked, speaking directly to Lily.

"You'll find, I think," Lily said smoothly, "that my forte is ice cream, taken at an ice cream parlor, with a dollop of chocolate."

"And you, Ruth, do you cook?" Crisp asked.

"Seldom," Ruth said. "But according to my mother, my coffee is acceptable."

"And what about potatoes?" Dev asked Lily. "Have you mastered boiling those yet?"

"Boiled potatoes?" Lily seemed to speculate. "What are they?"

"But you do know how to smash bananas?" Dev quickly asked.

"I believe I can manage it," Lily said.

"Let me put the poor creature out of his misery," Ruth laughed. "You may rest easy, Mr. Collins. Lily's pot roast is to die for, her potatoes are invariably done to a turn, and the bread she bakes and the cakes she makes are objects of glory. Lessons taken at her mother's knee, if you get my meaning."

"And you?" Crisp asked. "You've taken lessons at your mother's knee as well?"

"I can smash bananas," Ruth said. "My mother employed Mrs. Croft, a cook of renown."

"So wise," Crisp said. "Bottle of bubbly, anyone?"

Shepheard's dance that evening took place with the benefit of a good orchestra that did not play Vivaldi but did play an array of pleasing tunes that kept the four of them entertained until well past midnight. And then, as on the night before, each coupled boarded a separate taxi so as to deliver Lily and Ruth to their own flats.

"Thank you for a lovely evening," Lily said when the taxi stopped in front of her apartment block. "Won't you come up?"

"Your parents won't mind?" Dev asked.

"They're in Luxor, staying at the Sofitel Winter Palace Hotel for three nights," Lily said smoothly. "My father is there on business; my mother went along to keep him company."

"You aren't afraid that I might try to take advantage of you?" Dev laughed.

"If you do not try, and succeed, I'm afraid that I shall feel rather let down and despondent," Lily said, lifting her chin to give him a kiss before reaching for the door handle.

"I shall do my best not to disappoint you," Dev said.

The following morning, Dev returned to Shepheard's just in time to pack his grip, pay his bill, and join Crisp at the station. Lily and Ruth did not join them on the platform that morning.

"Sorry about last night," Crisp said.

"How so?" Dev asked.

"I expect you must have been wondering about me. Got back rather late, I'm afraid, and when I came in, I thought you might have already left to come here."

"I was never in," Dev said. "Lily and I are going to marry on my next leave. I shall need you as my best man if you can wrangle a day off."

"Funny," Crisp said, uttering a bit of a laugh. "Ruth asked me in for coffee, and when I got up there, I found that her parents had gone to Alexandria on consular business. I'm afraid I stayed the night."

"Cairo seems to have been good to us," Dev said, as their train slid into the station.

"Yes," Crisp said, as he reached for the handle to a compartment. "Who could ever have imagined it?"

10

Once they returned to Kantara, Dev and Crisp discovered that a change had taken place. St. Clair, promoted to Lieutenant Colonel, had moved from Ismailia to Cairo and been taken on to Murray's staff. Tuck, promoted to Major, had moved down to Ismailia and taken command of the squadron, and a new man—fresh from flying on the Western Front—Captain Broom, had taken over the Flight.

Broom, as Dev and Crisp found him, had a square jaw, steel gray eyes, a head of cropped dark hair, and the mien of a serious killer, a fact backed up by the revelation—something Wells picked up and conveyed to the rest of them—that the man had accounted for 11 Huns over the Somme and had announced that he expected to account for more in Sinai. Neither Dev nor Crisp found a single thing about their new commanding officer that they could have called warm or congenial. After meeting him the first time and finding themselves dressed down for being 10 minutes late back to station, the two of them came away from their interview with like minds.

"How we can be expected to hasten a train's return here is anyone's guess," Crisp said as the two of them walked to their tent and unpacked their grips.

"I don't think he quite understands what we're doing out here," Dev said. "Seems to think of himself as a hunter first and a recon and bombing pilot last. On the whole, I'm doubtful that's going to work out very well."

"Proof in the pudding, that sort of thing?" Crisp said.

"Or so I would imagine," Dev said. "The man's been flying scouts on the Western Front, so I'm wondering how he's going to find life when committed to flying the BE2c? Bit of a comedown, I think. With serious disappointment, I would imagine."

Captain Broom's tenure as the Flight's commander did not last long. In fact, it didn't last beyond that afternoon. When Broom led Symes, Wells, and Boy Stevens off on a mission to photograph Hun dispositions east of Bir El Mazar, he attempted to treat the BE2c that he was flying like the Sopwith Strutter that he'd flown over France, putting his plane into too steep a dive. One of its wings folded straight back, and he flew directly into the ground amid a battery of Archies, killing both himself and his observer in an instant.

Dev, Crisp, Boy Stevens, and Wells flew on the following morning, Tuck having sent up orders from Ismailia. With Crisp leading, and with a stop-off in Salmana to top off on fuel, they flew direct to Magdhaba and made four passes over the center and through the Archie fire, exposing every plate their observers could handle. On the way back, an Aviatik attempted to bounce them—something apparently flying out of El Arish or Rafa—but after a single pass, the Hun broke off the engagement, a clear indication that the Lewis guns of four observers, all of them firing together, constituted more of a threat that the Hun wished to contest.

"Looks to me," Dev said when they landed and as he and Crisp walked to the Flight's headquarters tent, "like the Huns are fortifying Magdhaba even more than before we left for Cairo. I count at least five redoubts being built, possibly six."

"Crouchback and I counted the same," Crisp said. "With, here and there, trenches in between."

"The question is, what's happening at El Arish?" Dev said. "I'd guess that Magdhaba's being fortified to protect El Arish's southern flank, because if Murray goes direct for El Arish, he'll have hell to pay on his own southern flank."

"From what I practiced as a ground officer before getting into the air," Crisp said, "I'd say that the battle for El Arish is probably going to turn into a battle for Magdhaba. Turn the position there, and the Turks at El Arish may have to withdraw all the way up to Rafa or Gaza."

"Concur, but the question is when?" Dev said.

"Well," Crisp said, "I think the Turks have withdrawn in large part from Bir El Mazar, although they've kept some Archies in the neighborhood, and from what Symes told me last night, the Light Horse and the Lowland Division are conducting both raids and reconnaissance missions east of the place. Meanwhile, other units are putting in fortifications along the rail line as it goes forward, so I'm guessing that either El Arish or Magdhaba may be on for sometime in November or December. You know Murray; he won't go until he feels he has overwhelming force, and that means he'll want both water and rail supply well up to within striking distance of El Arish."

In the Flight's headquarters tent, Boy Stevens, Wells, Dev, and Crisp came face to face with Captain Frome, just arrived from Port Said and just promoted from yet another assignment on the Western Front, his unpacked duffle and grip still resting on his cot.

Frome—young, younger than both Dev and Crisp—was a different man from Captain Broom. Pink-cheeked with a head of prematurely white hair, the man's eyes were deep set beneath bushy, equally white eyebrows. The man's ears stuck out, but the jovial expression on his face made his eyes sparkle above a row of exceedingly white teeth and the greeting of welcome that he extended.

"Good flight this morning?" he asked at once.

"Ripping, Sir," said Boy Stevens, not holding back.

"And satisfactory," Crisp said, showing more reserve. "Good weather for the observers, good exposure of plates, one Aviatik attempting an attack on the way back, but we scared him off, the four of us opening up on him together."

"I shouldn't wonder," Frome said. "Must have felt like he'd flown into a swarm of hornets. So, my lads, tell me, what's up in Magdhaba? I'm expecting a do there, sooner or later, because Tuck and the red tabs seem to be suggesting that we give it special attention."

"The Turks seem to be building redoubts," Dev said.

"My observer counted six of them," Wells said, "and he has good eyes."

"With trenches in between," Crisp added.

"Formidable position then?" Frome asked.

"It certainly has the makings," Crisp answered.

"Right then, we'll keep an eye on it," Frome said. "Now, what about the ships you're flying? Are they up to snuff for such a bevy of old machines?"

"Banes, his fitters, and his air mechs do a fair job of keeping them in the air for us," Dev said.

"And from what Banes tells me, you've helped him a time or two, if your name is Collins," Frome said.

"It is," Dev replied.

"Right," Frome said. "And Lieutenant Tiller, who has been a sort of materiel officer for the Flight, went off to Cairo almost as soon as you departed this morning. Permanent transfer to the sheds there—quick march for some reason that no one has bothered to explain. So, that leaves us an officer short. Mr. Collins, with your knowledge of engines—if I've heard Sergeant Banes right—you now have the collateral duty of looking after ours. That won't take you off flying, you can be sure, but it will give you something to occupy your mind during your idle hours."

186

"Thank you, Sir," Dev said, with good-humored sarcasm, Boy Stevens loosing a half-laugh even as Frome's eyes brightened with amusement.

"Yes," he said quickly, "no one is to be left out. Are you the one called 'Boy Stevens'?"

"Yes, Sir," said Boy, stifling his surprise.

"Right," said Frome. "From what I understand, and given the plate that was set before me at breakfast this morning, I'd say that the mess here is not up to par. Too much bully beef and that sort of thing. Too little care in the preparation. So, Mr. Stevens, in lieu of a qualified officer of supply, your collateral duty will confine your non-flying duties to an upgrade of our mess. I rather like to eat, and I'd rather like to eat something better. Catch my meaning, do you? Know how to use a hunting rifle?"

"Yes, Sir," Boy Stevens said.

"Right then," said Frome. "I will leave you to it and expect a possible gazelle or two along with game birds. And that brings me to Mr. Crisp and Mr. Wells. Mr. Crisp, I am today making you responsible for the Flight's Lewis guns, their upkeep and their ammunition. Mr. Wells, in the absence of an adjutant, you are to assist Mr. Symes and Mr. Bivin in the briefings they are to begin giving us on the contents of our various operations orders and the upkeep of our administrative papers. Understand how to write English, do you?"

"Hopefully," Wells replied.

"Well, then, you appear to be fully qualified," Frome said with no little amusement. "Leave schedule to remain as Major Tuck set it. No drastic changes otherwise in our operations. Good flying and a commitment to our missions remain standard procedure. There now, that's the drill, so off you go to write your reports on this morning's do, and I will look forward to reading them and forwarding them to Ismailia."

"Breath of fresh air, would you say?" Boy Stevens asked as the quartet left the tent and walked away.

"Vast improvement," Wells said. "Cold fish, Broom. No humor. Bad for morale. Sorry about his end. Nasty that."

"Yes," Dev said, "something to be anticipated and avoided."

"Always," said Crisp.

As October bled into the early days of November, Dev and Trent, flying beside Boy Stevens, Bivin, and Crisp over Magdhaba in order to re-mark the progress the Huns were making with their fortifications, caught a sudden jolt from an exploding Archie burst that nearly flipped the BE2c onto its side. Dev suddenly dropped nearly 1,000 feet in altitude before he managed to recover full control of the ship. As far as the engine was concerned, nothing seemed amiss, but nevertheless, Dev knew that he'd once more started to shake and felt something unusual about the plane's performance for which he couldn't account. And then, with Crisp and Biven rejoining him on one side and Boy Stevens on the other, he could see both the pilots and their observers stabbing the air with their arms and fingers, pointing toward his landing gear.

Extending himself out far over the side of the ship to the full length of his safety harness, Trent looked down and came up making hand signals to signify *kaput*. Dev knew, then, with a degree of certainty that the port wheel of his landing gear had been shot away by the Archie. The best he could hope for upon their return was that he would have enough fuel remaining to make Kantara without stopping at Salmana, because he would have no alternative other than to make a crash landing wherever he put down.

Boy Stevens and Bivin landed at Salmana, but Dev, with Crisp keeping him company, remained in the air, Crisp going along to offer escort and protection should he have to put down short of Kantara. In the event that he did so, Crouchback with his Lewis gun could try to keep any Berbers who might appear at bay and away from Dev and Trent.

Grateful for the protection, Dev was also relieved that he had enough fuel remaining with which to make Kantara. But as he approached the field, having wracked his brain to consider what he had to do to land safely and try to walk away from the crash, he nevertheless felt nearly every muscle in his body tighten and his heart begin to beat at twice its normal pace. He eased the throttle so as to slow the ship as much as he could without stalling her, and did his best to set her down on her rear skid before cutting his power and letting the forward section of the plane flop onto the runway. Then, very quickly, as the right wheel touched down, the empty axle on the port side of the plane dug into the earth, whirling the plane on a pivot while throwing Dev and Trent hard against the rims of their cockpits. The blow Dev received from the collision immediately and painfully cracked one or more of his ribs as the port wing folded up and the plane spun onto its side.

To Dev's relief, the petrol tank did not rupture and the fractured fuel line connecting the tank to the engine did not catch fire. But, in extreme pain from the rib or ribs that he had cracked, he was unable to do more than release his safety harness and use his feet to push himself out of the cockpit and onto the ground. Seconds later, the air mechs who had raced out with stretchers found both Dev and Trent, hoisted the both of them groaning onto the litters, and ran them to a Crossley tender that whisked them away for a bumpy and extremely painful ride to the infirmary.

"*Shit!*" Dev said, groaning with agony as he tried to apologize for the crash to the man beside him.

"Nay," Trent groaned back. "Ye got us down. We ain't dead. 'Tis all that matters."

"How bad you hurt?" Dev managed to ask between gritted teeth.

"Like as not, cracked rib," Trent groaned back. "Ye?"

189

"Same," Dev said.

At the infirmary, while Dev tried to lie perfectly still on the litter after demanding that Trent be treated first for his injuries, the doctor who finally came to look at him was the same who had treated him previously for the Mauser wound.

"A painkiller would be nice," Dev groaned, trying not to aggravate the needle-sharp rivets that seemed to be shooting through his side.

"Oh, for heaven's sake, I certainly hope not," the doctor said. "I seem to remember telling you that analgesics were saved for the seriously wounded. I could give you an aspirin, I suppose, but in your condition, I shouldn't like to upset your stomach. Try to be patient, lie still, and the pain will eventually subside. I'll just bind you up with a bit of a bandage in order to keep things in place, and then you're off to Ward B for rest and recuperation."

"Ward B is Nurse Cribbon's ward!" Dev protested.

"Well, of course it is," the doctor laughed. "Where else would we send an officer?"

When the orderlies finally wheeled Dev into Ward B and before she saw him heaved onto a bed, Nurse Cribbon studied his face. "I've seen you before, haven't I, for a bullet wound, for something legitimate," she said. "This rib business is nothing short of malingering, so you'd best mind your Ps and Qs, Mr. Smarty, because I intend to have you out of here quick march. The very idea that an able-bodied young man should take up a bed that might otherwise give comfort to the seriously wounded is something I will not tolerate."

Dev would have liked to have risen up from where the pains continued to shoot through him and strangled Nurse Cribbon with his bare hands. Instead, he merely closed his eyes, tried to ignore every word that came out of Nurse Cribbon's mouth, and thought of Lily. In the end, by lying perfectly still, that helped.

In the middle of the night, when Dev awoke and found that he needed a bed pan, Nurse Cribbon refused to give him one, demanding instead that he get out of bed, get onto his feet, and walk the length of the ward to the latrine. So painful was the maneuver that Dev thought he might pass out on the way back, the mere act of once more hoisting himself onto the bed he'd been assigned and lying back down bringing tears to his eyes.

As far as Dev could remember, he'd never met a woman who he thought actually hated men, but after two days of suffering Nurse Cribbon's ministrations, Dev knew that he wanted out of the hospital and back in his tent—dust, flies, and passing adders notwithstanding.

"Don't be ridiculous," the doctor laughed when Dev asked him if he could rise and depart. "You've got cracked ribs! You're here for a week at minimum, and possibly longer."

"That might make you a party to a homicide," Dev warned.

"If that implies a reference to the patient care that Nurse Cribbon has so graciously extended to you," the doctor said, "you may be thrilled to hear that she has been transferred to Cairo. Her brother appears to be a staff officer there, so she has been reassigned to the receiving hospital."

"Let the heavens be praised," Dev said.

"Funny you should say that," said the doctor. "Two of my patients farther down the ward said he same thing."

"Nurse Finnegan, when she arrived—with gentle hands, a pleasant smile, and a pleasing voice—spelled relief for everyone in the ward. Under her kind attentions, Dev made rapid progress, so much so that the doctor released him from the hospital at the beginning of the following week and sent him back to the airdrome to recover but with strict instructions not to fly again until he passed through a follow-up examination after yet another week of relative inaction.

Throughout the period that Dev had spent in hospital, he had continued to write to Lily, Crisp bringing him Lily's letters when they arrived, the two of them agreeing that neither Lily nor Ruth would be told of Dev's crash until Dev had fully recovered and discovered some way of breaking the news to Lily without needlessly upsetting her. Finally, once back on the airdrome and in his tent, Dev sat down and wrote her a letter explaining that he'd had *a little tussle* on landing one morning, *an equipment malfunction* causing the landing to be more *challenging* than usual, with the result that he would not be flying while the fitters saw to *minor* structural damage that had resulted in the event. Two days later, he received a letter back, part of it reading like a list: "How many bones did you break? Which bones are broken? How long will they require to heal? Will you have convalescent leave following? What is your temperature? What is your blood pressure reading?" and so on. To which Dev wrote back: "Two ribs slightly cracked and healing nicely. Temperature and blood pressure normal. Light duty for two weeks. No convalescent leave to be granted. Miss and love you, Dev."

"Now that you are back with us, footloose and fancy free," Frome said on Dev's second morning back, "I have a task for you which will come under the heading of 'light duty.'"

"Oh goody," Dev said flatly and without further comment.

"Yes," Frome said. "Well, with so much time on your hands, I thought I might set you to studying the Magdhaba problem. Hard to say when old woman Murray might want to make his move or the red tabs come up with a plan of their own, but best, I think, to steal a march on them if we can. Prepare a plan of our own. Something to do battle with in case the red tabs come up with some idiot undertaking of their own that's certain to get the lot of us killed. Something to negotiate with, if you see what I mean."

Dev saw and said so.

"Right, then," Frome continued. "We've got such a bevy of photographs that you can study the problem to your heart's content. And we've got the maps that HQ has developed to go with them. And just about now, the rail line and the pipeline are advancing into Bir El Mazar, which means that Murray will probably begin running up units of the Expeditionary Force and putting them into positions for whatever advance he's ultimately planning."

"Understood," Dev said.

"What's wanted, from our point of view, is an air plan. Whatever dispositions the red tabs make with the land forces have nothing to do with any attack we might make on Magdhaba in order to soften things up for them, so you need not consider or even inquire into what GHQ is planning. I merely want you to take a look at the photos and come up with a plan of attack from the air, the kind of thing that we might throw in either before our forces go forward or immediately upon their arrival in front of the enemy's gates."

"Something for El Arish as well?" Dev asked.

"Splendid idea," Frome said with a smile. "Keep the wicket covered, that. Goose in the bag, so to speak, should the red tabs try to drop a surprise on us. Maximum safety for the lads in whatever you plan, but maximum damage to result from whatever we do. You write the preliminary, and then, the two of us together will refine things and do the finals. Plans, that is. Up to the job, do you think?"

"Yes," Dev said.

For several nights in a row, while Crisp slept, Dev worked late under the glow of their hurricane lamp, studying the immense pile of recon photos that the Flight had taken and assembled—the same photos that he imagined the red tabs to be studying in Cairo. Then, in conjunction with the maps that GHQ had created from the photos, Dev went to work preparing a preliminary op-order for a possible operation.

What Dev's close study of the photos showed him was that the Turks were in the process of preparing a formidable position at Magdhaba—one that straddled Wadi El Arish, which ran north through the center of the village. On the west bank, Dev detected one small redoubt and three large ones stretching the length of the western approach. On the east bank, north of the settlement, Dev counted two very large and well-appointed redoubts, with a third, equally large redoubt located farther to the south almost directly east of the town. In the town itself, from what Dev could determine, the Turks had established a headquarters in a cluster of buildings that seemed to be set down directly in the center of the place. Rifle pits and trenches appeared to connect the redoubts, and both an artillery park and a supply dump seemed to be located directly behind the redoubts to the north.

In the beginning, Dev imagined an attack by the Flight's assembled formation, flying in from the north at 3,000 feet to drop Cooper bombs all over the settlement, but after considering the near impossibility of achieving any meaningful results from such a maneuver, he discarded the idea. For the purpose of self-defense, for the purpose of driving off and avoiding attack by any Huns that might descend on the Flight from El Arish or Rafa, Dev intensely disliked the idea of flying without observers whose Lewis guns would prove invaluable in such encounters. After studying the problem for hours, Dev came to the conclusion that the most effective attack the Flight could make would require dropping 100-pounders dead center on the redoubts with a follow-up that would plaster the positions with Cooper bombs. The weight of the payload would mean that the Flight's observers, for the good of the mission, would have to be left behind.

How, Dev next asked himself, might he minimize the dangers arising from that eventuality? After more thought and more turning ideas over in his mind, he combined two options into the plan that he thought most likely to catch the enemy by surprise. Rather than fly the mission from Kantara, the Flight would fly it from Salmana, all of the Flight leaving Kantara for Salmana on the day before the raid was called for and spending the night sleeping under the stars. With the railroad now in full and efficient operation, Dev foresaw no difficulty in having their bombs and necessary supplies of fuel shipped up to Salmana in advance of the operation. Their planes could then be bombed up and prepared the night before, in advance of an early morning takeoff—a takeoff that would require a flare path to be lit for them because Dev wanted the actual raid to go in at sunrise. But the thing that Dev most expected to contribute to the surprise that he hoped they would give the Turks would be their flight path. From the dispositions that the Turks had given, their redoubts and the artillery park they'd put in place, Dev reasoned that they expected attack from the direction of the railroad, from the northwest or north. Quite probably, whatever land forces Murray sent in might well take that approach, but that did not mean that 14 Squadron need take it, and Dev didn't plan for them to. Instead, leaving Salmana, he routed them south straight into the wastes of northern Sinai, straight down to the shifting dunes of Jebel Maghara. From there, where Turkish patrols seemed unlikely to spot them and alert Magdhaba, they would turn northeast and approach the Turkish positions from the southwest, coming up around the town to the south and making their initial bomb run from the east with the morning sun at their backs. And to give his fellows one more tiny edge, Dev planned for them to make most of the flight at 3,000 feet but descend to 200 feet at least 5 miles from Magdhara so as to make their attack at something approaching treetop level.

Frome, when Dev finally showed him the plan, read it, read it again, and declared it "more than satisfactory."

"Good job, Mr. Collins," Frome said with a smile. "Here and there, I want to make a refinement or two. I think eight Coopers per ship, rather than the six you have recommended, and an extra tin of petrol in the observer's seat to cover an emergency set down should the additional weight of the Cooper bombs make an increased demand on fuel consumption. And I have another idea or two which might help things along as well. I think I'll order our pilots carry very pistols on this one, to make up for the fact that we won't have observers with their Lewis guns along. The enemy don't like 'em, I'm told. Shoot off a flare in their direction, and they're apt to disengage. Fellow up at Port Said tried it once when a Rumpler got onto him. Exploded a flare in the Rumpler's direction, and the Hun turned tail. So, a flare gun and four rounds. Add it to the plan, and tell the clerk to get going on a typed copy so that I can fly down to Ismailia and show your handy work to Major Tuck."

Three days later, with his ribs mostly healed and with Trent reporting the same, the two men began flying once more, a photo recon mission heading the two of them, along with Crisp and Symes, all the way up to Wadi El Arish to photograph supposed gun emplacements west of El Arish proper. The trio were attacked there by an Eindecker and an Aviatik, the Eindecker sporting the Imperial cross on its wings, the Aviatik carrying the crescent moon of the Ottoman air services. The Eindecker—very good in a dive but not so efficient in a climb—made only one pass on the Flight before continuing straight down to the deck and escaping any further encounters, but that pass had been enough to wound Symes's observer and shoot his tailplane full of holes before Trent and Crouchback could, from the distance they were separated, throw out enough rounds to drive the Hun away. The Aviatik, foolishly circling while the Hun attacked—rather than joining him so as to come at the three from two directions—waited until the Eindecker had disappeared and then dove on them, catching the attentions of both Trent and Crouchback. The result was that he caught at least two tracers in his radiator and continued his dive streaming coolant in his wake. Neither Dev, Crisp, nor their two observers on the Lewis guns believed the Turk done for, but all four of them, after conferring following their return to base, considered the Aviatik put out of action. Symes, having a wounded observer and an uncertain tailplane, landed at Bir El Mazar rather than risk the long flight back to Kantara, and Frome had to send up a fitter and an air mech by train before Symes could get his ship back into the air and return to base.

Dev flew again the following day with Bivin, the two of them going out over the dunes of Jebel Magdhara to see if they could spot any Turkish patrols in the area. Twice they saw the fairly well secluded tents of isolated groups of Berbers, one or two of whom took pot shots at them as they flew low over their encampments, but of Turks they saw none and returned early after what Dev considered a routine flight.

Dev did not fly the following day. Instead, working alongside Frome, he made some additions to his plan for Magdhaba—additions that Tuck had suggested when Frome took the plan down to Ismailia for his inspection.

"The major intends to forward this to Cairo," Frome said when they finished their work. "The objective seems to be to get the door open before the red tabs reach it, steal their thunder, and fight it out with them on operational considerations. The major told me that the chief planner for air is an artillery colonel who has never so much as sat in a plane, much less in a BE2c and doesn't know the first thing about the trials and tribulations that we face. Seems to think we're flying pursuit ships, like the ones he's read about on the Western Front, all of them 40 miles per hour faster than what our boats can do, all of them armed with forward-firing machine guns. To make matters worse, his adjutant is cavalry, and the three or four dogsbodies assisting over there are infantry types. Not a flier among them, so you see what we're up against. Regular staff wallahs, the lot of them. Good for holding up the bar at Shepheard's and not much else in my opinion."

"Suspicions confirmed," Dev said.

"Unfortunately," Frome said. "I'd assumed that when Lieutenant Colonel St. Clair joined Murray's staff, he would be able to make a considerable difference over there, but Tuck tells me that he didn't last two weeks before he was promoted again, to full colonel, and shipped off to France to command a wing, or an air group, or whatever they're calling it. Several squadrons, that sort of thing."

"Good for St. Clair," Dev said, "but unlucky for us."

"Yes," Frome said. "Well, that's it for this morning. Let's adjourn for lunch. Boy Stevens, or so I'm told, went out with the bird nets and caught us some doves. Ought to make a very nice break from the bully beef, what?"

"Any break from bully beef is a day to be welcomed," Dev said. "I shouldn't like to exaggerate, but I'm not even sure that one of those Egyptian red foxes—well roasted and done up with a bit of chopped garlic and, perhaps, a hint of basil—might not be a tempting substitute."

"It is clear to me," Frome laughed, "that you have been out here too long."

"That is fairly clear to me as well," Dev said.

The late afternoon patrol that Dev and Crisp flew that day, Wells tagging along with a third camera, took the three of them south of Bir El Mazar to do another reconnaissance over the dunes. Almost without knowing it, October had given way to November, and while no one could ever accuse Sinai of being chilly while the sun was still above the horizon, Dev did detect a change in the temperatures, the air stilling and becoming more temperate as the evening approached. After sundown, as he well knew from flying during the previous winter, things could turn chilly and then downright cold in a hurry. So, at Kantara the sleeping bags had already been restored to the pilots' tents and had come in useful, particularly in the early mornings.

As on the preceding Flight, none of the fliers or their observers saw anything of note. Turkish patrols did not seem to be in the region, Hun scout cars had not been spotted, and the only evidence of human life anywhere turned out to be three camels and three Bedouin observed riding between dunes as the Flight turned and flew back toward Kantara.

But then, 15 minutes later, it became apparent that Wells's engine had started to falter, and three minutes after that, without warning, Wells signaled that the engine had packed up and that he was going down. Dev and Crisp stuck with him all the way down and saw him land on a pan of desert that seemed packed hard. Very quickly, Dev circled the position where Wells's kite had come to a stop, judged the condition of the pan for himself, and brought his own ship in to land alongside Wells. Then, he leapt out and ran at once to see if he could lend assistance.

"Coughed twice. Quit. No idea why," Wells said, fuming, to Dev who had raced to the plane and climbed onto the wing where he could speak to Wells and his observer. The observer, Dev noticed—a corporal whom he'd never met and did not know—looked as nervous as a cat with a pit bull chewing on its tail, and the reason quickly became apparent. Glancing to the south, he had failed to notice dust in the air and not far distant; that is when Dev knew that the dust he was seeing was being raised by horses rather than slower-moving camels.

Moments later, above them, Crouchback's Lewis gun began to bark. Dev knew then that the dust cloud he had seen was a clear indication that a Turkish patrol was approaching or that yet another group of Berbers were likely to try to attack and capture them.

Minutes passed as Dev crawled out onto the cowling to examine the engine. From what Wells had been able to tell him, Dev did not believe that the fuel line was clogged. He did wonder about one of the air filters and so called for a spanner, removed the housing, and found the particular filter that he was looking at to be thoroughly clogged with a residue of grease and sand. He immediately removed it, beat it against the cowling to dislodge as much of the corruption from it as he could, and slammed it back into positions just as the first rifle rounds from a dozen or more Berbers began to pass overhead.

From not high above, Crisp and Crouchback were doing what they could to hold the Berbers off. This time, rather than the handful that Dev had dealt with before, he saw that they were facing something close to the strength of a small clan—all of them spaced well out from each other so as to thwart Crouchback, who had no way of covering all of them at once.

"For Christ's sake!" Dev shouted at Wells's observer. "Open fire on them! Trent's on the wrong side; he can't shoot without hitting us, so quit sitting on your ass!"

The corporal, a man who appeared to be clearly shaken by the threat, froze.

"*Start shooting!*" Wells screamed over his shoulder. "Or I'll have you up on charges quick march!"

It was the longest sentence that Dev thought he had ever heard Wells deliver, but it had the desired effect. The corporal, snapped out of his trance, began to squeeze the trigger of his Lewis gun, and once started, he quickly discarded his reticence, took down two of the riders on the flank of the charge, a quick glance showing Dev that Crouchback, from the air, had accounted for at least one other more toward the center of the Berber line.

Working as quickly as he could, Dev did not take the time to wrench down the bolts on the air filter's housing as tightly as he could. He didn't care, because he expected that by not tightening the housing to its limit, the gasket that held it in place might let in more air and that the air mechs could replace the filter and finish the job later.

And then, in a flash, he was off the cowling, dropping straight to the ground and giving Wells's prop a twirl, the engine coughing, spluttering, and springing to life as Dev raced for his cockpit and took to the air not 40 yards behind Wells as Wells once more lifted off. All the while, Trent, with his Lewis gun unmasked at last, unloaded an entire pan of hornets among the oncoming Berbers.

Twice, between the point where Dev had made his hasty repair to Wells's engine and Kantara, the engine coughed, spluttered, and threatened to quit again. But in each case, after Wells lost altitude, the engine caught again, with the result that the three of them completed their return and landed safely, before the big machine packed up not 200 yards from the hangars.

"Many thanks," Wells said, as he came walking toward Dev and Crisp while his observer headed for the armory and the fitters went out to fetch his plane. "Near thing, that. Couldn't have done it. Wouldn't have known how. Owe you."

"What's owed," Dev said, "is a sharp bite on the ass of the air mech who tends your ship. That filter should have been changed before you went up. Not your fault, that. I'll put a flea in Banes's ear, and he can keel-haul the slacker and threaten a charge if it ever happens again."

"I suspect you nearly threatened a charge of your own on your observer," Crisp said, speaking to Wells. "Seemed to take him forever to get into action."

"Gorbals," Wells said. "Glasgow. Thick head. Slow wit. Nearly useless."

"But a fair shot, once he turns loose," Dev said.

"Swift kicks do wonders," Wells said.

And additional wonders were in store for them that night when they'd doffed their flying togs, had a wash up, and filtered into the mess tent. After a whiskey to wet their whistles, Boy Stevens stepped forward to announce that, rather than the curried bully beef they'd all been expecting, they would dine that night on a joint of gazelle, lately shot and fresh. Following the announcement, the mess erupted in a sudden and unrestrained cheer.

"You had a good day, then?" Crisp said to Boy Stevens as they sat down to dinner.

"I'll say," Boy Stevens bubbled. "Clean shot, 200 yards, not 10 miles south of here. And that's not all. That lad Grimsdale—the one who mans the counter in supply—he was driving and admitted on the way back that he has experience with pub cooking, in Sussex. Dragooned him at once. Things looking up, what?"

"Frome will be tickled pink," Dev said.

"Yes," Crisp said, "it looks like a new day has dawned."

11

Four days after Dev saved Wells, his observer, himself, and Trent from capture by the Berbers, Frome woke him at 0400 and told him to pack his grip.

"What's on?" Dev wanted to know, sitting bolt upright on his cot.

"We're going to Cairo," Frome said quickly. "The three of us—you, me, and the plan. Train departs at 0545, so look sharp. We present to the red tabs tomorrow, but we're going down today because I mean to take a day off after the last month, and you can do whatever you like until the two of us are to present ourselves and explain our plan tomorrow morning."

"Let me suggest that four of us go," Dev quickly said. "You, me, Crisp, and the plan. The red tabs will try to bully two of us. They will have seconds thoughts if opposed by three."

Frome gave the matter half a second's thought and then said, "Right. Get him up. Your responsibility to get the both of you ready and be at the station on time. I'll meet you there."

Awakened from a dead sleep, the news that he could expect to see Ruth waiting for him in Cairo brought Crisp instantly onto his feet and stimulated a flurry of hasty packing.

Disregarding the standing orders that governed the use of the base telephone, Dev put through an early morning call to Cairo, forced Lily out of bed, and delivered three words that he hoped, in the event that official ears were listening, would sound like the substitute for a telegram.

"Arriving Cairo 0900."

"Understood," came the reply in kind.

So, when Dev, Crisp, and Frome debarked from their train compartment in Cairo at 0900 that morning, they found Lily, Ruth, Mortimer, and Mrs. Winslow waiting for them on the platform.

"I'm about to be married," Dev said swiftly to Frome, "and you are most welcome to join our party if you wish to attend."

Registering no small surprise but offering hearty congratulations, Frome demurred. "Two's company, three's a crowd," he said. "This looks private, so I think I'll duck out. You just be sure that you and your best man are at GHQ in the morning, 0900 sharp."

"Done," Dev said.

And with that, Frome was away, his briefcase and their plan going with him.

One hour later that morning, without fru fru or music, in a bare office at the American consulate and with the consular chaplain reading the service, Lily and Dev exchanged their vows. Crisp stood beside Dev as best man, Ruth acted as maid of honor, the Winslows and the Steels were present as witnesses, and thereafter, the entire party adjourned to the Savoy for what Mrs. Winslow called the "wedding luncheon" that she had arranged. Conversation among the party bordered on the euphoric without ever stepping beyond bounds, and the lunch—a meal that combined cold pheasant with a cherry and whipped cream confection to conclude—seemed to satisfy everyone. The Steels seemed genuinely pleased to meet Crisp and dragooned him into accompanying Ruth to a supper at the Turf Club with them for later that evening. As the party rose to depart, Mortimer Winslow drew Dev aside and said, sotto voce, "It isn't much of a wedding present, I'm afraid, but I've arranged for you and Lily to have a room here at the Savoy until your leave concludes."

Dev, who had not had time to give the subject a moment's previous thought, felt genuinely grateful and said so.

And then, Crisp, Ruth, the Winslows, and the Steels, amid a plethora of good wishes and congratulations, said their goodbyes and departed, leaving Dev and Lily standing in the lobby of the Savoy with a multitude of hotel guests passing back and forth to either side.

"Well, Mrs. Collins," Dev said with a smile, "what would you like to do with the rest of our afternoon?"

"Well, Mr. Collins," Lily said without hesitation, "I rather thought we might like to go up to our room and do what we spent the night doing before you went back to Kantara after your last leave. I shouldn't like to rush you into anything, of course, but I hope what I have in mind won't disappoint you."

"Let's make haste for the stairs," Dev said quickly.

"Yes, let's," said Lily.

At 0900 the following morning, Dev and Crisp met Frome on the steps of GHQ, passed through the doors, and immediately found that they had to deal with an officious staff captain overseeing the front desk who made the mistake of trying to dress them down for wearing their flight uniforms.

"Maternity tunics are *never* worn at headquarters," the man said disdainfully as he looked Frome up and down. "I'm afraid that you will have to go dress in proper uniforms before I can admit you."

"I suppose," Frome said, answering in kind, "that you would like us to come back naked, for whether you like it or not or have sense enough to know anything about the Royal Flying Corps, these are the only uniforms we've ever been issued. Now, my good man, let us be about our business. So, if you will point us toward the office of Lieutenant Colonel Prince, we will leave you to sip tea or hold up the Long Bar at Shepheard's, whichever you prefer."

To Dev and Crisp's amusement, the staff captain turned red in the face and looked for a moment like he might have a stroke, but without saying a word, he threw up a stiff arm and pointed immediately down the corridor to their right. With Frome in the lead, head held high, the three of them turned their backs on the man and left him fuming.

Within moments, stopping in front of a door carrying a label that read "Air Staff," Frome knocked once, opened the door, and led the three of them inside. A sergeant sitting at a desk rose, looked them up and down, and said to Frome in respectful tones, "Sir, Colonel Prince won't like it. Service dress is required of all officers at headquarters."

"So we've heard," Frome said, "and it doesn't matter. Lead the way, Sergeant."

"Right, Sir," the man said, stepping quickly to an interior door, knocking once, and opening it for the trio.

Immediately, Frome, Dev, and Crisp walked inside to find Lieutenant Colonel Prince—an officer who looked to be in his late forties or early fifties—standing beside his adjutant, a man later identified as a Major Flemming, a 30-something individual with a pencil-thin mustache and slicked back hair, and a captain who appeared to be named Ballard as well as a lieutenant who eventually identified himself as Foy.

"Sir," Frome said, as Frome, Dev, and Crisp snapped to attention and saluted. "Captain Frome and Lieutenants Collins and Crisp reporting with plans for a raid on Magdhaba."

"Return to your hotel at once and change into proper dress," the major snapped. "Service Dress only at GHQ. General Murray's orders."

"Alas, Sir," Frome said diplomatically, "General Murray does not seem to be aware that the only uniforms the Royal Flying Corps has ever issued to the pilots of 14 Squadron are the ones we're wearing, and in lieu of appearing before you naked, I thought we had better continue to wear them."

Flemming looked like he might be on the verge of swallowing a frog. Ballard and Foy gasped to the point of sucking air. Lieutenant Colonel Prince broke into mild laughter.

"Point taken," Prince grinned. "Stand your ground, Captain, and let me make the introductions."

As the introductions were made, Dev couldn't help wondering if Flemming, red faced and fuming, might not be on the verge of a tiny stroke of his own. Ballard and Foy looked less red than bloodless, the apparent result of never before having heard Flemming answered in the way that Frome had spoken to him.

With the introductions completed, Flemming offering each of them only the most restrained of handshakes, Lieutenant Colonel Prince opened the conference by spreading out his own detailed map of the Expeditionary Force's operating areas and pinned it to the table.

"Now," he said, "we have read and studied your plan of attack for Magdhaba, and we have several reservations. Major Flemming will explain."

What Flemming explained instantly trashed everything that Frome and Dev had spent weeks working out.

"Air cavalry," Flemming said with authority, "is merely employed to do reconnaissance and support operations on the ground. What's wanted is a tight formation going in over Magdhaba at 200 feet, 100 yards in advance of the Light Horse when they charge. In that way, you will disrupt the Hun's trenches, destroy their wire, and open the door to the Allied advance on a broad front. As a result, the plan you have submitted is unsatisfactory and will have to be changed to conform to the needs of the engagement."

"Unless I miss my guess," Frome said with restraint, "you have never flown before, Major. Would I be correct in that assumption?"

"Yes," Flemming said with a sneer, "but the principles of attack are not altered by that eventuality, so the purpose of the action remains unchanged."

"We will be attacking with a total of seven ships," Frome began. "With a tight formation, that will give us a spread of approximately 200 yards for the bomb pattern that we are able to deliver. I hardly think that you expect to push an entire regiment through a 200-yard gap. Next, if we drop 100-pounders at 200 feet, we risk being blown out of the air by the concussion of our own bombs should we remain in a tight formation. But with that thrown aside, we will never have to face that eventuality because the Archies will blow us out of the air before we ever make our bombing approach. We are not, I submit, air cavalry, Sir. We can drop messages to the ground about what we see there, but we have no means at this time of receiving messages back, so your assumption that we can somehow coordinate our flying so as to go in over the Turkish positions 100 yards in advance of the Light Horse would strike any flier that I know as preposterous. We are as likely to bomb the Light Horse by trying that as the Turks, and as far as disrupting the enemy's wire, results show that our Cooper bombs are relatively ineffective in doing that, and it would be pointless to waste seven 100-pounders on the obstacles. The redoubts are the strongpoints at Magdhaba; 100-pounders dropped on those offer the possibility of doing them serious disruption, but surprise is called for if we are not to be shot straight out of the sky."

"The redoubts you may strafe with your forward-firing machine guns," Flemming instantly protested, "and at 140 miles per hour that should give you a decided advantage!"

Unable to stop themselves, Dev and Crisp broke into unrestrained laughter that stopped just short of being contemptuous.

"Begging your pardon, Sir," Dev said, "but none of us has ever seen a forward-firing machine gun on our ships, and if we are able to get them up to flying as much as 70 miles per hour, we almost have to shove our throttles through their stops. If you don't mind me saying so, Sir, you're thinking about the aircraft used on the Western Front. Our kites were obsolete two years ago and growing older as we speak."

"Do you not engage in air combat with the Hun?" Colonel Prince asked at once, his attention suddenly riveted to what Dev had said.

"When we can't avoid it," Dev said, "when we're attacked, and then we have to depend on our observers and their Lewis guns which are undependable. I've been out here for nearly a year now, and the only Hun I've engaged directly was one which flew into a flare that I fired in his direction with a very pistol. He caught fire and went down."

"I say," Flemming protested hotly, "rather unsporting, *that*, don't you think?"

"Oh, for Christ's sake, Major!" Frome snapped. "I'm sorry, Colonel, but your adjutant knows so little about the subject that he is supposed to have mastered that I'm not sure where any of this is getting us. Would you like for Collins to have been killed, Major, because the Huns, so much better equipped than we are, do have forward-firing machine guns, and they're deadly. We're relegated to doing what we can with what we have, and it's damn little in my estimation."

"All right," Colonel Prince said firmly. "That's enough, Captain Frome. You've made your point. Now, suppose you take out your plan for an attack on Maghdaba and go over it with us, because I'm sure that with an application of reason, we can work out something that will benefit the cause and be acceptable to all of us."

Across the two hours that followed, with tempers cooled, Frome, Dev, and Crisp outlined the plan Dev and Frome had designed, patiently explained what the BE2cs were capable of doing, what they were not capable of doing, and the probable successes in the attack that Frome and Dev believed that their Flight could bring off.

At one point in the discussion, Prince drew Dev aside.

"You seem to know a trifle more about the engines in your machines than the normal pilot might be expected to acknowledge," Prince said. "Where did you acquire your knowledge?"

"In my father's automobile business," Dev said, "and at Rutgers where I studied mechanical engineering."

"That would be in the States? The place once called Queen's College?"

"Yes, Sir," Dev said.

"So how did you find your way into the Royal Flying Corps?" Prince asked.

"I was born in Derry, Sir," Dev said. "I have family there who own a factory, and I was there helping to install new equipment when the war began. Product of two homes, two countries, if you see what I mean, and I joined up to help defend the first."

"Ah," said the colonel. "Glad to have you, of course. Stout fellow. Nothing's certain, of course, but I think the States may come in following the election over there. We hear rumblings, if you take my meaning."

"Yes, Sir," Dev said. "My father's letters have mentioned the same thing."

"And this plan, the one we're considering, is your own?"

Dev felt slightly taken back by the question. "Well, I think I'd have to say that it's *ours*, Sir," he said quickly. "I was down on light duty with some cracked ribs from a crash that I couldn't avoid, so Captain Frome put me to work with the photos and the maps, and I drafted a few ideas and then we worked with Major Tuck to refine things, so it's a joint plan as it stands."

"And not a bad one," the colonel said.

In the end, although Flemming fumed about one or two points, the plan was accepted, with only the start date left in the air pending decisions that still had to be made higher up about whether or not Murray would throw in an attack on Magdhaba, and when.

"If you don't mind me saying so," Crisp said as the three of them closed the door marked "Air Staff" behind them and started down the hall, "the Cavalry Major seemed a perfect horse's ass."

"But one who must have stellar connections and must have cut quite a figure on one of the hunt meets," Frome laughed, "or he would never have been allowed through the door by Murray's people. I'm afraid you lads missed the look on Prince's face when he made that 'sporting' remark to Dev, but it occurred to me that the good colonel might have liked to have given the major a very swift kick from behind and sent him sprawling onto his face. The two dogsbodies were speechless, which means that Prince is pretty much on his own in there and with absolutely no technical support to keep him informed."

"I'm guessing those three will make a real trio at the Long Bar," Dev laughed. "But no matter; looks to me like the plan's approved, and now, all we have to do is try to survive it when we put it into motion. So, when do we have to go back?"

"I was wondering when you might ask that," Frome said, "newlywed and all. Crisp and I are catching the train tomorrow tonight. Your leave is extended for three more days, and then, on Sunday afternoon, I will expect you to be suited up and ready to fly. Agreed?"

"The Saints and Mrs. Collins will praise you," Dev said.

"Oh, good fellow," Crisp said. "Miss Steel is bound to be euphoric when she hears the news."

"Never say that I don't have your welfare in mind," Frome said, "the both of you. But do keep out of the way of the Australians because they are liable to try to snatch those two lovelies right away from you."

At one o'clock that afternoon, Dev and Crisp joined Lily and Ruth at Alqamar, a unique restaurant running the length of a long city block but sandwiched down an alley between two buildings, so that the interior was long, dark—with only skylights to offer muted illumination—and only single tables spaced down one side of the long aisle. Where the kitchens might have been located, Dev never knew, but the food—lamb, saffron rice, and chickpeas—seemed particularly delicious.

"Your meeting went well?" Lily asked, as the four of them finished their meal and waited for their coffee, Turkish rather than the grayish tea that constituted the Arab variation. "The staff officers you met came up to the mark?"

Dev and Crisp both laughed.

"The colonel seemed a man of moderate intelligence and willing to listen to reason," Dev said. "I found that I rather liked him, but I don't think he knew much about flying."

"His adjutant spoke like a perfect idiot," Crisp said. "Time server, if you ask me, and the two buffoons in attendance, a captain and a lieutenant, didn't look like they had been to Eton. I rather think that someone snaked them in off the street and dressed them up to look like soldiers as one of those practical jokes that some people are supposed to enjoy."

"You three, of course, presented yourselves like recipients of the Military Cross, no doubt?" Ruth laughed.

"Oh, I say, this girl is spot on, isn't she?" Crisp said. "How perceptive of you to know that we came away covered with glory."

"Covered with glory?" Lily said. "Do tell."

"My friend and accomplice," Dev said, "sometimes dabbles in hyperbole. Let me merely say that we met, we spoke, and we came away without having been wholly shot down."

"Cheerful countenance then?" Lily prompted.

"Moderately so," Dev said. "But enough of the shop talk. Hush, hush, and all that. What, instead, have you beauties been up to this morning?"

"We've been browsing the bookstores," Ruth said at once, "searching for a copy of *Greenmantle*."

"*Greenmantle?*" Crisp said.

"The new thriller by John Buchan—John Buchan of *The Thirty-Nine Steps*," Lily said. "Ruth saw a review that gave the book high marks. Richard Hannay—the same Richard Hannay from *The Thirty-Nine Steps*—appears to play a major role, and from all accounts, he appears to be chasing the same Huns and Turks that you bright boys are attempting to turn back."

"I read *The Thirty-Nine Steps*," Crisp said. "Bit of the *Boy's Own* about the style, I'd say. Manly attitudes, manly adventure, that sort of thing. Almost reminded me of Alan Quartermain in a way. Cliff-hanger reading all the way through but compelling."

"Now you have it," Ruth said. "Sophisticated ladies, far from the paths of adventure, ladies like the two of us, need a bit of a thrill from time to time, particularly when their young men are absent for such extended periods."

"If adventure is what you seek," Crisp said instantly, "I believe that I can …"

"*Now, now,*" Ruth said, tapping her fingers on the table, "let's not get wholly ahead of ourselves. Over confidence can only lead to disappointment."

"I shouldn't like to seem suggestive," Lily said, "but in my experience, I find that marriage leads to endless adventure."

Suddenly, Dev felt like his ears had started to burn.

"Modesty," he said quickly, "will get you everywhere."

"Now stop," Lily said adroitly, "I fear you trifle with me, Sir"—a comment that left the four of them laughing as Dev and Crisp picked up their checks and walked their ladies onto the street.

In the late afternoon, invited by Ruth's father, the four changed and attended a consular soirée. After ten minutes' polite conversation with a Swiss diplomat and his wife about the lamentable facts that a hospital ship, the HMHS *Britannic*, had recently been sunk in the Aegean with the loss of 30 lives and that London had recently been bombed by the Huns—a total of six bombs falling near Victoria Station—the Swiss couple moved on. Left on their own, Dev, Lily, Crisp, and Ruth were surprised when they saw Sir Archibald Murray and a small entourage of staff officers enter the room.

"Good God!" Crisp said. "This certainly doesn't bode well for us."

"Not in the rigs we're wearing," Dev said. "Reckon we ought to make ourselves scarce?"

"Discretion is the better part of valor," Crisp said.

The expression on General Murray's face when he came in did not leave Dev with the impression that the man was a tower of strength. What Dev saw, something he kept to himself, were thinly pinched lips and eyes that tended to dart in several directions at once, indicating a mildly neurotic personality coupled with enough vanity to hide what the man might be thinking. And then, to Dev's intense displeasure, those darting eyes glanced in his and Crisp's direction, fixed on them, and showed Dev Murray's instant and intense dislike for what he saw. In the next second, Dev saw Murray turn to one of his staff officers, speak a word, saw the staff officer, a colonel, snap upright, look in their direction, nod his head slightly, and come walking straight toward them.

"Nothing for it," Dev said, "but to stand our ground, because we are in for it."

"You lot," the colonel said, sounding a sharp and official tone when he stopped in front of them, both Dev and Crisp coming to attention before their superior. "I regret to tell you that you are improperly dressed for an appearance in Cairo. The general has taken note, and if I were you, I would leave at once and get into the proper uniform."

Before either Dev or Crisp could make reply, and much to their shock, Ruth took a step forward and responded instantly.

"Colonel," Ruth said, showing no hesitation, "since you have chosen to include all four of us in your communication from General Murray, a social faux pas of the first order, I think it only fair that I should have a word. When you return to the general, you might inform him that he is a *guest* in the *American* consulate this evening, and the American consulate does not lay down rules to gratify his little peccadillos."

"You might also add," Lily said swiftly, sharply, and with murder in her eyes, "that service dress never made a flier one whit more of a marksman or one whit more courageous in the air. I should think, Sir, that the general should be more concerned about marshaling fighters than commanding dandified pansies."

Stunned to silence and with his mouth slightly open in shock, the colonel turned on his heel.

"Well," Crisp said with an attempt at a very restrained laugh as the colonel retreated, "I guess that's done it. My, my, but you girls are full of spirit."

"You realize, of course," Dev said, "that the colonel is never going to relay a single word of what you've said to the general."

"Of course we do," Ruth said, her face breaking into a satisfied grin.

"But it will be comeuppance enough for that colonel and his own effrontery," Lily said. "Ruth and I may not be in the service ourselves, but even we know that he should never have shown the bad manners to have delivered that demand in front of us."

"Nevertheless," Dev said, "I believe we would be wise to duck out."

"Agreed," said the other three in unison.

Helping the girls into a carriage on the street outside the consulate, Dev gave the driver orders to set a leisurely pace for the Berkshire Hotel, with the result that the four together finally enjoyed the carriage ride that the Australians' attempt at a chariot race had deprived them of during their previous leave.

At the Berkshire, seated amid potted palms beneath a sky-light through which the stars shone brightly, the service was almost—almost—so continual that it threatened to become oppressive. But the food mitigated the attention, and seeing that their glasses remained filled while the four of them feasted on a joint of splendidly cooked beef, Dev and Crisp were disinclined to complain.

"What is it, do you suppose," Dev said, "that makes Murray such a fastidious twit about such things as uniforms?"

"You mean, aside from any possible ramifications of his supposed breakdown? Crisp asked.

"Yes," Dev said.

"Time," Crisp said.

"Go on," Dev said. "Explain."

"You were probably too young to have picked up on this in Derry before you departed for the States," Crisp said, "but prior to 1871 when the requirement was dropped, officers in the Army had to buy their commissions. That meant, of course, that they had to be fairly wealthy, because each rank's commission sold for a higher price. It didn't take much account of ability, you understand, but it seemed to be a practice left over from the middle ages and connected to ownership of the land—which is where, until industry got going, we derived most of our wealth. Regarding Murray, given what little I know, I think he came into the Army as early as 1879, and most officers during that period still came from the landed class and still had money. They weren't issued uniforms like we were; they went to their tailors and came away with kits that would have required steamer trunks to carry, and not a few of them. I've seen photos of an officer's mess having lunch on the march in India. Train stopped on an embanked track in the middle of the desert—40 yards of table laid out, white tablecloths, silver, glassware, the entire cricket patch. No eating from mess tins for those men. They lived in a style that you and I can't even contemplate. But Murray, unless I miss my bet, still can, still remembers it, and still thinks war should be conducted in the same way."

"Rather a pain in the backside, isn't it?" Dev said.

"Murray calls it discipline," Crisp said.

"I call it looking forward to the past," Ruth said.

"Won't he be in for a surprise if we Americans get into it?" Lily said. "The boys commanding some of our National Guard units will be coming straight off the farm and straight from behind the plow. No grand estates to produce officers in Nebraska or Ohio. Only corn rows and store counters."

"But about that," Dev said, "we'll have to wait and see."

Following their meal and an after-dinner drink taken in the lounge, Crisp and Ruth went off in a taxi while Dev and Lily returned to the Savoy and went up to their room.

"Ruth and Crisp must envy us," Dev said, as Lily, clad in something silk and sleek, crawled into bed and snuggled down beside him.

"Oh, I don't think you have to worry on their account," Lily said blithely. "Ruth is spending the night with our friend Portia—Portia Parker, who you have not met."

"Oh," Dev said.

"Yes," Lily said. "Portia, as I discovered, happens to have been called away and is out of town in Alexandria for the evening.

"*Ah*," Dev said.

"Yes," said Lily.

Frome and Crisp returned to Kantara the following morning, but Dev was not at the station to see them off. In fact, Dev and Lily did not rise from bed until shortly after lunch, by which time both agreed that they needed to rise, take a late meal, and go for a restorative stroll before they returned to what they had taken to calling their "discussions."

"My dear," Lily said as the two of them took a late afternoon walk past the British legation, "when do you think that you might return here next for more of our most delightful discussions?"

"Just as soon as I can shake the dust of the desert free from my boots," Dev said. "What we might hope for is something around Christmas, because I will come bearing gifts and have what I hope will be some most delightful presents for you."

"Yes, that is what I was hoping you'd say," Lily laughed, "and I will hope that you will look forward to exchanging them with me as much and as often as possible."

12

Two days later, at the crack of dawn and with a staccato of machine guns splitting the air on all sides, Dev and Crisp leaped from their sleeping bags, snatched up their great coats, and ran pell-mell for the nearest slit trench just as two Rumplers and three Pfalz dove down to strafe Kantara and drop their bombs across the airdrome. Even as Dev dove for the trench behind Crisp, he could see three of the small German bombs in the air—all of them coming down one behind the other, all of them coming down in a way that marked a straight line directly toward where Dev and Crisp had taken cover. Seconds later, in perfect confirmation of his perception, the ground lifted and the two men came near to being buried by earth thrown up by one of the bombs, which exploded not a dozen yards distant, spewing dirt, rocks, and debris that came down all over them and left their ears ringing and their vision blurred.

"Bugger!" Crisp shouted, straining to hear his own voice. "Too close by half! Are you all right?"

Dev—dazed, spitting dirt from his mouth—clapped Crisp twice on the shoulder without saying a word, rubbing from his lips the muck that he'd had forced into his mouth by the blast.

"Where was the warning?" he finally said. "That's what I'd like to know. No siren. And chattering machine guns as our only alarm clock. Not very pleasant, I think. Someone should write a letter to *The Times*."

"Be sure to mention that to Frome. I'm sure he'll want to mention it to Tuck," Crisp said, standing to dust himself off only to once more throw himself to the ground upon seeing yet another Rumpler dipping toward the field for a second run.

Once more, the surrounding machine guns began to make a racket, so much of one that Dev, crushing himself to the earth at the bottom of their hole, believed himself hard pressed to hear himself think. Seconds later, the earth shook once more, two blasts lifting it in the vicinity of what Dev imagined to be the mess tent.

"Let's hope that one didn't do for the porridge," Dev shouted to Crisp. "After this lot, I'd hate to have to face bully beef for breakfast this morning and particularly not straight from a tin."

"Not to worry," Crisp shouted back. "The cooks built a sandbagged revetment around the stoves the day before you came back. If, however, they left the lids off the porridge pots, we're in for it. Oatmeal and sand, if you take my meaning!"

A Pfalz then made a run on the airdrome, but in the case of the Pfalz, the Hun aborted his attack, one or another of the machine gunners finally concentrating some fire on the target. As a result, the Pfalz dropped all of his bombs short, barely avoiding his own explosions before pancaking his ship directly onto the drome and skidding straight ahead over the dusty surface, until, with a resounding crash, he collided with the flagpole in front of Frome's tent. The pole tore straight through one of the Hun's wings and whirled the plane like a boy's top until it finally came to rest, whereupon Frome leaped from his own hole and ran with two of the air mechs to lift the stunned enemy pilot from the remains of his ship before it could catch fire.

From where Def and Crisp both lifted their heads above the edge of their trench, they could see that the Hun—a small man of less than medium height—did not appear to be wounded, and his plane, as the men sped him away from it, did not catch fire.

"Looks like we're to have a guest for breakfast this morning," Dev said.

"Let's hope the mess attendant serves him the bully beef," Crisp said, "presenting it as one of a multitude of English delicacies."

Given the two stars decorating the collar of the breakfast guest which the Flight entertained over porridge and eggs that morning, Dev took him to be an Oberleutnant, equivalent to his own rank, in the Austrian rather than the German air service. Judging from the thickness of the man's hair, the sparseness of the mustache he was trying but failing to grow, and the youthful exuberance with which the man spoke, Dev did not think him to be above 20 years old. Not in the least downcast by the fact that he was grounded and about to be sent to a prison camp, the man—one Ernst Pichler according to the name by which he identified himself—tucked in to the porridge, the bangers, and the eggs that the mess attendants sought to feed him with such gusto that Dev could not help other than to imagine that the Huns at El Arish or Rafa were on short rations.

To test the point, Crisp drew one of the mess attendants to his side. "Suppose you give him a heaping portion of bully beef," Crisp said in hushed tones.

"Captain Frome told us not to," the mess attendant said, also whispering, "so as to avoid leaving a bad impression."

"Suppose," Crisp said, "that you leave this one to me. Give him a bit, and let's see where it takes him."

Moments later, after Frome had taken his breakfast and left the tent, and while Bivin and Symes distracted the Austrian with small talk, the mess attendant set a healthy portion of bully beef before him on a plate. Without a second's hesitation when the Austrian's eyes lighted on it, he took up his fork, tucked straight into it, and devoured the mass with gusto.

"*Zee kaffee*," Oberleutnant Pichler said, downing the dregs of his cup and looking up with a satisfied smile on his face. "I make zee apologie, gentlemens, but not so good as Vienna. But zee *fleisch*, zee meat you say, zer goot! *Was ist los?*"

"*Delikatesse essen*," Crisp said at once.

"*Ja*," Pichler said, nodding his head in agreement, "*Ist goot! Danke!*"

"Proof positive," Dev said, out of the Austrian's hearing, "that the Huns have no taste."

"Absolute confirmation that their cooking is the worst in Europe," Crisp said, "with the possible exception of the Bulgarians. One never notices Bulgarian restaurants in London, if you take my meaning."

"Yes, well," Dev said. "And I believe that I may add to that the fact that I never once saw Austrian cuisine mentioned on any menu that I can specifically remember. Tells you something, I believe. Ever think of doing something in export following the war? Looks like the Austrians might be ripe for a market in surplus bully beef."

"Oh, I say," Crisp said, his smile brightening. "Rather brilliant, that. Entrepreneurial, what? There could be millions in it!"

"We must mention it to our ladies," Dev laughed, "and let them try to corner the market for us while we're away."

At 0900 that morning, Bivin, Symes, Wells, and Boy Stevens took to the air carrying racks filled with Cooper bombs in order to make a counter-raid on El Arish. In the meantime, the Red Caps showed up with a paddy wagon of sorts to take Oberleutnant Pichler in tow and deposit him behind wire, and less than an hour later, Frome called Dev to his tent.

"You weren't scheduled to fly today," Frome said, "but things have changed. Ask the mess to give you an early lunch, get on your flying togs, and fly down to Suez. D Flight has a spot of trouble down there. They're equipped with four antiquated Bristol Scouts and three even more antiquated BE2cs, and the BEs are all down with one sort of engine failure or another."

"So, what's the issue?" Dev asked.

"A passenger who has to go somewhere," Frome said. "Can't send him in a Bristol Scout because there's no observer's seat. Can't send him in one of their BE2cs because none of them can fly. Help has been called for—and you're it."

"Cairo?" Dev said, the thought of seeing Lily again coming instantly into his head.

"Ah ... not exactly," Frome said. "Other direction. You'll be flying well out into Sinai somewhere and putting down one of our intelligence types among the Berbers."

"You're joking," Dev said, beginning to laugh.

"I'm not," Frome said at once. "Serious business, Dev, demanding utmost attention. You fly down to Suez this afternoon and spend the night. You depart early in the morning and fly southeast to Nekhl where D Flight maintains some kind of emergency landing strip on the deep southern bank of Wadi El Arish. You refuel at Nekhl and then continue to fly southeast on a compass bearing until you are at least 10 or 15 miles east of Akaba, and out there, somewhere amid the wastes, you will find the Berbers, a devil of a lot of them, and put your man down. Not a word to anyone about where you're going or what you're going to do. All of this appears to be fairly hush hush. I'm not privy to the whole of it, but I rather think we're trying to stir up some kind of Arab revolt, and the man you're to carry out there has some part to play in it."

"And how," Dev asked, "in the middle of the wastes of Arabia, am I ever expected to get back?"

"Not to worry," Frome grinned. "Piece of cake, that. D Flight seems to have a ship or two already out amid those wastes with a supply of petrol with which to refuel you and send you back to Nekhl. The ships already on station out there are also down, so you will be carrying out a spare part or two, which their air mechs need to repair them, and ought to have no trouble getting back here. Given where you're going and the distance you'll have to fly, I think I'd carry some additional water as well, and it seems to me that going armed might be considered prudent."

"Yes, I'll just bet it would," Dev said. "I don't know how I'll ever thank you for offering me such a splendid opportunity for ending my life, dying of thirst, in no man's land somewhere."

"Oh, I could send Crisp in your place," Frome said, smiling from ear to ear, "but if his ship had trouble on the way back, he wouldn't have the slightest idea how to repair it. You, with your vast knowledge of engines, just might, so that's why you're elected to go. Any questions?"

"None that I can think of at the moment," Dev said, "but if I manage to return, I'm sure I'll have dozens at my fingertips. You and the others must try not to oversleep while I'm gone."

"I say," Frome said, coming to the edge of his chair with a look of mock-disbelief on his face, "is such a thing possible? I'm afraid that no one warned me."

Dev required nearly two hours to fly from Kantara to Suez but did not leave until nearly 1400 that afternoon—a departure he put off until he had collected his kit and left a letter for Crisp to post telling Lily that he would be going into the desert and that she might not be hearing from him for a few days.

The flight down to Suez went off without a hitch, Dev finding the airdrome, which he had never before seen, gauging the conditions for landing, and setting down without mishap. There, once on the ground, Captain Bertram Pugh, D Flight's commander, greeted him pleasantly, offered him a cot in his own tent for the night, and then took him into the mess where he met some of the other pilots in the Flight and found that one of them, Sandy Motram, had passed through Central Flying School with him, an eventuality that allowed the men to compare notes.

Sandy—a string bean of a man with huge hands and a broken nose from a recent crackup, according to what he told Dev—found flying from Suez to be a crashing bore.

"Occasionally the Turks send out cavalry patrols from Akaba," Sandy said, speaking listlessly. "We spot them, drop a Cooper bomb or two, and drive them back to their holes. Frankly, Collins, we've seen more action, the four or five of us who are down here, against the Bedouin. Here and there, we've had a plane go down, and then there has been hell to pay trying to hold those land pirates off while one or another of our air mechs has tried to repair whatever problem we've encountered. Riggsby, one of our lads, went down in a Bristol Scout out there. No choice but to burn it and try to walk, but the Berbers got him before he'd gone 5 miles, stripped him bare, lashed him a few times with some kind of whip, and sold him back to us for 50 pieces of gold."

"From what we've encountered in the north," Dev said, "I'd say you were damn lucky to get him back alive. The ones we've met have come at us hammer and tongs, rifles spitting, bent on drawing blood. Our lot east of Kantara seem to be allied with the Turks or the Germans, or both, and from what you tell me, your lot may not be. Either that, or they're willing to do business with whomever they meet. Know anything about this trip I'm supposed to be taking tomorrow?"

"I know that your passenger isn't down from Ismailia yet," Sandy said, "but that's about the limit."

"Been out to this place in the desert where I'm supposed to be going?"

"Truth told," Sandy said, "beyond the fact that you're carrying a passenger that we can't because our machines are down, Pugh hasn't said a word. We've got a couple of ships out there somewhere, Duffy and Benchard, but where they may be is something the rest of us don't know. At intervals, they seem to show up in Nekhl, but they haven't been returning here and have been gone for over six weeks. To change the subject, as I remember, you know a good bit about engines, don't you?"

"Some," Dev said.

"Want to have a look at ours?" Sandy asked. "Our air mechs mean well, but one's a former blacksmith who no doubt knows a lot about wagon wheel repair but not a lot about the BE2c. The other knows more but also drinks more when we can't find his bottle and put a stop to it. Pugh has had him up on charges twice already."

"All right," Dev said. "Let's go have a look. Maybe I can spot something that will help you get back into the air."

For the two hours that followed and prior to the evening meal which, owing to the proximity of the Red Sea, offered up genuine fresh fish for the main course, Dev looked over and then helped work on the engines on the BE2cs in D Flight's hangars. What he saw at once gave him a whole new respect for the work that Banes and his air mechs were doing in keeping his own Flight in the air. The people that Pugh had seeing to things were obviously not doing their jobs: plugs were dirty, air filters were clogged, fuel lines were equally clogged, engine controls were loose, and even the cables connecting the cockpit with the planes' control surfaces required greasing and tightening.

"Personally," Dev said to Pugh when the officers sat down to their fish that night, "I would complain to Tuck and have him find you a good sergeant to send down here. I think the two air mechs know enough to keep you flying, but like the fitters that are working with them, they're lazy. I'm no expert, but I can't see a thing wrong with the engines themselves; it's routine maintenance that's missing, and that can be remedied."

"Engines," Pugh said. "Flight School when I went through barely showed them to us. Ought to be a required part of the course, if you ask me. My fault for not knowing and not booting our lot up to the mark. I'll get in touch with Tuck in the morning and demand a sergeant with a basic knowledge of mechanics."

"I wonder," Dev said, "when this passenger of mine is supposed to arrive? I thought he'd be here by now. I want to look over the maps with him to get some idea of where we're going."

"This one," Pugh said, "a man who calls himself John Hume Ross and wears the uniform of a captain, flew out of here once before, and in the same way. The train that he took down here from Ismailia arrived in Suez at 1800, but we didn't see him here until approximately 15 minutes before he was scheduled to take off in the morning. Even when he did arrive, he hardly spoke a word and told Duffy—Duffy was the man flying him east—nothing more than to take off and that he would direct him where to go with hand signals. Duffy didn't like it much, nor did I, but with these intelligence types, one never knows what they're up to, and in my experience, they're apt to remain as tight lipped as stone. I can't be sure, but from the little I've been able to glean, I think the man is some kind of liaison with one of the Arabs of high estate. Someone like Hussein bin Ali or Faisal, or what have you. They're supposedly restive out there in the desert—a long way from Sinai—and from what we've heard, they have it in for the Turks, but I'm afraid that's the limit of what I know. Could be that we're trying to stir them up and get them to revolt. Could be that we're trying to enlist them to march on Mecca. Who knows? Ross might, but if he does, he isn't saying, and you're assigned to fly him wherever he wants to go and drop him off."

Sandy, following the meal and the departure of the other pilots, produced three bottles of beer.

"Sorry the port isn't handy," Pugh laughed, "but as a matter of fact, none of us has seen a full bottle of the stuff since we were last in Cairo. The shops in Suez don't seem to carry what one might call a regular supply, and I'd rather hate to try anything that they did put on sale. Our beer ration is more secure; Tuck ships it down to us by rail."

"That's the way we get ours as well," Dev said, "warm and intermittently."

At around 2215 that night—as Pugh, Sandy, and Dev polished off the last of the beer in their bottles and only about 15 minutes before the bugler sounded taps—the man calling himself John Hume Ross stepped quietly into the tent carrying a small duffle and threaded his way directly to where the three of them were sitting. Dev knew at once that he would be his passenger but that he was nothing like the man he had expected. The officer, with a head that looked both elongated and somewhat too big for the diminutive body that stretched out below it, struck Dev by his scholarly, almost ascetic demeanor, an appearance underscored by the condition of the uniform the man wore, which was atrocious for dirt, frayed fabric, and cut. The duffle he carried, equally atrocious for dirt and wear, Ross set on an empty chair, but rather than sit himself, he stood on the opposite side of the table from the three of them and greeted them with a pleasant smile.

"Hello, Pugh," the man said in an affable tone, "with you again, I'm afraid. Is this the man," he continued, looking at Dev, "who's to give me transport?"

"Hello Ross," Pugh said quietly. "Yes, this is Devlin Collins, down from Kantara. He'll be flying you. Care for a beer?"

"I think not, Pugh, but thank you," Ross said, extending his hand for Dev, who had stood to shake it. "Collins, is it? Splendid. Sorry to be a bother, but if we might have a word," and with that Ross indicated that he wished Dev to withdraw with him into the night.

Once outside the tent, Ross came straight to the point. "Take off at sunrise, or before, if you think it safe. After we refuel at Nekhl, continue on the same course. That should put us north of Akaba by several miles. Good idea, that. The Turks have Aviatiks at Akaba, six or eight of them. After Akaba, turn southeast down the coast. Another 30 miles into the desert will take us in the direction of Jebel Shar, and it will be in that vicinity where I shall want you to set me down. You'll find Duffy and Benchard down there and enough petrol to get you back to Nekhl. Nothing demanding, I think. I appreciate the lift. Any questions?"

"Do you know how to operate a Lewis gun, Sir?" Dev asked. "I wondered whether or not we ought to carry one."

"The answer to your first question is 'yes,'" Ross said, "but I think we need not bother to encumber ourselves with one. It would merely add weight to your ship for your trip back."

"Yes, Sir," Dev said.

"Well then," said Ross, "I'll leave you to it and fetch some sleep."

"Need for me to show you where you'll be sleeping?" Dev asked as Ross picked up his duffle and prepared to depart.

"I'll be sleeping out," Ross said, "as I did in Syria. Less bother, more stars. Good night, Collins."

"Good night, Sir," Dev said.

On the following morning, well before sunrise, when Dev went out to do his pre-flight checks on the BE2c, he found Ross rolling up his sleeping bag and stuffing it back into his duffle. Even as far south as Suez, the desert night had been cold, but Ross—clad only in the rag of the uniform that he had worn the day before—seemed to ignore the temperature, his only concession to it being a white silk scarf that he had wrapped about his neck.

"Do we fly now?" Ross said.

"Won't you prefer some breakfast first?" Dev asked.

"Fasting is sometimes a virtue," Ross said flatly, "and when flying, I find it doubly so."

"I'll have enough of a dawn to take off in ten minutes, Sir," Dev said. "If you would like to mount now, that will be satisfactory. There are some gaskets to the side of your seat which I am carrying out to Duffy and Benchard, so please be mindful of them. We think they'll restore the ships out there to flight."

Ten minutes later, with Pugh directing things from the side, one of his fitters swung Dev's propeller, the BE2c leaped to life, and Dev opened the throttle and took off, heading almost directly into the faint light of the morning's dawn.

By the time they reached Nekhl and set down to top off with fuel, the temperature on the ground had increased to the point where Dev would have liked to have discarded his leather flying coat. But, anticipating the usual momentary oil effusions from the engine and the dust that would be attending their next landing in the desert, and not wishing to make a mash of his uniform, Dev left the coat on and gave himself mild congratulations when he got the ship back up to 5,000 feet and found that the air there had not warmed as much as it had on the ground.

After an additional hour and a half, far to the south, as Ross reached from behind, clapped him on the shoulder, and pointed in that direction, Dev spotted what he imagined to be the outline of Akaba, located directly on the edge of the Red Sea. Alert and searching the skies with the eyes of a hawk, Dev placed himself on the lookout for any Turks that might be in the air. Eventually, without ever sighting anything that looked like one of the Aviatiks that Ross had mentioned, he turned southeast as directed.

On the desert floor, the appearance of the land mass began to look more and more broken, with long patches of what Dev imagined to be sand interspersed with what looked like bare, rocky mountains. Eventually, down between two of those imposing stands of utterly barren rock, somewhere north of Jebel Shar and with Ross clapping him several times on the shoulder and pointing down, Dev descended and found a long wide stretch of desert between the outcrops. Then, to his surprise, coming suddenly over what struck him as a wide wadi, he sighted tents—what looked like hundreds of them with horse lines and camels wedged into the spaces around them.

Following the hand signals Ross delivered to him from behind, on what Dev imagined to be a kind of mesa flanking the wadi, he set down and landed, putting the BE2c into a taxi pattern that soon brought him to the side of the two others that had been stranded in the open. Both of them were parked between an array of dark tents from which a uniformed British officer and what looked to Dev like a pair of air mechanics moved to greet them when the plane came to a stop. Once Dev cut the engine but before he could emerge from the cockpit onto solid ground, near the edge of the wadi some 100 yards distant, a cacophonous burst of rifle fire and a riot of screaming erupted. More than a hundred Berbers, their rifles raised, their robes stretching out behind them in the wind, spilled onto the mesa charging hellbent in Dev and Ross's direction. Dev flinched; he couldn't stop himself. For a second, with the most threatening onslaught that he'd ever faced before, charged by men with bearded faces and blood in their eyes wielding long, curved swords amidst the rifles that they were still shooting into the sky, he imagined that the game was over, that he and Ross were done for, that their throats would be cut in seconds. And then, as he glanced at the men he imagined to be Duffy and the air mechs walking casually toward him and realized that they were totally unmoved by the demonstration, he pulled himself together and recognized the onslaught for what it was—some kind of desert welcoming committee. The fact was underscored when the gathering Berbers reined to a skidding stop mere yards from the plane, all of them shouting together and at the top of their lungs, "*Orenz! Orenz! Orenz!*"

Immediately, Ross was over the side of the plane, down the wing, and in among them. Dev, somewhat to his surprise, never saw the man again, Ross's sudden disappearance into the Arab swarm being total as they escorted him away to their camp.

"Quite a show, aren't they?" the man who introduced himself as Duffy said, when he finally came walking up to receive the gaskets that Dev handed down to him from the rear cockpit.

"If I'd had a mass of Berbers coming at me like that east of Kantara," Dev said, "I'd have died an early death. We have to meet them with Lewis guns rather than with open arms."

"Yes, well," Duffy said, as Dev climbed down and stood on the desert floor while the two air mechs began refueling his plane, "we've got a different situation here. These are Ali's people; they're supposed to be our friends. An alliance of sorts, and all that, although I'm hesitant to go among them at night. Touchy, they are. Take offense easily. Different culture. Different customs. Quick to fight, and deadly when their blood is up. He's got their confidence, but we keep our distance. They refer to our kites as 'little birds.' Scared to death of them, of course. Once or twice, the Turks have given them a strafe, and they don't like it."

"What the hell is that *Orenz* business all about?" Dev asked.

"That's their name for him, for Ross," Duffy said. "For all I know, it might be his real name, but we've never heard him call himself anything other than Ross. I'm here to fly, so I don't inquire, but these intelligence blokes are in a class by themselves. Cloak and dagger, that sort of thing. Ever read John Buchan?"

"Yes," Dev said.

"Right," Duffy said. "Well, this is the real thing—*The Thirty-Nine Steps* in the flesh, if you see what I mean. Makes me tired, politics. I'd rather fly up and bomb Akaba if Ross would let me."

"Yes," Dev said, "closer to what we've been trained for. Any difficulties with the Turks?"

"We see them occasionally," Duffy said, "but usually at a distance. They don't come out here much. The Turkish rail line runs south from Tabuk to Medina, and they watch that, flying from both Tabuk and Medina. But we're sandwiched among the Sarawat Mountains—bare though they may be—and they don't like the idea of going down in here because they know that Ali's people will cut their throats, so it's not often that we're bothered."

"Sounds convenient," Dev said.

"Oh, it is," Duffy laughed, "but it's also a trifle boring. Suez, of course, is anything but lively, but on the whole I'd rather be back there with a chance of getting up to Cairo from time to time."

"Yes," Dev said. "Cairo has many attractions."

Thirty minutes later, with his plane refueled, and under atmospheric conditions that Dev found barely acceptable for getting into the air—something he would have imagined to be impossible in the middle of the Arabian summer—Dev left the ground, headed northwest for Akaba, and skirted the place, following his compass in the direction of Nekhl. But to Dev's surprise and somewhat to his consternation, some 30 or 40 miles west of Akaba and a good 50 east of Nekhl, he spotted a pair of Aviatiks flying on a reverse course toward Akaba two or three thousand feet above him. By diving at once toward the desert floor, Dev hoped that he would avoid detection. In that hope, he was disappointed when he glanced back and noticed that both planes had obviously spotted him and were diving to make an attack.

Virtually defenseless without Trent and his Lewis gun in the seat behind him, shaking under the stress of the moment, Dev did the only thing that he could think to do: snatched up the flare gun with which Pugh had sent him out, rammed a cartridge into the chamber, and waited. When he judged the moment right, as the two Turkish planes flattened out behind him and prepared to make a run on him with their forward-firing machine guns, Dev threw the BE2c into a tight turn and fired off the flare gun in his enemy's direction. The flare burst some 600 yards distant, the Turks, still

1,000 yards away, instantly breaking to both sides in order to avoid the burst and losing considerable altitude in the process. And that was the end of it. Neither of them wished to face the flare gun for a second pass, and as Dev watched from above while coming back full circle to his original course, he saw both breaking for Akaba in a straight line of retreat.

It didn't matter that the Turks had wisely chosen to break off and leave him to his flight. Once again, Dev was bouncing all over the sky, the fear of what had almost befallen him having gripped him momentarily in an iron fist. With sweat streaming into his eyes, he began to try once again to regulate his breathing so as to slow down and quell the stresses that he felt running through his body.

Dev had 50 miles to fly and three quarters of an hour in which to do it before he reached and put down at Nekhl. It took the whole of that time for him to bring himself back under what he considered full control; had he gone down in Sinai, after not only contending with the Turkish Aviatiks but after flying over at least three Berber encampments that he had seen below, he didn't believe that he could ever have walked the distance without being caught, stripped, and probably murdered between where he'd been attacked and the emergency strip at Nekhl.

"Uneventful flight?" asked the lieutenant who came out to supervise the air mech who refueled him at Nekhl.

"No," Dev said. "I was bounced west of Akaba by two Aviatiks."

"Really?" the lieutenant said, his eyebrows rising. "How'd you escape without an observer to defend you?"

"Not easily," Dev said. "Fired a flare gun at them as they started their attack. Upset them a bit, that did."

"Yes, stands to reason," the lieutenant said. "Lucky for you that Pugh sent you out with that thing. Red tab that was down to Suez last month called them unsporting. Pugh called the red tab a jackass, but not to his face."

"The description fits," Dev said. "I think I may know the red tab you're talking about, and I concur with Pugh."

Dev did not doss down in Suez that night. Instead, landing there at around 1500 that afternoon and after seeing his ship rapidly refueled by the air mechs, he said his goodbyes to both Sandy and Pugh, and took to the air swiftly so that he was once more able to land at Kantara as the last shades of twilight swept across the field. No one had been expecting him to return that day, so by the time he reached the mess, the stoves had gone cold. The best the mess attendants could do for him was a slab of hard cheese between two pieces of stale bread and a bottle of beer with which to wash it down.

Frome and Crisp, hurrying up from the armory when they saw Dev land, found him bent over his plate, his face still covered with a layer of grime and grease from his flight, his eyes red, his body slumping with exhaustion.

"Unexceptional flight?" Frome asked, pulling out a chair and sitting down across from Dev as Crisp slid into another beside him.

"Not exactly," Dev said. "Got bounced by two Turks west of Akaba."

"You went all the way to Akaba?" Crisp asked.

"And beyond," Dev said, his teeth crunching down on a piece of the hard cheese. "Went right out into the Hejaz and put down alongside a wadi between what I can only think of as pyramids of stone amid a couple of thousand Berbers. Didn't like that part of it much. About a battalion's worth of them came rushing up over the edge of the wadi screaming like banshees and firing off their rifles. Figured I was done for, but Duffy, the pilot that's stationed out there, said they were a 'welcoming committee' for the passenger that I carried out to them."

"And who was your passenger?" Frome asked.

Dev took another bite of the cheese, helped it down with a swig of beer, and looked back at Frome. "To tell you the truth, I don't know," he said flatly. "Small man, a captain in the forces with a very large, long head who called himself John Hume Ross, but when those Arabs came roaring toward us, all of them were shouting '*Orenz, Orenz*' at the top of their lungs, and I couldn't make hide nor hair of it. The uniform the man was wearing was so tattered and so filthy that I couldn't identify his regiment, and I don't think the two of us passed twenty words between ourselves the whole time I was around him."

"*Ah*," Frome said, a knowing smile curling at the edge of his lips. "*Orenz*, you say? Well, that toots a horn of sorts. I think I've heard of him. I think I may have met him once, long ago when I first came out here. I think he was doing something with maps, in intelligence, in Cairo. I believe the man had been some kind of archaeologist before the war. Picked up a snippet here and there—nothing you could put your finger on exactly—but I've heard rumor that he's some kind of liaison with Ali and his sons who consider him a very big mogul for their purposes. And for our purposes, he may be very big as well, but I don't know any more than that. And you say you were bounced by a couple of Turks?"

"Yes," Dev said, "flying Aviatiks with the crescent moon insignia on their wings. Fired a Very pistol in their direction, and that seemed to give them pause. Preferred not to risk it, if you see what I mean, and drew off toward Akaba."

"Tell Pugh about it, did you?"

"Yes," Dev said.

"Good," Frome said. "You don't fly tomorrow, so get some sleep and you can write your report in the morning. Best not to mention the name of your passenger. Merely say that you carried a passenger and leave it at that. Persona unidentified."

And with that, Frome rose and left Dev and Crisp sitting over the remains of Dev's sandwich.

"Two letters from Mrs. Collins waiting for you in the tent," Crisp said.

"Good," Dev said. "I'll get off a note to her to let her know I'm back and mail it in the morning."

"Wise move," Crisp said. "Otherwise, Ruth is liable to begin asking questions in support of her partner in crime, and I wouldn't know how to answer them."

"You're a true friend," Dev said.

"Yes, I know," Crisp laughed. "So, you saw a lot of Arabs out there?"

"I'd guess 2,000, if not more," Dev said. "Formidable force, that, if they get angry, I'd think. That Damascus to Medina railway isn't too far distant from them, and if the Turks upset them in some way, I'd imagine that they could give the Turks a lot of trouble by cutting it."

"I wonder if they'll try to?" Crisp said.

"Who knows?" Dev said. "With the Berbers of the desert, who knows anything?"

"*Orenz*?" Crisp said.

"Good guess," Dev said.

13

Dev did not fly on the day he returned from the Hejaz. Instead, as Frome had instructed him to do, he wrote his report and submitted it, leaving out any mention of John Hume Ross or the specifics of what he'd seen in the desert. He spent his day in the sheds and hangars, seeing to the work that Banes and his people were doing, and in the late afternoon—in contravention of almost every other day he'd spent on the station—he allowed himself a long nap. He woke to find himself refreshed from what he'd described to the others as his "travels."

Throughout much of November and early December, while D Flight continued to fly out of Suez, A Flight, flying from Ismailia and Cairo, provided transport services for innumerable numbers of red tabs and luminaries, while B Flight continued to watch the desert to the west in the event that the Senussi once more tried to raise a revolt. Frome's Flight, combined with 1 Australian Squadron, seemed to carry most of the combat responsibilities, the two squadrons combined into what Frome and Tuck began referring to as "the Wing." Often flying at least twice on any given day, Dev found himself doing at least three to four photo reconnaissance missions for every bombing and strafing sortie he undertook. The objective of the combined squadrons seemed to be twofold. The majority of their time they spent photographing the terrain between Bir El Mazar, El Arish, and Magdhaba to the south—a virtual triangle of desert—with the objective of reproducing on maps every bush, rock, and wadi, not to mention early warning outposts that the Turks tried to establish on the plain. When Turkish or Hun patrols were sometimes sighted, one or another of the planes in the Flight dropped down to strafe their columns and, if they'd flown out with Cooper bombs, to drop one or two of the 20-pounders where the pilots deemed they would do the most good.

On the less frequent days when Frome dispatched some of the Flight to make an attack, three or four of the pilots would bomb up with as many Cooper bombs as they felt safe to carry, form themselves into a loose gaggle, and head for El Arish and, twice, to Beersheba, where the Huns had established a new, larger airfield in support of their position at El Arish. The problem these pilots faced—something they learned early when they began to carry out their forays—was that the Huns seemed to be under a new command, a command that didn't intend for the German pilots to sit on cushions while the Royal Flying Corps bombed them at will. Instead, the Huns had taken to patrolling their airdromes, putting up at least two of their planes in the early morning and late afternoon—the times when they most expected to be attacked. Those aircraft, having invariably taken off early enough to climb for altitude in advance of a British sweep, seemed to have the height advantage that gave them the best terms for making attacks of their own on the marauding flights from Kantara or Salmana. And, as if the Hun planes in the air were not enough, whoever was commanding on the ground commanded with more machine guns and more Archies than the pilots of 14 Squadron had ever seen before.

During the first week in December, while making a dawn attack at El Arish, Dev had nearly thrown up on himself from stress-induced nausea when the tip of his port wing was shot away by a glowing piece of shrapnel and his tail plane was so severely shredded by yet another burst that he could barely control his ship in flight and nearly didn't make it back. Symes, flying three days later, and Wells, who flew with him, had so many of their wing ribs shot away while over Beersheba that they flew all the way back, never sure for a moment that their wings would not fold on them before they could put down and make an emergency landing at Bir El Mazar. And not two days afterward, Boy Stevens, coming home from a similar raid, didn't make it back and went down in the desert east of Bir El Mazar, walking a total of 8 miles during the night as he and his observer trekked back under cover of darkness, hoping to elude capture by any of the Berbers who lurked in the vicinity waiting to gather them in.

The combined effects of the work were telling, and even more telling when added to the months the squadron had spent in the air. Symes had developed a twitch of sorts that showed up in the blinking of his right eye when he came down from a flight. Wells complained more and more of gyppie tummy when on the ground. Boy Stevens, Bevin, Crisp, and Dev knew they were drinking more than they were wont to do in less troubled times, and the usually jolly Frome had shown himself to be increasingly testy. And in Dev's own case, he knew that his hands tended to shake more than at any time since he had come into the desert and started operational flying.

"I wonder," Boy Stevens said at table after a late afternoon raid in the middle of December, "if the Hun will have assembled as many Archies at Magdhaba, if or when we ever attack there?"

"I'd count on it," Crisp said. "Magdhaba, judging from what we can see from the air, may be not much more than a village, but the water source there is the key to the position, and it rather looks to me like the redoubts down there are set to defend it. To my way of thinking, that would mean a herd of Archies, all of them having given birth to a flock of protective machine guns with infant Mauser automatics in the hands of every gunner who serves them."

"Thank you for the thought," Bivin said acidly. "Makes a fellow feel splendidly secure to hear such optimism."

"Not at all," said Crisp. "Always one for sounding the upbeat."

"What's called for," Frome said quickly, "is a resounding downbeat, a 100-pound downbeat. Do a lot to interrupt the symphony, if you take my meaning. With the possible addition of a number of little Coopers' grace notes."

"Kettle drums most needed," Wells said. "Handley-Page monster. Big. Two engines. 250-pound thunder. Turks fleeing. Observers strafing. Archies silent. Best outcome."

"Don't hold your breath," Symes said. "The day we see a Handley-Page out here will be the day that pigs will be flying 180-miles-per-hour scouts with four machine guns to be fired forward."

Dev listened but said nothing. They were tired, the lot of them, utterly exhausted, trying to keep their spirits up by being witty, but the wit was thin and falling flat, and Dev quickly realized that he didn't have a thing to contribute to it. And then, with twilight falling fast, as they emerged from the mess tent and began to stagger toward their tents, they were bombed, a flight of four Rumplers escorted by three Aviatiks coming in low from the east and laying a crate of eggs across the airdrome that fell just short of the hangars and the planes stored inside them.

"Makes for a near perfect day," Dev said with disgust, as he and Crisp dove for the nearest rifle pit.

"Trenchant, that," Crisp said as the two of them cowered at the base of their hole. Babington Macaulay would be impressed. Old Thomas Carlyle might even show you a nod of approval."

Off to the side, one of the Hun bombs falling not far from their tent created enough of a concussion to lift the two of them a full foot into the air before dropping them back into the bottom of the hole as dirt and rocks showered down around them.

"Something tells me that Emerson would not be impressed," Dev said. "All your parts in place after that one? Ears still intact?"

"Barely," Crisp said, spitting dirt from his lips. "Must speak a word to Frome about early warning. We seem to be getting damn little."

"Not to mention the total failure of our machine gunners to get into action," Dev said. "I don't know about you, but I find that downright disconcerting."

"If forced to choose between shooting down a Hun or taking a tea break," Crisp said, "you ought to know by now which one is going to win out with the gunners."

"I doubt that I did," Dev said, "but I'll venture a note. Raids after the evening meal are to be ignored until one's tea has been brewed and taken."

"Oh, see there, you *do* know," Crisp laughed as another bomb exploded in the midst of the drome and one of the Rumplers, unopposed, roared overhead.

"Alas," Dev said, "yes."

During the two weeks prior to Christmas, Dev flew twice a day and, once, three times, joining the Wing in photographing everything in the triangle that he and his brother fliers could find and that the observers could catch on camera. Then, quite unexpectedly, on December 21, the Wing took off late in the afternoon, flew to Salmana, and landed before dark. Before anyone could give a thought to an evening meal, finding tent quarters, or so much as relieving themselves, Frome called his Flight for a briefing.

In Salmana's mess tent, when the fliers filed in, they found a map of the areas to the east and Frome standing before it, holding a pointer and looking serious.

"In case it has escaped your notice," Frome began, "things are on the move, and tomorrow, we will play a part in them. Already, the Light Horse is on the march and prepared to throw in an attack on the morrow against El Arish where, as things stand this evening, at least 1,600 Turks are in the trenches under the command of Khadir Bey. Starting at sunrise and carrying Cooper bombs, we are to patrol to the south to make sure that nothing gets up to him from Magdhaba. 1 Australian Squadron will be patrolling to the east to make sure nothing reaches him from Beersheba. The objective of the exercise is to drive the Turks and Huns out of El Arish, once and for all, and back to Rafa—and if not to Rafa, to Gaza, which will probably be the objective of some future attack for which we all may imagine that planning is in progress. Clear that from your minds, however, because with the pipeline and the rail line only now moving beyond Bir El Mazar, any move in the direction of Gaza is a long way in the future. Now, get some tucker, get some sleep, and be ready to fly at sunrise. Dismiss."

The following morning, Dev flew along with the entire Flight, but with regard to targets, movement, or the least sign of life between El Arish and Magdhaba, they didn't see as much as a lizard on the floor of the desert and returned to find that the Light Horse had been confronted with the totally unexpected. Rather than drive home an assault on the Turkish trenches, they found that the Turks had decamped, abandoning El Arish. The entire Turkish regiment that had been occupying the place had removed south to Magdhaba under the cover of darkness, leaving nothing behind them but a relatively empty village.

The Hun move, Dev and Crisp reasoned together, was not altogether foolish in conception. Instead, von Kressenstein had made rather a wise decision in their estimation. With El Arish at the limit for what Murray's pipeline and railroad could support until the Egyptian labor gangs advanced it many more miles, Rafa and Gaza were relatively free of danger. And with a Turkish regiment sitting on Murray's flank in the very well-fortified positions at Magdhaba, looking like a threatening sharp lance pointed at his side, Murray was not likely to move east or north, which would risk putting the Turkish threat even farther behind him. No, in the chess match that sometimes characterized war, von Kressenstein or Khadir Bey—or both acting together—had made a useful strategic move, wholly diverting Murray's attention from Palestine while channeling it down Wadi El Arish into the wastes of the Sinai desert.

"Bit of an anti-climax, what?" said Symes, as the Flight once more gathered upon their return, Frome intent on conducting another debriefing.

"For today," Frome said, seating them all behind one of the mess tables before once more addressing the map that he had pinned to the wall of the mess tent. "But if I may use the expression without causing undue laughter, 'the game is afoot.'"

Undue laughter followed, no matter how much Frome had tried to give his words a serious sound.

"Yes," Frome said, showing the merest trace of a smile. "Well, lads, here's the long and the short of it so that none of you gets comfortable. General Murray has made a decision. While most of the 2nd Light Horse Brigade occupies El Arish and guards our flank, General Chauvel has done a pivot and is marching the main strength of our force south under cover of darkness. Tomorrow morning at 0630, the 1st Light Horse Brigade, one regiment of the 2nd Light Horse Brigade, and the Imperial Camel Brigade will strike Magdhaba from the north and drive southeast down the wadi. The New Zealand Mounted Rifles and a regiment of the Rifle Brigade will circle more to the east and attack from the northeast, while the 3rd Light Horse Brigade circles even more to the east and hits Magdhaba from the east, while one of its regiments circles all the way to the south and drives up on the settlement from there. Chauvel intends to envelop the entire position and put Khadir Bey's regiment in the bag."

"Sporting of him," said Wells. "Red Cross girls expected? Donuts and char?"

"One imagines," Crisp said, registering more circumspection, "that we will be expected to play a part?"

"Most perceptive," Frome said, more of a twinkle showing about his eyes. "Good of you to ask. Yes, we will ... participate, according to the plan that Collins and I prepared and presented to the Air Staff at GHQ. 1 Australian Squadron will guard our flanks, both at El Arish and to the east, to attempt to dissuade any Huns flying from Rafa and Beersheba from interfering with us. A Flight at Ismailia and Suez are supposedly to guard the southern flank, to prevent any of the Turks at Akaba from attacking us from the south, but I'm doubtful that they will try, and if they do, I'm doubtful that our lads will be able to remain on station long enough to be of much help. Our job will be bombing. According to the plan that we've developed, each of you will be assigned a specific redoubt into which, it is hoped, you will drop your biggest egg. Then, with that done, we will have the pleasure of flying back and forth over the position so as to deposit our Cooper bombs where we believe they will do the most good—all of this only minutes in advance of Chauvel's attack."

Since Dev and Frome first developed the plan, it had not been kept a secret from the Flight. Time and again, the exercise had been discussed, the maps had been examined, and the aerial photographs had been studied so that each flier knew exactly which redoubt he was to attack and the altitude from which he planned to drop his bomb. But when faced with the actual fact of the mission, with the necessity for getting in and out unscathed, with the number of Archies and machine guns that the Turks were likely to have prepared for their reception, the impact of Frome's announcement seemed staggering. The Flight would not be headed for a picnic, and on the instant, the fact struck home with them in a way that it had not done before while it remained a mere mental conception.

During the following hour, bent over the maps and the photographs, each flier studied the potential for what he had to do with an expression on his face that showed the deadly serious nature of the operation. Recent photos taken only a day or two before showed them new Archie emplacements, and while the precise location of pits that might harbor machine guns could not be seen, potential sites could be anticipated, and each of the pilots made those calculations with as sharp an eye as he thought he could bring to bear. Frome, who intended to lead the attack, planned to strike the northernmost of the redoubts, Bivin would take the next to the east, while Wells would drop on the farthest to the east. Boy Stevens would drop Cooper bombs on the smallest of the redoubts to the west of the wadi, saving his 100-pounder for the larger position to its south, which Crisp would also bomb. Symes was to take the next most southern fixture, and the last, the farthest to the south—the redoubt whose reduction would close the door to the Turk escape—Dev had taken for his own. Notes were made, tactics were discussed, and in the end, Frome told them that he intended to bring them in for the attack from the northeast, all fliers splitting from formation some 4 or 5 miles out so as to make their way independently toward their targets. And then, if possible, the Flight would reform, following their exit, in order to return together. This would afford one another mutual protection in the event of a surprise attack from the air or the potential for overflight in the event that one or another of the pilots had to land in the desert and risk capture by the Berbers.

"This is more than a trifle discomfiting," Crisp said as the two of them walked away from the briefing toward the tent in which they expected to doss down.

"Yes," Dev said.

"Best you could come up with?"

"Yes," Dev said again. "Go in too high, and we risk a total loss of accuracy in our bombing. Go in too low, and we risk blowing ourselves straight out of the air with our own bombs. Going in just right risks the Archies and the machine guns, and God only knows what might get down there from Rafa or Beersheba if the Australians are not able to head them off."

"The plan looks sound to me," Crisp said, "but I am not going to like flying it.

"Nor I," Dev said.

By means of a lighted flare path, they took off before dawn, the Australians taking to the air first to establish some kind of air umbrella over Rafa, with another of their Flights patrolling to the southeast of Beersheba on the most likely flight path down toward Magdhaba. The Australians, much to Dev and Frome's relief, had managed to corral two DH1s with forward-firing machine guns, and another of their air mechs had devised a rig that allowed for two more forward-firing machine guns mounted forward, atop the upper wings of two Bristol Scouts. As long as the Lewis guns didn't jam in operation, Dev and the other fliers imagined that they might prove formidable in the air. If the observers in the BE2cs that they would be flying—observers that GHQ had demanded that they take with them—were given an even chance, Frome's Flight remained hopeful that it would be free from attack during their bomb runs.

Prior to takeoff, all of the Flight's wristwatches had been synchronized with Frome's intention to put in their attack at precisely 0630 that morning, at the same moment that General Chauvel was supposed to launch his own from at least half a mile's distance from the foremost of the Turks' redoubts and trench lines. The flight down to Magdhaba began well, each pilot getting into the air without difficulty, all of them gathering over the drome around a flare that Frome fired off to alert them to his position. Then, in a well-spaced-out gaggle so as not to risk collision, they turned southeast and flew the approaching leg at 3,000 feet.

The dawn, a gray and dim one that morning, allowed them to take their bearings. They arrived early in the area, flew one long circle in order to use up three or four superfluous minutes, and then, when he judged the moment right, Frome waggled his wings to alert the Flight, turned toward Magdhaba from the northeast position about which they had been flying, and headed in. Frome, Bivin, and Wells made their approach at 1,500 feet; Dev, Crisp, Boy Stevens, and Symes flew more to the west at 2,000 feet, to avoid any risk of getting in among the others and disrupting their approach. Then, when the time was ripe, Dev, Symes, Boy Stevens, and Crisp separated once more and went forward to dive and drive home their attacks at something below 1,000 feet.

Off to his left, Dev saw bomb flashes and heard the thunder of the Coopers that Boy Stevens dropped over his first target; then, very swiftly, he caught the flash of Crisp's 100-pounder as it blew over the first of the large western redoubts. At around the same time, farther back and more distant, Dev became aware of the sounds of Frome's, Bivin's, and Wells's 100-pounders. Almost before he knew what was happening, Symes dropped. Looking out ahead, Dev could see the redoubt that he was to bomb, dropped yet another 100 feet in altitude, flew a wiggling course to avoid the Archies that were beginning to burst all over the sky, heard machine-gun fire splinter something in his wing, and, arriving over the target, pulled the lever that released his own 100-pounder. And then he quickly pulled back on the stick in his attempt to lift himself out of the bomb's concussion circle.

Without being able to glance behind him, three of Trent's claps on Dev's shoulder told him that he had struck some part of his target, two claps having been designated for a near miss and one for a clean miss. How much of the redoubt Dev may have damaged, he could not say, but the satisfaction he took away from having hit any part of it lightened his mood. But before he could take so much as a smidgen more satisfaction from what he'd accomplished, he was horrified to see the plane that he knew to be Symes's streaking below him with its tailplane on fire and go skidding along the desert floor, kicking up clouds of dust from its obvious crash-landing not less than half a mile south of Magdhaba. With the clouds of dust that the crash raised, neither Dev nor Trent could determine whether Symes and his observer had been killed, knocked out by the crash, or survived to extract themselves from the remains of their ship and get away from it before it suddenly exploded on the ground, sending more dust and flames shooting into the sky around it.

Realizing that his hands had once more started to shake, Dev fought back the fear that Symes's crash had infused through his body. He bit down on what he could not control and turned so as to come up on his planned attack area from the southeast, maneuvering his kite all over the sky to confuse the Archies and the machine gunners as much as possible without utterly losing control of his plane. Sighting a trench line that he had not seen before in the photographs—a line that extended from the edge of the redoubt that he bombed to the edge of Wadi El Arish—Dev roared down to less than 100 feet, straightened his course at the last minute, and pickled four of his bombs along the trench, all the while flying straight toward the redoubt. From the redoubt itself, Dev could see what looked like machine-gun tracers coming straight at him, their green glow spaced out in the sky, the strong odor of cordite and phosphorus filling the air around him. Here and there a splinter from a strut or wing rib made a sound as it whipped past him, and then he was over the redoubt and beyond, once more dropping his remaining Coopers over yet another trench line—one he had seen in the photos he had studied the night before. Then, Trent behind him cut loose with the Lewis gun as Dev stamped on the rudder pedals, causing the plane to wobble on the path that a ruptured goose might fly. Dev slammed the throttle to its stops in an attempt to make a safe escape from the hornet's nest which he had disturbed in his wake and failed when, with sharp pain, he was struck from behind by something that drove him hard against the instrument panel and nearly knocked him unconscious.

Dev and Trent did not crash, but when Dev finally came back to himself enough to exert control over the stick, he knew that he was tearing away small branches of the desert thorn bushes that he was flying over. As he pulled back on the stick to gain altitude, he realized, glancing at the deck of his cockpit, that the ammunition pan of Trent's Lewis gun had been torn from its housing by a bullet or a shell fragment and thrown with a jagged edge against him where he sat in the cockpit. What Dev did not immediately apprehend is that the pan had not only ripped open his flight coat but it had also ripped open the flesh of his left shoulder, the pain only beginning to set in as he got control of the plane and felt Trent, working from behind him, clapping a battle dressing over the wound even as the muscles in his left arm began to stiffen.

"Ugly," Trent shouted at him from behind his ear, "but heal, it will!"

As the last Archies that the Turks were able to get off exploded on both sides of them—two or three pieces of shrapnel tearing fabric from the BE2c's wings but not severing anything vital—Dev felt grateful that his right arm had not been struck. He was able to control the ship's flight with his right hand regardless of the nausea that swept over him from time to time.

West of Magdhaba, beneath the rising sun, he finally found Frome circling, his tailplane shot through in more than one place, strips of fabric tearing back from the edges of his port wing. There, too, Crisp and Boy Stevens joined them, Crisp with gaping holes torn through the fuselage directly behind Crouchback's cockpit and both of Crisp's landing wheels shot away. Boy Stevens seemed to be missing part of his lower left wing, a fluttering hole ripped from its rear edge, while his tailplane seemed to be in shreds. No one else joined them that morning, Symes down, as Dev knew, with neither Bivin nor Wells in sight. After a delay, during which, in the far distance, Dev could see the dust from Chauvel's columns converging on Magdhaba, Frome signaled them to return to Salmana, and they were off, flying northwest in a tattered formation.

At Salmana, on Frome's hand signal, Dev landed first, his plane coming down hard and bouncing at least twice before he could settle into a taxi. Arrival at the hangar brought out medical attendants who, with Trent's assistance, helped him dismount from the plane as one of the Army's medical orderlies began to attend to his shoulder. In the meantime, Frome put down, one of his wheels folding up under him, the axle digging in so as to spin him in place. Curiously, the plane did not turn onto its side and finally came to a full stop after spinning Frome and his observer in a complete circle. The observer, Frome quickly discovered, had been wounded by a machine-gun bullet that had passed through the flesh of his calf. That man, placed immediately on a stretcher and loaded onto a Crossley tender, went off at once for the field hospital at Salmana. When Crisp brought his kite down, the struts that held the axle in place collapsed under him; he and Crouchback skidded across the makeshift drome for perhaps 50 yards before their kite came to rest, the two of them registering a degree of bliss while the medico patched them up, each having taken slight splinter wounds from tiny shell fragments that had passed through their plane over Magdhaba. Boy Stevens, upon landing, lost the entire tail of his ship, the whole construction simply folding up upon impact with the ground. It soon became apparent that both Stevens and his observer had also been wounded by Mauser rounds. Twenty minutes later, with the observer sandwiched into his own observer's cockpit and with Wells standing on the wing and clinging to the side of Bivin's cockpit, Bivin landed, none of the four wounded in any way but with Wells claiming that his hair would turn white as a result of the ordeal he had just survived.

Wells had in fact been shot down. A sizable shell fragment from one of the Archies had done for his engine—an eventuality that forced him to land in the desert 2 miles north of Magdhaba. That is where, putting down beside him and after discarding every ounce of extra weight in his plane—including the Lewis gun which his observer had totally disabled—Bivin had taken the risk of getting all four of them back into the air. He succeeded, Wells standing on the wing and hanging on for dear life all the way back to Salmana and fully expecting to be killed when Bivin set down.

"You are the only four to emerge unscathed," Frome said when the remains of the Flight gathered around the tender in which Dev happened to be sitting while a medical orderly finished bandaging his shoulder. "From what Dev tells me, Symes and his observer went down in a crash south of Magdhaba. His plane exploded, but whether or not he and his observer got out, we don't know. Anyone see anything?"

No one had seen anything at all. So when they went to the mess tent for a cup of morning coffee or tea and a late breakfast, all of them still in their flight togs, the atmosphere seemed subdued if not downright downcast.

Around noon, when Tuck flew in and assembled for debriefing those who had not gone straight to the hospital, the mood improved with the news that Chauvel's attack had gone off with near textbook perfection.

"On the whole," Tuck said, sounding a serious tone, "casualties were light. The Turks lost as many as 300 dead or wounded on the ground, and according to the latest message traffic, General Chauvel has taken more than 1,400 prisoners, including Khadir Bey. And you will be glad to hear that the 10th Regiment of the 3rd Light Horse Brigade stumbled upon Symes and his observer not 3 miles south of Magdhaba. The observer took burns on his arms, and apparently Symes came away black-faced with his flying coat singed, but they were attended to on the spot and ought to be back in Kantara with us in a day or two. No flying for you chaps until your kites are replaced. I'm trying to get new ships for you—something a little more advanced than what you've been flying—but don't hold your breath; as always, everything new and useful is going to the Western Front. In the meantime, until wounds heal and you're pronounced fit by the medicos, you're all grounded. Doss down here tonight. Catch the hospital train going back to Kantara in the morning, and once you do get back, let the Australians do the flying for the next week or two while the lot of you heal up. Any objections?"

There were no objections.

"Yes, well, I thought not. Written reports as soon as you can put them down, and if your wounds won't allow for writing, you can dictate them to the intelligence clerk. Well done, all of you. Your wounds excluded, it was a very successful mission which contributed hugely to General Chauvel's success."

Trent, to Dev's relief, had escaped injury during the mission. But when the doctor who chanced to look at Dev, Crisp, and Crouchback at the field hospital after their debriefing saw them, as a precaution against septicemia, he put them immediately onto the same hospital train that was scheduled to leave for Kantara that afternoon. They rode in the same compartment where Boy Stevens and his observer were supposed to be resting.

"So, what's the drill?" Boy Stevens groaned, for he was starting to feel pain from his wound, which amounted to a Mauser round in his thigh.

"Medico wasn't happy with us," Crisp said, nodding to Boy Stevens's observer, who'd taken a Mauser round in the foot and couldn't stifle a groan. "Said that Crouchback and I have splinters still embedded. Painted us with iodine and wanted us sleeping between clean sheets. Dev's got a gash. Deep that. Doctor talked about stitches."

"I recommended butterfly bandages," Dev said. "Told him I thought things would heal with less of a scar. He asked me where I thought I'd taken my medical degree and told me to get down to Kantara quick march where a surgeon could have a look."

At Kantara, riding in a Crossley tender tricked out as a makeshift ambulance, the five of them reached the hospital where the influx of General Chauvel's wounded were soon expected, the fliers from 14 Squadron being the first to arrive. There, while one surgeon took Boy Stevens and his observer into an operating theater to remove the Mauser rounds from their bodies, another looked at Dev. After putting in four quick stitches to close the gash on his shoulder, he consigned him to one of the wards for, as the man said, "as long as it takes for this gash to heal without any complications developing."

An hour later, wearing a hospital robe but with sticking plaster and gauze showing all up and down his arms and one of his legs, Crisp appeared and settled into a bed beside Dev, with his opening remark leaving Dev in no doubt about how unpleasant the previous hour had been.

"Lifted 19 bits of metal out of me," Crisp said, "and in each instance, it felt like I was having a boil lanced. Painful as hell. Enough iodine to have floated a boat. No painkiller."

"Ah yes," Dev said. "Last time I was here, I was told that painkillers are saved for the seriously wounded."

"I say," Crisp said, almost rising upright, "that's what the bastard told me."

"Jolly collection, aren't they?" Dev laughed. "Probably did their internships with the Spanish Inquisition."

Half an hour later, when Boy Stevens was carried in and placed on a cot next to Crisp, both Dev and Crisp asked him at once, "Give you a painkiller, did they?"

"No," Boy Stevens said flatly, tears still running from the corners of his eyes. "Told me that painkillers were for the seriously wounded and that I wasn't one of them. Damn near passed out, I can tell you. Felt like a red-hot poker had been thrust into my leg, that probe. Getting wounded was nothing compared to it. The treatment was hell."

"Perhaps the food will make up for it," Crisp ventured.

"I wouldn't put money on that," Dev said. "The last time I was here, we had bully beef, cooked up according to seven different recipes, all of them wretched. But we do have one thing going for us."

"Oh?" Crisp said.

"Yes," Dev said. "Nurse Cribbon has been dispatched elsewhere, and that is bound to be an improvement."

"Hear, hear," Crisp said. "I'd forgotten. Let the heavens be praised. Break out the fattened calf! If I didn't feel like a pincushion, I would be in the pink."

Nurse Felicia, the ward's current replacement for Nurse Cribbon, struck all three of them as several steps up from the ward's former attendant. To Boy Stevens—the patient she expected to attend in the ward for the longest period of time—she gave special attention.

"What a fine girl," Boy Stevens said, as their supper trays were taken away and Nurse Felicia left the ward after turning over to yet another nursing sister for the evening.

"Yes," said Crisp, "lovely bedside manner, and lovely to look at, which means—let me instruct you—that you are never to mention her should you happen to run into us in Cairo while we are attending our own lovelies, both of whom are in the same class for looks and poise."

"Make a particular note of that," Dev said, "and practice diplomacy. You do realize that we are leaving you a clear field of endeavor with regard to Sister Felicia, because the two of us are already spoken for."

"What good chums you are," Boy Stevens laughed. "It sounds to me like the two of you are more afraid of those creatures you have referred to as 'your lovelies' than you are of the Hun."

"And with good reason," Crisp said quickly. "As a lad like you will soon learn, it is never good to trouble calm and peaceful waters."

"What he is trying to say," Dev said, "is that we are loyal, true, and committed, so step forth and prosper, and we will leave you a clear path to joy."

By the time Dev and Crisp were released from the hospital and told that they could return to their squadron, Boy Stevens had made good progress down the path to joy, Nurse Felicia having consented to walk out with him somewhere in Kantara once the doctors allowed him back onto his feet.

When Dev and Crisp walked back into Frome's tent upon their return, they found him just rising from an early afternoon nap.

"Things," Frome said at once, "have slowed down here. As you will have noticed, we are without ships. Tuck tells me that several are presently being *reconditioned* for us in Cairo, so you know what that means: old planes of dubious performance, overhauled engines, reconstructed wings, uncertain flying characteristics."

"Doesn't sound promising," said Crisp.

"Not at all," said Dev.

"Twice repeated and underscored," said Frome. "Meanwhile, according to the photos the Australians are bringing back, the rail line and the pipeline are moving forward, none too rapidly, but moving forward, and brother Hun seems to have pulled back from Rafa and appears to be flying out of Ramleh and Beersheba."

"Ramleh?" said Dev. "That's a mite north, isn't it?"

"It is," said Frome. "Looks to me like the Hun has decided to play it safe, but what do I know. I've found that there's no accounting for his movements or for whatever tricks he's getting up to. It does, however, look like he's fortifying Gaza, and from all reports, that could be rough country for Murray to try to fight through. Nothing on that, of course. No reports of an attack pending; no intelligence that would indicate what Murray has in mind. Gaza, I'm guessing, but who knows?"

"And so," Dev said, "where is everyone? Place looks deserted."

"As you well know, Boy Stevens and his observer are still in hospital," Frome said. "Wells is around, and Symes, but I've sent the rest of them on leave, and the two of you are free to go yourselves, should the spirit move you."

"The spirit certainly moves me," Crisp said at once.

"The only question," Dev said, "is when does the next train depart?"

Frome glanced at his watch. "Rather thought you might be ready for a jaunt," he said. "So, here are your leave papers, and if you don't stop to do more than send a telegram, you can still catch the hospital train which leaves for Cairo at 1347 this afternoon."

At the station, Dev wrote a brief telegram: *Arriving Cairo station 1600. Love, Dev.*

And then, hurling their kit bags in ahead of them, Dev and Crisp leapt onto the departing train just as it started to pull out of the station.

14

Owing to the press of operations, the raid on Magdhaba, and their resulting stay in the hospital, Dev and Crisp had missed spending Christmas with Lily and Ruth, but New Year's 1917 turned out to be a holiday that the four of them celebrated in style together. After cooling their heels on the terrace at Shepheard's and with the January temperature in Cairo lowered in the late afternoon to the point where the two of them were grateful to be wearing their greatcoats while they sat for their drinks, Crisp departed to collect Ruth, while Dev returned to the Savoy where they were staying during his leave. As he walked into their room to collect Lily, he found her so stunning in a new ball gown that he nearly went weak in the knees.

"You are lovely to look at," Dev said, having gone almost breathless.

"All the better to encourage our forthcoming discussions," Lily purred.

"I can think of a few discussions that I would like to hold right here, right now," Dev said.

"Not to rush," Lily said. "Our absence would be a grave disappointment to Ruth and Crisp, and we most certainly wouldn't want to disappoint those two. Whatever would they do with themselves if they didn't have us to keep them company?"

"I shudder to think," Dev laughed. "But if you will take my arm, we can go down, and perhaps they will drop a hint."

"Oh, heaven forbid," Lily said, "for that would be telling."

"How very Victorian of you," Dev teased. "Marriage has made you so prim."

"I'll remind you that you said that not long after midnight," Lily said, teasing him back. "And then I'll give you a whole new appreciation of what it means to be 'prim.'"

"I shall look forward to it," Dev said, as the two went out the door and started toward the stairs.

Following what Dev and Crisp called a spectacular dinner, the four then went into the ballroom where the girls had shown the foresight to reserve a table for the evening. As the Savoy's New Year's ball commenced, they danced, shared a bottle of the bubbly, and talked together, drinking in the excitement of the evening, enjoying the music, and taking pleasure in each other's company.

"So what was it," Ruth finally asked, "that kept you brilliant young officers away from us during Christmas? Could it have been that little do at Magdhaba that we read about in the papers?"

"I defer to my fellow who is invariably equipped with all of the answers," Dev said.

"Routine flying," Crisp said at once. "Photo reconnaissance over empty desert, scouting for Turkish patrols which didn't put in an appearance, upkeep on our aircraft—that sort of thing."

"Yes," Lily said, that's what the papers mentioned, in some detail I might add. I gather that the photo reconnaissance went right along with dropping a series of bombs over the redoubts in Magdhaba amid what the paper called 'voluminous and deadly anti-aircraft fire.' You may be surprised to learn that the paper mentioned quite a number of you by name while touting what it called your 'heroic' achievements in advancing the Allied cause. I'm not sure that I can remember the specific wording, but I believe it said that Lieutenants

Collins, Crisp, and Symes as well as a Captain Frome were to be mentioned in dispatches."

"That couldn't have been us," Crisp said quickly. "We were out in the desert flying over total desolation."

"Whoever wrote that must have confused us with someone else," Dev said. "Probably some of the Australians. I understand that 'Collins' and 'Crisp' are common names in Australia."

"Irish-Americans have a terrible reputation for indulging in blarney," Lily said. "So, I suppose that gash that's healing on your shoulder suddenly appeared when you fell over a tent peg and accidentally injured yourself?"

"Quite so," Dev said.

"This one," Ruth said, lifting a finger in Crisp's direction, "looks like a duck hunter fired off a blast in his direction; he has little shrapnel wounds all over him."

"Is nothing sacred?" Crisp protested. "Doesn't it occur to you that you might shock these two with mention of what you have seen?"

Ruth and Lily broke out laughing. "For the two of you to think that you could keep secrets from us," Lily laughed, "is a dessert for our amusement."

"Which makes me think," Ruth said. "How is that Boy Stevens of yours getting along with that pretty Nursing Sister Felicia? Our sources inform us that she is attending him and providing tender, loving care."

Dev and Crisp nearly choked on their drinks.

"Now that," Crisp said, nearly fuming, "is cutting it a mite close."

"When we left," Dev said, "Boy Stevens seemed smitten and deep in conversation with your source. Where you happened to run across the delectable Sister Felicia is probably beyond our imagination, but we can say without fear of overstating the case that Boy Stevens is more than content to be in hospital."

"And lucky for the two of you that he is, and was, to take up the slack so to speak," Ruth said. "We shouldn't like to think that the two of you had let your minds wander."

"You needn't expect a disturbance," Dev said. "As I explained to Boy Stevens, Crisp and I are loyal, true, and committed. We are absolutely not the wandering kind."

"So good of you to mention it," Lily said.

"Yes," Dev said, "I think we might keep that idea as the foundation of our future discussions."

They danced, the four of them, drank some more bubbly, danced some more, raised their cheers as the Savoy rang in the new year, and after a final turn on the dance floor, saw Crisp and Ruth off to wherever it was that Ruth had the two of them hiding out for the evening. Then, they went up to their room where the Dev and Lily arranged to linger in their discussions until the early hours of the morning when they finally fell asleep tucked under the duvet.

Rising late on the day after New Year's, Dev and Lily took a late luncheon with Mr. and Mrs. Winslow, lingered in conversation with them for much of the afternoon, and finally departed before the cocktail hour to meet Ruth and Crisp in the lounge bar at the Savoy. There, the two couples shared two drinks each before removing to the dining room for supper. From there they went on to a concert in the later evening, which featured a string quartet playing music drawn from Italian operas that had been specially arranged for them. Following a nightcap, once more at the Savoy, Ruth and Crisp disappeared while Dev and Lily returned to their room to continue their discussions, the four of them agreeing to meet for a late breakfast at Groppi's the following morning.

In fact, the following morning, just as Dev and Lily emerged from their room and prepared to set off, a bellboy confronted them in the hall and met Dev with a telegram.

"It's from Frome," Dev said to Lily after reading it all the way through. "Orders." And then he read the message to his wife: *Report Central Aviation RFC Cairo 1400, Collins and Crisp. Ferry Duty.* "I can't be sure," Dev said, "but what that seems to mean is that our leave is over. I suspect that we will be flying new crates back to Kantara. Sorry, Love. I would like to have stayed longer."

"For several more discussions?" Lily teased.

"For endless discussions," Dev said, "with occasional meals in between. So, what say we go find the other unfortunate pair, break the dismal news, and have breakfast?"

"Lead on," Lily said, taking his arm.

After what turned into a brunch rather than a breakfast at Groppi's and after picking up Lily's suitcase and seeing both Lily and Ruth to the doors of their parents' flats, Dev and Crisp gave the taxi driver instructions to make for Central Aviation RFC Cairo—the airdrome to which Frome's orders directed them. After threading their way through any number of streets that seemed packed with pedestrians and traffic, the taxi finally reached the main gate of the base with half an hour to spare, negotiated an entrance with the gate guard, and deposited them in front of a series of hangars and an office that carried an unimpressive sign that read *Field Headquarters: Maintenance.*

"Do you suppose this is the spot?" Dev asked.

"Your guess is as good as mine," Crisp said. "Let's go in and find out."

Once through the door, Dev and Crisp instantly found themselves looking at four fresh-faced lieutenants with bright new RFC wing insignia sewn to their tunics and, behind a counter that appeared to separate office space from what looked like a waiting area, a bald, overweight captain wearing a soiled uniform who appeared to be smoking his pipe with pleasure while he studied the contents of a file.

"Excuse me, Sir," Dev said, coming to attention. "Collins and Crisp, reporting for ferry duty. Is this the right place?"

"You lot," the captain said, looking straight past Dev and Crisp to the four lieutenants, "up and at 'em. The agents of your deliverance have arrived. BE2cs departing for Kantara."

Instantly, the four lieutenants were on their feet, looking to Dev like a troop of boy scouts about to embark on an outing. And then, the captain turned to Dev and Crisp.

"New boys, for you, for 14 Squadron and your Flight," he said. "Six new ships for you waiting at the hangars. Well, let me amend that: six *reconditioned* ships waiting for you at the hangars. Good engines, acceptable airframes, fueled, tested, and ready to fly. Pity about the kites you lost over Magdhaba. Careless, that. Destruction of good government equipment, what?"

"Yes," Crisp said, "pity. We were doing our best to save them for a museum, but brother Hun seemed to have other ideas. Nasty Archies and such. You've equipped these new ... excuse me, these *pre-used* crates with synchronized, forward-firing machine guns, I suppose?"

"You had too much to drink during your lunch," the captain said, as he broke out laughing. "Where do you think you are, on the Somme, behind Arras, near St. Omer? Ships with modern equipment go to the men who are fighting the real war. But don't despair; we've given serious thought to issue each of you with fly swatters so that you can do some real damage out there when you go back."

"So thoughtful," Dev said.

"Right," said the captain. "And now, let me introduce you to the infant charges you will be taking out to Kantara with you," and pointing swiftly, he pronounced, "Ennie, Mennie, Minnie, and Moe," before walking around the counter and straight out the door onto the airdrome.

In fact, as far as Dev could remember, as he and Crisp stopped to shake hands, the lieutenants seemed to be named Hexley, Felder, Sitcomb, and Giles, but at that point in their acquaintance, the names more or less ran together for him. In their haste to follow the captain, their features failed to separate themselves for him.

"You want to take the lead, or shall I?" Crisp asked, as the two of them stepped out swiftly, following the captain, with the four lieutenants trailing along behind carrying their duffles and kit bags.

"Suppose you lead," Dev said, "and I'll follow along behind and try to make sure that none of them gets lost on the way up."

"There they are," the captain said, stopping finally beside the first of the reconditioned ships and throwing out his hand to indicate the six of them that were lined up in a row across the face of the hangars. "The air mechs have already done a pre-flight check on each of them, but you are free to repeat the process, and if each of you will just sign for one of these machines on the clipboard here, I will take my departure and leave you to it. And please, do try to preserve these machines in good condition. Government savings, and all."

"So thoughtful of you to ask," Crisp said. "Perhaps we should load them onto our backs and walk them up to Kantara."

"Why, what a splendid idea," the captain said. 'I wish I'd thought of that myself."

"I'll bet," Dev said.

With their signatures taken and with each man assigned to the BE2c he'd signed for, Crisp drew them together. "Do your own pre-flight checks," he said. "The air mechs are usually pretty good, but they don't fly these kites, and we do, which makes us responsible for our own welfare. I'll lead on the way up to Kantara; it will be about a two-hour flight, and Mr. Collins will bring up the rear in case anyone experiences trouble or starts to drift off in the wrong direction. If, by some remote chance, we should meet a Hun out there anywhere, the only defense we have is to run from him, so without an observer and his Lewis gun, evasion is your only hope.

I don't think we need to worry about that much, but keep your eyes open and remember that discretion is the better part of valor."

With each of them having completed their pre-flight checks, Crisp wasted no time. He signaled the air mech attending to twirl his prop, listened to the engine catch, and began to taxi; five minutes later, all six of them were in the air, flying northeast toward Kantara. They made the flight that afternoon at 3,000 feet, where the air was just cold enough so that Dev was pleased that he'd worn his greatcoat rather than depositing it with his grip in the observer's seat. Their flight—one in which the four new men showed a sound degree of discipline—turned out to be uneventful, all of them making Kantara in good time, all of them coming down safe, all of their planes behaving with perfect regularity.

On the ground, where Frome met them, Dev and Crisp reported themselves back—with six new ships in good condition, and with four new pilots to go with them.

"Sorry to have to call you back," Frome said, when he'd heard their report, "but the ferry assignment took precedence over everything else, and there was nothing for it but to have you do it because Bivin and Symes were already back."

"So suddenly we are fat on pilots but thin on aircraft," Dev said. "What gives? Will we take to port and starboard flying?"

"Probably not," Frome said, "but we'll know more about that in a day or two. In the meantime, you two are on for the morning patrol, and you'll be taking out these two lads, Hexley and Felder, with you, so don't let them get into trouble. Photo recon trip near El Arish, to make sure that the Turks aren't making any attempt to move back in there. Bivens and Symes will be taking out the other two … what are their names, Sitcomb and Giles, in the afternoon with the same objective east of Magdhaba. You'll all refuel at Salmana, so you need not worry about running out of petrol coming back. Oh, and there's one other thing that might be of interest. The lads down in the armory have worked out a new arrangement whereby your observers will now have dual Lewis guns mounted side by side. Just imagine what a surprise that will give brother Hun when he meets you for the first time!"

"Biffing," Dev said.

"When we asked for forward-firing machine guns in Cairo," Crisp said, "we were laughed at."

"Suggested that we'd mistaken Sinai for the Western Front," Dev said.

"No surprise there," Frome said. "One imagines that it will be a cold day in Hades before we ever join the mainstream. Now, suppose you send those new lads in to me. Let's have all four of them at once to start, and then I will interview each individually in turn."

"How do you like the new Lewis gun arrangement?" Dev asked Trent the following morning before they took off.

"Tidy," Trent replied. "More weight, but tidy."

Dev wasn't sure that he fully understood what Trent might have meant by 'tidy' but took the word as a mark of approval and didn't ask again. Minutes later, Dev, Trent, Crisp, Crouchback, Hexley, Felder, and their two observers were in the air making for Salmana, and around 0830 they were over El Arish and found it deserted.

The four planes involved in the Flight remained over El Arish for no more than 10 minutes, giving each of the observers plenty of time to expose any number of photographic plates. Then, as the four of them turned back toward Salmana, they were bumped from above by three Pfalz and two Rumplers which drove straight in toward them from, as far as Dev was concerned, the wrong direction. Instead of putting the sun behind them to blind the Flight, the Huns dropped on them from the west. Regardless of the surprise that the attack carried, the Flight's defense against it required them to do no more than make a 90-degree turn to unmask their observers' Lewis guns. Those Lewis guns—increased from four to eight by the work that the armorers had put in when mounting them—struck the Hun attackers like a broadside, almost instantly raising smoke from a Pfalz and a Rumpler, both of which turned away before they'd had time to do damage to the Flight. The others limited themselves to a single pass before dropping to the deck and striking a beeline toward the east. Whether or not the Pfalz and the Rumpler that showed smoke had gone down or not, none of them ever knew, because Crisp, leading the flight, did not attempt to follow the two of them down. Pilots, would-be aces on the Western Front, might be keeping score, but in Sinai, none of the Flight had fallen victim to what they called "that disease." Their objective, by common consent, was to complete the mission they were assigned and leave the Huns to lick their wounds as they might.

As far as Dev could tell from glancing at the others, none of them had been wounded by the German attack, but fluttering fabric on some of their ships indicated clearly that almost all of them had taken hits of some kind. For Dev, the most telling result of the attack had to do with the fact that his nausea had returned and that his hands were once more shaking. Cairo had been perfect, and being with Lily seemed like a dream, but being back amid the thick of things brought home to him the fact that he'd been a year flying in Sinai, living with the constant threat and fear of a swift death. As the thought stabbed at the back of his mind, Dev knew that he couldn't stop himself from wondering about how much more of it he could take before the shaking would become continual.

At Salmana where they put down, Hexley discovered that his observer had in fact been wounded, a machine-gun round having lodged itself in the man's side. By the time they discovered the wound, the man has passed out and had to be lifted from his cockpit before the medical orderly on duty had him put on a stretcher, loaded him onto a Crossley, and rushed him off to the field hospital for treatment. Their ships, showing signs of damage in several places, had to be carefully inspected while they were being refueled because no one wanted to take off with something that might set them down among the dunes. But aside from torn fabric and a few splintered wing ribs, the reconditioned planes they were flying looked sound, with the result that after an hour on the ground, all four of them were back in the air and made Kantara without mishap.

Once they returned, Frome listened to their reports, taking them orally from all four pilots, and then set them to making out the written copies that Tuck would expect at Ismailia. Later in the day, following lunch, he called for Dev and Crisp together, drew them into his tent, sat them down across from him, and asked them to report on Hexley and Felder.

"No complaints," Crisp said. "I thought they did fine."

"Same here," Dev said. "Looked to me like both of them demonstrated reasonable flying skills, and when we were bounced out there, both fell right in with the defense that we put up. The fact that Hexley's observer was hit had nothing to do with any of his maneuvers. That hit was simply bad luck and nothing more."

"All right," Frome said, showing them both a nod of agreement. "That's good to hear, because the next time they go off, they'll be going on their own. You two ... well, you asked me what we intended to do with all of these new pilots, and now, finally, I have in my hands a message that came in this morning while you were out that gives me the answer. Hexley and Felder are your replacements. You've been at it out here for nearly a year, and for the immediate future, your flying days seem to be over. Whether or not you realize it, Crisp, each time you come back here from a flight, your eyes are twitching to the point where I wonder how you can see, and Collins, you obviously have the same issue with a pair of hands that don't stop shaking until you've been on the ground for an hour. The flight surgeon has been over and had a look at the both of you from a distance, and he's reached the same conclusion. I might add, both Biven and Syme will be pulled off the line for similar reasons. It's a rotation, don't you see. Crisp, you're for a tour of duty at the School for Aerial Gunnery at Abu Kir. Bivin and Symes are to be sent to the School for Aeronautics at the same place. I gather that they're to instruct the pilots that we're training up on that airdrome. And Collins, quite frankly, I have no idea what the big boys have in store for you because they haven't told me, but it rather looks to me like you are going to be called on the carpet for something, because you are headed for an appointment with the eminent Colonel Prince at GHQ, at 0900 sharp on the day after tomorrow."

Neither Dev nor Crisp knew what to say, for Frome's announcement had caught them cold.

"I need not tell you that I'm going to miss having you in the Flight," Frome said. "As far as I'm concerned, you've done splendid work here, and with regard to the support that you've given me and the work we've done together, I couldn't have asked for two better subordinates. You may be interested to know as well, that you are both promoted to Captain with a suitable rise in pay, so I congratulate you on your well-deserved promotions and thank you for a job well done. Now, if I were you, I would pack up, say your farewells, and catch the afternoon train for Cairo where, one imagines, interested parties will be only too happy to greet the two of you and see you return."

Two hours later, having dispatched the appropriate telegrams, Dev and Crisp boarded the train and reached Cairo in good time.

15

With Dev's future totally suspended pending whatever it was that Colonel Prince intended to inflict on him, Mr. and Mrs. Winslow graciously offered the young Collins accommodation until Dev's affairs settled. So, later that evening, as Dev and Lily sat side by side on the Winslows' sofa, the two Winslows sitting in easy chairs flanking the couple, conversation developed in a pleasant but lively way.

"And you have no idea what he might be wanting from you?" Mortimer Winslow asked, referring to Colonel Prince.

"No, Sir," Dev said. "We lost every plane we flew on that raid. Some of us got home, but the ships were so damaged that they had to be written off, and if he's sore about that, there is absolutely nothing that can be done about it."

"But you were mentioned in dispatches!" Lily protested.

"That, my dear," Dev said, "is what we call public relations. Presenting a good report for public consumption. Support for the war effort. Keeping up public confidence, that sort of thing. What GHQ may actually be thinking promises to differ greatly from what is put out to improve morale for the folks on the street."

"There is that, one must admit," said Mrs. Winslow, "but I think it wise to look on the bright side until an ax is dropped. Best not to encourage a catastrophe through negative thinking."

Dev laughed. "Quite so," he said. "May be nothing more than an obligatory meeting."

"You met the man before," Mr. Winslow said. "What did you think of him at the time?"

"To be truthful," Dev said, "I thought Prince showed some sense. He asked us good questions, and he made decisions. His apparent Chief of Staff, a Major Flemming, struck the three of us as a perfect fool; as far as we could determine, he didn't know the first thing about flying or air fighting, and we imagined him to be a political creature who had been placed in the job because he was a cavalry officer who must have ridden well on some hunt or other. And there was a Captain Ballard in the room along with a Lieutenant Foy who looked to us like book ends—dense and made of lead."

"And it was Prince who approved your plan?" Mr. Winslow continued.

"Yes," Dev said. "Once the palaver ended, Prince made the decision."

"To my mind," Mortimer Winslow said, "that suggests a promising interview. After all, your mission succeeded with excellent results on the ground, and that was the objective all along."

"What you say is quite true," Dev said. "Perhaps I'm letting my last visit to the Air Staff Office too much color my expectations."

"Without question," Lily said emphatically, "and with me to come back to, and with the Huns so very far distant, we shouldn't let the mere thought of a meeting disturb our discussions."

"So true," Dev said. "So, what the news from home? Stock market still climbing? Pershing still chasing Pancho Villa? And did Boston really win the World Series? I'm a bit behind, you see. The lads I fly with are all hung up on cricket scores and test matches."

271

On the following morning, after a delightful night spent in bed with Lily at the opposite end of the Winslows' rather commodious flat, Dev trooped out early, found the tailor to which Lily had directed him, and saw to it that his RFC wings and his Captain's pips were fixed to a relatively well-tailored service dress blouse that he bought off the rack. Then, wearing the same, he collected Lily and took her to lunch, meeting Ruth and Crisp in the garden room of The Shire, a small but well-appointed hotel only two blocks from the American consulate.

"So," Dev said, "how many days were you given before you have to report to the School of Aerial Gunnery?"

"RFC Staff Headquarters for Personnel says two ... today and tomorrow," Crisp replied.

"A number which has not endeared them to me," Ruth said hotly. "Some of your cavalry and infantry types around here are being given entire months off. Are the Lewis guns not likely to pop off if this great man of mine is not there to oversee them? What, I ask, is the rush?"

"There's a war on, dear," Lily said, putting her hand on Ruth's wrist and showing her a smile.

"And it's liable to stop dead in its tracks if my bright and shining captain isn't there to direct it?" Ruth said. "You know as well as I do that there is some jackass in that personnel office who's behind this, and I'd very much like to give him a piece of my mind!"

"Loyal little thing, isn't she?" Crisp said.

"Yes," Dev said, "but if you would just turn her loose, I'd pay money to watch her tear in there and squeeze the life out of one of those officious toads."

"Oh, well put," Ruth said with enthusiasm. "What a treasure you've married, Lily. A regular agent provocateur, isn't he?"

"Alas," Lily said. "A man who must needs be watched with a close eye."

"Speaking of a close eye," Crisp said, "what might the two of you be doing this afternoon?"

Dev looked at Lily as Lily looked back at Dev. "Nothing very much," Dev said. "Have something in mind?"

"Oh, *ra-ther*," said Crisp. "If I may borrow for a moment one of your American expressions, Ruth and I thought we might get hitched at around 1600, in the consulate, if the two of you will stand up for us. The minister has been ordered. Additional witnesses have been summoned, and a room in your consulate has been made available for the hitching—"

"Nuptials!" Ruth snapped, "as I keep telling you, *nuptials!*"

"Yes, yes, of course, but *hitching* sounds so much more colorful, don't you think? And, as I was saying, bubbly will be waiting at the Savoy for afterward—if you can join us, that is."

The announcement left Lily and Dev speechless.

"Your idea, or Ruth's?" Dev grinned while Ruth and Lily indulged themselves in the obligatory hugging.

"Couldn't let the goods get away, if you see what I mean?" Crisp said. "Alexandria's too far distant for me to depart in comfort without her."

"If you ever refer to me as 'the goods' again," Ruth said, turning to her intended, "I will box your ears so hard that you won't know what time it is."

"Now, now," Crisp said, "don't ruffle a feather. Just a little joke for Dev's intake. Nothing more. Deep love and consideration intended."

"And you're going to set up in Alexandria?" Dev said.

"Just as soon as Ruth can make a break from our hotel and find us a flat, once we actually get up there."

"Perhaps your remarks about the personnel office were precipitous, my dear," Lily said. "One wonders if the mountain would have moved had not personnel cut the mountain's leave so short."

"There *is* that," Ruth admitted. "It's just that a girl likes to have time to pack. Lack of such time is the source of my ire. On the other hand, after considering how the office staff there has forced this man of mine into action, perhaps I should stop by and leave them a small contribution of some kind."

"On the whole," Crisp said, adopting an august tone, "I think it best that you avoid contact with Army offices. The people there—low types in many instances—may be apt to make suggestive remarks and immodest proposals."

"Oh ho," said Lily, "so does that explain where you and Dev have picked up your bad habits?"

"My lips are sealed," Dev said.

The "nuptials," as Ruth would have them, took place at 1600 that afternoon, in one of the quiet offices at the American consulate, with Lily and Dev standing up for the pair, while Ruth's parents and the Winslows looked on. Following, everyone adjourned to the Savoy for a glass of bubbly and a congenial early supper, and then, leaving the couple to enjoy their one-night honeymoon in one of the hotel's suites, Lily, Dev, and Lily's parents returned to the Winslow flat themselves, enjoyed a brandy, and retired for the night.

At 0855 the following morning, Captain Devlin Collins knocked once on the door marked "Air Staff" at GHQ, entered the outer office, where he found the same Army sergeant sitting behind the desk who had greeted him before, and announced that he was on hand for his appointment with Lieutenant Colonel Prince.

"It's Colonel, now," the clerk reported. "Himself was promoted, Sir, after Magdhaba."

"Ah," Dev said by way of acknowledgment.

Without hesitation, the clerk immediately knocked on the inner door, opened it, and announced, "Captain Collins to see you, Sir."

"Right," sounded Prince's voice from the inside of the office. "Send him in."

As Dev came to attention and reported himself, he also noticed that Major Flemming as well as Captain Bonnard and Lieutenant Foy seemed nowhere in evidence.

"Seat yourself," said Colonel Prince after reaching forward and giving Dev what seemed to Dev like an official handshake. "Do you prefer coffee or tea?"

"Coffee, if I may, Sir," Dev said.

"Quite right," the Colonel said. "Just the thing for opening the eyes and concluding the morning's slumber."

Dev said nothing about the fact that he'd had two cups at the Winslow breakfast table before leaving the flat that morning.

Less than a minute passed in utter silence before the clerk reappeared carrying two white china army mugs, the first of which he set before Colonel Prince before setting the other well within Dev's reach.

"Save for the loss of your aircraft," Prince said, "the raid you planned on Magdhaba went well. Targets struck as planned, no one seriously injured, all personnel returned to base."

"Yes, Sir," Dev said.

"The loss of your kites is to be regretted, but we now have an abundance of outdated BE2cs available in Egypt, so those were easily replaced. I regret that we don't have better ships for you men to fly, but London remains adamant about sending the up-to-date machines to the Western Front, and there is nothing either General Murray or I can do about it."

"No, Sir," Dev said.

"I have spoken with Captain Frome and Major Tuck, and I find that most of the work on the plan you submitted for the Magdhaba raid was yours, Captain—conception and detail. Your superiors explained one or two refinements which they added, but in my estimation, those were slight."

Dev kept his silence.

"What is needed here," Prince said, "what I need is a flying officer on my staff who is familiar with not only mechanical matters regarding the machines being flown on our front but with the operational considerations that our pilots face. Air Intelligence provides us with good and often exceptional information regarding the plans we seek to draft, but I very much want a planner who will work on these with me—a man who knows the ropes, so to speak, and who can anticipate the obstacles our fliers will face as they go forth to do battle. After seeing your work on the plan for Magdhaba, I'm convinced that you are the man I need in this office, so the reason I've called you in this morning is that I'm offering you the job."

It was the last thing that Dev had expected to hear, and for a moment, he didn't know what to say. Then, he posed the obvious question. "Do you not think, Sir, that some of the flight commanders or squadron commanders might be better suited—"

"No," Prince said firmly. "Those gentlemen are right now in positions where I want them to remain. You're the man with the obvious penchant for planning, and that's why you're needed here—to map things out and assist me."

"Will that mean working under Major Flemming, Sir?" Dev asked.

"Major Flemming, Captain Bonnard, and Lieutenant Foy are gone from this office," Colonel Prince said with a smile. "It seemed quite clear to me after I met with you, Frome, and Crisp, that those gentlemen would best serve the cause away from Shepheard's and in the trenches on the Western Front, and that is where I dispatched them. I speak ill of no man, but they don't hunt in Flanders if you take my meaning, which means that there is serious work to be done there, and that is where those gentlemen will best help to do it."

"Will our work keep us in Cairo?" Dev asked.

"For the foreseeable future," Prince said.

"Then I will try to do my best for you," Dev said, "with the understanding that you will send me packing if I'm not up to the mark."

"That goes without saying," Colonel Prince said, "but I don't think you need to worry about that. I've seen your work, so I'm confident that you're the right man for the job."

"Thank you, Sir," Dev said. "I will try to merit your confidence in me."

"One more thing," Prince said. "The post to which I'm assigning you merits a major in charge. Return to your tailor and have yourself properly fitted out. In the first place, as we brief others and carry our work forward here at GHQ, a crown on your shoulder will give you more clout than three pips. And as time goes by and we need to add staff members to assist us in our work, I should like for you to be ahead of them so as to maintain control over the planning process. Understood?"

"Yes, Sir," Dev said.

"Good," Prince said. "Any other questions before we begin work tomorrow morning?"

"One, Sir," Dev said.

"Speak," said Prince.

"Is it to be Gaza?" Dev asked.

"That is what I anticipate and what I intend you to plan for," Prince said, "but officially, silence is golden, so no one is to know what you are doing."

"Yes, Sir," Dev said.

When Dev returned to the flat, he found Lily alone, sitting on the couch, a writing tablet in her hands, her father still at the office, her mother out for the morning.

"Oh good, you're home early," Lily said, showing him a bright smile. "Are we staying in Cairo?"

"Yes," Dev said.

"I thought we might be," Lily said. "And as you know, idle hands are the devil's workshop, so I've found us a flat, one block over: small, furnished, compact, and comfortable. Two bedrooms, the big one for our discussions, the smaller one for my typewriter, a kitchen for cooking, and a dining and living space where I may lounge and display myself under your fervent gaze."

"You, my dear," Dev said, breaking into laughter, "are a beauty and a treasure."

"Keep that thought, always," Lily said, as she leapt up to give him a kiss.